Tales of the Barf Table

Book Two: Trouble Shooters

Tales of the Barf Table

Book Two:

Trouble Shooters

RAHN & TIMBERLEY ADAMS

Written by Rahn and Timberley Adams

Illustrations by Timberley Adams

Published by Gaillardia Press

Copyright © 2024 Rahn and Timberley Adams

ISBN: 979-8-9869431-3-8

First Edition, November, 2024

"It's not so important who starts the game but who finishes it."

— John Wooden

Chapter 1

THE HAZY FIGURE AT THE FRONT DOOR of the farmhouse looked and sounded like trouble. The knock alone—three sharp raps on the door frame, not on the door itself—rattled the hat rack on the inside wall and echoed down the hallway leading to the kitchen. Through the frosted window that showed the man's head and chest, the big farm boy who was alone in the kitchen could see that the visitor wasn't wearing a uniform. He wasn't a sheriff's deputy or an ordinary deliveryman. Despite the chill in the autumn air, he was wearing a white T-shirt without a jacket. He twisted his upper torso and nodded his head one way, then the other, as he waited to see if his knock would be answered. He wore no hat or cap. His hair looked long and unkempt. He held something below window level. The man looked back over one shoulder twice in the time it took the teenager to reach the front door from the kitchen.

Seventeen-year-old Artie Bauer opened the door a crack but didn't unfasten the chain guard. "Yes?" Artie said. "Can I help you?"

"Delivery," the man replied. "Pizza from Woody's Grill." He did, in fact, hold a large pizza box in one hand, extending it to the side so that the boy could see the restaurant's name printed on the brown cardboard. "You wanna open the door?"

Artie shook his head. "I didn't order a pizza," he said. "You're at the wrong house."

"Ain't this 5302 Ebenezerville Road? That's the address they give me."

Leaning to the side, Artie reached for the baseball bat whose smooth wooden handle protruded from the old milk can that the Bauers used as an umbrella stand. "Really?" the farm boy said. "There's been a mistake then. Nobody here ordered a pizza."

"Are you sure?" the man insisted. "Maybe Harry Bauer did. Or Mrs. Bauer. You mind if I come in and borrow your phone? I'll call Woody and double-check."

The man changed hands with the box and reached for the knob of the screen door, which would open outward if it were not latched. Artie saw that his ragged fingernails were caked with dark grease and that the joint of his right index finger next to the knuckle had been tattooed with the letter *K.*

"No," said Artie, pulling out the bat like drawing a sword from its sheath. "You wait out there while I call Woody and get this straightened out. I know Woody." He closed the front door and locked it. Then, bat in hand and his eye on the door, he eased back up the hallway toward the kitchen where the old telephone hung on the wall.

Before he could dial 9-1-1, he heard heavy footfalls on the front porch and saw the man running toward his vehicle, a primer-colored coupe with a missing rear bumper and tinted glass all around. The man fired up the car, made a three-point turn in the yard, and roared back up the farm road toward the main highway. Dust rose in the car's wake. In that part of Oleander County, there were no actual hills, just mile after mile of fields and swamps.

An old man's feeble voice came from a room off the kitchen. "Who was that?" the man asked. "Artie? Can you hear me?"

At the sound of the man's voice, Artie twisted his head around and did not see which direction the car turned when it reached the highway—to the left toward Monk's Landing, or to the right toward Ebenezerville.

"Hang on, Grandpa," Artie said. "I hear you, but I need to call the sheriff's department. That guy at the door was up to something. I think he wanted to rob us, but I didn't let him in. And I need to call Woody Woods as quick as I can."

"Why?" asked Grandpa Bauer, still in the side room. "What's Woody got to do with this?"

Artie shook his head. "Lay back down and get some rest, Grandpa—if you can. I'll tell you about it when I get off the phone."

Artie Bauer knew that Woody Woods would never, ever hire a deliveryman who looked like the guy at the door. Woody was proud of his "Grade A" health department rating. Besides, any delivery pizza that left Woody's Surf Shop & Grill at the beach was always carried in a red, insulated bag, even if it was going to a cottage just up the strand from the grill. Also, anyone who knew the Bauer family well—even most deliverymen who didn't—never used the open front porch and actual front door of the farmhouse to call on the Bauers; visitors knocked at the back screen door and then entered through the enclosed back porch where Grandpa liked to sit when Grandma was in the kitchen cooking.

No, said Artie to himself as he dialed the rotary phone, *that guy was nothing but trouble—with a capital T. I just hope he doesn't come back before a deputy gets here.*

Chapter 2

AS THE LATE BELL SOUNDED, Woody Woods peeked into the Arbor High cafeteria from the breezeway. He saw through the plate-glass window that one of his son's friends had already taken her seat at the round table down front near the trash bins. Two others—a tall couple, a boy and girl—were headed that way, carrying bag lunches. Woody recognized Brett's other friends waiting in line to get their lunch trays across the big room. One was a laughing, talkative boy in a wheelchair pushed by a husky, straw-haired youth. The tall helper leaned down to rest his elbows on the chair's hand grips as they crept toward the serving area. Behind them was a diminutive boy with a wide smile, especially for girls whose attention he could catch in line or at the tables they passed.

Woody knew that this was the so-called Barf Table gang, of which his son had become a reluctant member that fall. It wasn't because Brett Woods had been unpopular like most of the others at the round table down front. In fact, Brett—a good-looking surfer boy—had become a varsity football star and a school heartthrob during the season just ended. He could have sat anywhere he wanted at the long 10th-grade tables in the Arbor High lunchroom, maybe even at one of the rows of seats in the junior and senior level that looked down on the lowly freshmen and sophomores. Brett had started out that school year sitting with the popular 10th graders, until his best friend took advantage of his trust and got them both into big trouble. That was when Woody Woods's easy-going son decided he'd sit wherever he darn well pleased—at the Barf Table, with teenagers who wouldn't treat him as they'd been treated at the start of the year. Besides, the freshman girl who was sitting there, Leah Russo, was smart and cute.

Woody Woods, owner of Woody's Surf Shop & Grill at nearby Sandpiper Beach, might as well have been carrying a large cardboard tray of pure gold that day as he waited to enter the cafeteria. Instead, the tray held seven white bags of Woody's famous golden fries from the deep fryer in his strand-side grill. After making them, he had hopped into his van and rushed them the four miles inland to the high school in Monk's Landing so they'd still be fresh when he presented them to the Barf Table gang. They would be Brett's goodbye gift.

Of the eight tablemates, only senior Artie Bauer was absent. Like Brett, Artie sat there out of choice, not because he had to. This was Artie's fourth year at the Barf Table. But all that week—Thanksgiving Week—he'd chosen to stay home to be with his elderly grandfather on their farm in rural Oleander County, and no one blamed him one bit.

"Dad?" said Brett Woods, sticking his head out the door to the breezeway. "Sorry I'm late meeting you. I had to talk to my teacher. You want to come in? Or do you need to get back to the grill?" Brett stepped aside and held the door open for his father.

Woody Woods smiled and nodded. "No problem, son. Sure, I'll carry this tray over to the table while I've got a good grip on it. It's heavy, and I'd hate to dump these bags on the floor."

"Gotcha," said Brett, a glint in his eye. "Don't want any oil spills."

The father chuckled. "Hey, now. This isn't that kind of oil. It's Vitamin G, and everybody needs a good dose of grease now and then. Keeps things moving."

"Whatever you say, Dad." Brett waited for Woody to enter, then let the metal door shut behind them. Like a good blocking back on the gridiron, the boy hurried ahead to clear a path through the milling throngs of students for his father and the wide load of fries.

Tommy White and Bennie Pressler, the boy in the wheelchair, were rolling up just as the father, son and seven bags of deep-fried heaven arrived at the table. Little Ricky Duran was hot on their wheels. He sniffed the air and exclaimed, "Hey! Woody's fries! Yes!"

The couple—Nicie Evans and Ty Green, both seniors—saw the grease-spotted white bags and glanced down at the plain brown ones they had carried to the table. They looked at each other. "These sandwiches I made can wait, Ty," said Nicie. "Peanut butter don't spoil."

"No jelly today?" Ty Green said. "How soon love fades." He winked at her, and she smacked his arm. He rubbed his bicep even though her playful slap hadn't hurt him. She could have inflicted some pain, though, if she'd wanted, because Nicie Evans—a recent transfer from Mimosa Beach High—had a reputation for fighting.

Still standing, Woody set the tray of fries down and looked at the faces around the table. "Gee, guys," he said. "I wish Artie was here." Woody laid his hand on his son's shoulder. "Brett has some big news, and I hate for Artie to hear it secondhand. But you go ahead, son. I'll go talk to your guidance counselor while you all eat. Enjoy the fries." He turned and left.

Already seated, Brett Woods passed the bags around the table, but made no move to open his own. Before anyone could dig into their food, Nicie piped up, "Well, now you gotta tell us. What's going on? Something big?"

"Yeah, Brett," said Ty Green. "Is it good news or bad news? We've had enough bad news for a while."

Brett shrugged. "Depends on how you look at it, I guess," he said. Turning to Bennie Pressler in the wheelchair next to him, Brett added, "You've had all night to think about it, buddy, after our dads talked on the phone. Is it good or bad?"

"Well," began Bennie, "it's bad news for the Barf Table—you know, since we'll have to do without your shining presence and brilliant repartee all winter. And you won't be here to attract cheerleaders for Ricky to flirt with. But Ricky's doing okay on his own. Right, Ricky?"

Ricky Duran frowned. "Wait, what?" he said. "Where are you going, Brett?"

"And you'll be gone all winter?" asked Tommy White. Though he lived with the Pressler family as a foster child, Tommy seemed surprised, even hurt, that Bennie hadn't already shared Brett's plans with him.

Brett shook his head. "Huh-uh," he said, "this isn't a bad thing, not at all. It *is* big, Nicie—the biggest thing I've ever done in my life. And, Ty, it's *good* news for a change." He took a deep breath. "Tommy—and, well, Ricky, too—my dad didn't want anyone other than Bennie and his family to know about this until it was all set. Our families have been friends for a long time. We go way back—in spite of the bad stuff that happened after Bennie's accident."

Quiet until then, Leah Russo also looked hurt. "Will you just tell us?" she said. "You guys finally get me wanting to eat something, and now you're letting it get cold." But the thin girl didn't care so much about the food as she did the prospect of losing Brett's company that winter. They had just started getting close enough to have good talks despite the difference in their ages—him in the 10th grade, her in the 9th.

Brett Woods gave the girl a worried glance but sat up straight for the big announcement. "I'm going to Hawaii," he said. "My whole family is. Plane leaves tonight. We get to Honolulu late tomorrow, and by Friday I'll be surfing the North Shore. Isn't that great? Great waves, great surf competitions, great weather! And we'll be there all winter—the greatest time of the year to surf! It's a great chance to see if I'm any good at this thing."

Leah shook her head. "That's just, well ... great," she said without emotion. "Really." She went ahead and started on her fries.

"But what about the surf shop?" asked Ty Green. "And the grill? Everybody hangs out there, even in the winter. It's the best place to eat on the beach—the *only* place to eat."

"Yeah," said Tommy White, looking down at his untouched plate of food and bag of fries. "Who's gonna feed all the teams that eat their pregame meals there? I was looking forward to wrestling this winter just to eat at your dad's grill."

"Nobody told you?" Bennie Pressler said to Tommy. "Wrestlers don't eat, not on match days, anyway—not unless you're a heavyweight. And that's Artie."

Brett Woods held up his hand for quiet. "Yeah, I know," Brett said, "but Dad says he and Mom are looking forward to this vacation, too. It's the first time in years they've been able to close the business, and take some quality time off.

That big lawsuit and the other problems with our old pal Josh just about wore Dad out."

"No pal of mine," said Ty Green. "I'm glad he left—even though he came back and acted like a monkey at the homecoming dance, not to mention how he ruined our Halloween festival." He opened his bag and reached inside for a handful of fries. "So, you *are* coming back, right? Me and Artie figured you'd make a good third baseman for us in the spring."

Brett's eyebrows rose. "I hadn't really thought about it," he said. "About baseball, I mean. But, yeah, we're coming back. Dad wants to reopen the shop and grill before Easter, and he needs to do some cleaning and fixing up. That'll take some time. When does baseball start?"

"Middle of February," said Ty. "That's when Nicie won't get to spend so much time with me." He winked at her. "Baseball is my best shot for a scholarship—Artie's, too, if he doesn't get something in football or wrestling. So we'll be putting in extra time on the school diamond and in the bullpen."

Nicie Evans popped him again, harder this time. "Well, you just remember I'll be keeping an eye on you two from the softball field. If I see any prissy little heifers hanging around that bullpen—like that gold-digging Vicki Duke—you won't be seeing diamonds long; you'll be seeing stars." She nudged him, then looked up and her eyes widened. "Well, speak of the devil," she said. "If it isn't Digger herself."

A popular senior, Victoria Duke was Arbor High's head cheerleader and homecoming queen, but she had been laying low since the homecoming dance. Though the vivacious blonde had gone to the formal with Brett Woods, she had met up with her old boyfriend—Josh, the troublemaker—in the school gym and had shown a new side of herself. Basically, she and Josh drank too much of the liquor that Josh had smuggled in. His drunken antics brought the dance to a halt. In the excitement, she threw up all over herself and the rest of the homecoming court. From then on at school, she ate her lunch every day in the guidance counselor's office with Miss Thelma Hopper, who was also the cheerleading advisor. That was so the other kids couldn't tease her or, worse yet, banish her from her seat in the senior section. But now she was crossing the cafeteria on a beeline toward the Barf Table.

Bennie Pressler, always the comedian, was first to greet her. "Hi'ya, Vicki," Bennie said. "You'll forgive me if I don't stand up." He reached down to release the brake on his wheelchair so that he could move and make room for her between himself and Brett. "To what do we owe this honor on this beautiful Waisin Wednesday?"

She knew exactly what he was referring to—the day when raisins were served for lunch and when everyone showered the freshmen section with clumps of the sticky, dried fruit. The Barf Table always got the worst treatment, even from fellow 9th graders.

"No, Bennie," said Vicki. "I'm not staying long. I just heard that Brett's going on a big trip, and I wanted to say goodbye—and to wish you luck, Brett." She bent down and put her arms around his shoulders and gave him a quick hug.

Brett blushed. "Thanks, Vicki," he said. "How'd you hear?"

"Your dad," said the girl. "He was talking to Miss Hopper in the guidance office. He said this is your last day until … when? Sometime in February?"

Brett gave her a confused look. "I don't know," he said. "I guess so. Why do you care?"

"Yeah, Digger," said Nicie, who had never liked the cheerleader. "What's it to you? Aren't you still dating Josh?"

Vicki surprised them by smiling. "Of all the names I've been called since homecoming," she said, "that's my favorite, Nicie. It beats Icky Vicki or Vicki Puke. I so glad you transferred here from Mimosa Beach." She looked around the lunchroom. "I mean, I'm surprised nobody has come over here to fake-barf a handful of raisins or mouthful of milk on me."

Leah Russo spoke up. "Well, you *are* standing here at the Barf Table with us. If you're still here when the bell rings in a couple minutes, you'd better watch out."

"I don't plan to be," Vicki said. "And, no, Nicie, I'm not dating Josh now— that loser." She studied her spotless tennis shoes for a moment. "While I'm here

I want to apologize—to all of you," she began, now blushing herself. "I—well, *we*—ruined the homecoming dance, and you all got punished because of my bad decisions. Well, I'm gonna make it up to you—to all of you."

Little Ricky Duran glanced over at Brett Woods before announcing, "Victoria, since you are no longer dating Josh, and since Brett is leaving for Hawaii tonight, I would like to ask if you need an escort to the next school dance. The next dance is at Valentine's Day—is that right? As your escort, I would be happy to save all my dances for you, Victoria."

Bennie Pressler spat out his sip of Yoo-hoo; Tommy White grimaced from being hit by the spray; and Ty Green almost choked on his fries. Nicie patted her boyfriend on the back and laughed. "You'd better grab that little man, Digger, before he gets away," said Nicie. "You ain't gonna get a better offer than that— not at *this* school. Ricky here is a dancing machine—unlike *someone else* I know." She slapped Ty again.

"Not feeling the love," said Ty with a straight face. Then he laughed.

Leah Russo swallowed a fry and raised one eyebrow at Brett Woods. "Are you okay with that?" she said.

"Why shouldn't I be?" said Brett. "That's up to Digger—I mean, to Victoria. Sorry, Vicki."

The cheerleader's smile appeared genuine, as she laid her hand on Brett's shoulder and squeezed it a couple of times. "Oh, Leah," said Digger, "don't you worry about our Brett. He's gonna be surrounded by pretty surfer girls and Hawaiian princesses all winter long. We'll be lucky to get him back by Valentine's Day." She patted his shoulder.

"And the only dance he's gonna do," added Bennie Pressler, "is the hula—or whatever they call that dance those tough-looking guys do at luaus."

Right then, the release bell rang for upperclassmen, and clumps of raisins— like molten lava from an erupting volcano—rained down upon the Barf Table. Digger shrieked and covered her hair with her hands as she ran away. Nicie and Ty snatched up their bags and hurried out of the danger zone. Bennie, Tommy and Ricky covered their food as best they could. Leah flipped up her hoodie as she rose to leave, and Brett held above his head the wide cardboard tray that had carried the fries.

As she passed his seat, Leah ducked her own head under the tray and leaned close to Brett's ear. "Will Bennie know how to reach you?" she asked.

"Yeah, I guess so."

She felt her face flush. "Good," she said. "We can be pen pals this winter—that is, unless you're too busy learning how to do the hula."

Leah's eyes twinkled, and Brett smiled.

Chapter 3

ON HIS WAY HOME from basketball practice that Wednesday night, Ty Green slowed his car on the highway as he saw the Bauer family's farm road up ahead. Two rural mailboxes stood there like silent sentries—one for the farmhouse about a quarter mile down the coquina- and marl-covered lane, the other for an older, smaller cottage across Ebenezerville Road. The nearer and more battered mailbox—the one with "Mr. & Mrs. Harry Bauer" stenciled on the side—also bore a wreath of still-white carnations fastened to the wooden post beneath the large metal box. The newer mailbox bore the name "Duran."

Ty parked his old white Ford LTD at the farmhouse and jogged through the yard to the Bauers' back door, peering inside to see if anyone was sitting in one of the stuffed chairs on the enclosed back porch. He knocked lightly twice and saw a light come on in Grandpa Bauer's makeshift bedroom off the kitchen. Artie, not Grandpa, appeared in the doorway and looked out through a kitchen window to see his best friend and teammate standing at the back door. Ty saw that Artie was holding a baseball bat as the big farm boy turned on the porch's overhead light and came to open the back door to let him in.

"Grandpa pitching you some batting practice?" Ty said as he entered. "Kinda late for that, isn't it? Or early, if we're talking about the season."

Artie shook his head but smiled. "You're a funny man, Ty Green." He locked the door behind Ty and offered his friend a seat on the porch. "It's kinda chilly out here," said Artie, "but I don't want to disturb Grandpa. What's up?"

"Well, a couple of things," Ty said, "but, seriously, why are you armed with a baseball bat? You expecting visitors tonight—besides me, I mean?"

"I wasn't expecting *you*," said Artie. "No, a sketchy guy came out here around noon. I think he was checking to see if we were home—you know, to break in."

Ty was quiet for a second. "Yeah, I've heard about people doing that—seeing in the paper that someone died and then robbing them when they're at the funeral. You think that's what the guy was doing?"

"Yeah, but he didn't see anything in the paper," said Artie. "That white wreath on the mailbox probably pulled him in off the highway. I should've taken it down Sunday night after Grandma's funeral, but I didn't want to stop and do that with Grandpa in the truck. I needed to get him home and back into bed. And I haven't been out since then—just not in the mood."

Ty nodded. "I don't blame you, buddy. So, how did you handle the guy off the highway? You didn't let him into the house, did you?"

"Are you kidding?" replied Artie. "He said he was delivering a pizza from Woody's, and he tried to get into the house to use the phone. But he was filthy, and he looked like he'd slept in his clothes. His car was sketchy, too, but I couldn't get a tag number because the back bumper was gone."

"Did you call Woody and tell him?" Ty asked. "I mean, he was over at the school about then, but he didn't stay long. Matter of fact, that's part of what I was going tell you—about Brett and his folks. They're going to Hawaii for the winter."

"Yeah, I know. Brett and Woody and Ms. Woods came out here this afternoon and told me. It was out of their way, but they wanted to drop some food off here before they went to the airport up in Iron Harbor. They told me all about their trip, and I told Woody about my visitor."

Ty Green sniffed the air. "I *thought* I smelled something good—better than you can cook, anyway. What is that?"

"A whole pork roast," said Artie, "and there's a big tub of slaw in the fridge, a huge bag of fries, and another big bag of hush puppies. All we'll have to do is heat them up tomorrow."

"Speaking of tomorrow," Ty said, "what time do you want us to be here?

I mean, what would be too early? We don't want to catch you and Grandpa lounging around in your drawers." He grinned.

Artie shook his head. "You aren't gonna catch me undressed," he said, "*or* Grandpa. I have to milk the cows at zero-dark-thirty, and we'll be lucky if we can get Grandpa up out of bed and into his wheelchair. He really misses Grandma. So do I, but somebody has to do the work."

"What about the Durans?" asked Ty. "Aren't they helping out? I mean, they live right across the highway in your family's old homeplace."

"They've been doing more than their share ever since Grandpa's accident this fall," Artie said. "The work that Ricardo and little Ricky do is worth twice what the rent would be on that old place if we were making them pay to stay there. And Gabby Duran is the best cook in Oleander County—almost as good as Grandma was."

Ty was quiet again for a few seconds. "How's *she* doing?" he finally asked, referring to Gabrielle Duran, who was Ricardo's wife and Ricky's mother.

"Okay, I guess," said Artie. "That was really a shock for her—to find Grandma like she did. And I think Gabby blames herself for not coming over here sooner—like she could've called for help in time to save Grandma. Your mom told me in the ER that it wouldn't have mattered—that she passed away sometime in the middle of the night."

Ty nodded. "Mom would know. She's a good nurse." He quickly changed the subject. "So, the other thing has to do with basketball," Ty began. "They told us after practice who the new boys' coach is gonna be, and I'm not exactly thrilled with the decision."

"Why not?" Artie asked. "Did Mr. Church decide to keep coaching you guys for the rest of the season? I didn't think the principal was supposed to coach a sport."

"Lurch Church *thinks* he knows everything about high school basketball," said Ty, with a snort, "but at least he's smart enough to hire someone else to fix all the damage he's done over the past few weeks. I wish Coach Jones hadn't quit."

"So, who's the new coach?"

"You're gonna love this," said Ty. "It's Nicie's old girls' coach from Mimosa Beach High. His name is Jimmy Foxx, and he's a real piece of work—at least, that's what Nicie says. I told her the news after practice. The guy meets us on Monday, and then our first game is Tuesday. Lurch said he'd help coach that game and then get outta the new guy's way."

"So, how's Nicie handling that?"

Ty Green's eyebrows shot up. "Not very well," he said. "Actually, the coach isn't her main problem. He's bringing his daughter with him, and she'll be on our girls' team. Nicie absolutely *hates* her. They got into some fights last year."

"Arguments?"

"No, *fights*. Fistfights. The worst one was in the locker room after a big game they lost. It was at Iron Harbor. Remember?"

"Yeah, now I do," said Artie, "because it made the local sports that Nicie got suspended. And then Mimosa Beach came here and played us. Without Nicie in their lineup, we beat them bad. The coach's daughter wasn't all that good on her own."

"Well, she's a lot better this year," Ty said. "The girl's a junior now, and Nicie says she went to one of the best basketball camps in the state last summer. Colleges are already looking at her—*big* colleges."

"What about Nicie?" Artie asked. "Have any college coaches contacted her?"

"No," said Ty, "and we aren't sure why. Probably all the fights, because she wins them and always comes off looking like the bad guy—or girl, I mean. But these aren't ordinary chick fights, not by a long shot." He shuddered at the thought of taking a real punch from his girlfriend, who could bench-press more weight than any girl he'd ever known. "Or maybe it's the beach volleyball she plays in the summer."

"I don't know," said Artie, "but I need to go check on Grandpa. He's being awfully quiet." The two friends rose from their chairs and moved toward the back door. "Do me a favor?" Artie continued. "Stop at the mailbox and take down that wreath, will you?"

"Sure," Ty said. "I can bring it back tomorrow when we're all here for Thanksgiving—if you want to show it to your granddad or hang onto it a while longer. And, hey, I'll tell everybody to come between eleven-thirty and noon, okay?"

Artie Bauer nodded and waved goodbye to his friend. "That sounds good," he replied. Then he shut and locked the back door behind Ty Green and watched him walk to his car.

"This is gonna be some kind of Thanksgiving," the big farm boy murmured, shaking his head sadly at his choice of words, though no one else was there to misunderstand him.

Chapter 4

'I LIKE THIS CAR,' said Leah Russo, looking out the passenger-side window at the barren fields they whizzed past. "How does it handle?"

Nicie Evans smiled. "Like a dream," she said. "Daddy saw this one at the auto auction Saturday night. He said he could just see me in it, cruising at the beach with the top down. But he'll sell it before long." She glanced over at her passenger. "How old are you, anyway?"

"Fifteen," said Leah. "I turn sixteen next October." Despite the oversized gray hoodie she wore, the snugness of the black seat harness and belt revealed her thinness, making her look younger than she was. Leah Russo had basically stopped eating almost a year earlier when her family had suffered the kind of tragedy that everyone fears—a fiery car crash that took the life of her big brother, everybody's hero at Arbor High.

Leah adjusted her green and gold Arbor Bruins cap and pulled her ponytail through the hole in back. "I'm signed up to take driver's ed in the spring," she said. "I don't know if I want to, though. Dad says he's tired of hauling me around, but Mom's acting funny about me driving. I think she's afraid the same thing will happen to me that happened to Reuben."

Nicie Evans grunted. "I'm sorry," she said, "but you are *not* your brother, and your daddy doesn't haul you around all *that* much." Her dark eyes flashed. "They been too busy going off on their little trips every weekend and leaving you to make do for yourself. You need to do what's right for you, girl."

Leah nodded but kept looking out her window. She missed her big brother. He had been Arbor High's best athlete—star quarterback and senior captain of the Bruins football team, high-scoring forward in basketball, and slugging third baseman in baseball previous years—and always the most popular boy in his class. Reuben Russo had everything going for him until that icy January day when his car skidded into the path of an overloaded logging truck on Ebenezerville Road near the high school.

"You need your driver's license, girl," said Nicie. "You got too many things you wanna do to be standing around waiting for somebody else to give you a ride. Me and Ty are graduating this spring—Artie, too. So, who you gonna catch rides with when we're gone? Bennie Pressler's daddy? You're older than Bennie, aren't you?"

"Yes, I am," Leah said, "but he'll have his own car before I will. His family is so rich, I bet he already has a Ferrari or Corvette picked out for his folks to buy him."

Nicie shook her head. "Nah, I figure that boy will be lucky if he gets out of that handicap van his daddy drives him around in. That horse therapy you're doing with him don't seem to be helping all that much." She signaled and shifted down to make the right turn onto the road to the Bauer farm.

"It takes time," said Leah. "It's helping me, and it'll help Bennie, too, once he gets out of that chair for good. He can stand up now, but he needs to do more weight training to get his leg muscles working right again."

"Speaking of which," Nicie said, eyeing her passenger, "you could do a little weightlifting yourself, honey—like lifting a spoon or fork to your mouth three times a day. Awright?"

Their eyes met for an instant, and Leah nodded. Then they both looked ahead as they passed the red barn and other farm buildings, and they saw the white, two-story farmhouse just down the road. The Bauers' old red pickup and the Durans' white work van with ladders atop sat along the edge of the yard.

Nicie was parking her blue sportster behind the van when one of the work vehicle's back doors popped open and little Ricky Duran hopped out.

"Hello, girls," Ricky greeted. "You're just in time! You can help me carry these boxes of food into the house."

Nicie huffed. "Do I look like a deliveryman? Come on, little dude. You can help us carry *our* food into the house, and then we *might* help you with yours."

Always eager to please a pretty girl, Ricky smiled. "I can do that, Nicie. What did you and Leah bring?" He closed the van door.

"Well, Leah brought a case of sodas," said Nicie, "and I baked a sweet potato casserole and two big pumpkin pies. What did your mama make?"

Ricky beamed. "My mother sent two loaves of bread, a pot of *pepian* stew," he said, "and the best Magdelana cake you will ever eat in your life. Mm-mm."

"She *sent* it?" Leah asked. "Where's Ricardo? You didn't drive over here by yourself, did you? I didn't know you had your driver's license."

He grinned. "I do many things that are surprising," he said. "Besides, all I had to do was cross the highway. It is not illegal for me to drive on the farm road. My father said I could drive his van here this morning, and Mr. Bauer always gives me permission when my help is needed. I drive his big tractor and the farm truck."

"That does it," said Leah. "If little Ricky is driving, I'm gonna *have* to learn just to keep up with him." Then she laughed. "Come on. Let's get all this stuff inside. I want to see how Artie's doing. And Mr. Bauer will be so happy to see you, Nicie. You know you're his favorite, right?"

Nicie gave a curt nod. "Me and Mr. Bauer are tight," she said. "I felt so bad for him on Sunday. He looked so pitiful, sitting there in his wheelchair next to the casket. He was always so rough and gruff before Mrs. Bauer died, even after his tractor accident. But at the church he just looked so sick at heart. I wanted to keep on hugging him."

The three friends gathered up the food and drinks from the sportster's trunk and carried it into the house, then returned for the boxes that Ricky's mother had sent. As they took on that second load, they heard another vehicle approaching them on the farm lane and saw the dust it kicked up on the road. It was Ty Green's white LTD, with Ty at the wheel and two passengers on board, one up front, the other in back.

"Who's with Ty?" asked Leah. "That looks like Tommy in the front seat. Is the other one Bennie? I figured his dad would bring them in their van."

"Yeah," Nicie said, "that wheelchair is a bear to deal with. I don't think there's enough room in the White Whale's trunk to hold it, what with the spare tire and Ty's sports equipment back there—everything you can imagine. He could open a sporting goods store. But maybe he cleaned it out for Bennie."

Like a racecar driver, Ty Green raised his hand out the driver-side window as the car rolled to a stop in the yard next to the sidewalk. "Good morning, ladies," said Ty, nodding to the girls, "and greetings, young Ricardo. Happy Thanksgiving."

Ty put the car in Park, set the parking brake and began rolling up his window, even though no one usually parked in the yard. Tommy White exited the car and hurried around to help Leah with the box she carried. Bennie remained seated in back and, uncharacteristically, kept quiet. In fact, he seemed happy sitting there, and neither Ty nor Tommy made a move to help their friend get out of the car or to open the LTD's trunk to remove his wheelchair.

As the five teens walked up the handicap ramp to the back porch door, Nicie Evans stopped and looked back at Bennie Pressler sitting alone in the car. "You guys not gonna help him?" Nicie asked. "He looks like Jonah in the White Whale—except he looks happy as a clam. What are you boys up to?"

Ty Green and Tommy White exchanged a knowing look, and Ty nodded to the younger boy, giving him permission to explain. "It's tough love," said Tommy. "We all agreed that Bennie needs to stop depending so much on everybody else."

"That's right," Ty added, "and that was Mr. Pressler's idea, not ours. He said we should make Bennie open his own doors and get wherever he's going without so much help."

Leah sputtered, "But that's mean. He can't unload his wheelchair. He might fall and hurt himself again. You know he had a stroke when that surfboard hit him. He can't do that yet."

Ty shrugged and held the back door open for the others. "Then he'll have fun eating his lunch in the Whale," said Ty. "His mother sent a kugel—I think that's what he called it. It's sitting on the back seat with him. It looked filling."

"What did *you* bring for lunch?" Nicie said, eyeing her boyfriend with disdain. "I don't see you carrying anything. And don't say, 'I brought my appetite.' That's lame."

Seeing that his girlfriend was losing patience with him, Ty remembered the saying about discretion being the better part of valor. "Hold on, hold on," he said. "I need to get Artie out here—and his grandpa, too, if he's able."

"Oh?" said Nicie. "You aren't gonna make Mr. Bauer get out of bed all by himself and not use his wheelchair anymore, are you?"

Ty held up his hand to quiet her—a move that infuriated Nicie even more. "Not hardly," he said, calming her. "We've got a surprise—well, Bennie does. But that's all I'm gonna say. Just take the food on inside and come back out here and wait for me and Artie. We'll get Grandpa, but it might take us a few minutes. Just be cool. You'll see."

Following his friends through the enclosed porch and into the house, Ty stuck his head into Grandpa Bauer's makeshift bedroom off the kitchen and saw Artie sitting in the easy chair at the head of the bed. "Hi, buddy," said Ty Green in a low voice. "Thanks for unlocking the back door for us. How's he doing?" Ty nodded toward Grandpa, whose eyes were closed.

"About the same," Artie whispered, "but I think this will help him—give him a reason to keep working. I'm glad you gave me a heads up. Where'd you call from?"

"Front seat of the Whale," said Ty, with a chuckle. "Bennie's cell phone. I'm not sure I want one of those things. I kinda like 'running out of gas' and not getting help quick, you know?"

Artie Bauer smiled and shook his head at his best friend's joke. "You're hopeless," Artie said, then added in a louder voice, "Grandpa? You awake? You ready to get up?"

The gray-haired old fellow—already dressed in clean pajamas—grunted his assent and opened one eye at the tall teenager standing beside Artie. "Run out of gas, huh?" Harry Bauer croaked, with a grin that stretched across his bristled cheeks. "That still work?"

"Grandpa!" said Artie. "You're telling on yourself." With a laugh, the big farm boy rose and leaned down to put the old man's slippers where he could slide into them. "Okay, Grandpa, let's get up and go see the surprise that Bennie has for us."

After the two boys helped Grandpa into his wheelchair, Artie pushed his grandfather through the kitchen and around the long table full of food with eight place settings of paper plates, plastic flatware and red cups. Ty held open the doors onto and off the enclosed porch so that they could join the others standing outside on the ramp and in the yard. They took care not to brush up against the thorny, old rosebush growing against the house near the back door. Bennie still sat quietly on the back seat of the white LTD parked in the brown grass of the back lawn. He grinned—not mischievously, but in anticipation of something hopeful and good—as he watched Artie and Grandpa emerge from the back porch.

"We're ready!" Ty shouted to Bennie, as the kids on the ramp parted so that Grandpa Bauer could see the boy in the car. Tommy, standing in the grass, moved closer to Bennie's car door but gave no indication of offering help.

Remaining seated a few seconds longer, Bennie gathered himself for this act that he had practiced alone over the previous couple of weeks but had never completed without two or three epic failures. Finally, he leaned toward the car door, pulled the latch and pushed it open, blocking the spectators' view somewhat. Then he straightened up and brushed his dark, curly hair from his eyes, and took hold of something in the floorboard behind the front seats. He twisted and set the large object on the sidewalk just outside the car, then turned and leaned out to make two separate adjustments, each with a distinct, metallic click as the hollow aluminum tubes of the walker snapped into place. Bennie set one sneaker-clad foot, then the other outside the car onto the concrete path and within the frame of the walker. Then he began to rock forward, and, on the count of three, he rose to stand on his own, with only the walker's support. The others encouraged him as they realized what he was doing for the first time in public. They cheered as he walked slowly toward the ramp and closer to them.

Even Grandpa Bauer understood the significance of what young Bennie Pressler had then achieved, and he also knew how difficult the feat had been. When red-faced Bennie came face to face with Grandpa just outside the door to the porch, the old man said, "I'm proud of you, son." His voice cracked as he added, "It's a Thanksgiving miracle. Next time you're here, we'll walk up the ramp together."

Chapter 5

WARMING IN GRANDMA'S OVEN, the Thanksgiving turkey had been roasted overnight by Ty Green's mother and delivered to the farm before sunrise. Rachel Green was used to caring for people, as she was a nurse at the hospital in Ebenezerville. She was working her regular shift that day and would eat a late Thanksgiving dinner with her husband and son that evening. To the Bauers, she was more than just Ty's mother. She had become a member of their family ever since the tractor accident that had almost taken Harry Bauer's life. Her patience and guidance, especially in hospital-related matters, had helped Pearl Bauer through her husband's brush with death and had eased the elderly woman's fears about dealing with a situation that seemed out of her control. Rachel Green, like her son and his friends, was part of Artie's *farmily*, as Ty had dubbed the group's kinship. Other Barf Table parents—like Woody Woods, Ricardo and Gabby Duran, Abe Pressler, and Donnell Evans, Nicie's father—were also extended farmily members.

With potholders in each hand, Nicie Evans lifted the roasting pan from the oven and carried it to the table. For her part, Leah Russo had already finished microwaving the pork roast and fries from Woody Woods and the other potluck dishes that needed warming. It would be a feast.

Nicie placed the turkey near Grandpa Bauer at the head of the table and smiled down at him. "You do the honors, Mr. Bauer," she said. "That's a fine turkey—and I even helped stuff it."

"I'm happy to say the blessing," said Harry Bauer, "but I think somebody else needs to do the carving." He nodded at his grandson sitting on his right.

"Artie, son, you're the man of the house now," said Harry, "at least until I'm back on my feet."

"That's the spirit, Mr. Bauer," said Nicie. She patted him on the back, leaned down and gave him a peck on his whiskery cheek.

Harry blushed. "Young lady, that was my daddy's name," he said. "You call me Grandpa, just like that big old boy you're dating does and *has* ever since he was a little scutter."

Just then a knock came at the back door. Artie rose from the table and hurried out onto the porch to see who was holding up their special meal. He recognized the tall, middle-aged woman in a slouch hat and work clothes right away. Her name was Minnie Marecek, a therapist who had been working with Bennie Pressler and Leah Russo on the farm twice a week for over a month—in the stable and corral, to be precise. Minnie was an expert in equine therapy. She also was the unmarried aunt of the only other heavyweight besides Artie on the Arbor High wrestling team. For that reason alone, Artie knew Dr. Marecek from the wrestling matches she had attended the past three seasons, even though Artie was the only Bruins heavyweight who got to wrestle as a starter since his junior year. Minnie was one of Artie's biggest fans.

"Hi, Doc," said Artie, as he pushed the screen door open for her. "What's up?"

"Did I miss the surprise?" she said, stepping onto the porch. "Abe Pressler called me this morning and said I should come out here and see Bennie for some reason. He wouldn't tell me why, exactly, just that I shouldn't miss it. But it looks like I did."

Artie nodded. "Yeah, but come on in. I'll let Bennie tell you about it himself. We're getting ready to eat, but you can join us, can't you?"

"No," she said, shaking her head. "I'd better not, but I can stick my head in and say 'hi' to everybody. Looks like you've got a crowd."

Minnie let Artie step around her and return to his seat in the kitchen. As he sat down, she stopped in the doorway and waved to Grandpa Bauer first, then to the rest of the gathering. "Happy Thanksgiving, everyone," she said, looking around the table. "I came out to check on one of the horses, but, Bennie, I understand you have something special to tell me."

Bennie Pressler's eyes lit up. "Yes, ma'am," he said. "I left that old wheelchair at home this morning, and I *walked* all the way from that big white car outside to this kitchen chair, the one I'm sitting in. And I did it *all by myself*—well, with a walker, anyway."

"That's great," Minnie said. "Before long you'll be hopping on and off horses like a rodeo cowboy."

"Or rodeo *clown*," interrupted Leah Russo, who shared therapy sessions with Bennie, her buddy since the start of school that year. Because the two were 9th graders and shared similar interests, they were always paired in school-related activities—Leah, as a budding sports reporter; Bennie, as a gadget guy, aspiring announcer and wannabe comedian. Only Leah—and maybe Nicie—could have gotten away with zinging Bennie like that, because they all had grown so close as Barf Table mates.

"Either way," Bennie said, with a grin, "I'm not gonna need that big old lift soon to get me on and off my horse. And even if I fall down and look like a fool, rodeo clowns are great athletes, *and* they're funny. I can handle that."

Dr. Marecek wished them farewell and returned to the barn to check on the horse she had mentioned. Weeks earlier, Ricardo Duran had expanded the stable area and tack room. The Bauers' big workhorses—Tom and Dick—had always been kept there, but that fall Abe Pressler, Bennie's father, had arranged for the psychologist to board two of her therapy horses on the Bauer farm for Bennie and Leah to ride during their Wednesday evening and Saturday afternoon sessions. Minnie's work with Bennie involved mainly physical and occupational therapy. With Leah, the hours riding and caring for her horse provided her with emotional support to overcome her eating disorders and anger issues that stemmed from the loss of her older brother.

Until the start of wrestling practice at Arbor High, Dr. Marecek had brought an assistant along to help with Bennie's therapy sessions, in particular. Tommy White, who lived with the Presslers, had always come to the farm, too, but he was still learning how to lead the horse and to walk next to the rider as the assistant had been trained to do. When wrestling season started, Dr. Marecek lost both her assistant and Tommy to the wrestling team on Wednesday evenings and on the occasional Saturday when tournaments were scheduled. The assistant, a senior at Arbor High, was Minnie's niece—Wilma Marecek, the team's other heavyweight besides Artie Bauer.

This was Wilma's fourth year as the wrestling team's only female member. Not only was she big and strong, she was smart and talented. In fact, Wilma was Artie's main competition for the Ebenezer Endowment, a four-year college scholarship that went to the best senior student-athletes in Oleander County. The recipients had to attend Iron Harbor A&M, but that was where Artie wanted to go anyway so that he could study agriculture close to his family—or what was left of it after Pearl Bauer's death. Wilma wouldn't mind going to A&M either, because her father was an officer stationed at the Iron Harbor Naval Base. When he was deployed overseas for months at a time—as was the case right then— Wilma and her mother would move into Minnie Marecek's house in a quiet subdivision on the river between Port Oleander and Monk's Landing. Wilma had chosen to attend Arbor High because she liked the school's size and because it had been easy enough for her aunt to drop her off there on Minnie's way to the stable space she rented near Mimosa Beach. The stables there were owned by a wealthy local developer whose spoiled son had been Brett Woods's former friend and had ruined homecoming at Arbor High.

All the Barf Table friends had talked their families into delaying their usual Thanksgiving gatherings until later in the afternoon. That gave the teenagers a couple of hours to spend on the farm with Artie and his grandfather before they all had to go their separate ways.

Leah Russo was the only one who wouldn't be going home to another family get-together, as this was the first Thanksgiving since her brother Reuben Russo's death, and her parents had left town yet again to trick themselves into not thinking about him. They never took struggling Leah along on these trips, because her very presence and appearance reminded them that they weren't hurting as much as she was. The girl's depression—she was in Stage 4 of her grief, according to Minnie—was becoming less of a burden for her as she learned to open up to her friends and to the therapist. She also shifted the weight of her worries onto the strong back of Micki, the chestnut mare she rode and cared for under Dr. Marecek's guidance.

After the plates, utensils and cups were collected in a garbage bag and the leftover food was stowed in the refrigerator, the group retired to the back porch, where Ty Green and Tommy White helped Grandpa into his favorite easy chair. Artie Bauer collapsed the wheelchair and set it aside to clear a path for Bennie Pressler's walker. Once all the teenagers were seated on the old sofa and loveseat and in the other old chair—all of it cast-off furniture from decades past—the after-lunch conversation turned to Brett Woods, the farmily member who was absent.

"I wonder if Brett has gone surfing yet," said Ricky Duran, seated between Leah and Tommy on the sofa.

Sitting at the far end next to one sofa arm, Bennie leaned forward and looked around Tommy. "No way," Bennie said to Ricky. "They aren't even there yet. He's gonna send me a message after they get settled in their rental house and he has time to find a computer to use. It'll probably come in the middle of the night or even tomorrow morning—you know, the time difference and all."

Leah's eyebrows rose. "How's he gonna do that from Hawaii—send you a message, I mean." Then she said, "By messenger pigeon?"

Bennie laughed. "It's about that fast," he said. "It's called FidoNet, and it's like America Online or CompuServe, but it's free."

"FidoNet?" said Tommy. "Is that what you're always messing with at home?"

"Well, kind of," Bennie said. "My BBS is hooked into FidoNet. It's a network of computer bulletin boards, and it *fetches* electronic messages—you know, like a dog."

Artie spoke up. "You can do that from the computer lab at school," Artie said. "Coach Johnson gets a bunch of email messages every day, and he has me sort through them and print out the important ones for him. He doesn't like messing with computers."

"The man's a dinosaur," said Bennie. "Before long, that'll be the *only* way we send mail."

"I hope not," Nicie Evans said. "I like a good, handwritten love letter now and then." She elbowed Ty Green sitting next to her on the loveseat.

"What?" Ty said. "You always say you can't *read* my handwriting. At least you could read my sweet nothings on a computer."

"*Nothing* is about right," said Nicie. "My mama still has the letters Daddy sent her back when he was in Vietnam. She wouldn't give them up for nothing."

At that, Grandpa Bauer lifted his hand on the chair's armrest. "I used to write Pearl—Artie's grandma—a love letter every day when I was in Korea," he said. "She saved every last one of them. She tied them up with a yellow silk ribbon and put them in her hope chest." He took a breath. "I guess she was *hoping* I'd come home safe so we could get married finally."

"Can we read them—your letters?" asked Nicie. "Or are they too mushy?"

Some color rose into Harry Bauer's pale cheeks for a change. "No, ma'am," he said, but with a chuckle. "Over my dead body. Matter of fact, I told Pearl to burn them things back when I was in the hospital, thinking I wasn't gonna make it out."

"That bad, huh?" said Bennie Pressler. "Now, you see? If they'd been email messages, you could've just deleted every last one of them by pushing a button. By the way, where's Mrs. Bauer's old hope chest now? I hope it's locked." He cut his eyes toward Nicie.

It was Grandpa's turn to laugh. "Nobody's gonna get into that old cedar chest," he said. "It was in our daughter's room until Artie here came along. Then we moved it up to the attic to make room for his crib. Far as I know, it's still up there under a pile of junk." He thought better of giving the teens that information. "I'd better not hear any bumping around up there in the attic," he said. "You know it's haunted, right?"

Artie snorted. "Don't listen to him," Artie told the group. "That's what he always said to keep me from snooping around when I was little—or that there was an escaped convict hiding up there. But he's right about all the junk. It's a big mess." He grinned and added, "Besides, Nicie, you wouldn't be able to read Grandpa's bad handwriting, either. It's worse than Ty's."

"Hey, now," said Ty Green, acting hurt. "Guys like me and Grandpa don't waste our time practicing our penmanship. We're lovers, not writers. Ain't that right, Grandpa?"

Harry Bauer frowned and nodded his head once in a big way, but he couldn't hide the twinkle in his steel-blue eyes. "That's right, son," he said. "And speaking of Fido-whatever-it-was, I need to go see a man about a dog. Pardon my French, ladies."

Grandpa's announcement broke everyone up, as well as the gathering itself. They were still laughing as they piled back into their cars to go home—Ty Green, with Bennie Pressler and Tommy White; Nicie Evans, with Leah Russo, who had decided to spend the long weekend with the Evanses; and Ricky Duran, in his father's work van.

Artie Bauer still had milking and other late-day farm chores to do, but after helping Grandpa to the bathroom and back to bed, the big farm boy took a few minutes to sit, rest and watch part of the pro football game on TV. He paid attention to the offensive linemen and wondered if he'd ever be good enough to play in the NFL. He knew, though, that the odds of becoming a pro linemen were one in a thousand. He wasn't even that good at wrestling, though he enjoyed the sport and looked forward to the high school season ahead. His real chance to shine was in baseball, as his best friend Ty Green's battery mate. Both he and Ty had the opportunity to go somewhere in baseball, either to the college ranks or to the minor leagues. But they'd both have to get through their respective winter sports before baseball season rolled around in the spring.

* * *

On the road home, Nicie Evans glanced at Leah Russo in the blue sportster's passenger seat. "You and I need to have a talk," said Nicie, returning her attention to the highway ahead.

"I ate," Leah said. "I ate a lot—for me."

"No, not that," said Nicie, "but I *am* proud of you for eating some vegetables, at least. No, we need to talk about ... guys."

Leah frowned. "What? Are you having trouble with Ty?"

"Ty Green?" Nicie said. "Not hardly. We're both whupped." She shifted gears. "No, you and I need to talk about *your* boyfriend."

"I don't have one."

"Well, I think you do," said Nicie. "I think you like Brett Woods, but you don't want to hurt anybody's feelings—like Artie or Bennie. Right?"

Leah shrugged and turned her head to look out her window. "Yeah, maybe," she said. "Artie's like a big brother, and I think he feels the same way about me. But I'm just not sure. And then there's Bennie. Well, he's funny and smart and all, and we're *always* together at school and now after school. But I'm pretty sure we're just friends. I don't *feel* anything else."

"Is it because of his accident?"

"You mean, because he's learning to walk again?" asked Leah. "No, that isn't it—at least I don't think so." For a moment, she wondered if Bennie's disability had, in fact, affected the way she saw him. "No," she continued, shaking her head, "there's just no ... spark ... between us, not like you and Ty."

Nicie smiled and nodded. "Do you feel that spark with Brett?"

"Maybe."

"Well, girl," said Nicie, "now you're gonna get a chance to see just how much you miss that boy, and how much you like Bennie Pressler. You know, his family has money—well, Brett Woods's folks do, too—but not like the Presslers. That's why ol' Digger Duke was after both of them at one time or another. Remember? She dumped poor Bennie after his accident, and she was stringing Brett along pretty good at homecoming. You ready to compete with her?"

Leah turned her head toward Nicie and studied her serious expression. "I don't know," Leah said. "I don't care about money. And I'm don't care how popular a guy is—or how popular dating him makes *me*. But I can't compete with Vicki Duke, and I sure don't want to set myself up for that kind of pain. I hurt bad enough now."

That ended the conversation until they got closer to home. But as the little blue car rolled past brown cornfields and leaf-strewn woods, Leah Russo wondered if she were waiting for the wrong young man to heal the ache she felt in her heart. Maybe that person had already been a part of her life and now was gone, never to return.

Chapter 6

BLACK FRIDAY DAWNED like every other fall morning in the Evans household, with Nicie's parents leaving early for their respective jobs. Her mother Alicia worked in a big hotel on the strand at Mimosa Beach, and her father Donnell ran his own garage and wrecker service in a building he rented on Coastal Highway connecting Mimosa Beach and Monk's Landing. The girls—Nicie and Leah—had no intentions of going shopping that day, as the beach mall and large department stores would be packed with bargain hunters and kids out of school for the long holiday weekend. No, Nicie Evans and Leah Russo decided to spend the morning at the beach—at smaller and less touristy Sandpiper Beach near Monk's Landing.

For late November, the weather was mild—sunny and warmer than usual, with a chill in the air only until the sun rose above the tree line. The Evanses' house was an older, red-brick rancher that sat at the end of a cul-de-sac off Shore Drive, the winding road that followed the actual shoreline and connected all the beach communities in Oleander County. Nicie and Leah stowed their sand chairs and beach towels in the sportster's trunk. They didn't bother taking a cooler of sandwiches and drinks, because they had to be back home by noon. The Arbor High Bruinettes basketball team had practice at one o'clock, and both girls had to be there. Nicie was the team's star forward; Leah was team scorekeeper and unofficial assistant coach, as she'd been for the varsity football team that fall.

They left the sportster's convertible top up for their short drive to Sandpiper Beach. After parking in the public lot near the fishing pier, the friends grabbed their gear and hurried onto the strand to get situated before other beachgoers took the choicest spots. At that hour, mainly dog walkers and the occasional surf fisherman were the only other people on the beach. Since fish weren't running close to shore right then, only the least serious anglers with nothing better to do sat bundled up at wide intervals on the rickety wooden pier. Some of the older men smoked and drank coffee to pass the time; others just stared at the tips of their long poles and waited to see if a stray fish took their bait.

"Look at those guys," said Nicie Evans as she plopped down into her sand chair. "How many of them are married, you think? And how many didn't want to go Christmas shopping with their wives today? Daddy would be here if he didn't have the garage to keep him busy."

Leah Russo laughed. "I know I'd rather fish than shop." Sitting only inches above the wet sand of mid-tide, she leaned forward in her chair and peered up the strand toward the volleyball court outside Woody's Surf Shop & Grill. "I wonder what Brett's doing right now," Leah said, seeing that the volleyball net had been removed and that the picnic tables on the patio outside the grill were gone.

"I don't know," said Nicie Evans. "I've never been to Hawaii. You?"

Leah shook her head. "I wish," she said. "I mean, I saw *Endless Summer*— not because I wanted to, though. Dad rented that video for us to watch one Saturday night, and the next thing I knew, he was out there in a wetsuit on a board with a couple of Reuben's friends." She pointed toward the breakwater. "It was embarrassing."

"Only time we get good waves here," said Nicie, "is when storms are coming in. I watch the boys—and a few girls—surf in the summertime when I'm playing volleyball at the hotel, but that's not my thing, sitting out there in that deep water."

"Why not?"

Nicie humphed. "You ever been to the docks and seen what those boats catch in their nets?" She made a face. "Not just fish and shrimp. They pull in some stuff that would curl your hair if you knew it was swimming around out there under your toes."

Restless, Nicie pushed up from her low chair and stood next to her friend. She shed the light jacket she wore over a T-shirt and shorts, took off her sneakers and socks, and tossed it all in her empty seat. Leah took the hint and removed her own shoes, but left on the oversized gray hoodie and jeans that she always wore. The wet, hard sand was cool on the soles of her feet.

"We going for a walk?" asked Leah. "Up the beach or down?"

Nicie nodded toward the vacant surf shop. "Let's go see if there's a note on the door," she said. "Maybe it has a phone number you can use to call your boyfriend in Hawaii."

Leah slapped at her friend but missed. "Stop it," said Leah, as they started up the strand. "I thought about that all last night—about that *spark* you were talking about yesterday in the car—and I don't think I've ever felt a spark for any boy except my brother."

"Excuse me?" Nicie said, her eyes wide. "Girl, you know you aren't supposed to have those kinds of feelings for your brother, not even a good-looking one like Reuben Russo. He really was fine, though—rest his soul."

"Noooooo," Leah groaned. "That's *not* what I meant." She shook her head and tried to explain. "Reuben was the best big brother ever," she said. "He told me the truth about things—about what I was good at and what I needed to work on. He spent a lot of time with me when I was little, and he taught me how to do all the things he was learning how to do—to play sports and like good books and not be afraid to be myself. He read to me all the time. But he didn't treat me like a kid, the way Dad and Mom do. My brother treated me like I was his best friend, and he taught me what's important—even if he didn't mean to." She was referring to his death.

"I understand," said Nicie, still walking. "The spark between you two was love, but it was the best kind of love. I always wished I had a big brother like that. But after Mama and Daddy had me, they called it quits, I guess."

Leah smiled and reached over to touch Nicie's shoulder. "Can't top perfection, huh?" Leah said, then looked up and stopped in her tracks. "Hey, we've got company."

Still without his wheelchair, Bennie Pressler had walked with Tommy White around the surf shop and up the alley from Beach Street. They had been dropped off by Bennie's mother, who didn't work a nine-to-five job as she handled the family company's charitable efforts. The boys were headed toward the fence railing that separated Woody's patio from the sand where the bare volleyball poles stood. Tommy was first to look down the strand and spot the two girls, as Bennie was focused on placing the feet of his walker on solid ground. Leah saw Tommy wave, turn and say something to Bennie, who looked up and shouted, "Hey, ladies! Come over here! I've got something to show you!"

Bennie wasn't kidding around this time. In fact, it was as if he had overheard Leah and Nicie's conversations about boys. When the girls reached the pair on the patio, Bennie took a square of paper from his pocket, unfolded the sheet and extended it to Nicie for her to read. "Go ahead," he said. "Read it out loud. It's from Brett."

Nicie glanced over at Leah, who nodded for her to proceed. "Okay," Nicie said. "Here goes. It's pretty long." She squinted down at the big block of dot-matrix printing on the bright white paper and started reading the words that Brett had sent from Hawaii:

"Hey dude. OK to share this note with everybody so I only have to write one. Got here after dark and moved into our house. Not big like home but mom and dad like it and its 10 minutes from beach. But everywhere here is 10 minutes from a beach! Havent seen the waves yet but this is hawaii right? Before I forget, I need you to ask leah something for me."

With that, Nicie stopped reading and started to hand the paper to Leah, in case that part was personal. "No," said Bennie, "it isn't anything bad. It's about school. His parents are making him keep up with his schoolwork. They know better than to rely on me to get his assignments for him. I might give him *my* homework to do."

Nicie nodded and continued: "Ask her to go see miss hopper every fri to get my work and send it to me over the weekend so I can do it and fax it back to school. Its gonna cost a bundle but mom said if I dont do my work we will have to go home. Dad told me I better not mess up his time here in paradise so I will try to do my work (when ocean is flat haha). Say hi to tommy and good luck with wrestling. Hi to everybody at the barf table. Thank leah for helping me. See you. Brett."

Bennie took the paper, refolded it and stuck it back in his pocket. Turning to Leah, he asked, "So, can you do that for him—get his assignments together and email him? You can use the computer and modem in the lab at school to get on my bulletin board. Or maybe I can rig something else up."

"Why can't Miss Hopper just fax the assignments to him?" said Leah. "Wouldn't that be the easy thing to do?"

"Yeah," Bennie said, "but I guess Woody didn't want to lug a fax machine and big old laptop all the way to Hawaii. I'm pretty sure Brett's books were enough trouble. And the school probably doesn't want to spend that kind of money on long-distance fax calls—not for a kid who's basically skipping school to go surfing. Before they left, I gave Brett a list of free BBSes on Oahu, but I have no idea how he even sent *this* message. I guess he found a library or internet cafe."

Leah felt conflicted—pleased that Brett was thinking of her, but annoyed that he would take her help for granted. "Well, he should've asked me himself *before* he flew off to Hawaii," she said. "I'm busy with my own stuff, and doing that for him is gonna be a lot of trouble. What if I can't get into the computer lab right away? There's only one computer there that's hooked to an outside phone line, and I'll have to wait behind all the coaches who use it—you know, like Artie does for Coach Johnson."

"Oh, don't worry," said Bennie, holding up a hand to calm her. "I said we can work something out. Maybe we can—"

Just then, a loud banging came from the alley next to the surf shop, where a large green dumpster sat. The garbage receptacle was used by Woody's two businesses, mainly the grill, and by the real estate office across the alleyway. Sandpiper Realty, however, was still closed for Thanksgiving and wouldn't reopen until Monday. The sound of something heavy hitting the trash container's metal sides and bottom rang out again and again.

"Who's doing that?" Bennie said. "It sounds like they're using a baseball bat."

Tommy straightened up and started moving toward the alley, where he and Bennie had walked minutes earlier. "I'll check," said Tommy. "Probably just some bum dumpster diving."

"I'll go with you," Nicie volunteered. "These two need a minute to work things out, and you might need some backup."

They both laughed and disappeared around the corner of the building, the banging still going on.

Though they were alone, Bennie turned back to Leah and said in a lower voice, "I didn't want to say anything in front of Nicie and Tommy, but this thing with Brett isn't just about his schoolwork." He hesitated for a second when the noise in the alley stopped. "That's better," he continued. "Look, I think Brett just wants to stay in touch with you."

"Why?" Leah said, though she knew the answer to her question.

"I think he likes you," said Bennie, "and I think you two would be good tog—" An angry shout from the alleyway startled Bennie and made him fumble for his walker.

Recognizing Nicie's voice, Leah reflexively started moving in that direction. "Just stay here," Leah told Bennie. "You'll fall. And we don't know what's going on." From the alley, a car engine roared to life, and tires squealed on pavement.

But before Leah reached the corner of the building, Nicie appeared and beckoned for her to follow.

"Come quick," Nicie said. "That delivery guy Artie told us about just hit Tommy. He needs help."

"Hit him? With his car?" shouted Bennie from the patio. He was already reaching for his cell phone. "I'll call for an ambulance."

"No," Nicie said. "I mean, not with his car—with the pipe he was digging through the trash with. But call 9-1-1. He's bleeding."

Leah hurried to Tommy's side next to the dumpster. The husky, straw-haired boy lay motionless on the ground, his face covered in blood. It streamed from a gash to his forehead near the hairline and turned some stray blond locks dark red.

Looking up as Nicie joined her, Leah struggled to remove her own gray sweatshirt, the one she always wore. She wound it into a loose bundle and handed it to her friend. "Here," Leah said. "I'll hold his head up. Put this underneath."

At that point, Leah Russo didn't care if the blood stains ever came out of her brother's old hoodie or not. Right then, she knew what was important and what was not.

Chapter 7

TOMMY WHITE HAD BEEN KNOCKED OUT COLD, but his head injury wasn't as bad as it appeared. After checking him out, the EMTs in the ambulance that arrived assured the husky boy's friends that head wounds—even less serious ones—could be bloody, and that his vital signs were all good. In fact, he was groggy but awake when the EMTs prepared to leave with him. He objected when Nicie Evans said that she and Leah Russo would follow the ambulance in her car to the closest hospital, which was the medical center in Mimosa Beach. He said they needed to wait there for the police and that Bennie should call Mrs. Pressler, because she, as Tommy's foster parent, would have to sign some papers in the emergency room before taking him home.

When the whole gang gathered at the Bauer farm on Saturday afternoon, Nicie thought back to the previous day's excitement and laughed. "Tommy had it together more than any of us," she told Artie Bauer, Ty Green and Ricky Duran, "and he was the one with blood all over his face and head. He looked scary."

The friends stood together outside the barn as they waited for Dr. Minnie Marecek and her niece to arrive. Nicie had brought Leah, who was spending the whole weekend with her, to the younger girl's Saturday horse therapy session. As usual, Tommy accompanied Bennie to continue his training as a therapy assistant. He did so despite his bandaged head and bruised ego, not only because he'd been knocked out by the dumpster diver in front of two girls, but because an ER nurse had cut his long, blond hair so that the doctor could patch him up.

"Oh, that mullet needed to go, anyway," said Nicie. "No one who's *anyone* these days has a mullet. I bet your hair will look nice short—kinda like Artie's, once the stitches are gone and it grows back out some."

"Yeah," Ty said, "the only good mullet is a dead mullet—in my mama's frying pan, with plenty of bacon grease!"

Leah turned up her nose. "That's horrible," said Leah. "You had to kill *two* animals to make that meal—the fish and the hog."

Ty hooted. "More than two," he said. "When Dad and I go fishing, we come home with a whole mess of mullet, enough for a big meal—a feast. Mullet is good eatin'. Dad says they call it 'Biloxi Bacon' where he comes from."

Ricky Duran, who was there to help Artie do chores, inched closer to Tommy and peered up at his bandaged head. "Why did they shave your *whole* head?" Ricky asked him. "You could have washed the blood out of your hair in back and left it long."

"Because," Tommy began, cutting his eyes at the girls, "I didn't want to look like a clown, with a big bald spot in front when the bandages come off. I told them to shave my whole head—like Michael Jordan." He blushed. "I have enough trouble getting girls to take me serious."

Bennie Pressler grinned. "Well, you know what they say?" he joked. "Bald in front, you're a thinker. Bald on top, you're a lover. Bald all over?" He paused a beat. "You *think* you're a lover—unless you're MJ. Then you're the greatest basketball player ever."

"I don't play basketball," Tommy said. "I wrestle—well, I will once I get over this." He pointed to his own head and turned with the others as they heard Minnie Marecek's pickup truck approach on the farm road. The doctor's niece, Wilma Marecek, sat in the passenger seat. "But I'm not even as good as Wilma," added Tommy. "She's pretty tough."

That made Artie Bauer chuckle. "Wilma Marecek's been wrestling longer than me," Artie said, "and she has it in her blood—wrestling, I mean. She told me once that her granddad was a champion wrestler in Czechoslovakia, that he even tried out for the Olympics back before World War Two. That's why she wrestles—to honor him."

Wilma and her aunt exited the pickup truck and met near the tailgate to walk side by side toward the gathering. "Dawg," said Ty Green, with a low whistle. "She's bigger now than the last time I saw her." The hefty girl stood half a head taller than rawboned Minnie and outweighed her by twenty pounds. Wilma usually wore her dark brown hair long but had chopped it off shoulder length for wrestling season. "What do you know," Ty added. "Wilma got a haircut, too."

"She looks good," said Nicie. "I just wish she'd stop wrestling and play basketball. We need a big center who can push people around in the paint. That new girl we got now—what's her name?—is too skinny and too scared of banging under the boards."

Leah waved at Dr. Marecek and Wilma as the pair turned at the corner of the barn and headed toward the stable and corral in back. "Ann Marie is doing the best she can," said Leah. "She told me she's afraid of starting as a ninth grader. Did I tell you I'm writing a feature story for the school newspaper on new winter athletes?" She pointed at Nicie, then at Tommy and Ricky. "I need to interview you guys, too," Leah added, "when you get a chance to sit down with me."

Nicie Evans frowned, as a newspaper story might jeopardize her chances for a fresh start at this new school. Tommy White turned green at the thought of having his picture taken before his hair could grow back out. But Ricky Duran gave a wide smile and said, "I look forward to my interview." He nodded. "I like long walks on the beach, dancing in the moonlight and cooking my favorite Guatemalan dishes for all the girls I love."

Artie Bauer spoke up. "Yeah, well," he said, "you won't be *eating* any of those dishes, not if you're trying to make weight. That's the hardest thing about being on a wrestling team."

"That's what I told Tommy," said Bennie, "that only heavyweights like you and Wilma can eat anything you want."

Artie shook his head. "I wish," he said. "When I weighed myself before football season, I was too heavy for wrestling. But that's not the case now—not with everything that happened this fall." He motioned toward the white farmhouse where Grandpa Bauer was still resting in bed. Everyone knew Artie was referring to Grandpa's injury and to Grandma Bauer's recent passing. Those tragedies and other difficulties faced by the family that fall had put stress on seventeen-year-old Artie. So far, he had handled the added pressure with grace and courage.

Ty Green was under additional stress as well, though not from family circumstances like the ones Artie had suffered. As quarterback of the Arbor Bruins football team that fall, Ty had finished his senior season as co-captain with Artie of the most underrated and overachieving team in the Suncoast Conference, which was composed of Oleander County's five high schools. Three of the schools were public—Iron Harbor High, Port Oleander High and Mimosa Beach High. The other two—Arbor High in Monk's Landing and Solid Rock Christian Academy in Ebenezerville—were public charter and private schools, respectively. In football and basketball, Arbor worked hard to finish second in the conference to Iron Harbor. But in baseball over the past three seasons, the Arbor Bruins had been the class of the league on the diamond, thanks in large part to hurler Ty Green on the mound and catcher Artie Bauer behind the plate— the Suncoast Conference's best battery. So, baseball—not football and certainly not basketball—was where Ty Green's future lay. He just hoped that the new basketball coach he would soon meet wasn't the jerk that Nicie Evans had said he was. Ty didn't want basketball that winter to ruin baseball in the spring for him.

With Ricky in tow, Leah, Bennie and Tommy left for their therapy sessions in the corral around back, leaving Ty and Nicie to talk with Artie in private. "We have a problem," Ty told his best friend. "Nicie just found out why she hasn't got any basketball offers yet—you know, from colleges." Ty looked over at Nicie and asked, "You wanna tell him?"

She shook her head. "No, you go ahead. I don't wanna get upset again."

"It's her old coach," said Ty, "and my *new* coach, Jimmy Foxx, who's taking over on Monday. He's the problem. Coach Carson asked Nicie after practice yesterday if having Coach Foxx and his daughter around was gonna be an issue. She said 'no,' but then Coach Carson told her what he's been hearing about her from colleges."

Artie could tell that Nicie was trying hard not to cry, an emotion that was out of character for her. "What's he heard?" asked Artie.

"That Nicie's uncontrollable," Ty said, "and some other stuff that Coach Carson wouldn't repeat. But he said it was very 'unflattering'—that was the word he used. He said Coach Foxx had been putting the word on her to college programs, and that's the real reason she hasn't got any scholarship offers."

Artie waited to see if Nicie had anything to add. When she was silent, he asked her, "You and Joe Carson get along okay, don't you? I know he's kinda slack as a teacher, but he's a pretty good basketball coach and a decent guy. He and Coach Johnson are best buddies. You know he also coaches girls' softball in the spring, right?"

Ty answered for her again. "Yeah," Ty said, "it's hard to keep those two old codgers apart during baseball season. They're always sneaking off to dip snuff and smoke cigarettes." He laughed. "Ol' Jug Johnson and Bozo Joe Carson are a couple of characters—but they're good coaches."

Nicie tried to smile. "Coach Carson and I get along fine," she said, "and I like all the girls on this team—so far. Even that timid 9th-grade center of ours—Ann Marie? She's a sweet girl. But everything's gonna change Monday when Jamie Lou Foxx gets here. I just don't like that girl, no matter how good she is. She talks way too much trash, especially to her teammates." Frowning, Nicie took a deep breath to settle herself before they rejoined the others.

In the corral, Dr. Minnie Marecek was leading the horse carrying Bennie Pressler, with Wilma Marecek walking alongside him. Leah Russo brushed her chestnut mare Micki in the door to the stable area. Tommy White, still dizzy from the previous day's excitement, and Ricky Duran sat on bales of hay and watched as Leah prepared to saddle the quarter horse. It was all Ricky could bear to let Leah do all her work without offering to help.

Minnie threw up her hand when she saw the other three teens join Tommy and Ricky. "I wish we had a larger paddock and corral here," she said. "In fact, an office and waiting room would help. Then I could move my other two therapy horses here from Stark Stables. It would make things a lot easier." She looked up at her patient. "You still doing okay, Bennie?"

With one white-knuckled hand gripping the pommel and the other trying to hold the reins loosely, Bennie nodded and managed to say, "Maybe Dad can help."

"With what?" said the therapist. "With getting you to loosen up a bit?"

Wilma giggled but took up for Bennie. "Oh, Aunt Minnie," said Wilma, "he's made a lot of progress. Right, Bennie? Why don't you show everybody."

With that, Bennie nodded and laid the reins on the horse's dark mane near the saddle and released the pommel, sitting up straighter, closing his eyes and extending his arms outward as if he were about to take a highway sobriety test. Instead of touching his nose with alternate index fingers, he held the same pose as his bay mare Belle took four more easy strides.

"No, Doc," he said. "With the space problem here." He opened his eyes and retook the reins, this time with both hands. "Dad said something the other day about a trailer that's being moved off a construction site—you know, where we're building a new store. That could be an office and waiting room—and our clubhouse even—if Artie's granddad doesn't mind."

Minnie looked over at Artie seated on a hay bale and said, "Did you hear that, young Mr. Bauer?" When he said "no," she told him Bennie's idea, even the part about the trailer serving as a clubhouse for the Barf Table friends.

"Clubhouse?" interrupted Ty Green. "How big is this trailer? Is it big enough for a weight room? That's what we need—I mean, what *Bennie* needs and Grandpa, too."

Leah Russo chimed in. "And could the office have a computer in it? With a phone line and a fax modem? That sure would help me out—you know, with sending Brett his homework every week. And he could send it back to us instead of to the school."

Artie Bauer's eyes lit up as he considered the possibilities of having a place other than the barn and farmhouse for all his friends to gather outside school. "Bennie?" called Artie. "You talk to your dad about that trailer, and I'll talk to Grandpa." Artie glanced at Ricky and added, "I'll talk to Ricky's dad, too. He's our foreman and needs to know what's going on. Okay?"

Bennie nodded and looked down at Dr. Marecek. "Are you serious?" he asked. "You'd move your whole business here if there was enough room?"

"I sure would," Minnie said. "It might cost a bit more, but what I'd spend on the office and waiting room and extra stable space, I'd save on travel back and forth to Mimosa Beach every day." She nodded toward Wilma. "And my niece there would love being a part of your great little group. What do you call yourselves? The Barf Table?"

Wilma winced. "Thanks, Aunt Minnie—really," she said. To herself, the big girl added softly, "I *almost* made it four years. Now I've *got* to sit there." With a bemused smile, she nodded her head slowly, as if having to sit at the "unpopular" table in the school cafeteria, even with new friends to ease her pain, had been her fate all along.

Chapter 8

IT WAS MEATLESS MONDAY in the school cafeteria at Arbor High. On any given Monday, that meant a soup and a sandwich, sometimes a small salad with oil and vinegar dressing. The idea was to clear the cooler of leftover vegetables from the previous week and ready the counters for the coming week's menu of meals. That way, no food was wasted—at least in theory—and the lunchroom staff was able to stretch its tight budget.

Savings aside, the cafeteria's homemade tomato soup and toasted cheese sandwiches were popular menu items in winter months. But when the weather hadn't yet turned cold and when leftovers were in short supply—as was the case on this particular Monday—the lunchroom ladies resorted to that old faithful of teenage fare, peanut butter and jelly sandwiches. Two sandwiches per brown paper bag, in fact. That meant they also didn't have to worry about washing plates and trays.

Two grandmotherly women in white pantsuits handed out the bags as kids filed past them; and cashier Frankie, the only man on the cafeteria staff, collected their lunch money. Frankie also stood out because he refused to wear a white uniform. He preferred black jeans and black death-metal T-shirts to go with his long, dark hair and black moustache and goatee. But he was a nice guy, and the kids loved him once they got past his intimidating appearance.

For convenience's sake, Nicie Evans often made peanut butter and jelly sandwiches for her and Ty Green to eat at lunch. They usually wolfed down their sandwiches and then took off to be alone as soon as the upperclassmen's release bell rang midway through the lunch period. But after the homecoming dance debacle, Principal Jerry Church had rescinded Nicie and Ty's early-release privileges indefinitely and hadn't restored them yet. While the pair thought nothing of eating PB&J sandwiches on a regular basis, the rest of the Arbor High student body saw this occasional Monday lunch as a skimpy substitute for a well-balanced meal. And coming on the first school day after Thanksgiving break, they found the menu choice particularly insulting. So, many students ate one sandwich and saved the other to use later as a projectile or some other form of weaponry when the release bell rang.

This was an exceptional Monday for another reason. It was the day when former Mimosa Beach High girls' basketball coach Jimmy Foxx would finally meet the Arbor High boys' team at practice after school, taking the reins from Principal Church. It was also when the new coach's hotshot daughter, Jamie Lou Foxx, would transfer from Mimosa Beach and join the Arbor girls' team. A surprise bonus for the Bruinettes was Russian exchange student Yuliya Safin, a 17-year-old tennis phenom who had been placed with the Foxx family for the school year by the women's tennis coach at State College, a friend of the Foxxes. Arbor High didn't have a tennis team, but that didn't matter, because Yuliya was almost as good at basketball. She could always play junior tennis outside school on the weekends.

Leah Russo had spotted the coach and the two new girls in the building before school that morning. None of the other Barf Table buddies had seen either Jamie or Yuliya because the pair had spent most of the day so far in the guidance counselor's office getting their class schedules squared away. Coach Foxx himself wouldn't meet his math classes until Wednesday, as Mr. Church had given him two days to get settled in his new office near the gymnasium and to prepare for the Bruins' first game on Tuesday night against the Solid Rock Harvesters.

Any other year this would be a big rivalry game—Arbor High versus Solid Rock Christian Academy—but this season the home matchup was little more than a dress rehearsal for Arbor's second game, a Friday meeting with Mimosa Beach High on the road. Having lost three key players (including Nicie Evans) and a head coach to Arbor High that season, the Mimosa Beach Lady Waverunners would be loaded for bear or, rather, for the Bruinettes.

For the first lunch period since before Thanksgiving week, all the Barf Table friends were seated and accounted for—that is, everyone except Brett Woods, whose presence was already missed at school. "I got another FidoNet email yesterday from our boy in Hawaii," announced Bennie Pressler, in his wheelchair again to keep from being jostled in the busy hallways. "I didn't print it out, but he asked me about everybody and said to say '*mahalo*' for helping him with his assignments."

"Everybody?" said Leah Russo. "Or just me? I'm the one doing the work. Miss Hopper almost bit my head off this morning when I stuck my head into her office. I just wanted to remind her to round up Brett's assignments by Friday."

Bennie grinned. "Now you know why *I* didn't want to do that," he said. "Thelma Hopper hasn't liked me ever since the homecoming dance. We butted heads over everything—like where I could set up my deejay booth and sound system. I wanted to be out of the way, but, no, she wanted me to be front and center. And then she blamed *me* for the big mess later. I mean, I wasn't the one who swung across the gym like Tarzan and crashed into my PA. And I wasn't the one who got Vicki Duke drunk and made her throw up all over the homecoming court."

"*Digger* Duke, you mean," said Nicie Evans. "Remember how bad she treated Brett that night? And then she lied about who brought the liquor to the dance." Nicie turned to Leah. "So," the older girl continued, "why was perky Miss Hopper in such a bad mood this morning?"

"She didn't say," Leah replied, "but I guess it had to do with our two new students. I saw them headed toward the guidance office as I was leaving. They'd been with Coach Foxx in his gym office. He was there when I went to see Coach Carson."

Just then, Thelma Hopper herself entered the cafeteria with Jamie Lou Foxx and Yuliya Safin close on her high heels. *Perky* was, in fact, the best word to describe the short and fit Miss Hopper. As guidance counselor and cheerleading advisor, the thirtysomething bachelorette was always in motion and always encouraging students to be their best selves—which made Leah's run-in with her that morning unusual. But now Miss Hopper and her two charges were headed straight for the Barf Table. She appeared to be in a better mood, though the brown, layered hair that framed her perky nose, blue eyes and fuchsia-pink smile looked a bit mussed for a change.

Miss Hopper led the two newcomers around the table and stopped next to Leah. "Miss Russo," said the guidance counselor, "I want to apologize for being short with you this morning. And I want to introduce these two new students to you personally." She indicated Jamie and Yuliya, and continued, "I understand you're writing a newspaper story about new winter athletes. Well, both Jamie Lou and, uh, *Yooliyah* are new basketball players here at Arbor High."

Yuliya winced. "I'm sorry, Meess Hopper," said the dark-haired exchange student clearly, yet with a definite Russian accent. "I weesh to go by *Julia*—J-U-L-I-A—the way my name would be pronounced and spelled here in America. I should have told you earlier."

Blushing, Miss Hopper smiled again and blinked once, as if this long day would never end. "No, *I'm* sorry—Julia," Miss Hopper said, before turning to Jamie Foxx. "Well, *Julia* and Jamie Lou—you do want to be called Jamie Lou, don't you?—they'll be joining the gir—"

"Just *Jamie*," said the new coach's daughter. The hint of a smile was on her thin lips, and her brown eyes narrowed when she saw Miss Hopper close her own eyes and shake her head just a bit.

From their dealings the previous year on the Mimosa Beach squad, Nicie Evans knew that tomboyish Jamie hated being called *Jamie Lou*, even though it was her full name and the one that both of her parents—James and Louise Foxx—insisted upon using in public.

"Well, girls, I'll leave you to have some lunch," said Miss Hopper, turning to head back to her office. She nodded toward the cashier at the end of the lunch line. "Go see Frankie Hughes over there—the man in the black clothes—and he'll let you jump the line. Tell him I said it's okay because you're both upperclassmen."

Miss Hopper turned to Nicie and added, "I'm sure you'll want to take these young ladies under your wing, Nicie, and help with their transition to Arbor High. After all, Jamie and Julia are your teammates now." The guidance counselor kept looking at Nicie as if she expected a reply.

Nicie shrugged. "Miss Hopper, I'll give them the same great guidance you gave me when I got here," she said. "Oh, wait. That was Mr. Church who told me I had to sit here—but I'm glad he did." She pointed at the single empty chair at the Barf Table. "We only got one seat, though."

"Oh," said Miss Hopper, "I'm sure these young ladies will want to sit on the upper level with their classmates. It's part of our Arbor Bruins tradition, right?"

Bennie Pressler watched Miss Hopper and the two girls turn to go their separate ways. "Yeah, right," Bennie muttered. "Kinda like the Barf Table and Meatless Monday and Krakatoa Tuesday and so on."

"Speaking of which," said Artie Bauer, "it's just about time for the release bell. Anybody heard what the juniors and seniors are gonna do with their extra sandwiches?"

They all shook their heads. "Any guesses?" asked Artie. "I've seen it all in my four years. I'm just glad they put a stop to *Meatball* Mondays before it took a turn for the worse." They all remembered the Monday after Grandpa Bauer's accident earlier that fall, when the student body used the Barf Table for good will instead of ill. The kids had gone "bowling for dollars" with their extra meatballs and had given the pot of money to the Bauer family. This Monday, however, an ill wind blew through the Arbor High cafeteria.

Their first clue as to the prank on tap came when two senior boys picked up two of the gray garbage cans next to the tray-return counter and carried them back toward the lunchroom's long, regular tables. They stopped just in front of the Barf Table to survey the airspace between the garbage cans and the upper level of seating, where two long lines of junior and senior boys were already forming. The two seniors placed their trash containers at four o'clock and seven o'clock in relation to the round Barf Table.

Bennie Pressler, whose wheelchair sat at twelve o'clock high next to Leah

Russo, was the first to see what was up. "You guys had better move!" he told the three seniors sitting at the Barf Table. "You're right in the line of fire!"

Artie Bauer, Ty Green and Nicie Evans all turned to look over their shoulders. They saw their classmates holding their extra peanut butter and jelly sandwiches like flying discs, some smashed flat and rounded for better aerodynamics. Many of them were pantomiming their tosses, like golfers taking practice swings on the tee.

Leah Russo glanced up at the big clock on the far wall above the cafeteria entrance. "T minus 60 seconds, guys," said Leah, rising to leave. "They're not gonna give us any time after the bell rings. Just look at them up there."

Despite his own injuries from the holiday weekend, Tommy White got up to help Bennie with his wheelchair. Ricky Duran rose and took off the letter jacket he had earned as the football team's first-year kicker. "I do not care if they give me another ugly T-shirt to wear," Ricky said, referring to free shirts that the school receptionist handed out when students soiled their clothes. "I love this jacket. Brown and purple are not our team colors."

Artie Bauer had also worn his letter jacket that day, but he had taken it off and draped it around the back of his chair while he ate. With the threat at hand, he decided to fold the jacket, lay it on the seat that Ricky had vacated, and push the chair up under the table. Ty Green had left his coat in his car that morning.

"Come on, guys," said Nicie Evans. "We don't have to sit here and wait to be harassed. I don't care if Lurch Church did tell us we couldn't leave." Nicie started moving away because she stood to lose the most in a food fight, as she wore new blue jeans and an off-white sweater.

In their rumpled jeans and flannel shirts, both Artie and Ty looked like they wouldn't mind taking a couple of direct hits as long as one or two stray throws hadn't been smashed too badly and might be edible. They were still hungry—Ty was, anyway. "Just sit back down and scoot your chair over behind me, babe," Ty told his girlfriend. "I just wish I'd brought my ball glove."

Nicie laughed. "Well, sweetie," she said, "if you don't mind, I'll just sit behind Artie. No offense, but you're a pitcher. He's a catcher."

Before they could take cover, the release bell rang, and two flattened sandwiches spun through the air toward the garbage cans. Both doughy discs fell short of their targets, but the players next in line adjusted the height of their throws for better distance. Several tosses flew well over the Barf Table and splat against the block wall above the tray-return window. With only one or two throws coming at a time, the tablemates easily dodged the projectiles, whether they were standing or seated.

None of the offerings were deemed lunch-worthy by Artie and Ty. Still, Nicie had to scold Ty twice when he reached out to inspect sandwiches that landed atop the table. Those tosses were declared the overall winners by the senior boys who had stayed to judge the contest, even though the throwers had overshot their marks—or so the champion PB&J disc golfers claimed when coaches Jug Johnson and Joe Carson finally came back into the cafeteria from the breezeway and broke up the fun.

Jug checked with his wrestlers—Artie, Tommy and Ricky—to make sure they hadn't been splattered by any stray peanut butter and jelly. That might keep them from making weight, Jug joked. Being the girls' basketball coach, Carson nodded to Bennie and Leah, who were the varsity basketball teams' scoreboard operator and scorekeeper, before leaning over to Nicie and Ty to make sure they were both okay.

"Have you seen the new girls yet?" Carson asked his star player. "They came to the gym with their daddy first thing this morning, but they took off before we could have a good talk. And ol' Jimmy boy has kept me and Jug busy during our free periods moving stuff for him—like he's our big boss or something." He studied Nicie for a moment. "You listening to me?"

Nicie was looking past her coach at someone approaching. "Well, you can talk to one of them right now," Nicie said, without taking her eyes off the girl coming toward them. "Jamie Foxx is headed this way. I don't see that Julia girl." Nicie waited a few seconds before introducing her once and future teammate. "Coach Carson," said Nicie, "I'd like you to meet Coach Foxx's little girl— Jamie Lou."

The tomboy's eyes flashed again as she extended her right hand to Carson, her left hand still in a fist by her side. "Hi, Coach," she said. "I'm sorry I was in such a hurry this morning in the gym. It's good to meet you, sir." She moved closer to Nicie and reached out with her open left hand to pat her old nemesis on the back. "And *Donicia*," she added, using Nicie's full name, "I'm looking forward to us being on the same team again. Last year was such a blast."

Nicie kept quiet, though something didn't feel quite right about the usually cold-blooded Jamie Foxx's suddenly warm behavior. Once Jamie and both coaches left, Nicie turned to Ty and Artie. "That's not the girl I grew to know and hate last year," Nicie said. "Maybe it won't be so bad playing with her again."

"Yeah, maybe not," said Ty, leaning to put his arm around Nicie to give her a quick hug. But then he pulled back and looked at the once-clean sleeve of his flannel shirt. "Well ... maybe you were right about her to start with," he added, holding out his arm and revealing a smudge of peanut butter and grape jelly from the back of Nicie's sweater.

"Turn around, babe," Ty said. "Let's see the damage." In the middle of Nicie's back, Ty and Artie saw a perfect brown and purple handprint staining the sweater's off-white fabric. "That ain't gonna come out," Ty noted. "What do you think, Artie?"

Artie shook his head sadly. "I think it's gonna be a lo-o-o-ng basketball season," he said, and retrieved his own letter jacket for Nicie to wear to the office.

Chapter 9

WITHOUT JUNIOR VARSITY TEAMS to take up court time, the Arbor High Bruinettes always practiced first after school in the gym. Old Joe Carson's practices usually lasted about ninety minutes. Then the boys' team would hit the court around five-thirty and practice until at least seven o'clock, depending on whether or not they had won their last game. Losses meant longer practices, which usually ended with additional "suicides"—running drills that were meant to be punishing. But that was how the old coach had done things. On this particular Monday, the Bruins were meeting their new coach, Jimmy Foxx, who would be coaching high school boys for the first time. He'd had success at Mimosa Beach High as the girls' coach, but now he was in uncharted territory without his daughter on the team to give him inside information on the other players' attitudes and behavior.

As the school newspaper's sportswriter, Leah Russo was on hand to take some action photos of Nicie Evans and the two latest Mimosa Beach transfers for the article that Leah was writing. Also, she wanted to interview Jamie Foxx and Julia Safin right after practice, knowing she could talk to Nicie anytime. But there was one other motivation for being at practice that day—to remind Nicie not to retaliate against Jamie for the peanut butter and jelly incident at lunch. Leah's role as basketball scorekeeper meant that she needed to attend the girls' and boys' games at home and on the road; however, she wouldn't have been at practice if not for her newspaper job.

Sitting on the single row of bleachers that had been pulled out, Leah called Nicie over when the players emerged from the locker room. They started loosening up at the four baskets on the gym's two practice courts, set crossway over the regular floor.

"Nicie, come here," called Leah to her friend, who grabbed a basketball off the rolling ball rack and dribbled it at a walking pace toward the basket near Leah's seat. Leah fiddled with the camera she held, hoping she'd loaded its fresh roll of film correctly.

"Want me to pose?" Nicie said with a smile. She balanced the ball high in one hand and stood with her legs as wide apart as she could, to look as much like her favorite NBA player as possible without jumping.

"No," said Leah, "I'll take some shots when you guys start playing. It'll be good practice for me. I'm not used to this zoom lens." She twisted the long camera lens to lengthen it, then to shorten it. "I have to shoot from the scorer's table when I can."

Nicie laughed. "You're gonna be more fun to watch than us," she said. "Are you a good juggler, little girl?"

"Guess I'm gonna have to be—big girl," said Leah. "Anyway, you keep your head on straight today. Okay?"

Tossing the ball off the backboard and catching it, Nicie pretended she didn't understand. "Why wouldn't my head be on straight?" she asked, putting the ball on her hip under one arm and turning to watch Jamie Foxx and Julia Safin leave the locker room. They grabbed balls off the rack and drifted toward the opposite basket to shoot.

"That's why," said Leah, also watching the newcomers at the other end of the court. "You know what I mean. Come here." She motioned for Nicie to move closer. "Look, you don't want to mess anything up for yourself," Leah said in a lower voice. "Just let that business today in the lunchroom go. That girl's gonna try her best to get you kicked out of school."

Nicie bounced the ball hard on the court but caught it. "She ain't getting me kicked out of school," said the big girl. "Not again. I'll fix her."

"No, you won't," Leah said. "That's the *old* Nicie, and you're not that person anymore. She wants you to lose your temper and start a fight—yeah, I know, she *started* it—but it'll look like you did, because she was so sneaky about messing up your sweater."

Nicie nodded. "Yeah, you're right," she said. "Out on the court, the girl that throws the first sneaky elbow doesn't get caught. It's the one who gets mad and pushes back."

"Right," said Leah. "Just give her time. If she wants to fight with you, she'll eventually screw up and do something out in the open. *Then* you push back. You need witnesses—so don't put yourself in a bad spot with her or, for that matter, with Julia, since we don't her yet."

A few minutes later, Joe Carson pulled himself up from the easy chair in his office and joined his girls in the gym. Old Joe didn't believe in using an actual whistle on a lanyard; he could whistle just as loudly by putting two fingers to his lips. One long, shrill blast signaled the official start of practice.

"Happy Thanksgiving Monday, gals," Carson told the group as they gravitated toward him near mid-court. "Let's take our positions and do some stretching before layups and the fast-break drills. Don't worry. We'll take it easy. We don't want to pull any muscles the day before our first game. Get us started, Mel."

Carson kept walking as senior captain Melanie Grayson took the coach's place at mid-court and indicated which stretch to begin with. Since her sophomore season, Mel had started at point guard for the Bruinettes. With dark, shoulder-length hair pulled into a short ponytail, she was average height—about five-five—but had always been about ten pounds heavier than her best playing weight. Still, she was the best ball-handler, best passer and best outside shooter on the Arbor High squad—good enough to have earned second-team All-Suncoast Conference honors her junior year.

"While we're stretching," continued Carson, "I'll keep talking at you and save us some time." He had walked the length of one row of players and was starting along the next row. "We want to welcome two new players into our midst today, from Mimosa Beach High School—Miss Jamie Lou Foxx and Miss U-LEE-uh Safin—I think I said that right."

As Leah expected, Jamie Foxx immediately spoke up to correct the old coach on the two girls' names. Leah was surprised, though, by how graciously Joe Carson took being corrected by this player he didn't really know yet.

"I'm so sorry, little lady," said Carson, "but I've been hearing your daddy say, 'Jamie Lou this' and 'Jamie Lou that' all day long. And I don't know how to speak Russian. So Miss Julia, I hope you'll forgive me, too."

Julia Safin simply nodded and continued stretching. Jamie Foxx frowned and said, loudly enough to be heard across the court, "Yeah, well, my *daddy* is an idiot."

Leah thought she saw a smile appear at the corners of Carson's mouth, but he didn't acknowledge the girl's insult. "Anyway, ladies, you'll find that my coaching style may be different from what you're used to. I'm not going to scream at you and throw towels and chairs—that isn't what I do. Is it, Mel? Is it, Nicie?"

Carson waited for his two seniors to respond, even though Nicie Evans had been on the team for only a few weeks that young season. Almost as one, the two girls said, "No, sir," and moved on to the next stretch.

"We have a system here," said Carson. "We learn our offensive patterns and special plays, and we learn our defenses. They're the nuts and bolts of our system. But it's based on something else—something bigger than playing offense or defense. What's it based on, girls?"

Again, the old coach turned to his seniors, and they responded in kind with the same two-syllable word. He nodded and said, "That's right—*respect*. I respect you, you respect me, we respect each other, and we respect our opponents. As long as we do that, we'll be a winning team, no matter what the scoreboard says at the end of the night."

Leah noticed that Jamie seemed bothered by the coach's indirect approach. But before the new girl could blurt anything else out, Carson added, "Now, you might wonder how showing respect puts the ball in the hoop or stops the other team from scoring baskets." He paused next to Jamie Foxx. "It's very simple," Carson said, as he looked her in the eye. "Respect means that each and every one of us needs to do our absolute best for one another on the court and off the court. And that respect depends on trust. We have to trust each other to say and do what's right. Any questions?" This time he didn't call on his seniors but also didn't redirect his gaze.

"No, sir," said Jamie Fox.

Practice went much as Leah expected. To his credit, Carson made it clear that Jamie Foxx and Julia Safin would not play the following day against the Solid Rock Lady Harvesters, because they did not know the Bruinettes' plays and defenses yet. "We'll have our practices on Wednesday and Thursday," the coach said, "and then we'll see how things shape up before we play Mimosa Beach on Friday—that is to say, who'll play on Friday and who'll ride the bench."

Julia seemed to take Carson's admonition in stride; however, the look on Jamie's face told Leah that her interview with the two newcomers after practice might be more challenging than she had expected. Leah knew that her friendship with Nicie would make Jamie defensive right off the bat and that the new girl would wonder if Leah had an ulterior motive behind every question. But now Leah suspected that Jamie resented being at Arbor High, even though the move had been good for her father's coaching career—moving from being the girls' coach at a public high school to the boys' coach at a charter school that could basically "recruit" players from other parts of the county. This resentment also called into question how Jamie might play on Friday against Mimosa Beach High, her old team. Leah had no doubts about Nicie Evans's loyalty, because Mimosa Beach had expelled her at the start of the school year for fighting with Jamie Foxx and other mean girls there.

Practice itself went as well as could be expected. Jamie and Julia assumed spots on the second team and caught on quickly as the first string ran through the team's offensive patterns and special plays with the backups on defense. Tuesday's prospective starters included seniors Mel Grayson and Nicie Evans at the point and shooting guard positions; juniors—and identical twins—Sara and Clara Harmon at the forward spots; and timid freshman Ann Marie Childers at center. Another promising 9th grader would be first off the bench at guard—a wiry, redheaded spitfire named Sandy Cuthbert who would never, ever be described as "timid" on the court. She could shoot almost as well as Mel and Nicie; however, little Sandy's height—at 5-foot-nothing—made her shots easier to block and kept her from hitting the boards with the big girls. But she was scrappy, so much so that Coach Carson started calling her "Cutthroat" on the third day of tryouts. Carson knew her scrappiness would be good until she got into foul trouble.

For her part, Nicie Evans could play any position, though her preferred spots were on a wing at either shooting guard or small forward. She was a good ball handler and could run the offense at point, if needed. Also, Nicie was tall enough and strong enough to play on the front line—at either power forward or center— and she had no trouble rebounding against taller girls.

Shooting action photos during practice, Leah Russo could already tell that Jamie Foxx would eventually take Nicie Evans's guard spot and push the taller senior to the other wing. At forward, Julia Safin would replace one or the other of the twins—probably Clara Harmon, who wore contact lenses and was always losing one during practices and games. Her sister's eyes also needed correction, but Sara wore prescription goggles and looked like she was ready to either go into battle under the boards or dive for oysters off the Sandpiper Beach pier. Next to Sandy "Cutthroat" Cuthbert, Sara "the Fly" Harmon was the player most likely to foul out of any game. On the other hand, Clara Harmon's nickname was "Cookie," because she enjoyed baking in Home Ec class and often brought cookies, cakes and pies for the team to eat after practices and games. That was one reason point guard and team captain Mel Grayson was overweight.

"What are you doing in here?" Coach Jimmy Foxx shouted at Leah Russo, as he walked onto the gym floor from his office in the hallway next to the boys' locker room. Still seated on the single, pulled-out row of bleachers, Leah had just watched Coach Carson and the Bruinettes disappear through the door into the girls' hallway on the opposite end of the gym. She had told Jamie Foxx and Julia Safin that they could do their interview there in the gym, once the girls had showered and dressed. She had also hoped to get a picture of Jamie and Julia with Jimmy, as well as photos of the boys' practice.

"Hi, Coach Foxx," said Leah. She introduced herself and added, "I'm waiting for your daughter—well, for *both* your daughters, Jamie *and* Julia. They're meeting me out here for an interview. It's for the school paper—for *The Grapevine.*"

Foxx eyed her suspiciously as he continued to approach from across the court. "I don't care who you are, honey," he said. "This is a closed practice—period—so you're gonna have to talk to the girls somewhere else. How about in Coach Carson's office?"

Leah nodded. "Oh, okay," she said, standing and holding up her camera, "but I also want to take a few pictures of you and the boys' team—if that's all right."

"It isn't," said Foxx. "I'm not taking time out of my practice for you or anyone else to take pictures. We have a lot to do and don't need any distractions."

"But I'm your scorekeeper, too," explained Leah. "I also helped Coach Johnson and the football team this fall."

Foxx hissed. "This isn't football," he said. "And, young lady, I do know who you are. Just for the record, I wasn't a fan of your brother like everyone else—your *late* brother, I mean—so don't kid yourself. You aren't gonna get any special favors from me. This is my program now."

Confused, Leah couldn't help but ask, "What did Reuben ever do to you—other than score a gazillion touchdowns against Mimosa Beach's horrible defense? And, by the way, I'm not asking for any special favors. It's my job."

"Don't smart-mouth me," said Foxx. "If I need to take this up with Principal Church, I will. He'll be here in a minute to officially turn the team over to me. And as far as *helping* me goes—as scorekeeper or anything else—you'll do as you're told, period. If I don't ask for your help, you need to stay out of my way." He jerked his thumb over his shoulder toward the girls' locker room door. "Now clear out of here, and don't come back unless you're invited."

"Can I stay just for *that* picture," she asked, "of Mr. Church turning the team over to you? That would be great."

"What did I just say?" said Foxx. "Get out. Now. It's either my way or the highway."

Leah was tempted to say, *Yeah, your daughter was right—you* are *an idiot,* but she bit her tongue and left the gym, waiting in the hallway outside the locker room for Jamie and Julia. She now had more empathy for Jamie's negativity about her father, though the young reporter knew better than to broach the subject with either girl.

Sitting in Coach Carson's office—he had taken off right after practice—Leah left the door to the hallway open while she interviewed first Julia, then Jamie. Yuliya "Julia" Safin explained matter-of-factly how she had come to live with the Foxxes. "My family lived in Siberia," Julia said in her sultry voice, "and then we moved to Moscow so that I could play for the Tennis Federation—vell, it is called the Tennis *Association* now."

"What was Siberia like?" asked Leah. "Did you like living there?"

Julia smiled patiently. "Meess Russo," she said, shaking her head, "no one *likes* living in Siberia. My father and mother *had* to live there." When asked why, she said, "My father was an athlete. My mother is a dancer—or she teaches dance now. They wanted to live in America. But the authorities did not like what Father said once about the Soviet Union. That is why we moved to Siberia when I was a small child."

Seated in a corner of the office, Jamie Foxx spoke up when her exchange sister fell silent. "Go ahead, Julia. Tell her what else happened. It's okay."

"Vell," Julia continued, "my father died in Siberia when it was still the Soviet Union. So, when Russia was reborn, Mother and I moved to Moscow so that she could teach ballet and I could play tennis for the best coaches."

Leah wrinkled her forehead. "But how did you get here—to Oleander County, I mean?" Leah asked. "Why didn't your mother come with you to the United States? We have good ballet companies here—like in New York City."

Julia turned to look at Jamie before replying. "My mother does not wish to come to America now," said Julia. "She has a new husband and a new son and a new life in Moscow. They are very rich. She and my stepfather helped me come here. I hope to play tennis at least one year at State College and then become a professional. I play basketball only because it was my father's sport, and I am good at it. It helps me remember him."

A lightbulb went off in Leah's head. "You have a lot in common with another athlete at Arbor," said Leah. "A girl here named Wilma Marecek *wrestles* because her grandfather was a champion wrestler in Czechoslovakia."

"She wrestles?" asked Julia. "I did not know that Arbor had a girls' wrestling team."

"No," interrupted Jamie Foxx, "she's an oddball—the only girl on the team. We always laughed at her when Arbor wrestled at Mimosa Beach. It's probably the only way she can get a guy to hug her. I'm not saying she's ugly, exactly, but she's more boyish looking than I am."

"That wasn't nice," Leah said. "Wilma is a really sweet person, and I think both of you would like her if you'd just give her a chance."

"Yeah?" said Jamie. "How do *you* know her?" Jamie arched one eyebrow, as if she didn't think Wilma—or Leah—could have a wide circle of friends like anyone else.

Just then, the muffled sound of someone shouting in the gym caught the three girls' attention. Jamie's neck turned bright red. The color rose into her cheeks when she realized that the yelling was coming from her father.

"What's going on?" Leah asked, not expecting the other girls to answer. "That's weird."

The hallway door from the gym flew open and then slammed shut behind Ty Green, wearing his green and gold Bruins practice uniform. He stormed past the coaching office where the girls sat and glanced at them in passing. That made him stop and back up to address Leah.

"Where's Nicie?" he said, fuming over whatever Coach Foxx had said to the boys' team in the gym. The yelling, in fact, had grown louder now that Ty had left the gym floor. Ty Green knew who Jamie Foxx and Julia Safin were, but right then he didn't care.

"She's waiting for me out in the parking lot—to give me a ride home," said Leah. "We'll be done in a few minutes. But what happened in there? You can tell us." She glanced over at Jamie, whose whole face was beet red now.

Ty shook his head. "*Huh-uh*," he grunted. "Nothing to tell—not until I talk to Nicie. She'll still be waiting on you out there, but I've had enough. I'm going home."

This time Jamie had questions. "Going home? You're still on the team, aren't you?"

Ty stared through her. "Like I said—I've had enough. I'm going home."

"But did you quit," Jamie asked, "or did he kick you off the team? It makes a difference."

He gave an angry laugh. "To who?"

"To me," Jamie Foxx shot back. "He was looking forward to coaching you. He told me so. He says he wants to coach you this spring, too—in baseball."

Ty Green was incredulous. "That ain't gonna happen for *two* reasons," he said. "One, Jug Johnson's the baseball coach here. And, two, I wouldn't play for Jimmy Foxx now if he or Lurch Church paid me—and I'm sure you know why. I'll be back in a minute to get my stuff."

With that, Ty stomped out of the building and headed straight toward Nicie's sportster in the parking lot.

Still inside, Jamie asked Leah, "So, are we done now? Do you still want to talk to me?"

Leah shrugged. "Yeah, I do," she said. "It's my job." Then the young reporter smiled. "Besides," she added, "the story just got interesting. Really interesting."

Chapter 10

LEAH FINISHED THE INTERVIEWS and hurried out to Nicie's car, finding her alone. "Where's Ty?" asked Leah. "I didn't see him come back in."

"Nicie was so angry that her lip trembled as she spoke. "He went around the building," she said. "He doesn't want to see that jerk again. He's afraid he'll hit him."

"What did he say?" Leah asked. "Foxx, I mean."

"He was talking trash," said Nicie. "He was bragging about how he *fixes* players who don't *get with the program*. That's what he always says—that, and *my way or the highway*. He's a real piece of work, like I said before."

In her mind, Leah could hear Foxx talking like that, because he had used those very words and phrases with her. "Yeah," Leah said, "but what does that have to do with you? He isn't your coach now. He's Ty's coach—or was."

"I'm afraid that jerk will mess up Ty's chances for a scholarship—even in baseball," Nicie explained. "And what did his trash talk have to do with me? *I* was the example he used—how he had a player last year at Mimosa Beach who wouldn't *get with the program*, and how he put the word on that player to college coaches. That was *me* he was talking about, just because I didn't let his spoiled-brat daughter push me around."

Leah shook her head. "No, that isn't cool," she said, "but I understand why Ty has to quit the basketball team now—especially after Jamie told us her dad is going after Coach Johnson's job next spring. She said he wants to coach baseball here, too."

"Yeah, Ty told me she said that," Nicie replied. "Fat chance, though. Without

Ty Green, the basketball team is gonna stink. And then Lurch Church wouldn't dare replace Jug Johnson with a loser like Jimmy Foxx. The old Jugster may be old-school, but he's a winner."

Leah nodded. "You're right," she said. "Coach Johnson has a lot of support from parents and the booster club. I can't speak for Artie, but I don't think even *he* would play baseball if Foxx stole the team away from Coach Johnson." Then she added, "But I don't trust Mr. Church—not anymore. He lost my respect after that homecoming mess."

"Word," said Nicie. "I wouldn't trust Lurch as far as I could throw him. He turned into a real slimeball when he started selling real estate on the side this fall. You know he works nights and weekends at—what's it called now? Sandpiper Realty? Is that it?" She was referring to the real estate office located next to Woody's Surf Shop & Grill on the beach.

Leah nodded. "Yeah," she said, "but isn't that place still owned by Stark Realty? They just changed the name, right? I guess they had to after Josh Stark and his dad got into so much trouble a few weeks ago. So, Mr. Church is working for Joel Stark. *Hmm.*"

"I heard the Starks are laying low these days," said Nicie. "They don't go out much now." She smiled, her anger subsiding. "I also heard that they pulled Josh out of Solid Rock Academy before Thanksgiving and that they shipped him off to military school. It was either that or take a chance on the court sending him to the School for Troubled Youth in Capital City." She laughed. "Josh won't be swinging like a monkey in their gym—not at that military school."

Leah winked. "That's what he gets for messing with us," she said. "With the Barf Table, I mean. You feeling better now? Are we ready to head home?"

"I guess so," said Nicie. She cranked the sportster's engine and touched her foot to the gas pedal to warm the car up. "I'm glad you're here with me, Leah. It helped to talk it through. I usually just explode—or that's how it feels, anyway." She put the car in gear and slowly pulled out of the parking spot toward the school drive.

"I keep things bottled up inside for too long," Leah countered, "and *then* I explode. No, actually, I just punish myself for things I can't control." She paused to reflect, as the car stopped at the main highway to let a line of traffic pass. "You know," continued Leah, "that's what I'm learning from Dr. Marecek and my horse Micki—to live more in the moment. You hear people say that all the time—that they're *living in the moment*—but it's true. You can't change anything that's already happened, and you don't really know what's going to happen until it does. The only thing you can control is what you do right now—like when you ride a horse."

The last car in the long line that passed on Ebenezerville Road was a primer-colored coupe with a missing rear bumper and tinted glass all around. As soon as the traffic left the school zone headed out of town, the coupe jumped out into the passing lane and roared past three other vehicles, barely getting back into line before meeting an oncoming truck.

"Hey!" said Nicie. "That's the car from the beach Friday! The guy who assaulted Tommy was driving that car. It has to be the same one." She leaned forward and craned her head to the right to check the gray car's position in line. "What should I do? Follow it? I can catch him—in this car, I can." She revved the engine like a racecar driver.

"Hold on, Fireball," Leah cautioned, taking out the cellular phone that her vacationing parents had left with her. "I'll call the sheriff's department and report the car. Remember, the deputy we talked to Friday said to call him if either you or Tommy saw the guy again, or his car. Maybe the state police can stop him on the highway between here and Ebenezerville."

Nicie let her foot off the accelerator for the moment. "Yeah, girl, you're right," she said with a sigh, pushing down the left-turn signal and checking for traffic both ways. "We've got the horsepower to catch him, but it could be a rough ride." She glanced at her younger friend. "And I sure would hate for either one of us to get bucked off."

* * *

Late that night, Leah Russo lay on her bed and stared at the ceiling. The ceramic lamp on her nightstand illuminated the room despite the pleated lampshade that dimmed its light. No sounds emanated from anywhere in the large house, not even from the brass alarm clock sitting on the nightstand next to the forlorn teenager. Her parents had been gone for days—on another trip to somewhere she didn't care to visit—and they wouldn't return home until week's end. She rolled her head to one side on her pillow and studied the Princess telephone beside the lamp. A slip of paper bearing the ten digits of an unfamiliar number lay next to the sky-blue phone.

She guessed that the sun had just set in Hawaii and that Brett Woods and his loving mother and supportive dad were sitting down to a meal of poi and raw fish. *Or maybe they're at a luau,* she thought, *and they're having roast pork with their poi. Brett and Woody do like their barbecue.* Her stomach growled as she remembered the tossed salad she had thrown together from a bag of lettuce in the fridge and then had picked at for her own supper. Having just spent the long holiday weekend with the Evans family, Leah had turned down Nicie's invitation to stay until Leah's parents got back home. *I have to act like it doesn't matter,* Leah told herself, though she knew that it did. *My selfish parents care more about themselves than about me, their own daughter.* She wondered if they would ever love and support her as they had treated her brother Reuben. Or did she herself have anything to say on the matter?

Leah looked again at the slip of paper. *I can't make anyone love me who doesn't want to,* she thought. *I can't control another person's feelings.* But she was certain of one thing she could do right then, without worrying about its repercussions down the road.

"Why not?" she murmured. She sat up and reached for the phone's handset, ready to dial Brett's number.

Chapter 11

IT WAS KRAKATOA TUESDAY at the Barf Table. The Arbor High upperclassmen always had two ways to go on this day of the week—to take the name literally and do something volcano-related, or to interpret the pun figuratively and crack a few 9th graders' toes. In the past, they had sculpted volcanoes of mashed potatoes with lava-like gravy. They had shaken freshman tables—and, most of all, the Barf Table—like volcanic mountains rumbling before erupting. Now and then, they had sacrificed a pretty 9th-grade girl in one creative way or another. Or they had simply stepped on the toes of helpless freshmen boys and inflicted as much pain as possible.

On this Tuesday, however, the collective mind of the student body was on that night's season-opening basketball games at home against Solid Rock Christian Academy. Located in Ebenezerville—not that far from Artie Bauer's and Ty Green's family farms—the private school had a reputation for poor sportsmanship and gamesmanship despite its religious affiliation, from its coaches, in particular. In fact, the Solid Rock Harvesters baseball coach had tried in previous years to lure both Artie and Ty away from Arbor High, but the Bruins' beloved old coach, Jug Johnson, had always shut those recruiting attempts down cold and kept the boys on his roster. It was no different in basketball, as Solid Rock always tried to attract the best players—on both the boys' and girls' teams—that might have otherwise gone to Arbor. The county's other three high schools—Iron Harbor, Port Oleander and Mimosa Beach—were all publicly funded, and their teams were limited to student-athletes who lived in their respective districts.

Artie Bauer and Leah Russo were first to seat themselves at the Barf Table.

Artie asked her with a grin, "So, have you heard any, uh, *rumblings* about what's up today?" He picked up his fork and moved some French fries off the disc of mystery meat in the entree compartment of his plate. "You know, this ugly old piece of whatever-it-is would have flown a whole lot better than those mashed-up sandwiches yesterday."

Leah smiled. "Yeah, that thing does look like a UFO," she said, "an Undigestible Fried Object." She opened the brown paper bag before her and took out what was left of the previous night's salad. "Nope," she said, "haven't heard a thing. Of course, I wasn't listening."

"You know," Artie began, "this is the first time I've seen you bring food to school. You're usually too busy reading a book here at the table." When she frowned, he added, "But I'm glad. You're making progress. Now if I can just get *my* appetite back."

She looked up at him, trying to understand how he had meant that remark. "Are you okay, Artie?" she asked. "Is your grandpa okay?"

Their eyes met as he paused before replying. "We're getting there," he said. "I was just referring to this plate of food—well, to the meat, anyway. The fries look okay. The green beans aren't nearly as good as Grandma's. She seasons hers with...." He stopped, realizing he was speaking about his grandmother in present tense. "Never mind," he said, dropping his head.

"I'm sorry," said Leah. "I was just afraid you were making Grandpa eat *your* cooking. Then you both would lose your appetites, right? Every day isn't Thanksgiving, you know."

Artie smiled at her attempt at humor. "You need to stop hanging around Bennie Pressler so much," he teased. "He's rubbing off on you. But, no, Gabby Duran does most of the cooking for us. She's keeping all us men out there well fed—me and Grandpa and, of course, Ricardo and little Ricky. She's a great cook—and a brave woman to put up with all of us guys."

Leah glanced toward the cafeteria door and saw Nicie Evans and Ty Green enter, late as usual after spending some stolen moments together outside. But instead of coming straight to the Barf Table, the couple turned and headed toward the senior tables on the upper level of the lunchroom. They took seats at a table where two other Bruins basketball players sat.

"Have you talked to Ty?" Leah asked Artie. "Did he call you last night?"

"No, I called him," Artie said. "I asked him what all the screaming was about in the gym. We could hear Coach Foxx yelling, even up in the wrestling room with the doors shut." Artie shook his head. "I mean, geez, Wilma almost pinned me while all that was going on."

Leah snickered. "But why are they sitting up there with the seniors?" she asked, serious again. "Did one of us say something wrong?" She didn't want to ask if Artie and Ty had gotten into a fuss over Ty's decision to quit playing basketball, or maybe over Coach Foxx's plans to steal Coach Johnson's baseball job that spring.

"No," said Artie, shaking his head. "He told me last night he needed to explain to the other guys—to the other seniors, anyway—why he did what he did. That's what he's doing now, I guess. I don't know if they'll come down here today or not—but that's okay. Ty's always been like part of my family, you know?"

"Yeah, Artie," said Leah, "he's your brother from a different mother." Then she realized that Artie had never known his own mother and that the whole topic of motherhood was, at best, awkward for the big farm boy. "Sorry," she said. "I did it again, huh?"

Artie waved her off. "Oh, don't worry about it," he said, "but I do wish Ty's mom was my mother—or Nicie's mom, or Ricky's mom, or Bennie's mom, or Brett's mom. They're all better mothers to their children than mine was to me. She left when I was a baby."

Before she could stop herself, Leah blurted, "Well, I notice you didn't name *my* mom. But, hey, that's okay, too. I'm right there with you, buddy."

Artie's eyes narrowed. "I didn't mean it that way," he said evenly, "but, you know, I didn't name Tommy's mother, either."

"She's in prison," said Leah, "with Tommy's dad. They had no choice about abandoning Tommy—not like *my* parents."

"Are your folks are in prison, too?" Artie said, a sparkle in his eye now.

"Have any idea when they'll get paroled?"

Leah harrumphed. "As far as *they're* concerned," she said, "our house is their prison. All these trips they take to get away from me are like work release." She studied her friend's face to see how he was taking her honesty.

"I was just teasing you, Leah—and I shouldn't have," said Artie. "Don't give up on them. Your folks are still hurting just like you are. And, you know, I miss Reuben, too. He was my hero and my friend." Artie paused for a second. "But I didn't know just how bad losing someone close to you feels until now—with Grandma gone. She was a mess, but she was the closest thing to a mother I've had all my life. And if she was still here fussing at me and Grandpa, I wouldn't trade her for anybody else's mother, no matter how great they are."

The two were silent while they waited for their other tablemates—Bennie Pressler in his wheelchair, bald-headed and bandaged Tommy White with the two boys' food trays in hand, and little Ricky Duran—to get through the lunch line, pay death-metal cashier Frankie, and take their seats at the Barf Table. By the time they arrived, only ten minutes remained before the upperclassmen's release bell. That meant the juniors and seniors had to hurry and finalize plans for their Krakatoa Tuesday observance. Three senior boys—Ty Green, surprisingly, and his two former teammates—rose from their seats and walked straight down into the 9th-grade section.

"What are they doing, Artie?" Leah asked. When he raised his eyebrows but kept his lips pressed shut, she looked around the table from one boy to the next. "Bennie? Tommy? Ricky? Did you guys hear anything? What's going on?"

They all shook their heads—but smiled knowingly. The two senior hoopsters with Ty split up, one bending down to whisper in timid Ann Marie Childers's ear and the other walking toward Sandy "Cutthroat" Cuthbert's seat. Leah was still confused—until she realized that her friend Ty Green was headed her way.

When Ty reached the Barf Table, he stopped behind Artie's chair and beckoned to Leah, who was sitting across the table. "Rise, sweet maiden," said Ty, with a straight face. "Prepare to be sacrificed to the gods of Krakatoa Tuesday."

Bennie burst out laughing. "*Sweet* maiden?" he said, elbowing Leah beside him. "Just don't say anything, or the gods will throw you back."

Leah rolled her eyes at Bennie but stood and extended her hand to Ty, who said, "Come with me, freshman scorekeeper. Krakatoa awaits." Then he leaned close and murmured, "Don't worry. You'll be okay."

Not entirely convinced, Leah let Ty lead her across the lunchroom and up the three steps to the upperclassman section where the other two 9th-grade girls already stood. The two "maidens" had been joined by a pair of senior girls who were winter sport athletes—Bruinette captain Mel Grayson and wrestler Wilma Marecek. The two basketball boys had returned to the lower level and stood just below the 9th graders who waited to be "sacrificed."

When they neared the "altar" where the other girls had gathered, Ty stopped, turned to Leah, and bowed. "A high priestess will assist us with this sacrifice." He winked, turned on his heel, and joined the senior players on the floor below.

Nicie Evans, who had remained seated until then, stood to greet her young friend. "Ah, Kiki-a-loni-a-leah Russo," announced priestess Nicie to the throng. "Would you like to go first?"

"No!" interjected Sandy Cuthbert. "Not her! I want to go first! This looks like fun!"

Ann Marie heard the excitement in Sandy's voice and volunteered weakly, "And I'd rather go last—if that's okay."

Leah just shrugged. "Whatever," she said. "Who decides?"

Nicie stepped forward again, this time pointing to another senior girl seated nearby who had donned a grass skirt, a pair of coconut halves over her green and gold "Bruins Spirit" T-shirt, and a brown paper bag bearing the image of a frowning tiki face in crayon. "The goddess Pele will decide," Nicie said, loudly enough for everyone to hear. "Let us welcome goddess Pele back into our midst."

Nicie bowed and motioned to the table of seniors sitting around the grass-skirted girl. "Pe-le, Pe-le, Pe-le," they chanted. On cue, the girl stood, stepped away from the table and twirled in place, making her grass skirt stand out like a whirling dervish's gown.

Goddess Pele stopped spinning and sashayed over to Ann Marie. In a clear voice that later that day would be directing cheers in the crowded gym, the girl proclaimed, "The first shall be last, and the last shall be first. Thus sayeth Pele—even though I *still* don't understand what all this has to do with soccer."

Nicie smacked her own forehead. "Oh, Digger," said Nicie to the goddess. "Just go back to Miss Hopper's room. We'll take it from here. But thanks."

To her chagrin, Ann Marie allowed Mel, her priestess, to help her onto the two-foot-high brick wall that served as a safety barrier for the upper level. The tall 9th grader turned to face the seniors, who now drummed on their tables and chanted, "Kra-ka-TO-a, Kra-ka-TO-a." But instead of falling backwards into the arms of her senior ballplayer, Ann Marie turned again to face the tall boy on the floor below, squatted on the low wall, motioned him out of the way, and unceremoniously hopped down.

"Boo-o-o-o," jeered the student body, even the 9th graders sitting at Ann Marie's table.

Now it was Leah Russo's turn. Before helping her onto the wall, Nicie gave Leah a hug and said, "Don't be afraid. He'll catch you. Just cross your arms and fall straight backwards—like a tree falling."

Standing on the wall and hearing the Krakatoa chant again, Leah looked down at her friend Ty, who was braced to catch her. The other senior athletes stood by to help him, if necessary. Ty smiled at her and nodded with confidence. "I got you," he said, and nodded again. For the first time since her brother died, Leah knew she would indeed be okay and that she could trust her strong friend to have her back.

Without delay, she turned, crossed her arms, closed her eyes and fell backwards. She knew Ty had shifted position a few inches during her fall, because she felt his muscular arms wrap around her and then set her upright. She finished by giving him a quick hug around the neck before scooting back to her seat.

"Ru-sso, Ru-sso, Ru-sso," all the kids chanted, before turning their attention to the last sacrifice on the cafeteria's Krakatoa Tuesday card—Sandy "Cutthroat" Cuthbert, five-foot-nothing but full of vim and vigor, with red hair, a wide smile and a face full of freckles.

Sandy whispered to Wilma, her priestess, who then had a quick word with Nicie. The two senior girls shrugged at one another and helped the wiry 9th grader onto the low brick wall. She grinned at her high priest on the floor and motioned for the player to back up, back way up, even more, so that she could attempt a dismount that would be the talk of school for years to come.

"Have you seen that dancing movie?" Sandy shouted to her priest, who had backed up almost to the Barf Table. She wiggled her chest and hips suggestively and held her arms up like a ballroom dancer. "We're gonna do The Lift. Okay?"

The boy laughed and nodded, but also waved Ty and the other player over to help him. Before they could chicken out, Sandy hopped into the "volcano" and took off like a shot toward her partner, leaping into the air toward him with her arms raised in a swan dive. Her tiny body's forward motion carried her up and onto his awaiting hands, his arms lifting her up over his head, where he held her long enough to complete the move. As he and the other two athletes let her back down to the floor, the entire crowd—even death-metal Frankie and the lunchroom ladies—clapped and cheered, ready for anything the Solid Rock Harvesters had to throw at them during the basketball games that night in the Bears Den.

Chapter 12

IN THE PREGAME LAYUP LINE before the six o'clock tipoff, Nicie Evans turned to Sandy Cuthbert and asked, "Where did you learn to do that lift, little girl?"

Sandy grinned. "Gymnastics camp," she said. "My dad fell in love with Mary Lou Retton and decided I was gonna be a gymnast." She watched Nicie take off toward the basket from the right, catch the rebounder's pass, and with her right hand toss the ball up off the glass into the basket. Seconds later, Sandy did likewise, even though she was left-handed and barely made the layup from her weaker side.

At the back of the rebounding line after Sandy's layup, Nicie turned again and said, "How did you end up playing ball then?"

Still annoyed at how difficult her layup had been, Sandy shook her head and muttered, "Because people said I was too short."

"You *are* a little squirt," teased Nicie, as she drifted toward the basket to snag a rebound and feed the next shooter on the right side.

When Sandy rebounded, passed and returned to the layup line, she poked Nicie in the back and replied, "Yeah, well, tell that to Muggsy Bogues and Spud Webb."

Nicie laughed, and when the ball came to her, she tossed it back to the left side for left-handed layups. "Okay, Cutthroat," Nicie said with a smile. "Now let's see how you do on your strong side." And when Sandy joined her again in the line on the left, Nicie added, "Muggsy and Spud can dribble and shoot with either hand. You've got some work to do."

Sandy nodded. "I know," she said. "Already am. I want to start next year."

At the other end of the court, the Solid Rock Lady Harvesters were already practicing free throws and jump shots to get used to the unfamiliar basket there in the Bears Den. Both coaches—Joe Carson and the Solid Rock lady coach—stood at the scorers' table and watched as Leah Russo and the Solid Rock student scorekeeper swapped books to record each other's lineups. Bennie Pressler sat next to Leah and fiddled with the scoreboard controls and the PA system. When the scoreboard buzzer sounded to end the warm-up period, Bennie tapped on the big microphone on the tabletop before him to make sure it would work when he introduced the starting lineups.

Coach Carson called his girls to their bench on the first row of bleachers just beyond the scorer's table. The starters—Mel Grayson, Nicie Evans, Clara and Sara Harmon, and Ann Marie Childers—sat at the head of the bench where Carson would be. They removed their warm-up suits as Bennie Pressler introduced the Lady Harvesters starters one by one. Jamie Foxx, Julia Safin, Sandy Cuthbert and the other Bruinettes subs stood solemnly at their end of the bench as each Lady Harvester first-stringer loped over to shake Carson's hand before rendezvousing with their teammates in the center jump circle. The Bruinettes starting five followed the same routine and returned to the bench for Carson's final instructions before the tipoff.

The coach knelt in front of his starters, and the substitutes gathered behind him. "These girls aren't as quick as we are," Joe Carson said, "but they got some size. So—Clara and Ann Marie—you girls box 'em out on the boards, and get the ball out quick as you can to Mel or Nicie or Sara, and you gals fill your lanes on the fast break. Let's keep 'em running 'til their tongues are hanging out. We ready?"

Still on one knee, he looked from one starter to the next and held out his hand, palm down. The five seated girls laid their hands on his hand, and the subs leaned over or around Carson to place their hands atop the others. "We're ready," the coach said, nodding his head. "*Team* on three." Once the ritual "team" cheer was done, the subs and coach sat. The starters rose and took the floor for the opening tipoff.

The Bruinettes did, in fact, get off to a fast start, with Mel Grayson pushing the ball up the floor, penetrating the Lady Harvesters' zone defense, and then either driving to the basket or flipping the ball back out to Nicie Evans or Sara Harmon for three-point shots or long two-point jumpers. On defense, the Arbor High girls matched up one-to-one and gave up points only when Clara Harmon or Ann Marie Childers let their players outmaneuver them close to the basket. But when Solid Rock shots missed, Clara and Ann Marie followed their coach's orders and blocked out, keeping their taller but slower opponents from getting into position for offensive rebounds and second shots at baskets. Then the Bruinettes were off and running, fast-breaking just like their drills in practice. They filled all three imaginary lanes to the basket—the center lane for the ball handler and the two outside lanes for her hard-charging teammates—and finished with easy layups more often than not. After one quarter, the score was Arbor 18, Solid Rock 6. At the half, Arbor was up 34-14.

Leah Russo double-checked her numbers in the team scorebook, while Bennie Pressler rummaged through his backpack for the bottle of Yoo-hoo he had brought from home. Looking up, Leah nodded at the bottle Bennie was now shaking. "You aren't supposed to bring glass into the gym," said Leah. "Better keep it out of sight for another minute."

"I know," Bennie said, "but we were all out of cartons at home, and a hardworking man's gotta have his Yoo-hoo. You know?"

Leah shook her head. "Just go on outside and drink your chocolate milk," she said. "I'm gonna be a minute."

"Chocolate-flavored *drink*, thank you very much," Bennie corrected, stowing the bottle in a coat pocket. "Okay. I'll go get us a place in the concession line. Don't be long, or you'll have to eat whatever I buy for you." Without Tommy White there to help him, Bennie had to scoot from behind the scorer's table on the third bleacher and then almost crabwalk backwards down to the floor. There, he pulled himself up into a standing position, reached back behind the table for his aluminum walker, and unfolded its sides with two snaps. He nodded to Leah and started moving toward the gym lobby as quickly as he dared.

The pep band was getting on Leah's nerves as she tried to tally the point totals to make sure they matched the scoreboard and the Solid Rock book. By the time she joined Bennie in the lobby, the 15-minute intermission was half over. Seven minutes and change counted down on the scoreboard clocks mounted high on the walls at opposite ends of the gym.

"Guess who I just saw?" Bennie asked his friend, handing her a hotdog wrapped in red and white paper. Before Leah could guess, he blurted, "Doc Marecek."

Annoyed, Leah looked at the hotdog and pursed her lips for a second. "Veggie dog?" she asked. "I didn't know they sold them here. And why'd you tell me to guess?"

With his elbows on the arms of the walker, Bennie reached for the hotdog. "No, sorry," he said. "That's mine." He took back the hotdog, hugged it against himself with the hand holding the Yoo-hoo, and reached into his coat pocket. "I bought you a box of Milk Duds—to sweeten you up a little." He tossed her the small box of chocolate-covered caramel balls.

"Thanks," said Leah, catching the box with one hand. "I didn't know you ate the hotdogs here at school. They aren't kosher, are they?"

He laughed. "Are you kidding? The only kosher things here at school are the dill pickles. Just stepping on campus makes me unclean, so I don't worry too much about it while I'm here." He unwrapped the dog and took a big bite. "No, I heard some good news from Minnie—from Dr. Marecek. She said Dad and Mr. Bauer came to an agreement with her about pulling an office trailer onto the farm so she can move her whole business out there. That's great, huh?"

Leah's spirits rose. "Best thing I've heard all day," she said. "When are they gonna move the trailer in?"

Bennie took a sip of his drink, then said, "Dad told me last night that if Mr. Bauer agreed, we have an old construction trailer ready to be moved any day now. It's in Iron Harbor near our new store at the mall."

"How old?" asked Leah. "And how big is it?"

"It's a double-wide," Bennie said. "It's big enough for Minnie's office and for a good-sized waiting room, with heat *and* air-conditioning—and *two* restrooms. Plus, there's another big room for whatever *we* want to use it for."

"*We?*" asked Leah. "You mean, us? The Barf Table *farmily?*"

"Well, sure," said Bennie. "Why not?" He leaned to one side to look into the gym, and he saw that there was just enough time for him to walk back to the scorer's table before the buzzer sounded. He gobbled down the last bite of hotdog and drained the last of his drink. "Anyway," he said, "Minnie was here to pick up Wilma from wrestling practice, so she's already gone. We can talk to her tomorrow night at our therapy session. Let's get back inside, okay?"

With Leah's help, Bennie was able to navigate the line of fans returning to their seats and the Solid Rock players milling between the court and bench. Both teams would be playing offense that half in front of their respective benches. Bennie reached the scoreboard controls just as the buzzer went off. In the stands, the pep band was playing the last strains of the school fight song. The Arbor cheerleaders, led by Vicki Duke, had just finished their halftime dance routine and were gathering up their jackets to take a break of their own. Bennie, Leah and the Solid Rock scorekeeper had all climbed back into their seats at the table and were ready for another half of basketball dominated by the Bruinettes. That was the expectation.

But this was girls' high school basketball, and what was expected wasn't always what happened. With a 20-point lead and the ball, the Bruinettes seemed content to play a slower, half-court game at the start of the third quarter. Mel Grayson walked the ball up the court and passed to Nicie Evans on the right wing. Nicie held the ball high and watched the Solid Rock zone shift toward her before passing back to Mel at the point. As the captain threw the ball to Sara Harmon on the left wing, Nicie cut through the lane to the corner below Sara and waited near the baseline for the junior forward's pass—which never came. Instead, Sara tossed up a long three-point attempt that caromed off the rim into the hands of the Lady Harvesters center. The tall girl flipped an outlet pass to one of the Solid Rock guards, who led the fast break for a layup. Then, when Clara

Harmon tried to inbound the ball after the basket, the Lady Harvesters showed their full-court, trapping defense. They intercepted the weak pass from Clara and put another quick score on the board.

Joe Carson rose from his seat on the bench and squeezed the rolled-up white towel he held. Leah watched to see if the coach would call a quick timeout or let his two seniors do what they could to calm the younger girls on the ensuing possession. Clara managed to inbound the ball to Mel, who was immediately double-teamed in the corner. As they had practiced, the other Bruinettes drifted toward their captain but kept some distance between themselves so that she'd have at least three open receivers away from the Solid Rock basket. With two defenders' hands in her face, Mel got a pass off toward Nicie near the top of the key—the top of Solid Rock's lane, that is—but the ball was intercepted again and ended up as two more Lady Harvesters points.

Now, with Arbor leading 34-20, Coach Carson called a timeout. Leah tried to listen in as he ran through each girl's responsibilities against the full-court trap, which was not an ordinary press. "Mel," Carson said, tapping his captain on the knee, "you take the ball out and try to get it in to Nicie." He turned his head toward his shooting guard. "Nicie, get the ball right back to Mel and then head toward Sara at center court. If you don't get the ball back, Nicie, set a pick for Sara." He touched Sara's knee. "You come off Nicie's pick, and either you or her should be open if Mel still needs help with the double-team. Let's go."

As the starting five headed back onto the floor, Leah saw Carson take Sandy Cuthbert by the arm and say something that elicited a smile and nod from the backup guard. Sandy had spelled both Mel and Nicie at two different points in the first half, playing nearly a minute each time. She had even scored once on a steal and breakaway layup. But now her role in breaking the Solid Rock press would be more vital, especially if the Arbor starters couldn't get the game back under control.

Bennie sounded the buzzer to end the timeout, and Leah sneaked a look farther down the bench at Jamie Foxx and Julia Safin. Both were already seated and still wore their warm-up suits. The dark-haired Russian looked calm and collected, almost asleep, her head and eyes turned down. Jamie appeared agitated, as if she couldn't believe that the coach wasn't putting her into the game. But Leah knew that Joe Carson was a man of his word, and if he'd said Jamie wouldn't play that night, she wouldn't, unless the circumstances were beyond his control.

Little by little, the Arbor girls learned to handle the Solid Rock press, and the lanky Lady Harvesters soon grew tired of pressing quite so hard. The half-hearted traps that they set pulled them out of position enough to open up the floor for the attacking Bruinettes, who withstood the initial surge and went on to extend their lead at the end of the third quarter. Going into the final period, Arbor led 46-24. Joe Carson cleared the bench—except for Jamie and Julia—and let the remaining girls play the last minute of the game. The final score was Arbor 58, Solid Rock 30.

Leah finished with her scorekeeping duties as quickly as she could and packed up to leave the gym.

"Hey, where you going?" asked Bennie, surprised that Leah wasn't staying to fill out the boys' scorebook in preparation for their game. In fact, both teams had already come onto the floor for pregame warm-ups at opposite ends of the court, just as the girls had done two hours earlier. Bennie added, "I thought you were working both games—like me."

Leah shook her head as she donned her coat. "Nope," she said. "My job here is finished. I need to catch a ride home with Nicie after I take care of a few things for Coach Carson. I'll talk to you tomorrow, Bennie."

She walked down the sideline past the cheerleaders and pep band, turned at the baseline and walked along the far wall toward the girls' locker room and Carson's office. Before she left the gym, she turned her head and saw the two Bruins coaches—incoming Jimmy Foxx and outgoing Jerry Church—exiting the door from the boys' hallway and heading across the court toward the scorer's table and home bench. Then she looked at Bennie and saw that he had figured out what was going on, because his look was like hers earlier in the day when she'd realized that she was about to be sacrificed to the gods of Krakatoa Tuesday.

Chapter 13

FOR A WAISIN WEDNESDAY, the lunchroom was quiet. The Arbor Bruins had lost the night before to the Solid Rock Harvesters in Jimmy Foxx's first game as Bruins coach. And the loss had been ugly—a 40-point blowout in the second half after the two teams had played on even terms throughout the first half. As he had promised, Principal Church had started the game on the Arbor bench and had helped Foxx manage the first two quarters of the contest. Jerry Church knew what the Bruins starters could do, even without senior Ty Green in the lineup, and so the principal passed along offensive plays and defenses for Jimmy Foxx to call. Most everything that Church suggested worked—to Foxx's irritation, especially when it became obvious to the home crowd who was actually running the team that night. Foxx addressed that problem—for himself, anyway—in the locker room at halftime, and he paid the price of arrogance and pride.

Seven of the eight seats at the Barf Table were filled that day, with surfer dude Brett Woods's chair still empty. As usual, Artie Bauer and Leah Russo got to the table first, followed by Ty Green and Nicie Evans with their bag lunches. Then, with only a few minutes left before the 11th- and 12th-grade release bell, the three freshman boys—Bennie Pressler, Tommy White and Ricky Duran—arrived with their trays from the long lunch line. On this early December day, Tommy still carried both his and Bennie's trays; however, Bennie had decided that if he could use his walker at a ballgame—as he had done the night before—then he could use it at school as well. Besides, he was tired of being called The Wheelchair Boy.

"Well, if it isn't the Three Stooges," said Ty Green, greeting the freshmen as they took their seats at the Barf Table. "Bennie has got to be Moe, and Tommy's bald head makes him Curly. So, Ricky, I guess that makes you Larry."

"Three little pigs, you mean," said Leah. "Look at all that food." She hadn't brought lunch for herself that day, so any amount of food seemed excessive to her.

Artie chuckled. "Nah," he said. "They're our Three Musketeers. We couldn't do without these three fellows—especially on the wrestling team."

"Bennie? On the wrestling team?" said Nicie. "I gotta see this. When's your first match at home? Tomorrow night?"

"Yeah," said Artie, "but Bennie doesn't wrestle. Tommy and Ricky do—and they're good. Bennie's the *voice* of the Fighting Bruins. Right, Bennie?"

The usually boisterous Bennie just nodded and took a bite of his lunch. Leah nudged her friend with an elbow and said, "What's wrong, Bennie boy? Saving that golden voice of yours for tomorrow night's match?"

Bennie slowly turned his head and looked at her without speaking, and took another bite of food. That was when Leah figured out part of what was bothering Bennie. "Oh, I get it," Leah said. "You're mad at me for leaving last night. Is that it?"

Bennie kept chewing and finally swallowed. "You think?" he said. "That jerk acted like it was *my* fault you'd left—like I'd given you permission or something."

"You're gonna have to narrow that down a bit," said Leah. "Which jerk are you talking about—Lurch Church or Foxx?" The others at the table knew better than to interrupt.

"Both," Bennie said, "but mainly Foxx. He yelled at me for five minutes in front of the whole crowd."

"What did Mr. Church do?"

Bennie shook his head. "He just stood there and let that idiot scream at me. Then I had to sit beside Foxx's wife for the whole ballgame. She smelled like an ashtray—and didn't know what she was doing. I tried to show her how to keep score—like you're supposed to do."

This time it was Leah shaking her head. "Oh, no," she said. "The last thing Jimmy Foxx yelled at *me* was, 'Your job's to do as I say' and 'Don't come back unless you're invited.' Well, he didn't say one word to me between then and last night's game. And I certainly didn't get an invitation from him or anybody else to keep score for the boys. My job was done when the girls' game ended. I'm sorry Foxx yelled at you, Bennie, but that's on him, not me."

Now Ty Green spoke up. "You also didn't call the TV stations with the boys' score last night," Ty said to Leah. "I saw the girls' score on the late sports—well, I knew it, anyway—but I didn't find out what happened with the boys until I got to school this morning." He looked around the table. "Did you guys hear about that—I mean, about what Foxx said to Lurch at halftime?"

No one other than Nicie knew, so Ty continued, "The boys told me that Foxx really lit into Lurch in the locker room—told him he didn't need his help and that he was just in the way."

"Yep," said Bennie, "I wondered why Mr. Church wasn't on the bench during the second half." Bennie laughed. "It got downright comical—and *I'm* the comedian here. Coach Foxx didn't know who could do what, and he didn't know any of the special plays. He'd call something, and the team didn't know what he was calling. He didn't know who to substitute or when to put them in. It was a mess—not to mention we needed Ty out there against Solid Rock. Any chance you'll come back, Ty?"

"No way, no how," Ty said. "Not as long as Jimmy Foxx is the coach. And from what the boys said, he ain't going nowhere no time soon."

"Oh, don't be so negative," chirped Leah. "Surely Mr. Church won't let him keep talking to him that way. Lurch still has a little bit of a backbone, doesn't he?"

Ty shrugged. "I'm beginning to wonder," he said. "The boys told me he just stood there and looked at Foxx as he was getting fussed at. And when it was over, he said something like, 'Well, okay, you're the coach,' and left the locker room."

"That's right," Bennie said. "Lurch came out of the locker room while the cheerleaders were still doing their dance number. He stood at the door there and watched them like he didn't know what to do with himself—like he might go back into the locker room. But when the routine ended, he walked across the floor to the scorer's table and whispered something to Mrs. Foxx, and then he left. I don't know what he said to her, because I was headed back from the lobby, and he didn't even look at me when we passed each other. I guess he went to his office until the game was over. I saw him come back to turn off the lights and lock up the gym."

Leah looked across the cafeteria at the clock on the far wall. "Well, in about two minutes, I'll ask him myself," said Leah.

"Ask who?" Bennie said. "About what?"

"Mr. Church," she replied. "About what happened between him and Coach Foxx. I got a note last period telling me to report to the principal's office when the release bell rings. I guess I'll get to explain why I left last night after the girls' game. If he asks, I'm gonna tell him exactly what Foxx said to me the other day."

"You go, girl," said Nicie Evans, who had been quiet through most of the discussion. "That man needs to be put in his place. Foxx is a bully, and he taught his daughter to be one, too. She's gonna ruin our team. It'll be just like last year—except Coach Carson is a good guy. I just hope Foxx doesn't bully him and Coach Johnson into quitting. At their age, they shouldn't have to put up with that kind of mess."

Artie Bauer perked up at her mention of Jug Johnson, who was Artie's football, wrestling and baseball coach, as well as a surrogate father. "Yeah, Ty told me about Coach Foxx saying he wanted Coach Johnson's baseball job," Artie said, glancing over at his best friend. "We aren't gonna let that happen—no way, no how, as Ty says." Artie smiled and winked at Leah. "You tell Mr. Church *exactly* what Coach Foxx said to you. That was disrespectful—especially the remark about Reuben."

The release bell rang. Raisins rained down upon the 9th-grade seating area and the Barf Table in an impressive, if unimaginative, hailstorm of sticky brown droplets. Leah Russo flipped up her hoodie and scurried toward the exit, brushing stray raisins from the gray sweatshirt fabric once she was in the cafeteria lobby.

She looked back toward the Barf Table and saw Ty Green and Nicie Evans leaving, too, despite the principal's revocation of their senior privileges. Good-hearted Artie Bauer and the three freshman boys were still seated. Leah smiled at the thought of Artie reminding the 9th graders about the bright side of losing their lunches in the raisin maelstrom. *Gotta make weight*, she guessed Artie was telling the two wrestlers. And he was probably trying to convince Bennie that fasting would give him a better PA voice.

Artie Bauer, the eternal optimist, Leah said to herself with a smile. Then she realized that Artie had referred to something that she had told only her friend Nicie—about Jimmy Foxx's cruel remarks about Leah's late brother and everybody's hero, Reuben Russo. So now Leah knew that she had to be careful about what she told Nicie Evans, that whatever they discussed might be repeated, at least to boyfriend Ty and his best friend Artie. Her own buddy Bennie Pressler's uncharacteristic reserve, however, was even more troublesome for Leah. It wasn't just her behavior the previous night, her leaving between games without explanation. It was also the secret she was keeping from Bennie and everyone else, one that she was certain Bennie would find out about, if he hadn't already. There was no good reason for Brett Woods not to tell Bennie that Leah had called him on Monday night. What not even Brett Woods knew, though, was how deep Leah Russo's feelings for him were becoming.

* * *

As soon as the Bruinettes' practice ended on Wednesday, Leah hopped into Nicie's blue sportster, and the girls zipped up Ebenezerville Road to the Bauer farm for that evening's horse therapy sessions. Dr. Minnie Marecek was already there, as were Bennie Pressler, his father Abe, and Ty Green. Leah and Nicie found the four walking through the old office trailer that had been moved that day to the farm from the new Pressler's construction site in Iron Harbor. Artie Bauer, Tommy White, Ricky Duran and Wilma Marecek—all of them wrestlers—would be there shortly after their practice ended.

"What do you think, Minnie?" asked Abe Pressler, holding the metal door open for the other three to exit the trailer. "Watch your step, folks. A crew will be back out here tomorrow to get the place shipshape—mainly the plumbing and electrical—and I'll have them build ramps on both sides for Bennie and Mr. Bauer and any other clients that need that assistance. We'll make sure the trailer is ready for you by the end of the week."

Ty Green was happiest of all. "I can't wait to set up my weight room," Ty told the man. "Is that floor in there strong enough to hold all my weight equipment?"

"I'm sure it's strong enough to hold the little barbell my Bennie boy can lift," said Abe, as he held his son's walker and helped him down the makeshift steps. "Bennie isn't exactly Arnold Schwarzenegger, you know."

"Hey!" said Bennie. "I'm walking here, I'm walking here!"

Abe smiled and added, "But I'll have my work crew put in some extra bracing under the floor on that side—just in case Artie and Miss Evans here want to pump some iron."

"Yes, sir," said Nicie Evans, showing off the muscle in her right arm. She put the other arm around Leah Russo's bony shoulders. "We're gonna get this little girl lifting weights, too."

Minnie Marecek's eyes sparkled at all the enthusiasm she was hearing. "Thank you so very much, Mr. Pressler," she said. "I can't wait to move my other horses here. It'll make things so much easier for me and Wilma."

"Well, I'm happy to do what I can," said Pressler, "but this is all possible thanks to Artie and his grandfather. And please, Minnie, do call me *Abe. Mr. Pressler* is my name at work. This is my pleasure—to help the folks who are helping my son. It's a good investment for us as well."

The two of them walked off together to talk with Harry Bauer in the farmhouse, leaving the teenagers at the doublewide trailer, which had been pulled into a newly cleared lot behind the barn and next to the corral. Ty Green took his girlfriend inside the empty trailer to show her the space for their new weight room. Bennie needed to rest from the exertion of walking through the trailer and climbing down its rickety steps, and so he and Leah took seats on bales of hay just inside the barn door. Leah told Bennie to keep an eye out for Artie's pickup truck, which would be carrying the big farm boy and the other three wrestlers.

"How are they gonna do that?" asked Bennie. "Four people in the cab of that pickup?"

Leah smiled. "I guess little Ricky's gonna have to sit on somebody's lap," she said. "He won't mind, as long as it's Wilma's lap and not Tommy's." When Bennie didn't crack a joke, she studied his somber look and asked, "Are we okay, Bennie—you and me?"

Their eyes met. "I don't know," he said. "Are we? I'm not the one keeping secrets—well, not about stuff that matters."

She frowned. "What?" she said. "I'm gonna tell you right now about my little visit to the principal's office. There's nothing to hide. Mr. Church asked me why I didn't stay for the girls' game, and I told him—even the part about Reuben. That embarrassed him, and all he could do was apologize. He said he'd talk to Coach Foxx about it."

Bennie shook his head. "No, not that."

"Then what are you talking about?" she said. "Is it about me not telling *you* I was gonna leave the other night? I figured the less you knew, the better off you'd be."

"*You* figured?" said Bennie. "Or *Brett* figured?" His hurt look told her that the incident at school involving scorekeeping and Coach Foxx wasn't what truly concerned him. So, he *did* know about Leah's long-distance telephone call to Brett in Hawaii, and he knew at least part of what they had discussed.

"What did Brett tell you?" she said. "That I called him Monday night? And that I asked him for advice about how to handle Coach Foxx? What's wrong with that? I also told him that Nicie and I had just seen that fake delivery guy—the man who assaulted Tommy—driving past the school when we were leaving for home. I figured Woody needed to know that."

Bennie nodded but gave her the same hard look. "So, you don't trust me anymore?" he asked. "Nicie and Ty and Artie all knew about your run-in with Coach Foxx, but you didn't even bother to tell me about it—and I was the one who got yelled at after you disappeared."

"I apologized to you for that."

"No," Bennie said, "you apologized for Coach Foxx—just like you said Lurch did. You *didn't* apologize for not telling me about things to begin with. Aren't we best friends?" He waited for her answer, then added, "Or is Brett your best friend now?"

She looked away. "I don't know how I feel," she said. "We're best friends— you and me—but Nicie and I had been talking about, well, about boys and all, and she said something about feeling this *spark* whenever she's around Ty." Knowing she was changing the story somewhat, Leah paused to see how Bennie was taking this explanation. "She asked me if I feel that spark when I'm with you."

"Do you?"

Leah looked down again. "No," she said softly. "I mean, I love you, Bennie— as a friend. But right now I'm feeling so many different things, and I...." Her voice drifted off, and her thought was left unsaid.

"Well," he began, "all I ever wanted was to be your friend, Leah, and to know you trust me. I meant it when I said you and Brett would be good together. Things are hard enough right now for me—learning how to walk again and all. And it isn't like I didn't have problems *before* my accident, but I figured I could count on you for support. That's why Brett's email message kinda bugged me. I just wish FidoNet was faster and I'd gotten it *before* last night's game and not first thing this morning."

She looked up at him. "I *am* sorry, Bennie—about the whole mess. I do trust you, but I was at home all alone, and I was mad at my parents for going away again, and my feelings were hurt. That's really why I called Brett. I mean, I did want to talk to him and to tell Woody about that skeezy delivery guy, but I guess I mainly wanted to get back at my parents, to get their attention when they have to pay for a long-distance call to Hawaii."

A grin started on Bennie's lips. "So, they don't know about it yet?" he asked.

"They won't be home until sometime this weekend," she said. "Besides, they won't get this month's phone bill until after Christmas—so I guess I wasn't quite thinking things through, at least not as far as getting their attention goes."

"Well, not until next month," said Bennie. "But cheer up. They'll probably go on another long trip over the holidays and leave you at home all by yourself again. Maybe that'll be when the phone bill's delivered to your house."

"Home alone?" Leah said. "On Christmas Eve and Christmas morning? Now that's a cheery thought."

"It could be worse," said Bennie. "You could be Jewish like me and have to give yourself a present *eight straight* nights—but my folks would never do that to me. As a matter of fact, we may go on a trip over the holidays ourselves—all of us, to Hawaii."

"Really? When did *that* happen?"

"It isn't written in stone yet," Bennie said. "Brett mentioned it in his note, that his mom and dad are going to call mine and invite us to go stay with them in Hawaii for a few weeks—Tommy, too. But Dad doesn't like being away during the holidays, because this is when our stores do their best business. I mean, he could run everything over the phone or by fax or by computer if he wanted to. But he says it doesn't look good if the boss takes off when everyone else is working so hard. And Tommy has wrestling now, so that complicates things. They can get somebody else to run the scoreboard for me, so that's not a problem."

Now Leah was downcast. "When will you know?" she asked.

"I'm not sure," Bennie said, "but I *promise* I'll let you know as soon as I find out. I mean, you're my best friend, after all."

Chapter 14

THIRSTY THURSDAYS AT ARBOR HIGH were a mixed bag for 9th graders. Sometimes the upperclassmen would do nothing more than pick one unlucky freshman boy—usually sitting at the Barf Table—and pour out his carton of milk (or Yoo-hoo, in Bennie's case). Other Thursdays they might swipe the drinks of an entire table of freshmen; or collect tiny salt packets and empty dozens of them on one or more 9th graders' plates of food; or hold a chug-a-lug between two or more unfortunate kids, with the chugged drink being water or milk or an exotic mixture of liquids. That last option was what occurred on this particular Thursday, because the boys who devised the prank were senior wrestlers who wanted to promote that night's first home wrestling match. It also meant that the chug-a-luggers were freshman wrestlers Tommy White and Ricky Duran.

"What do you want us to do this time?" asked Ricky. "We can stand on our heads and drink something, or do one-handed pushups and drink through a long straw." He was excited to be the center of attention—Tommy, not so much, because of his shaved and bandaged head.

"Don't give them any ideas," hissed Tommy to his little friend. "They don't need any help coming up with something crazy."

Nodding to Artie Bauer as they passed, the two senior wrestlers walked their freshman teammates to the spot in the 12th-grade section where the three 9th-grade Bruinettes had been initiated two days earlier. When they were in place, Artie rose from his seat at the Barf Table and turned to address everyone in the lunchroom.

"Your attention, please," said Artie, waiting for the clatter of trays and chatter of students to subside. "Tonight in the Bears Den, our two newest varsity wrestlers—Ricardo Duran Jr. and Thomas White—will hit the mat for the Arbor High Fighting Bruins for the first time."

He paused to watch and laugh as little Ricky clasped his hands above his head as if he had already won his match. Tommy, too embarrassed to do anything that bold, managed a weak wave to everyone.

Artie continued, "But first, our young grapplers will begin their quests for victory by doing what every champion wrestler does on match day—making sure they're good and hydrated!"

As the senior wrestlers lifted two five-gallon water coolers onto a nearby tabletop, Artie addressed Ricky and Tommy: "These two water coolers have been filled for you to empty as you hydrate for tonight's matches. You both have until the release bell to either win or lose this competition. The prize will be a cooler bath right after the bell—but for which competitor? For the winner or the loser? We shall see. Good luck, men!"

He motioned for the contest to begin, and the seniors began handing paper cup after paper cup of water to Ricky and Tommy. Both boys gulped down their first few cups of water without spilling any on the floor, but soon started sloshing out half of each cup on themselves as the cups came faster and faster. The two seniors and their assistants weren't even counting the cups that each boy drank. So, when the release bell rang, they loudly declared the competition a tie, unscrewed the lid of one cooler that oddly had not been used to fill cups, and dumped its entire contents on the already drenched boys being held—not more water, to everyone's shock, but green and gold confetti that Artie later swept up without too much trouble.

* * *

Both Arbor High basketball teams held shorter practices after school that day and were off the court in time for the wrestling team to set up the gym for its first match of the season. The Fighting Bruins hustled their green and gold mat onto the court from the wrestling room upstairs, rolling it out, taping down its individual sections, and cleaning its entire surface with sanitizer. All the boys had setup duties, though the older team members—Artie Bauer and the other three senior wrestlers including Wilma Marecek—bore the most responsibility and supervised the job for Coach Jug Johnson. Jug stayed in the locker room to complete weigh-ins and skin checks until around six o'clock when the home team warm-up on the mat would begin. Ten minutes later, the Arbor High Fighting Bruins would yield the mat to that night's opposing team, the Solid Rock Christian Harvesters for their warm-up, followed by team introductions.

As he had done for the basketball teams, Bennie Pressler was again at the microphone to introduce the teams and announce the opposing pairs in each individual match, starting with the lowest weight divisions and ending at heavyweight. With Leah Russo's help as statistician, Bennie also announced running scores between each match's three two-minute periods, as well as the eventual winner after a pin or decision. Leah's main job was to record on paper individual points are they were announced by the referee's left- or right-handed signals from the mat, and to tell Bennie what to announce over the PA. The referee wore a red band on one wrist to represent the visiting wrestler and a green band on the other wrist to represent the home wrestler. The opposing grapplers wore appropriately colored bands on their ankles so that the home statistician would be less likely to misinterpret the referee's calls.

Whether on or off the mat, preparations for that night's wrestling match went smoothly until Jimmy Foxx decided to cut back through the gymnasium on his way home from basketball practice. Leah Russo saw the brash new coach stop in the boys' locker room hallway door and look across the floor at the scorer's table where she and Bennie sat. Foxx watched Artie Bauer and the other seniors giving the mat another going-over with sponge mops after the Bruins were done with their team warm-ups. His chin high and head back, the aggravated basketball coach sniffed the air three times and then made a beeline for the senior wrestlers, stomping across the clean mat in his street shoes to reach them. He grabbed Artie by the arm.

"What are you all using on this mat?" Foxx shouted, pointing at the mop in Artie's hands. "That stuff's gonna ruin my floor! Get it out of my gym! Use water, kid."

Leah could see the confusion in Artie's face. But before he answered, Jug Johnson himself lit across the gym floor faster than anyone expected possible for a man of his advanced age and rotund size. His nickname was an apt description of his physical shape.

"What in the Sam Hill do you think you're doing?" Jug yelled at Foxx. "We're hosting a wrestling match here, buddy, in case you didn't know, and now we have to mop the floor *again*, thanks to you."

Jimmy Foxx grabbed Artie's mop away from the big boy. "Not with this corrosive stuff," said Foxx, almost as loudly as he'd yelled at Artie. "This is my basketball court and my gym, and I say what goes on in here. Got it, big guy?"

At first, Leah thought Jug was going to pick Foxx up and snap him in two like a dry twig. The new basketball coach had been a good athlete in his high school and college days, but his physique had never been especially impressive, as he was of medium height and weight. In his brand new Bruins warm-up suit, Foxx even looked somewhat soft, with his youthful good looks, rosy cheeks and sandy brown, gelled-back hair. Jug looked like a high-strung Sumo wrestler in street clothes. He wore a forest green V-neck sweater over a light yellow, button-collar shirt and a green tie, baggy khaki pants, and polished brown Oxfords.

Jug's face was bright red as he stared at the younger coach. But he shook his head, as if he were trying to settle the wild thoughts percolating in his brain. Jug looked over at Leah and Bennie sitting at the scorer's table, then at Artie, Wilma and the other two senior wrestlers on the mat with him and Foxx. He seemed to be looking for someone else, either the referee or maybe Principal Church, when he turned back to his antagonist.

"Coach Foxx," Jug Johnson began, "this ain't the time or place for this discussion. But we're using state-approved disinfectant on our mops, and we ain't got no choice but to clean the mat like we're doing now. It's in the rulebook, and I'll show it to you tomorrow, if I need to." He glanced again at Artie and turned back to Foxx. "One other thing," Jug added. "This may or may not be your basketball court, 'cause I imagine Joe Carson would have something to say about that, too. But I know for dang sure you're standing on our team's wrestling mat, and I'll thank you to get your dirty sneakers off of it, this instant—so we can get started here."

Now Foxx looked like *he* might explode, but he sneered at Jug and threw down Artie's mop before storming off the mat.

"I'm sorry about that, boys—and girl," Jug said to his seniors. "Let's hurry and finish up with the mops. We need to get this show on the road." He managed a weak smile. "Oh," he said to the four, but mainly to Artie, "and I'm proud of you all for not letting that young fella get you in any trouble—for staying out of it. He don't know what he's doing yet, but he'll learn."

In her seat at the scorer's table, Leah Russo wondered if Jug Johnson knew yet that Jimmy Foxx wanted his baseball coaching job, and if Foxx knew that Artie Bauer was the best catcher in the entire Suncoast Conference. She leaned over to her friend Bennie Pressler and whispered as much in his ear.

Finishing off a granola bar and popping a straw into his snack-sized carton of Yoo-hoo, Bennie chuckled. "I almost hate to miss all this," he said, referring to Brett's invitation for him to join the Woods family in Hawaii. "You can't beat this. Dinner *and* a show."

Chapter 15

THE BRUINS BOYS' BASKETBALL TEAM took the spotlight on Fishy Friday at Arbor High. It wasn't exactly dinner and a show—more like lunch and an afternoon matinee. Once again, Ty Green participated with his two former senior teammates as they combined a lunchroom prank with an impromptu pep rally. Their intent was to honor their former coaches—the one who had left earlier that fall and Principal Church, who had filled in until Coach Foxx came on board. The boys did not want to include Foxx in the frivolity—in any capacity—because the jury was still out as to how long he would last at Arbor High after Tuesday's second-half collapse and Thursday's embarrassment at the wrestling match. Coach Jones, the old coach, wouldn't be attending, as he had resigned unexpectedly and moved out of state to care for an ailing parent. Jerry Church would be on campus but would only come to the cafeteria if there were some disturbance that required administrative support. Frankie, the death-metal cashier, took care of that.

"Yeah, I need some help in the lunchroom," black-clad Frankie said into the handset of the phone on the wall next to the cashier's stand. He winked at Ty standing beside him. "This is a job for Principal Church. He needs to see what they're doing with the fish sticks today."

Ty slapped Frankie on the back and lifted a tray stacked high with nothing but golden brown, oven-fried fish sticks. He hurried back to a table on the 11th- and 12th-grade level where a group of seniors had cleared everything off the tabletop and head cheerleader Vicki Duke had unrolled a large paper sign. The students were frantically arranging the brown fish sticks on the off-white poster paper when the principal burst into the cafeteria.

"What's going on in here?!" Church bellowed, scanning back and forth in the large room for troublemakers.

Still at the cashier's stand, Frankie pointed toward the lunchroom's upper level, which was out of Church's line of sight from where he stood. "It's the seniors," shouted Frankie. "They said they aren't gonna stop until you go up there."

Church moved forward far enough to turn and look back toward the upper level, where he could see the gaggle of seniors still hunched over the table bearing the poster. All he could see, though, were the students' backs, not what they were working on.

"Stop that!" Church shouted. "Whatever you're doing—or whoever you're doing it to—stop it right now!" He turned back to check the Barf Table and count heads there, just to make sure one of the 9th graders wasn't missing.

Ty Green was the only Barf Tabler not sitting in his usual chair. Instead, Ty stood at the top of the upper-level stairs, beckoning the principal to come that way. "Hurry, Mr. Church," said Ty. "It's getting *ugly* up here—really *ugly*."

That was when the cheers began—first *Jer-ry! Jer-ry! Jer-ry!* and then *Church! Church! Church!*—until the principal waved his hands to make them stop and headed around the corner to mount the stairs. At the top, Ty Green stopped him.

"Hold on, Mr. Church," said Ty, "while we get into formation." He placed his hand on Mr. Church's chest while an "honor guard" of senior athletes—three per side—lifted fish sticks like swords for the principal to pass beneath. "You may proceed," Ty said, withdrawing his hand and hurrying around the fish stick arch so that he could join his former teammates behind the table of honor. The poster now read "THANK YOU, COACH!" in carefully placed fish sticks.

By then, Jerry Church knew that he'd been pranked—in the best possible way. With a smile, he walked to the table, where he was greeted by Vicki Duke. She rose on her toes and kissed him lightly on one cheek. "Thank you, Mr. Church," she said. "The boys have some gifts for you, too—to show their appreciation.

Do you like our sign?"

"I sure do," said Church. "Thank *you*." He looked up at the three senior boys across the table, each one hiding something behind his back. "Okay, now," the principal said. "What have we got here? A copy of *The Old Man and the Sea*? A big bottle of cod liver oil to drink in my old age? You know fifty isn't that old, right? I enjoyed working with you boys." He smiled again.

Ty waited as the other two boys presented Jerry Church with an Ugly Stik fishing rod and a nice spinning reel—the principal's "mace" and "scepter." Then Ty stepped forward with the temporary coach's "crown," a green and gold bucket hat covered with fishing lures and flies. "You'll probably use live bait on the pier," Ty said as he handed the hat to Church, "but it'll be good for inland fishing, if you're into that. We're sending the same stuff to Coach Jones."

The principal was visibly touched by the students' generosity, and he looked as if he wanted to say something to Ty, in particular, but managed only to shake their hands and croak, "Thank you, boys." He turned and looked around the lunchroom again—his eyes resting for a few seconds on Artie, Leah and Nicie at the Barf Table—before walking back down the stairs, turning the corner and heading back to his office as the release bell rang.

Back at the Barf Table, the seven friends continued celebrating the wrestling team's big win from the night before. As usual, Artie had won his heavyweight match. Little Ricky regaled the others with every move of his surprise victory over Solid Rock's all-conference wrestler at 113 pounds. Ricky pinned the champion grappler in the latter minute of the first period. And both Tommy and Wilma had made good showings in exhibition matches, though both narrowly lost on points, with Tommy at 220 pounds and Wilma at heavyweight.

"I could have wrestled at 108," said Ricky, "if you guys hadn't made me drink so much water yesterday at lunch. But it was okay. I beat that guy, anyway." He beamed and flexed his biceps again, as he'd done the previous day for the whole lunchroom.

Just then, Vicki Duke walked up behind Artie's chair and stopped. She rested her hands on his broad shoulders and turned to address Ty. "That was really sweet of you guys to do that for Mr. Church," she said. "Thanks for letting me join in on the cheerleaders' behalf. Mr. Church is such a teddy bear. I just love him."

Leah and Nicie looked at each other and rolled their eyes. Ty gave Vicki a crooked smile and said, "Yeah, I wish Coach Jones hadn't left, but I have to admit, ol' Lurch did a pretty good job filling in until, well, Foxx got here."

"Does this mean you're playing tonight?" Vicki asked Ty, her hopes rising for the Bruins' showing that night at Mimosa Beach.

"I miss my guys," Ty replied, "but I can't play for that man—for Coach Foxx. Me and the boys, like me and Artie, have been playing ball together—football and basketball and baseball—ever since we were kids. But that guy isn't gonna come in here and push everybody around and expect me not to speak up. He's not my daddy."

"That's right," said Nicie, though she chose not to say more despite being irritated by the topic. Leah reached over and touched Nicie's hand to acknowledge her restraint.

"I'm sorry to hear that," said Vicki, as she turned to address Bennie. "Oh, my, Benjamin, you aren't using a wheelchair now. That'll make your trip to Hawaii so much more fun!"

Leah and Tommy both shot looks at Bennie, who suddenly seemed more interested in opening another Yoo-hoo than responding to Vicki's remark. "We aren't sure we're going—not anytime soon, anyway," Bennie said finally. He glanced at Leah and Tommy, then added, "How did you know about that, Dig—uh, Vicki?"

The cheerleader smiled. "Brett told me last night on the phone," she said. "I sure do wish *I* could spend a month in Hawaii in the winter, but I have too many basketball games to cheer at. I'm looking forward to the Christmas tournament in Iron Harbor. We're working on a new dance routine for it, kinda like the one I did Tuesday here in the cafeteria—you know, with grass skirts and coconuts and tiki torches."

Leah could just see the newspaper headline—*Fire Dance Destroys Iron*

Harbor Arena—but she kept her lip buttoned. Bennie, though, couldn't resist questioning the head cheerleader further about her phone conversation with Brett, who had been her date at homecoming. "How did you get Brett's number?" Bennie asked. "I didn't give it to you."

"I got it from Miss Hopper," replied Vicki. "Well, actually, I saw it on her desk. She has a file she keeps for his assignments." She turned to Leah. "I heard Miss Hopper say you're going to come by this afternoon for Brett's file, and I should give it to you if I'm there and she's not."

Leah nodded. "Great," she said. "Thanks ... Vicki." Leah wanted to ask why Vicki hadn't passed along Brett's assignments to him over the phone the night before, but she didn't want to encourage more communication between the surfing football star and his old flame.

"Well," Vicki said, patting Artie's shoulders absentmindedly, "is everybody going to the game tonight in Mimosa Beach? We need all the support we can get there. Right, Nicie?"

Nicie's eyes narrowed, but Ty spoke up. "I'll be there," he said, "well, for the girls' game, anyway. Leah, you can ride home with me and Nicie, if you want. Since it's Mimosa Beach, she doesn't have to stay for the boys' game or wait to ride the activity bus home. Coach Carson's cool. He knows the score."

Leah nodded again. "Thanks," she said. "I'll do that, too."

"How about you, Artie?" Vicki said, massaging his neck muscles. "Are *you* coming to the game tonight? We could use your help."

Now Bennie was confused. "What do you want Artie to do?" he asked. "Be a hula dancer in your new dance routine?" He giggled. "Or stand by with a fire extinguisher? I mean, I'm going to the game tonight. Dad said he'd take us. So, I could do that—can't dance just yet, but I could put out any fires all you hot cheerleaders start." He winked at her.

Artie took Bennie's teasing comments in stride, though the big farm boy's face did begin to turn red at the unexpected attention Vicki was giving him. "No," Artie told the girl, "Ricky and I need to get home as quick as we can after wrestling practice. I have work to do on the farm, and I want to make sure the office trailer is ready for Dr. Marecek's sessions tomorrow."

"Well, we'll miss you tonight, Artie," said Vicki in her sweetest voice. "Now, you tell that handsome granddaddy of yours 'hello' and give him a big hug for me." The blond cheerleader leaned forward and wrapped her arms around Artie and gave him a good squeeze. "Bye-bye, now," she said, before turning and walking away.

Leah Russo was afraid to say much about Vicki's curious visit to the Barf Table, because Leah didn't want to hurt her friend Artie's feelings. Tommy White, however, wasn't afraid to ask the question that was on all their minds. "What was *that* all about?" asked Tommy. "I think she was coming on to you, Artie."

"No," Artie said, shaking his head, "I think I know what she's after—and it isn't what you guys are thinking."

"What?" Bennie Pressler teased. "That she wants you for your body?"

Artie laughed. "Yeah, well, maybe she does," he said. "I did hear that Miss Hopper and the cheerleaders need somebody to wear that stinky old bear suit and be Bruno the Bruin at all the basketball games. But I don't have time to do that." He looked at Tommy. "Hey, bud, you're big enough to fill out that suit. Interested? I can call her back here."

Tommy White shook his head, even though his neck *was* sore from the previous night's exhibition match and he would have enjoyed getting a neck rub from a pretty cheerleader. "No," he said. "I don't have that much school spirit—not yet, anyhow. I don't even want to go see the games in Mimosa Beach tonight." He nodded at Ty and Nicie. "No offense," Tommy added, "but I just want to chill out tonight. I'm bushed."

"How are you gonna get home?" Bennie asked him.

Tommy shrugged and turned to Artie. "Can you give me a ride home—to the beach?" Tommy asked. "I'd hate to make Mrs. Pressler have to come after me."

"How about this?" said Artie. "Why don't you ride home with Ricky and me, and spend the night on the farm? Then you can go back to the Presslers' house tomorrow after Bennie's session with Dr. Marecek. You can talk to Grandpa while I do my chores and work at the trailer. He'll enjoy talking to somebody besides me. We'll all have fun."

Bennie made a joke about the boys having a pillow fight, but he liked the idea of Tommy visiting the farm and making a new friend. Also, Bennie wasn't afraid of using his walker without Tommy's assistance after Mr. Pressler dropped him off at Mimosa Beach High that night.

"I think I'm ready to solo," Bennie said, "but if I have any problems, I'm sure Digger Duke will make sure I have a soft landing. She won't let me crash and burn."

Again, Leah and Nicie looked at each other and rolled their eyes. Little Ricky Duran, who hadn't said much after bragging about his win, put Bennie in his place. "You shouldn't trust her," said the little wrestler, becoming serious for a change. "The feather pillows on our farm make a softer landing than anything you will get from Vicki Duke—and much less expensive. Vicki looks soft and is very pretty, but she is a hard person deep down inside. You do know that, Bennie, as does Brett. That is why you call her *Digger*."

Bennie studied his diminutive friend for a second and admitted, "Yeah, you're right, Ricky." Then he motioned toward his folded walker leaning against the table. "But when I finally get rid of this thing, I'm gonna find *somebody* to dance with and hold in my arms—even if I have to wear a stupid bear suit to do it."

Chapter 16

LEAH KNEW NICIE WAS HURT when the Mimosa Beach student section jeered her during the pregame introductions. These were students she had known since kindergarten, many of them her neighbors and playmates. Also, she had represented Mimosa Beach High on the basketball court the previous three years, ever since her 9th-grade season as a Lady Waverunner, and as a starter the past two years. Despite all the problems with her MBHS coach and his daughter—Jimmy and Jamie Foxx—Nicie had earned all-Suncoast Conference honors her junior season and should have merited attention from college recruiters. But now Nicie knew why scholarship offers weren't rolling in—because Coach Foxx had blackballed her with the collegiate coaches who had contacted him about her.

For whatever reason, Nicie was off her game throughout the first quarter. The Bruinettes' two newcomers—guard Jamie Foxx and forward Julia Safin—had learned most of Arbor High's offenses and defenses, and, as promised by Coach Joe Carson, had started that night's game. Oddly enough, Jamie and Julia had as many boisterous fans on the home side of the gym as on the visitor side. Leah couldn't quite understand why the Mimosa Beach students received Jamie and Julia so warmly—even waving and clapping when Coach Foxx himself entered the gym toward the end of the first quarter with the Bruins boys team—but gave Nicie such a hard time for the first eight minutes of the contest.

In the team huddle between quarters, Coach Carson got down on one knee in front of the five starters on the bench. "Okay, ladies," he said, "we're only down by three, thanks to our two new gals." He nodded at Jamie and Julia seated side by side. "Good shooting, Jamie. And that's the way to get those offensive rebounds and put-backs, Julia."

Then he looked up at Nicie. "Hang in there, girl," Carson said. "I know the shots aren't falling right now, but they will. You keep taking your shots when you have them." When Nicie raised her head to acknowledge his instruction—and his faith in her—he patted her knee and added, "Don't let them get under your skin, young lady. You're too good for that."

Twins Sara and Clara Harmon—who had lost their starting spots to Jamie and Julia—had played a couple of minutes apiece that first quarter, going in once for Nicie and twice for Ann Marie Childers, the second time when timid Ann Marie picked up her second foul on a questionable call. When the Harmons were on the floor, Julia switched to center but didn't do much better down low against the taller Mimosa Beach post player.

Nicie had also played out of her usual position throughout the first quarter, moving from shooting guard to small forward so that the shorter Jamie wouldn't have to go to the low post or baseline quite as often as Nicie would at forward. Against zone defenses, the two girls started most offensive plays from the opposite wings—that is, from the areas to the left and right of point guard Mel Grayson. But Mel often dribbled to the right, her strong side, against a zone. That pushed Nicie to the baseline and pulled Jamie to the point just beyond the three-point line at the top of the key, where Jamie sank treys—three-point jumpers—like a machine.

When the Lady Waverunners had switched to a one-to-one defense to counter Jamie's outside shooting, Nicie had been forced to begin each play down low toward the right baseline, with Mel starting out on the right wing. On the left, Jamie had played the wing, and Julia had set up toward the left baseline. Ann Marie had moved back and forth across the lane, and up and down from low-post spots to high-post spots, though she had struggled to free herself from the taller and stronger Mimosa Beach center's aggressive defense.

At the scorer's table between quarters, Leah Russo tallied her players' points and saw that Jamie Foxx led the way with nine, followed by Mel Grayson and Julia Safin with four apiece. No other Bruinettes had scored thus far—a fact that the Mimosa Beach student section didn't let Nicie Evans forget the first two times she ran downcourt on offense in the second quarter. Her third trip down the court was the charm.

The Lady Waverunners center had just scored on their second possession to push their lead to five. Ann Marie grabbed the ball and carried it past the baseline for her inbounds pass to Mel, with Jamie just upcourt. Mimosa Beach was still in a one-to-one defense, but they weren't pressing, instead picking up their assigned players in the forecourt past the center line. That took pressure off the guards and off inexperienced Ann Marie, but required Nicie and Julia to be more reactive to Mel's and Jamie's decisions in bringing the ball across midcourt. Against a one-to-one defense, the guards' basic choices were dribbling the ball with intent, driving to the basket, passing to a teammate, or pulling up and shooting a jumpshot from either long or short range. The Bruinettes big girls—Nicie, Julia and Ann Marie once she jogged up the court—had to adjust to whatever choice either Mel or Jamie made.

Mel took the inbounds pass, turned and fired upcourt to Jamie at the center jump circle. Jamie took the ball on the run and dribbled to the left where she usually set up. She picked up her dribble and held the ball high, looking for Julia on the left baseline or expecting to hit either Mel or Ann Marie after they crossed midcourt. But the defenders surprised Jamie by moving forward and picking up their players early, cutting off both Mel and Ann Marie.

Seeing that the official nearer to Jamie had started his five-second count on her stalled possession, Coach Carson whistled sharply and shouted, "Cross! Cross!" at Nicie and Julia. The instruction was so loud that even Leah heard it—though her ears rang from his whistle—and she knew what the coach wanted the forwards to do.

Nicie heard and understood, but she hesitated for an instant, not knowing how Julia would react—or if she would react at all. Before Nicie could move, she saw the dark-haired Russian headed her way with a defender in tow. Instinctively, Nicie held up to let her teammate cross the lane and stop just out of the paint. There Julia planted both feet and braced to screen Nicie's defender. Moving in an arc toward the lane, Nicie brushed past stationary Julia and left both defenders a step behind. She looked for a pass from the harried Jamie and curled toward the painted block low on the left side. But before Nicie could get across the lane, Jamie heaved a desperation three-point shot that was partially blocked by the girl guarding her.

In the gym lights, Nicie could see that the basketball would fall short of the orange rim. To this athletic young woman whose off-season sport—and summer job—was beach volleyball, the large brown sphere's inhibited flight looked something like a set shot she might see from her partner on the beach strand. Nicie leapt high to meet the ball with both hands at the apex of her jump. For a fraction of a second the ball rested on the pads of her fingers before she popped it toward the back of the iron, off the glass backboard, around one side of the rim and through the white net. Nicie Evans was on the board in more ways than one.

At the scorer's table, Leah Russo sniffed when the Mimosa Beach scorekeeper noted that she had credited Jamie Foxx with an assist on the play, not a missed shot attempt. Sitting right behind Leah in the stands, Bennie learned forward and quipped, "Great pass, huh? I bet she planned that when she picked up her dribble too soon." The MBHS scorekeeper gave him a dirty look and turned back to the action on the court.

Nicie's first basket—an accidental "alley-oop"—settled her down and renewed her self-confidence. At the same time, Jamie's blocked shot and inadvertent assist called into question her own abilities as a leader on the team. The same Mimosa Beach fans that had laughed at Nicie and lauded Jamie fell quiet, at least where the two former Lady Waverunners stars were concerned.

Except for Ann Marie Childers, the Bruinettes players outmatched the girls guarding them for the remainder of the first half and took a four-point lead into the locker room. All that kept Mimosa Beach in the game was the Lady Waverunners' ability to pass the ball time after time to their big center in the pivot for easy baskets. The big girl would hip-check Ann Marie or simply shove her out of the way for a close-up bank shot or hook shot. No whistles were blown for offensive fouls—at least, not when Mimosa Beach had the ball. Nicie Evans tried to sag off her own player to double-team Ann Marie's girl, but that resulted in open shots for the forward Nicie had been guarding.

Coach Carson wasn't one for big halftime speeches—especially when the Bruinettes were leading—so Leah Russo wasn't surprised when the Arbor girls exited the locker room after only a few minutes and jogged to the end of the court in front of their bench to loosen up and get used to shooting at the different backboard and goal. The coach returned to his spot at the end of the bench and looked up at Leah, who was studying the scorebook and taking notes for her school newspaper article.

"Well, that was a new one for me," Coach Carson said to Leah. "Mel and Nicie tried to encourage Ann Marie to get tough in the low post, but our new girl shot them down—shot *all* of us down, I'm afraid."

Leah wrinkled her brow. "How'd she do that?" she asked. "We're talking about Jamie, right? Yeah, I've noticed she's good at peeing on people's Wheaties."

"She did more than that this time," said Carson, shaking his head, "and sooner or later I'm gonna have to do something about it—exactly what, I don't rightly know."

Carson explained that Jamie had laughed out loud at Mel and Nicie's encouragement of Ann Marie. "Don't know what she said," he added, "but she even muttered something under her breath that made the poor girl cry. Jamie apologized—said she was just fussing at herself—but there was more to it than that."

"How do you know?"

The coach replied, "Her buddy Julia just up and said, 'Maybe *you* should not have talked so much, Jamie'—you know, in that funny accent of hers? I don't think she meant 'talking to *Ann Marie*' or 'talking to *us*.' I think Jamie's been talking to her old teammates—probably *about* Ann Marie and even about Mel and the twins. They already knew about Nicie from last year."

"What are you gonna do?"

He shook his head again. "Like I said, I don't know," he replied. "This isn't the time or the place for that little talk—even though not having it could cost us the game."

Leah looked cross-court once more, this time focusing on the Bruinettes' young center. "How's Ann Marie now?" she said. "Can she play?"

"I'm not sure about that, either," said Carson, "but I'm gonna give her a couple minutes to see. We're also gonna come out in a box-and-one zone, with Nicie guarding that big girl. We didn't practice that defense this week, so if Jamie *has* been talking to her old buddies, she didn't know to warn them ahead of time. Matter of fact, *Jamie* doesn't know about it just yet herself, so she—and Julia, too—may be coming out if they can't figure out what to do in the box-and-one."

Leah smiled at the thought of Jamie Foxx getting paid back after thinking she had been so sly in the locker room. From what Leah had learned about her that week, Jamie was quick to blame others for her own failures, but she relied on deceit off the court and passive-aggressive behavior on the court to avoid getting into trouble for her own words and deeds. Julia Safin, on the other hand, was blunt to a fault. Leah wondered if the Russian exchange student was afraid of anyone or anything short of being sent back home, whether to Moscow or Siberia.

The game's second half started with Mimosa Beach on offense. As Coach Carson had indicated, the Bruinettes came out in a box-and-one zone defense, with Nicie Evans guarding the Lady Waverunners center. The "box" was comprised of Mel Grayson and Jamie Foxx at the "elbows"—opposite corners of the paint at the free throw line—and Julia Safin and Ann Marie Childers on each side of the lane near the low blocks. In the huddle before the third quarter began, Julia hadn't reacted when the coach called for the new defense. Jamie, however, had initially balked and questioned—in her passive-aggressive way— whether or not the defensive change made sense, given that the Bruinettes were ahead by four points. Carson had simply smiled and said, "Well, we'll give it a try and see."

At her guard slot, Mel knew how to play the box-and-one, having used it previous years and having practiced it with the team that season, just not that week. Jamie, at the other guard, didn't keep in mind that Nicie—playing the center position on defense—might not be behind her in the paint, as would be more likely in a regular two-one-two zone. Nicie's job was to guard the Mimosa Beach center wherever the big girl went—high or low, inside or outside, to one corner or the other, even to the point or a wing, if that's where the offense took her. Also, Nicie wasn't going to let this girl—whom she had played with the previous three seasons—push her around. Nicie Evans knew where her loyalties lay, as did Arbor newcomer Julia Safin, who caught onto the new defense with no problem.

However, Ann Marie Childers and, surprisingly, Jamie Foxx had trouble adjusting to their new defensive responsibilities. Ann Marie was outmaneuvered twice for offensive rebounds and put-backs by the Lady Waverunners power forward, and Jamie let her player drive right past her down an open lane to the basket once. When that happened, she gestured at Nicie with a frown and mouthed, *Where were you?* From their vantage points, both Leah and Coach Carson could read Jamie's lips. That was when Carson rose, walked down the bench and told Sara Harmon and Sandy Cuthbert to check in at the scorer's table for Ann Marie and Jamie. The two starters would come out the next time the clock stopped for a dead ball. The score was now tied.

Jamie couldn't believe she was being benched so soon, especially since she had scored the Bruinettes' lone basket that half. She glared at Sandy when the excited little sub tossed her a towel. Jamie walked to the end of the bench without looking at anyone, covered her head with the towel and began to sulk. Coach Carson motioned for Ann Marie to sit next to him to talk for a few seconds, and the tall 9th grader did so. Leah thought she looked almost relieved to be off the floor right then.

Just back from the lobby, Bennie Pressler leaned forward and said into Leah's ear, "Did I miss something while I was out? Is Jamie taking a schvitz or what?"

Leah turned to look at him and raised her eyebrows but didn't explain. "Tell you later," she said and turned her attention back to the action on the floor.

What the Bruinettes lost on offense with the substitutions, they gained on defense. Sara Harmon—spelled by her twin sister every three or four minutes—

was experienced enough to do what was required of her down low in the box-and-one. At the top of the zone, Sandy Cuthbert's quickness and energy kept the opposing guards off balance and resulted in two turnovers and a steal, all of which translated into Arbor baskets on the other end of the court. Ann Marie settled down next to Coach Carson on the bench and subbed in at different times for Julia and Nicie when they needed quick breathers. The two older girls were playing hard and well.

Late in the third quarter, Coach Carson wanted to sub Jamie Foxx in for Mel Grayson at point guard—Mel had played the whole game so far—but Jamie refused to leave her spot at the end of the bench, preferring to sit askew on the bleacher so that her back was to the coach and her teammates. In fact, she even traded a look or quick comment now and then with students in the home bleachers—or so it appeared to Leah from the scorer's table.

Jamie's misbehavior stopped, though, late in the fourth quarter when her father, the new Arbor boys' coach, left his team's locker room and stuck his head into the gym to see how much time was left on the clock. When Jimmy Foxx realized what was happening—that his daughter was acting up on the bench—he placed two fingers in his mouth and whistled even louder than Coach Carson was capable of doing. Jamie had heard that shrill whistle before and knew what it meant. She removed the towel from around her neck and sat up straight. Now it was the father's turn to glare across the court, but not at his coaching colleague—at his 16-year-old daughter for letting her father and herself down.

With a minute left to play and Arbor leading by one, senior captain Mel Grayson dribbled across the midcourt stripe and called timeout for the Bruinettes. Coach Carson met the five on the floor in front of the bench, not wanting them to sit during the brief break in the action. "Okay, ladies," he said, "it's crunch time. This last minute is what it's all about."

Leah could see that all five girls were wet with sweat and breathing hard, even energetic little Sandy Cuthbert. The Arbor High subs, including Jamie Foxx, had risen from the bench and stood in a loose huddle around the five players and Coach Carson.

"What defense are they in, Mel?" the coach asked his point guard, not because he didn't know the answer, but because he wanted to be sure that his players were thinking on their feet, not just standing there staring at the floor.

"They were in a zone, Coach," said Mel, "but I think they'll switch to man now."

"Right," Carson said, "so let's shake things up a bit. Let's stay in our *zone offense* when they switch to one-to-one. Okay? I said, *stay in our zone offense*—with you, Mel, staying at the point. Nicie, you're on the right wing. Sandy, left wing. Sara, you start out at high post, and Julia you set up down low. Does everybody understand?"

All five girls nodded, and Carson continued, "If they stay in the zone, we just pull the ball back, and you three girls up top—Mel and Nicie and Sandy—you three gals just dribble and play catch with one another and run out the clock. That's if they stay in the zone for some reason—*but they won't.*"

At that point, Leah saw Coach Carson turn his head and look at Jamie Foxx, who stood to his immediate right and was paying close attention to his instructions as if she expected him to send her into the game. He made no such move.

"Here's what they're gonna do," the coach said. "They're gonna switch back to a one-to-one, and they're gonna double-team us wherever they can. So stay out of the corners, and keep moving, just like you were working the ball against a zone. And I want you two girls playing high and low post—Sara and Julia—to keep moving and to set picks back and forth for each other so that one of you gets open. But don't get caught camping out in the lane, okay? We don't wanna give up the ball on a three-seconds call."

Then he looked down at Sandy Cuthbert. "Little girl," Carson said, "you're on the left, and that's your strong side, being lefty and all. So don't hesitate if they give you a lane to the basket. Take it to the hoop and put it in." He motioned to Nicie. "Same goes for you on the right. And both of you girls on the wings look for a pick from whoever's at high post. We can do this."

He reached out to end the timeout with the ritual cheer, and the girls touched his hand. "*Team* on three," he said. "*One, two, three—*," and they shouted their mantra as if they believed it would deliver the team a win.

The scoreboard horn blared, and the Arbor High five took their positions in the frontcourt. The subs had returned to their seats on the bench, but Joe Carson remained standing within the coaching box in the painted area along the sideline, down from the hash mark closer to midcourt where Nicie Evans would inbound the ball.

As they had rehearsed in practice, Nicie first looked for Mel, then for Sandy, and she was prepared to get the ball right back from either one. Meanwhile, the two post players—Sara and Julia—drifted forward and tried to break free for the inbounds pass in case neither guard got open. The Lady Waverunners didn't contest Nicie's throw-in, instead using that defender to double-team Mel. With Mel covered and Sandy scrambling up, back, even over the center line and into the backcourt, Nicie looked left toward the basket and saw Sara waving for the ball near the foul line. Julia and the big Mimosa Beach center were tangled up fighting for position behind Sara.

Holding the ball high with both hands, Nicie snapped the inbounds pass at Sara, whose defender had sagged backwards to guard against another alley-oop pass. Sara caught the ball and prepared to throw it right back to Nicie on the wing, but the twin hesitated for a second, letting her opponent recover. The Lady Waverunner reached forward and poked the ball out of Sara's grasp, sending it scooting toward midcourt where Mel, Sandy and their three defenders had converged. Closest to the loose ball, Mel dove toward it. Her left arm and shoulder hit the floor first and screeched like clean sneakers on a newly lacquered court, but she managed to gather the ball in with her right arm. One defender bent low in an attempt to snatch away the ball but succeeded only in jostling her teammate and causing her to tumble onto Mel, still smarting from the dive to the floor seconds earlier.

An official's whistle sounded, and the game clock stopped. With the whistle dropping to his chest, the man in black and white stripes made a rolling motion with his hands to signal that Mel had traveled. He awarded the ball to Mimosa

Beach.

Even without his walker for support, Bennie Pressler jumped to his feet on the bleacher behind Leah and screamed at the official. "That was a foul!" Bennie yelled. "You can't travel if you have somebody on your back!" He leaned down to Leah at the scorer's table. "That's the same guy who made the bad call in the first half," said Bennie. "That's home cooking."

Leah agreed with her friend but said nothing. A few Suncoast Conference officials had crooked reputations, but Leah had attended all her late brother's games, and this particular man didn't have a bad name yet. She thought it was more likely he didn't want any trouble getting to his car later that night after the boys' game, whose crowd promised to be even rowdier.

Fifty-one seconds remained on the game clock. Arbor led by a single point. Still on the floor, Mel pushed the ball away to make the official chase it down. She rolled over and tried to sit up but couldn't put any weight on her left arm, wincing in pain and lying back down. Coach Carson and the girls on the floor hurried to their captain to give aid.

"I'm okay," Mel said through clenched teeth, in obvious pain. "Just give me a minute. Help me up. I'm gonna finish this thing." She rolled onto her right side and tried to push up, but she had trouble standing, even with help from her teammates.

"Absolutely not," said Coach Carson. "You're going to the locker room to have somebody take a look at your arm. Mimosa Beach has a trainer—he's a doctor, even—and we'll get you to the ER if we need to. You're what's important, young lady, not this durn game." Carson motioned to the Mimosa Beach coach to send assistance, and they helped Mel off the court.

Ball in hand, the same official approached Carson. "We need a sub, Coach," the official said, "unless you take another timeout. It would be your last one." The coach nodded and turned to scan the players on the bench for someone to replace his injured point guard.

"Yeah," Carson said, "I need to call that timeout." He called the girls back to the bench and addressed them. "They'll take good care of Mel in the locker room, and we'll do whatever we need to about her arm. But right now we need to finish this game."

Again, Jamie Foxx looked like she expected to be subbed in, but the coach pointed at Clara Harmon and told her to check in at the scorer's table when they finished talking. "We're on defense," he reminded. "Nicie, Julia, Clara—you guard their big girls. Sara and Sandy take the guards. Okay, we're matching up full court, so get with your girl as soon as we break huddle and stick to her like glue as long as they have the ball. You know how to play defense."

He glanced at Jamie, then looked back at Sandy Cuthbert, whose blue eyes sparkled in anticipation of leading the team on offense. Carson continued, "When we have the ball, I want Nicie and Julia on the wings—Nicie right and Julia left. Sandy, you'll be at the point. I want you to push the ball to the left—to your strong side—and if you can't penetrate, look for Julia at the low corner baseline or Nicie moving toward the top of the key. Sara and Clara—you guys are playing the post positions, high and low. Give Nicie and Julia room to work if either one gets the ball, but be sure to follow up any shots."

The horn sounded, calling the teams back out onto the floor. Mimosa Beach inbounded the ball, got it across midcourt and set up their attack despite the Arbor girls' stubborn one-to-one defense. The Lady Waverunners point guard passed to a forward at the high post and lit out for the corner baseline. The forward wheeled on Julia Safin and hooked her with her free arm so she could drive toward the basket. Nicie Evans cut her off, forcing the Mimosa Beach forward to put up a short floater that used every part of the cylinder before dropping in.

The same official blew his whistle again. "Foul," he shouted, raising one arm to stop the clock. He twisted to check the guilty player's uniform number before turning to face the scorer's table once more. "Foul on three-zero," he said, showing three fingers and then a fist to the girls keeping score. "That's three-zero … green." He repeated the hand signals for Nicie's number. Then he said, "Basket good," making that sign before holding up one finger. "One shot."

With their team now trailing by a point, the Arbor fans seated across the court howled in derision. Leah shook her head at the bad call. Bennie, standing again, leaned down and said, "I told you so. Home cooking. They're cheating us."

The Lady Waverunners forward bounced the ball three times at the free-throw line and calmly sank the shot, putting her team in the lead by two with fifteen seconds left on the clock. Arbor had no timeouts left, and the new Mimosa Beach coach chose not to call timeout himself, instead waving his players back down the court and yelling at them not to foul.

As Coach Carson had instructed, Sandy Cuthbert pushed the ball across midcourt, then to the left side. She couldn't find an open lane to the basket, and Julia was covered in the lower corner. Before the little guard could turn to look for Nicie at the top of the key, two Mimosa Beach players converged on Sandy and forced her to pick up her dribble. It was much the same situation as Jamie Foxx had faced early in the game on Nicie's alley-oop basket. But instead of throwing up a desperation shot in the waning seconds, Sandy trusted that Nicie was following Coach Carson's orders and was near the top of the key.

It wasn't exactly a desperation pass. It was more of a Hail Mary throw like one a football quarterback might purposefully sling downfield on a game's final play, because Sandy Cuthbert had faith in her teammate.

With two seconds left, the ball sailed through the air and hit Nicie's soft hands head high. The Bruinettes' newest star made sure she was behind the three-point line before squaring up and arching her long jumper toward the goal. The horn sounded and the in-laid lights around the edges of the backboard flashed red as Nicie's shot snapped the cords without touching the rim. This time there were no whistles from the officials. Both held their arms high as if the Hail Mary pass had resulted in a touchdown. The three-pointer gave Arbor High the win.

Chapter 17

AS THE BRUINETTES CELEBRATED on the court, Ty Green waited for his girlfriend and her teammates at the door to the team's locker room. Leah Russo and Bennie Pressler had spotted Ty sitting in the visitors' stands across the court, but the Arbor senior had not approached either of them during the game. Leah figured Ty was just laying low—maybe because he didn't want to be mistaken for still being on the Arbor boys' team or be questioned about why he had quit. Another possibility was that he felt this was Nicie Evans's time to shine, and he didn't want to steal any of the spotlight that was focused squarely on her right then.

Leah finished her work at the scorer's table and started packing up to leave, knowing she was catching a ride home with Ty and Nicie. Still seated behind Leah as he waited for the rush toward the concession area to thin, Bennie reached down and tapped her on the shoulder.

"So, you guys are taking off now?" Bennie asked. "Think there will be room for me in the Whale? I'm having second thoughts about staying."

"Why?" Leah said, turning toward him as she slid out from behind the table. "I thought you wanted to flirt with Vicki Duke during the boys' game. But, I've got to tell you, if you keep jumping up and down like you've been doing tonight, Digger *will* make you put on that stinky bear suit and be Bruno, at least for the away games." She laughed.

Bennie frowned. "Oooh," he said. "That's *another* good reason not to stay. No, I have a feeling things are gonna get out of hand during the boys' game. These Mimosa Beach folks are already upset about losing to our girls. And I don't want to get caught in the middle of a fight or something—not with me using a walker. They know who I am and where I go to school."

"But you'd be sitting over there on our side," said Leah. "You'd be okay."

"Yeah, as long as I stay here in the gym," Bennie said, "but I'll have to walk outside and wait for Dad sooner or later. He's checking on things at the Mimosa Beach store while I'm here, and I don't know exactly when he'll be done. So, how about if I tag along with you right now, and then Ty and Nicie can take us—you and me—over to the store to meet Dad. I can call and tell him what we're doing. It would save Ty from having to go out of his way to take you home. Your house is already on our way home to Sandpiper Beach."

Leah shrugged. "Okay," she said, "and, yeah, I'm guessing Ty and Nicie wouldn't mind having some alone time tonight, anyway. Weren't those great shots? I mean, the game-winner, but the alley-oop, too. They were both poster shots! I wish I'd brought my camera."

Bennie agreed and followed Leah onto the floor and across the court toward the visitors' locker room. She went inside to find Nicie and to see about Mel's injury. Bennie stayed outside the door and talked to Ty, who said taking Bennie and Leah to the Pressler's Department Store there in Mimosa Beach would be no problem. Just as Bennie finished calling his father to have him wait at the store for them, Leah and Nicie emerged from the locker room.

"Great game, babe," Ty said to his girlfriend. "I'm proud of you. That shot was money."

Nicie smiled at Ty's praise but still looked worried. "Mel's hurt pretty bad," she said. "Her parents are taking her over to the emergency clinic here at the beach."

"That's near the mall, isn't it?" asked Ty. "Well, we can stop and check on her in a few minutes since we're taking these two over to Pressler's. You know about that, right?"

Nicie nodded and handed her duffel bag to Ty for him to carry. The four headed toward the twin doors to the concession area in the gym lobby, then outside toward the White Whale in the parking lot. With Bennie using his walker, they couldn't move as quickly as they would have liked. But no one gave Nicie—or any of them—any real trouble. A few Mimosa Beach fans saw Nicie and started to say something, then stopped when they recognized Ty walking with her. No one bothered with either Bennie or Leah.

Once they were seated in the Whale—Nicie up front, the other two in back—Ty headed for the beach mall with its Pressler's anchor store. It was a mile away and only a block from the emergency clinic. Ty dropped Leah and Bennie off at the curb near Pressler's east entrance. As they waited for Bennie to climb out of the back seat and get his walker unfolded again, the 9th-grade comedian tried to make small talk.

"Hey, Ty," said Bennie, "do you want to borrow my cell phone for the rest of the night? Or maybe Nicie would like to have it."

Ty looked confused. "Why would we want to borrow your cell phone?"

Bennie snapped his walker into place and grinned. "Oh, I don't know," he said. "Maybe for when you, uh, run out of gas?" He would have put air-quotes around that last phrase if he hadn't been gripping the walker so tightly.

Ty hooted and waved Bennie off. The White Whale was rolling through the parking lot toward the main drag through the beach town before Bennie and Leah reached the Pressler's entrance and got through the revolving door. With Christmas just around the corner, shoppers came and went in good numbers even at that late hour. It was, after all, a Friday night when the mall was a popular destination for kids and young couples looking for amusement, as well as for shoppers looking for bargains.

Bennie and Leah found Mr. Pressler busy working upstairs in the store office. He told them to sit right there and wait for him to finish—that he'd be ready to go in fifteen minutes or so. Thirty minutes later, the two were still seated on an upholstered bench in the hallway outside the office when Leah's own cell phone rang. She studied the caller's number and showed it to Bennie, but neither recognized it.

"Hello?" Leah said, wondering if the call had anything to do with her parents' expected arrival home. Maybe they'd been delayed and were calling from wherever they had stopped for the night. Maybe something worse was wrong. Maybe they'd had an accident.

But it was Nicie, calling from the emergency clinic. "Hey, girl," said Nicie, "thought I'd give you a call and tell you about Mel—so you don't worry. Where are you right now?" When Leah told her, Nicie continued, "Yeah, we're waiting, too. But the ER people told Mel's parents that her arm's broken—well, it's only cracked, a hairline fracture, but her arm will be in a cast for six weeks, they said. She has some bruised ribs, too. We're waiting for her to come out before we leave. Coach was here, but had to go back to the gym to be with the team. He wanted me to stay and let Mel know we all care about her."

"Which arm?" Leah asked.

"Her left arm," said Nicie, "so she might not be out for the whole season—at least, that's what Coach told us. She'll miss the next Mimosa Beach game, but she should be back for the last one against them." Nicie changed the subject. "So, you're staying at your house tonight? Will your folks be home, finally?"

"I don't know," Leah said. "Either tonight or tomorrow—at least, that's the last I heard. I'm gonna call them in a minute to see if they're home already. They probably are."

"Okay, then," said Nicie. "I'll plan on picking you up tomorrow morning at your house so we can go out to the farm for your horse therapy. You and Bennie behave tonight."

Leah heard a muffled remark and laugh in the background. "You tell Ty Green that I said the same thing about you guys," Leah said, with a smile. "Bye, Nicie."

She closed the phone and turned to Bennie. "Nicie says we need to *behave* tonight," Leah said, glancing up and down the empty hallway. "I think even she would have a hard time finding trouble here. I didn't know retail was so exciting." She rolled her eyes.

"Just wait until Christmas Eve," Bennie countered. "That's when the excitement *really* starts. Then everybody gets to catch their breath for twenty-four hours before all heck breaks loose the day *after* Christmas. It's fun just to walk around and watch everybody go crazy." He paused. "Too bad I won't get to see it this year."

"Why not?" she said. "Is the trip to Hawaii on for sure?"

He nodded. "Yeah, I think so. Dad said that if he can take care of some stuff tonight, he'll feel better about us being away over Christmas—and over Hanukkah. And I think he was gonna call Woody Woods in Hawaii, too—you know, to make sure things haven't changed. Say, do you want him to go ahead and fax Brett's assignments from here? He can do that, you know—fax the papers wherever Woody says to send them. Do you have them with you?"

"Yeah," said Leah, "but I don't want to bother your dad with that right now, and I want to get on home. We can fax them from the farm tomorrow, can't we? Is Dr. Marecek's office set up yet? She has a fax machine, doesn't she?"

Bennie shrugged. "I don't think she does—not right now, anyway, but she does have a phone line. Tomorrow I'm taking an old laptop, a scanner and a fax-modem out there to set up in our section of the trailer, and you'll be able to fax stuff to Brett from there every Saturday—or whenever you're out there on the farm. I just figured Dad could fax the stuff tonight and save us the trouble tomorrow."

She nodded. "I know, but you can show me how to scan papers and how to fax them with that laptop—also, how to send emails—and then we can make absolutely sure it all works." She smiled. "Besides, I'm gonna be sending you *your* assignments and Tommy's, too, right?"

"Wait, *I'm* supposed to do homework like you regular people?" said Bennie, pretending to be shocked. "I'll have you know I'm smarter than the average Bruin. But, yeah, if you don't mind adding me and Tommy to your to-do list, we'd appreciate it. You can send me a FidoNet message every now and then, too—or one note for all three of us. I'll even read the mushy parts to Brett in a *sexy* voice." He batted his eyelashes at her.

She smacked him on the shoulder just as Abe Pressler flipped off the lights in the office and stepped outside into the hallway. "Are you two ready to hit the road?" the man asked. "Bennie, I'm glad to see that you still have a way with women. Leah, do I need to intervene here? I can double Bennie's chores—make him take out the garbage, wash my car *and* clean the garage. Of course, that'll be after he gets home from the farm and finishes his homework."

Leah laughed. "Yeah, just like a *regular* person, huh?" she said.

Pressler grinned and replied, "Exactly. We wouldn't want Bennie to get a big head." He squeezed his son's shoulder. "It's been hard enough keeping him humble at just the *thought* of missing school for our trip to Hawaii. But now it's definite—or as definite as something can be in this world."

"Really, Dad?" Bennie said. "So, when do we leave?"

"I talked to your guidance counselor today," said Pressler. "The last day of school before winter break is Friday the 18th. Miss Hopper said you and Tommy could take your tests early—if you have any—and miss the last two days of school that week. Then we can get to Hawaii before the start of Hanukkah and be there with our friends when we light our first candle. It'll be a special holiday for all of us, Tommy included."

"Sounds like a winner to me, Dad," said Bennie. "So, did you talk to Miss Hopper about, uh, anything else today?"

Pressler laughed. "Yes, I did," he said. "First of all, Miss Hopper said that you can't afford to fall behind in any of your classes—that you need to keep working hard these next two weeks, *and* you need to do all the work your teachers send while we're in Hawaii, just like Brett Woods is doing." He waited to see Bennie's reaction and continued, "I also heard something about a *need* that the school has right now—something I'm told you can help with."

"What's that, Dad," the boy said. "I always do what I can for the school—like running the scoreboard and PA at basketball games and wrestling matches, and deejaying at dances. You know that."

The father smiled again. "Well, actually, the person who answered the phone and took my name was the person who broached this particular subject. It was Vicki Duke, that girl who came over to our house once or twice a while back. Do you know where I'm going with this?"

Leah laughed out loud, but Bennie ignored her. "Yeah, I think I do, Dad. So, does this *need* that the school has have anything to do with a stinky old bear suit?

If it does, I guess I can wear it at away games—if you want me to do that—but I can't be a dancing bear just yet. Maybe I'll be walking better when we get back from Hawaii—you know, all that water therapy."

Pressler gave his son an odd look. "So, then, you're willing to be the cheerleaders' new mascot—at away games, at least?" The boy shrugged and nodded. "Okay, then," Pressler continued, "I'll call Miss Hopper next week and tell her you'll be helping me pick out a new bear suit for her, and that you'll also be Bruno when we get back from Hawaii—a part-time, non-dancing Bruno, that is."

Bennie was speechless. Leah leaned closer to him on the bench and said, "Smarter than the average bear, huh?"

The ride from the Mimosa Beach mall to the Russo family's subdivision between Monk's Landing and Sandpiper Beach was uneventful. No matter how hard Bennie tried to back out of his offer to be Bruno, the part-time, non-dancing bear mascot, his father seemed to like the idea more and more. Abe Pressler even suggested that Bruno wear a green and gold Hawaiian shirt and swim trunks with "Pressler's" embroidered across the seat of the shorts. In the middle of a cold winter, that outfit would be especially appealing, the department store owner teased. Leah had some suggestions of her own—like getting Bruno a special scooter so that he could "dance" with the cheerleaders, in case Bennie didn't feel up to standing some nights.

Leah stood in the driveway of her darkened house and waved to Bennie and Abe as the Presslers' van backed out into the street and turned toward Sandpiper Beach. She had tried to call her parents shortly after leaving the mall, but they hadn't answered either their cell phone or the house phone, and they hadn't returned the voicemail and answering machine messages she had left. Abe had questioned whether or not he should leave Leah alone—even offering to let her stay with them at the beach until her parents arrived home. But Leah had insisted that she'd been staying alone for the past week and that she would be okay. "Mom and Dad were probably on the road when I called," she had told Abe, "and they'll probably get here soon. I'll be fine."

The Russo cottage was a light green, two-story Cape Cod at the end of a cul-de-sac in the Arbor Woods subdivision. Though unused since his death, Reuben Russo's old basketball backboard and goal still stood above the white garage door on the left side of the house, just below the window to Leah's bedroom on the second floor. Leah walked up the driveway and saw the fan-shaped backboard shining in the moonlight. She remembered the evenings when her brother would spend hours thump, thump, thumping a basketball on the concrete drive to practice free throws and jumpers, even though his best sport was football and his favorite sport was baseball. He had told Leah once that he wanted to be an all-conference athlete in all three sports—a dream he realized by his junior year at Arbor High—and he'd practiced long and hard at basketball to be the best all-around athlete anyone in Monk's Landing knew.

On some of those evenings years earlier, Leah would peer down from her bedroom into the near darkness and see Reuben dribbling and shooting by porch light. She also remembered hearing the telephone downstairs ringing on occasion with a call from the neighbors on that side for her brother to stop making so much repetitive noise. Before Reuben's fatal car crash, Leah's own athletic ability had consisted of cheerleading, either baseball or softball, depending on the age when girls were allowed to participate, and even football, as she had won a second-place trophy in the county Punt, Pass & Kick competition under Reuben's tutelage. Although she possessed only a budding sportswriter's interest in basketball and had never really used the driveway goal herself, she refused to let her parents take it down. To Leah, the rim and board were sacred. But her parents couldn't bear to look at it without seeing and hearing the ghost of their son on his quest to be a triple-threat athlete. For all the survivors, the razor's edge of grief was remembering their loved one, but not thinking about his loss every moment of every day.

In bed late that December night, Leah Russo awoke from a fitful sleep to the sound of a car pulling up outside in either the Russo driveway or that of the neighbors. She assumed it was her parents, though they still had not called to let her know when they would arrive home. Lying in bed, she waited to hear the big garage door open so they could pull inside, but it did not. Without turning on her bedside lamp, she rose and padded over to the window to look out, her concern beginning to rise for her parents' safety. In the driveway sat an indistinctly colored car. Light from the night sky above and from a distant streetlight was absorbed in the automobile's dark and dull finish. Its glass all around was even darker, though the windshield did reflect the waxing moon behind the white, fan-shaped backboard above the garage door.

Moving to one side to keep her silhouette from being seen, Leah stayed by the window to see if the driver or a passenger got out. Minutes passed and no one left the car. In her mind, Leah tried to visualize turning the locks in both the front doorknob and deadbolt. She knew for certain that she had not used the security chain on the front door, because that would have then required her to come downstairs later and unchain the door for her parents.

Just then the driver's-side door swung open and a wiry man with long hair stepped out onto the concrete driveway. The car's courtesy lights shone weakly into the night, but the man's features were obscured by the darkly tinted windshield as he reached over the driver's seat into the back. He took out a large, square, thin object—a pizza box, just like the ones at Woody's—stood up straight again and closed the car door, holding the empty box loosely by his side. As the man walked from the drive toward the walkway to the front porch steps, he raised the box and balanced the container as if it held an actual pizza.

Leah Russo was not thinking about her brother Reuben or her parents right then. At this chilling moment, she was remembering Artie Bauer's story about the phony pizza deliveryman who had come to the farm the week before and had tried to enter the house. She also recalled the description of Tommy White's assailant in the alley outside Woody's Grill after Thanksgiving. She hadn't felt thankful for too much then, as she and her friends had sat around the farmhouse table. Now, eight days later, she thanked her lucky stars that she had seen the car pull up in the driveway and that she'd had time to call for help and to hide.

Chapter 18

IT WAS ALMOST NOON THAT SATURDAY when Leah Russo and Nicie Evans finally arrived at the farm. Nicie's blue sportster raised dust as it sped down the farm lane to the barn and new trailer, where Dr. Minnie Marecek, her niece Wilma, and the rest of the Barf Table gang waited. Just from seeing the two friends hop out of the little car, there was no clue about what either of them had experienced the night before. As usual, Leah wore faded jeans, her oversized Bruins hoodie and old tennis shoes, and Nicie wore a warm-up suit and nice sneakers. Neither carried a big winter coat, though the official change in seasons was only two weeks away. The late fall weather had been mild in Oleander County.

"We've been worried about you, Leah," said Artie Bauer. "A sheriff's detective called me this morning and said that my name—and Tommy's—had come up in connection with a home break-in last night between Monk's Landing and Sandpiper Beach. Was that near your house?"

Leah nodded. "It *was* my house—in Arbor Woods," she said. "The robber was that fake pizza delivery guy you met—the one who beat up Tommy at the beach. He was in that same old car as before, with the messed-up paint job and the dark windows."

"Yeah," said Nicie, "and no back bumper. We saw that fool drive past the high school the other day, and I wanted to chase him down, but little Miss Leah here wouldn't let me." Nicie turned to her friend. "Now, don't you wish I'd gone after him and found out where he's staying? You wouldn't be mixed up in this mess now—having to stay all night at the sheriff's department."

Ty Green looked concerned. "So *that's* why you weren't at home this morning," he said to Nicie. "I tried to call your house early, but no one answered."

"Leah called me around midnight from the sheriff's office in Iron Harbor," said Nicie. "We went up there to get her, but the detective handling the case said he had some more questions for me about the man I saw in the dumpster, the guy who hit Tommy. And then they asked Leah to go back to her house to see what was missing."

"What did the pizza guy get, Leah?" asked Bennie Pressler.

Leah shrugged. "Just the money that Dad had left on the kitchen counter for me and the jewelry boxes from their bedroom—Mom's and Dad's. I think the guy went into Reuben's room, too, but all the trophies looked like they were still there. But they're not gold or anything."

She stopped to catch her breath, then continued, "He came up the stairs and was in my room when, all of a sudden, the phone rang—my princess phone on the nightstand. I don't know who was calling—might have been my folks, might have been the police calling me back—but the phone ringing scared him. He ran back down the stairs and then out of the house before the cops got there. The phone had stopped ringing by the time he left, but I wasn't going to come out of hiding until I heard the patrol car's siren."

Little Ricky asked, "Where did you hide?"

"Under my bed," Leah replied. "He was even looking under it when the phone rang, but it was dark because I never turned on a light."

Ricky's eyes were wide. "Did he see you?"

"I don't know," said Leah. "Maybe so. He got down on his hands and knees, and lifted one side of the bedspread to see what was under there, but I'd rolled all the way to the wall, and the other side of the bedspread was between me and him. So, maybe he didn't see me."

"Did you see him?" Ricky said.

Leah shook her head. "I didn't see his face clearly—that's for sure. To tell you the truth, I held my breath and closed my eyes."

As usual, Bennie looked at the scientific angle. "Did they dust for prints?"

"Yeah," said Leah, "and they made a bigger mess than the guy did. I'm glad Nicie and her mom were there this morning to help me clean up. I still don't know where my folks are, but at least the house will be clean when they get home. For all I know, they could be anywhere."

"I hope they're okay," Artie said to Leah. "You're welcome to stay here on the farm until you talk to your parents, but the detective that called this morning wants me and Tommy to go up to Iron Harbor and answer more questions about the pizza guy. We're heading up there this afternoon. You can come with us—but I guess you've had enough *Law & Order* for one day."

Leah agreed that she didn't want to go back to the sheriff's department with them. "I'm staying with Nicie," Leah said, "because Mr. and Mrs. Evans promised they'd be responsible for me. Otherwise, the deputy would have turned me over to child services, and I didn't want that, even for one day." She looked and saw that Tommy was listening.

Nodding his head in agreement, Tommy said, "Yeah, foster care can be bad. But I got lucky with the Presslers. That was only because my mama and daddy both had worked for Mr. Pressler in Ebenezerville at different times, so he knew them—or knew *of* them—and he wanted to help out."

Putting his hand on Tommy's shoulder, Bennie corrected, "I'm the one who got lucky, buddy. After my accident last summer, I needed a friend my age to be close by all the time—like a brother, really. I'd still be in that wheelchair, Tommy, if you hadn't come to live with us. We're gonna have so much fun in Hawaii."

At Bennie's mention of their family's upcoming vacation, Tommy's face grew somber, but he said nothing more. Leah noticed the sudden change in the tall, husky boy's expression, and she wondered if he wasn't as excited as Bennie about leaving Arbor High, even for an extended holiday break.

Dr. Minnie Marecek and Wilma emerged from the office trailer and joined the teenagers in the shade of the barn. "Bennie," said Minnie, "your father is a miracle worker. This office is so nice—and the waiting room! It's perfect."

Minnie noted Leah and Nicie's presence without asking why they'd been late. The doctor continued, "Well, now that everyone is here, let's get started. Leah? Bennie? Wilma and Tommy will help you with your horses in the stable, and we'll meet in the corral. Don't be in a rush. We want to do things the right way—the less stressful way." She smiled.

While the therapy sessions were underway, Artie, Ty, Nicie and Ricky walked on down the farm lane to check on Grandpa Bauer. The four friends were gone the whole hour. When they returned, they carried four large objects from the farmhouse's attic: three wooden, straight-back chairs, one with arms, two without; and the old cedar-lined chest that Grandpa had told them about at Thanksgiving—Grandma's "hope chest" containing Harry Bauer's old love letters that he had dared Nicie to find and read.

Artie and Ty carried the dusty cedar chest between them, then turned sideways—one teenager in front of the other—to haul the coffin-like box up the new ramp on the back side of the trailer and through the metal door into the gang's section of the doublewide.

"How'd you talk Mr. Bauer out of that?" Leah asked Nicie once everyone had gathered inside. "I didn't think he wanted us snooping around in it."

Like a queen on her throne, Nicie moved the straight-back chair with arms over next to the hope chest and took a seat. "Oh," she said, "we gave him the love letters, and he's reading them now. He said we could have all the other stuff—whatever we want to keep. There's some neat old things in here." She patted the chest's rounded front edge.

"We can use it like a coffee table," Nicie added. "There's an old sofa and easy chair up there, too. They'll look good here—and some cool old lamps, you know, with the fringe around the bottom of the lampshades."

Artie spoke up. "Yeah, this is gonna be a nice clubhouse," he said. "There's even a big, old, round table up there—not quite as big as the Barf Table, but it'll do." He turned to Ty. "So, do you think there's enough room in here for your weights and other workout equipment?"

"Yeah, buddy," said Ty. "I'll haul my bench and free weights over here tomorrow, and we can bring that other furniture down from the attic. So, we can get started with Grandpa's training as soon as he wants. Tommy and I don't have to worry about working Bennie out for a month or so. Right, guys?"

"Hey!" Bennie said. "We still have almost two weeks before we leave for Hawaii. We can get a lot done in that amount of time. Who knows? It might mean the difference between being stuck on a boogie board like a little kid and standing up on a real board like a surfing god." He winked and slapped Tommy on the back.

Their therapy sessions now over, Bennie and Leah went to the smaller room on the Barf Table gang's side of the trailer and set up his computer equipment. Bennie showed Leah how to scan papers—in this case, Brett Woods's school assignments—and how to use his spare laptop computer and modem to fax the digital copies anywhere in the world. Finally, he demonstrated how she could write and send FidoNet messages to Brett right then, and to Bennie himself and Tommy later. He also set up a new computer bulletin board system—The Virtual Barf Table BBS—on the laptop with Leah as the administrator. That way, any member or friend of the gang could log onto the BBS and leave a message, like an actual bulletin board. Using her sports reporter's notebook, Leah jotted down all of Bennie's instructions so that she could cruise the information superhighway on her own after he left for Hawaii. She wanted to be as confident steering this new vehicle through cyberspace as her friend Nicie Evans was behind the wheel of her fast car.

Chapter 19

FOR ALL INTENTS AND PURPOSES, Meatless Monday at Arbor High was cancelled—not the school day, but the cafeteria capers. Artie Bauer and Tommy White had learned Saturday at the sheriff's department that Leah Russo's burglar—the phony pizza delivery man—had hit several other homes late Friday night and early Saturday morning around Monk's Landing. Ordinarily, most crimes of that nature would have had little effect on the Arbor High student body; however, these weren't simple home break-ins—the thief had also killed four dogs. Two of these pets were inside the houses awaiting their owners' returns when the burglar struck. Two other dogs were outside in fenced-in yards, and were killed so that they wouldn't bark at the intruder and alert neighbors. To most of the students, losing a pet was like losing a family member. So, that Monday, neither the bereaved nor their friends were in the mood for hijinks of any kind.

Once all seven friends were seated around the Barf Table, the main topics of discussion were what had happened to Leah's parents that weekend and how the fake pizza delivery guy's burglary spree had billowed into a wave of dog killings. Mr. and Mrs. Russo had finally returned Leah's call on Saturday afternoon. They'd had car trouble on Friday and had been forced to stay where they were until Monday when a mechanic could get them back on the road. At the same time, they hadn't seemed to know the reason for the delayed repairs, and they hadn't bothered to tell Leah where they were or why they hadn't called her cell phone sooner. When she'd told them about the Friday night burglary, they'd sounded more disturbed about the jewelry box thefts than the danger that

Leah had faced. Hearing about the canine deaths hadn't affected them, except to make them thankful that they always took the Russo family's black Labrador retriever puppy on their car trips. They had, however, seemed relieved to learn that Leah would be spending the rest of the weekend with the Evans family—or so they'd said.

"My parents are so out of it," Leah told her friends at the Barf Table that Monday. "They care more about the puppy than they do about me—I mean, they take better care of her. Mom got Lady last summer and won't let the dog out of her sight. Me? They don't want me around. I'm so tired of them making me feel like I don't matter."

Nicie Evans sat up straight. "Well, let me tell you something, girl," she said. "You matter. Me and Mama and Daddy drove up to Iron Harbor in the middle of the night on Friday to go get you, because you matter. Your folks should be the ones riding horses out on Artie's farm."

"Hey, now," Artie Bauer said with a chuckle, "don't drag me into this. But I agree. Leah, your mom and dad are just having a hard time right now—with everything. I know how they feel, and how *you* feel. Heck, I'm feeling that way about losing Grandma, and I'm watching Grandpa deal with it, too. It's not something you flip on and off like a light switch."

The seven teenagers around the table were quiet for a few seconds. Artie looked up again from the steaming bowl of tomato soup on his tray and addressed his two wrestling teammates. "Hey, guys, are you ready for tonight?" asked Artie. "Be sure to stay hydrated this afternoon, but don't overdo it. Remember, you've got to make your weights tonight before the match."

Ricky Duran stuck out his chest. "I don't care who I wrestle," said the tough little fellow. "I will beat him." He took a big bite of his grilled-cheese sandwich and chewed furiously, turning to Tommy White. "I will eat your sandwich, too, Tommy, if you think you can lose down to 195."

"No," said Tommy, "Coach Johnson told me I'll be at 220 again tonight, and it may be a *real* match this time, not an exhibition. He might move Jimmy down to 195 since we don't have anybody at that weight. Jimmy's pretty close to 195, anyway." He looked down at his tray and added, "So, I'm eating my sandwich, buddy—if you don't mind." They both laughed.

Artie smiled at the change in mood. "I'm really impressed with both of you so far," Artie said. "Tommy, once you put on a little more muscle, you'll be our heavyweight next year after Wilma and I graduate. And, Ricky, you're so quick on the mat. You can already shoot as well as I can—maybe better."

At that, Bennie Pressler couldn't keep quiet. "Shoot?" he said. "I wondered what Coach Johnson was telling you guys to do the other night against Solid Rock. At first, I thought he was saying that instead of cussing—but you weren't wrestling *that* bad."

Artie shook his head but laughed. "No, 'shoot' means to crouch low and step toward your opponent to go for his legs," Artie explained. "It's when you're both standing up and facing each other. And there's a certain way to *shoot* so you don't put yourself in a bad position. That's what Ricky is so good at already—going for a takedown without getting off balance. That's two quick points, right off the bat."

The sports calendar that week would be a challenge, with the basketball teams playing the Port Oleander Pilots on Tuesday and the Iron Harbor Gray Dukes on Friday. From year to year, Port Oleander's hoop squads were respectable, and the Iron Harbor teams were the best in the conference more years than not. The Arbor High wrestling team, with basically the same schedule, would meet Mimosa Beach High that Monday and Port Oleander High on Thursday, then cross the county line for a four-team "quad meet" on Saturday at Oakmont Prep School. So many matches in one week, not to mention in one Saturday, always tested the Bruins grapplers at every weight classification, but especially at heavyweight. Artie Bauer was in the best shape of his high school wrestling career, but he already knew he would probably let Wilma Marecek, his backup, wrestle at least one of the Saturday matches. Artie wanted to be ready the following Monday when he would meet Iron Harbor's undefeated heavyweight, the defending Suncoast Conference and state champion. Even though Artie had suffered minor injuries during football season, his body was now strong. But after his grandmother's recent death, his mental game—his focus—was what everyone including Artie wondered about but did not discuss.

"Hey, guys," said Artie, "are we gonna meet at our new clubhouse on Wednesday after our practices? And after Leah and Bennie do their horse thing, I mean." He was basically asking Ty Green and Nicie Evans that question, because the others—Ricky Duran, Tommy White and Artie himself—would already be there on the Bauer farm.

Ty nodded. "The weight room is shaping up real nice," he said. "I'm gonna haul another weight bench and some other equipment out there tonight. Coach Johnson is loaning us some of his personal stuff from home—said he hasn't used it in years." He looked at Nicie. "You don't have anything else planned Wednesday night, do you?"

"You mean, for *us* to do?" Nicie said. "No, I want to keep working on *our* section of the clubhouse—*our*, as in everybody, including us girls. That big room isn't just *your* weight room, buddy. We need something in there other than your torture equipment."

"I know," Ty said. "That's why Artie and I hauled that furniture you wanted down from the attic yesterday—the old sofa and big, stuffed chair, some end tables, and some lamps. We even got that round dinette table and some chairs to sit around it. They don't match, but they'll do."

Artie chuckled. "Yeah," he said. "Grandma and Grandpa used to have that table on the back porch, and we'd eat out there in the summertime when it was too hot in the kitchen after she'd been cooking all afternoon. We moved it up to the attic when Grandpa finally broke down and bought us an air conditioner. The chairs never did match. They came from yard sales."

"I don't care where they came from," said Nicie. "We're gonna make that clubhouse our home away from home. We can even look for one of those little dorm-sized refrigerators and a cheap microwave—maybe even a TV—and then we'll be set."

"Good," said Leah Russo. "I have a feeling I'm gonna *need* a home away from home—other than *your* house, Nicie. I can't keep imposing on you and your folks." Before Nicie could protest, Leah looked up and saw Jamie Foxx and Julia Safin approaching with their empty trays. "Incoming, six o'clock," Leah hissed toward Nicie.

The two "sisters" looked as different as two girls could—short-haired Jamie, in a Mimosa Beach sweatshirt and faded jeans; the taller Julia, in a nice blouse and slacks that accentuated her figure. The Russian had pulled back her dark hair into a loose ponytail with a black, velvet scrunchie. She wore just enough makeup to highlight her full lips and brown eyes. Jamie used only lip balm, if that.

Jamie stopped at the Barf Table, while Julia kept walking toward the tray return window. "I heard about what happened at your house, Leah," said Jamie. "That must have been scary." When Leah nodded, Jamie looked at Nicie. "And I heard you and your parents drove up to Iron Harbor Friday night to help out. That was nice."

"Yeah," said Nicie, with a suspicious eye, "but how'd you know about that?"

Jamie looked up as Julia rejoined her empty-handed. "Well, actually," Jamie said, "Dad had to drive up to Iron Harbor himself Saturday morning. Our little dog was one that got killed by that maniac. I mean, who would shoot a sweet, little dachshund?"

Nicie frowned. "I'm sorry, Jamie. That's horrible. Did the guy break into your house, too?"

"No," Jamie said, "our neighbor's house. But little Nathan—our dog—was in our fenced-in yard when the break-in happened next door. He'd gone out the doggy door in the middle of the night. We didn't see or hear anything. Isn't that right, Julia?"

The Russian girl nodded. "Yes, you are right," she replied to Jamie, then turned to the others, "but, no, not even the shot. And I am a light sleeper. I heard when leetle Nathan went outside, but that was all I heard. I went back to sleep and did not awaken until Meester Foxx—Coach Foxx, I mean—got up early and found leetle Nathan dead."

Jamie further explained that her father called the sheriff's office to report the shooting and was told about the spate of burglaries in the area. That was when they discovered the break-in at the house next door, finding a back door jimmied open while the neighbors were away for the night. "They came home that afternoon," Jamie said. "The thief got all their jewelry and an old pistol that they kept in a nightstand. But that wasn't what he used to shoot Nathan."

"What did he use?" asked Bennie Pressler, the budding investigator.

"Dad couldn't really tell," Jamie said, "and the cops wouldn't tell him, either. They know, but they don't want to say."

Bennie continued, "Did your dad take little Nate up to—"

"*Nathan*," Jamie snapped. "Like the hot dog." She pursed her lips.

"I know, I know," said Bennie. "Great name. But did they examine Nathan? Did they put him in cold stor—"

"Just shut up," Jamie said, annoyed by the questions. She shook her head and turned to leave. "Come on, Julia. Let's go." They left without saying anything more.

Watching them walk away, Bennie called, "Hey, I'm sorry, Jamie. My condolences."

Leah saw Jamie just shake her head again without stopping to acknowledge Bennie's apology or his expression of sympathy. "Let it go, Bennie," said Leah. "She was being nice, and then you had to start your forensic pathologist routine."

Bennie tried to argue. "Yeah, but—"

"No," Leah said. "Why do you need to know that stuff? Were you gonna offer to go dig up Jamie's poor little dog and do an autopsy if the sheriff's department doesn't still have him? Hasn't your family ever had a dog?"

Bennie understood her point. "I know, I know," he said again. "It was too soon. But the more we know about that guy, the better off we'll be if we run into him again. Now we know he has at least two guns—the one he stole and the one that has a silencer or something on it." He let that sink in, before adding, "But, no, we've never had a dog. We're cat people."

Chapter 20

MONDAY NIGHT'S WRESTLING MATCH at Mimosa Beach saw Arbor win their second match as a team. Little Ricky Duran and big Tommy White came into their own as Bruins grapplers. As he'd predicted, Ricky beat his opponent—in the first period, even—shooting from the standing start and scoring a quick takedown. Like a cat playing with a mouse, Ricky would let the boy escape, only to take him down again and again. He pinned him near the end of the first period.

Tommy White did, in fact, wrestle in the 220-pound weight class. His match was nip and tuck, but he toughed out all three periods and won on points. Coach Jug Johnson told Leah Russo afterwards—in her role as team statistician—that Tommy would stay in the regular lineup at 220 so long as Jimmy, the upperclassman that he'd replaced, kept making the lower weight. It was good strategy, Jug said, because several upcoming teams had good wrestlers in the 220-pound class that Jimmy had never beaten.

As usual, Artie Bauer won his heavyweight match at Mimosa Beach without trouble. In her exhibition appearance, Wilma Marecek wrestled poorly against the backup Waverunners heavyweight, who pinned her near the start of the second period. On the bus ride home after the match, Wilma told Leah that she was having second thoughts about wrestling during her senior year, when so much else was going on—college applications, scholarship applications, college-prep courses, and therapy work as her aunt's assistant. "And Artie's so good," Wilma said, "the team doesn't need me. Besides, Artie can practice with Tommy now."

Unlike the wrestlers, the Arbor basketball teams fell short of their expectations in their first contest of the week. On Tuesday night at home against Port Oleander, the Bruinettes couldn't get on track with Sandy Cuthbert replacing the injured Mel Grayson at point guard. No matter how hard Nicie Evans and Jamie Foxx tried to take control of the offense and score, a miscue on a teammate's part would turn the ball over and lead to points for the Lady Pilots. Port Oleander wasn't an especially good team—just good enough to score a big road win on this Krakatoa Tuesday night.

The Bruinettes' weakest link wasn't point guard Sandy Cuthbert, as most observers expected. It was freshman center Ann Marie Childers, whose toes were stepped on—both figuratively and literally—more than anyone else's. The Lady Pilots big girl pushed Ann Marie under the basket, away from the basket, anywhere she pleased on both offense and defense, and the officials called a minimum of fouls. To her credit, Jamie Foxx was frustrated at halftime about the team's performance, but she didn't make Ann Marie or anyone else cry this time. That didn't help, though, because the beating that the tall freshman took under the basket wore her down so much that Coach Carson sat her on the bench for good late in the third quarter and let the Harmon twins share the pivot position during the game's final stanza.

The Bruins boys team still hadn't gelled with their new coach, who himself was out of sorts due to the recent crime spree in his neighborhood and the loss of his family's pet. The Bruins trailed from the opening tip-off and never came close to making the game competitive. Bennie Pressler heard Coach Foxx tell his wife afterwards—she was still his scorekeeper—that he was beginning to regret having made the mid-season move to Arbor from Mimosa Beach. "We're gonna have to start from square one," Foxx told her, referring to the team, not to the family, though they, too, were mapping out new routes in uncharted territory. Their daughter Jamie was under more stress than her father was.

Whenever the Barf Table gang noticed Jamie Foxx in the Arbor cafeteria, she was rarely ever sitting with or talking to anyone except her exchange sister, Julia Safin. Jamie wasn't the outgoing type, especially with the opposite sex, but Julia—in her sultry, Russian way—attracted boys like bears to honey. She also got along well with her Bruinettes teammates and most other girls in school, including head cheerleader Vicki Duke. The talk around campus was that Vicki was after Julia to share the mascot duties with Bennie Pressler once the new bear suit arrived. Since Benny had agreed to be Bruno at away games, Julia could be the bear at home, changing into the costume after the girls' game and coming back out for the boys' contest. The irony of this Russian beauty hiding inside a bear suit was lost on everyone except the Barf Table crew, who considered offering their empty chair—Brett Woods's old seat—to Julia Safin. They didn't, though, because Nicie Evans said the move would cause Jamie Foxx even more pain.

That week's Waisin Wednesday finally arrived, and Arbor High Athletics took a collective breather from interscholastic competition that night. After their respective team practices ended, the Barf Table's winter athletes piled into Artie Bauer's old red pickup truck, Nicie Evans's blue sportster, and Minnie Marecek's new white pickup as the full moon rose in the dark December sky. The caravan on Ebenezerville Road was short-lived, though, when Minnie, bringing up the rear, turned into a convenience center parking lot.

Ty Green, driving the White Whale, had left school right after the last bell and had given Leah Russo and Bennie Pressler a ride to the farm. Leah and Bennie wanted to do more work with the newly installed computer equipment, and Ty wanted to put the finishing touches on his weight room. He also wanted to repaint and put a new net on a rusty old basketball goal that Artie had bolted above the rear barn door years earlier. When asked why, Ty told Leah that even though he had quit the basketball team, he missed shooting hoops because it helped him focus on a simple task and calm himself down. It was a mindless activity that he could do all by himself. He added that snapping the cords of a basketball net was more satisfying than hefting any barbell in the weight room.

"I've never thought of sports like that," Leah said. "Maybe I should find Reuben's old ball and start using his backboard and goal in the driveway."

"Maybe so," said Ty. "It's like meditation for me, and *swish* is my mantra—until baseball season, and then it's the sound of my fastball popping Artie's catcher's mitt for a strike."

"The sound of one hand snapping shut?" asked Leah, with a sly smile.

"Exactly," Ty said, though Leah doubted that he'd caught her play on words.

Catching up with them on the walk from the car, Bennie heard Leah's last question and Ty's response. "So, what *is* the sound of one hand clapping?" Bennie asked his two friends. "I never can figure that riddle out. It makes no sense."

"It isn't a riddle," said Ty. "It's a Zen koan, and it isn't supposed to make sense. You can't hear silence if your mind isn't quiet. At least that's what my guru always says."

"You have a guru?" asked Leah, surprised at Ty's breadth of knowledge.

"Yeah," said Ty. "Jug Johnson. He's even shaped like the Buddha." He smiled.

"And he says wise stuff like that?" Bennie said. "Gee, who'd a-thunk it?"

Ty shrugged. "Well, those aren't his *exact* words. What he always says to me is more like, 'You're thinking again. Stop it. Just throw the ball.'" They all laughed and went about their tasks to get ready for the Barf Table's first real meeting in its new clubhouse.

About ninety minutes later, the other teens arrived on the farm from wrestling and girls' basketball practice. Dr. Marecek and Wilma would be there in a few minutes, Artie said, as they apparently had stopped to get something to eat and drink. He opened the rear barn door, looked outside into the growing darkness and turned on the trio of spotlights illuminating the corral and barnyard outside the stable.

"Wilma didn't have a good practice," said Artie to the gang as they joined him in the open doorway. He looked Bennie in the eye. "So don't tease her about *anything*. Okay?"

Bennie held up his hands. "I'm not about to say anything to upset Wilma," said Bennie. "She's the one who leads my horse—or walks beside me in case I'm about to fall. I *love* Wilma Marecek. She's the man."

"*Wo*-man," corrected Nicie. "That's woman, buddy, and don't forget it. That woman could kick your scrawny butt all over this barnyard, so you'd better keep that trap shut tonight. Got it?"

"Yes, ma'am," said Bennie. "So, Artie, why's she upset—Wilma, I mean."

Instead of answering, Artie looked at Tommy and nodded for him to explain. "It's kinda my fault," said Tommy. "Well, not really, but, well, Artie and Wilma and Jimmy and me were all practicing together—you know, wrestling two minutes and then switching partners. When it was my turn to wrestle Wilma … well … I pinned her right off. Artie and Jimmy didn't pin her, because we weren't supposed to pin the other guy—I mean, person. I just got carried away."

Leah knew that Wilma was already questioning her participation on the wrestling team and that this latest development could push her to quit, just as Ty had done with his basketball career when push came to shove. Sure, Wilma wrestled to remember her grandfather's athletic achievements, but he had been a champion. As Wilma had told Leah Monday night on the bus ride home from the Mimosa Beach match, she at least wanted to know that she was helping her team be successful. She wanted to be needed. If she couldn't even give newbie Tommy White a good practice match, then she didn't need to be on the team. Before the Mareceks arrived on the farm, Leah took Nicie aside and told her what she knew about Wilma's doubts and fears.

"Nicie, she just wants to make a difference," Leah said. "I think she was hoping things would be different her senior year. She's been working so hard, and she's been helping Artie get better by giving him a good practice partner, but now her heart just isn't in it, you know?"

"Well, like I said before," replied Nicie, "she needs to quit that ol' wrestling team and play basketball for us. I tell you what. As big as she is, I wouldn't care if she could hit the broad side of a barn as a shooter, as long as she could grab a rebound and throw the ball out to somebody wearing the same color jersey."

Leah glanced up at the newly painted goal above the barn door and said, "When she gets here, you can try her out, Nicie—as soon as the paint's dry. But I really don't think she'll quit the wrestling team. It would look bad on her scholarship application. You know, she's in the running for the Ebenezer Endowment. Artie is, too. That's a full ride for four years."

"Yeah, I know," said Nicie, "but we do need someone tough like Wilma down low. I know Ann Marie's trying hard—like you told me the other day—but she just isn't big enough or strong enough to hold her own with the other centers in the conference. They're all juniors and seniors, and Ann Marie's just a freshman. They're beating her up. She'd be better coming off the bench."

"I agree," Leah said, "but you need to let Wilma make her own decision about wrestling and about basketball. Don't put any extra pressure on her. She'll figure it out for herself. I don't like being pressured into doing things, and you don't either."

Nicie simply nodded, and the pair joined the others inside the trailer as they waited for the doctor and her niece to arrive. It wasn't quite time for Leah's and Bennie's therapy sessions to begin, and so Leah and Nicie started looking through Grandma Bauer's old hope chest in the clubhouse lounge area, while the boys huffed and puffed, clunked and chunked with Ty's weight training equipment on the other side of the big room.

Seated side by side on the old sofa, the two girls lifted the hope chest's heavy lid and locked the hinges at each side to keep it from slamming shut on them. They peered into the box and saw a jumble of papers, spiral notebooks and paperback novels, as well as a stack of blue crocheted squares, a blue baby outfit and an assortment of mementos that a teenage girl might keep. There was a diary whose title page identified "Ingrid Ann Bauer"—Artie's mother—as its author and a framed, eight-by-ten prom picture of three young couples standing in front of a big rosebush, pregnant with red blossoms, in the yard of the Bauer farmhouse. Tall clumps of two-toned bearded irises—their dark, velvety, tongue-like falls lolling in full bloom—surrounded the rosebush. Five of the six prom goers were squinting into the sun. The sixth—a short, wiry boy on the far left—was preoccupied with fending off a large German shepherd that appeared ready to jump at him.

"Which one do you think is Artie's mom?" asked Nicie, tilting the photograph toward her friend. "The tall girl in the middle—the one that's frowning?"

"Nah," Leah said, "I think it's the little one on the left. Look at those eyes. She's looking daggers at whoever took this picture. Mr. Bauer, maybe? Or Mrs.

Bauer?"

Nicie giggled. "Yeah, that's how I'd look on prom night if my mama or daddy lined us up in the yard and wanted to take a picture. That crowd looks like they're headed to jail, not to the prom. Look at the big guy with the tall girl. He's trying to look tough, staring into the sun."

"What about the boy with the mad little girl on the left—the one getting ready to kick the dog?" said Leah. "I wouldn't trust that guy with *my* daughter. He looks like a little weasel. And look at that pizza face."

Nicie laughed, then looked closer at the photo and froze. "Wait a second," she said. "*Pizza* is right. You know who that looks like?" Before answering her own question, she called across the room for the boys to stop lifting weights and to come look at the framed photograph. She turned to Leah. "I've seen this guy—recently. You have, too, but not up close like I have."

"The pizza guy?" asked Leah.

"I think so," Nicie said, as the boys joined them around the open hope chest. "Artie and Tommy have seen him, too." She held up the photo for the two boys to study. "Hey, guys, do you recognize the scrawny boy on the far left?"

Artie scratched his head, as he took the picture in hand and tilted it to cut down on glare from the fluorescent ceiling lights. "You think this is the pizza guy?" Artie said. "I don't know. I didn't get a good look at this face through the window and screen door—just his hand, the one holding the pizza box, with the tattoos."

Artie shrugged. "It could be that guy—all cleaned up—but that's definitely my mother standing next to him. I've seen other pictures of her. And the German shepherd is Grandpa's dog, Sergeant. He still talks about that dog—said ol' Sergeant was the best dog he ever had." Artie handed the framed picture to Tommy White.

The younger boy with the shaved head took a quick look at the photograph and then raised it to within inches of his face for closer inspection. "I agree with Artie," said Tommy. "That *could be* our guy, but it's hard to tell—he's looking down at the dog. I got a *better* look at the pipe he hit me with than his face, but that could be him."

Tommy's head moved from left to right as he slowly scanned the other subjects in the lineup. Then his eyes stopped on one couple—the big, tough boy and tall, frowning girl standing side by side in the middle. "I've got a question, though," he said, looking at Artie. "Why are my parents in this prom photo?"

"Your parents?" said Artie, taking back the picture for another look. "I have no idea. I've never seen this picture before, and I've never heard any stories about my mother going to the prom with anybody. I guess I need to ask Grandpa about all that. Or maybe I cou—"

Footfalls on the handicap ramp out front interrupted Artie's train of thought. The group heard the door to Dr. Marecek's new waiting area open and close, and then exclamations from both Minnie and Wilma about the trailer and its possibilities for the horse therapy business.

Artie turned to Leah and Bennie, and patted Tommy on the arm. "I guess it's time for your sessions, guys," Artie said. "While you're all doing that, I'll go talk to Grandpa about this picture. He's still pretty sharp. He'll probably remember every last detail of that night."

Nicie picked up the diary again and extended it toward Artie. "Here, take this with you, too," she said. "You and Grandpa should read it before any of us do. There's no telling what your mama wrote in it—about boys and about prom night and maybe about some other things you don't want other people to know about, or not just yet, anyway. But maybe the pizza guy's name is in it."

Artie thanked her and took the diary. "I'm just wondering, though," Artie began, putting his hand on Tommy White's shoulder, "do you visit your parents very often, Tommy? Is it hard to get into the, uh, facility to see them?"

"It's okay to say *prison*," said Tommy, "because that's where they are. They're in two different prisons, though—one for men and one for women—but both are in Capital City. I haven't seen them in six months. It was right before I went to live with Bennie and his folks."

"If you go see them," Artie said, "you could ask about this picture."

"Look," said Tommy, as he followed Leah and Bennie toward the door. "I need to think about it—whether or not I want to see them, I mean. There's a lot more to this than them just being in prison for a long time. But I'll talk to you later, Artie."

The tall, stubble-headed boy followed his friends out the door. They were met at the doorway to the Mareceks' side of the doublewide trailer by Minnie and Wilma. Ty Green and Ricky Duran went back to the weightlifting area, leaving Nicie alone with Artie at the hope chest. Leah Russo stopped at the door and looked back, as if she were still listening to the pair.

"Do you want me to walk with you, Artie?" asked Nicie. "I can stay out on the porch while you talk to Grandpa. Or I can fix you guys something to eat. You haven't had supper yet. None of us have." She looked at Leah and winked, knowing food might be just the ticket for them all.

Artie considered her offer and nodded. "Yeah, that's a good idea," he said. "You can fix sandwiches for everybody. There's plenty of bread and stuff." He paused. "But I do need to talk to Grandpa by myself. Reading those old love letters from this hope chest got him all upset, and he keeps reading them over and over, like they're the Bible or something. I can't get him to put them away. I'm afraid seeing this picture will upset him, too. I've heard him say my mother broke his heart when she got in trouble and then broke it again when she ran off."

As Leah hurried toward the stable where Wilma and Tommy were preparing to saddle the two therapy horses, Leah heard Artie and Nicie leave the trailer to walk down the farm lane toward the house. Light from the farmhouse's kitchen window illuminated the portion of the yard nearest the house, as well as the dormant red rosebush where eighteen years earlier six young people with hopes and dreams—if not for their futures, then at least for that one night—had held still and stared into the sun for one brief moment in time. On this night, however, Artie and the Barf Table gang had too many worries complicating their young lives. The craziest, or looniest, complication—an effect of the December full moon lighting Artie and Nicie's walk down the farm lane—didn't bother them that evening, but only because it had not yet occurred.

Chapter 21

'HAVE YOU GUYS HEARD?' Nicie Evans asked her friends at the cafeteria table. "Coach Foxx is out today, and Lurch is gonna run the boys' practice. Coach Carson told me last period."

"Any chance Foxx is gone for good?" said Artie Bauer. "I'll have to ask Coach Johnson about it. I haven't talked to him yet. That sure would solve one big problem—not that we don't have others to deal with."

"What do you mean?" interrupted Leah Russo, looking up from the paperback novel she had been reading. "The drama here at school? Or the stuff going on outside school?"

"Yes," said Artie, in all seriousness.

Leah pressed him for more information. "Well," she said, "did you talk to your granddad this morning about that old picture we found in the hope chest—I mean, since you guys said last night that he was asleep when you went to talk to him?"

"No, I didn't," said Artie. "He refused to wake up and look at it this morning before I left for school. I guess he's in such a funk over those old love letters we gave him that he just isn't ready to talk about any of it yet. That's all I can figure, anyway. We can try again this weekend."

Leah started to say something, but thought better of it and went back to reading her book. Ty Green finished his first peanut butter and jelly sandwich, and unwrapped his second one. He was listening to the conversation at the table, but had heard it all before and was trying not to let it ruin his lunch.

Artie turned back to Nicie. "So, Foxx isn't here today?" he said. "I wonder why not."

"Who knows," said Nicie, "but I saw Jamie and Julia at their lockers this morning. They wouldn't still be here if Foxx quit. Jamie didn't want to come here in the first place. She'd already be back at Mimosa Beach if she didn't *have* to be here."

Leah interrupted again. "*I* know why Coach Foxx isn't here today," she said, "but I didn't want to say anything until everybody was here at the table. It's a touchy situation—for Coach Foxx *and* for Jamie and me. And it's a long story— what happened last night." She closed her book and laid it on the table next to a pack of saltines and bottle of water.

Taking a deep breath, Leah began her story. "You know how I've been mad at my mom and dad for not paying attention to me lately?" she asked. "Well, last night they made up for ignoring me—big time—or Dad did, anyway.

"You know," Leah continued, "they got home from their trip on Monday, but we didn't really sit down and talk until Tuesday night when I got back from the basketball game. I kinda surprised them by getting home so early, and they wanted to know why I didn't stay for the boys' game—like, why I wasn't keeping score for the boys, too. So, I told them—everything."

"Oooooh," said Nicie. "You told your daddy about Coach Foxx fussing you out? I know what *my* daddy would've done."

Leah smiled just a bit. "Yeah, well, nothing probably would have come of it," she said, "except that Mom and Dad drove down to Mimosa Beach last night for a late dinner and ran into Coach Foxx. They were at the restaurant in the hotel where your mom works, Nicie. Anyway, he was in the bar there with some Mimosa Beach coaches after practice. They were having a little Christmas get-together for old times' sake, I guess. It was crowded, and Mom and Dad couldn't get a nice table in the dining room, so they had to sit at a little table in the bar."

Ty Green chuckled. "And your dad just walked up and cold-cocked him?" he guessed. "That's what I would've done after the way that jerk talked to you."

"Well, it wasn't just what Coach Foxx said about *me*," Leah corrected. "It was also what he said about Reuben—and he repeated all of it, loudly, to his coaching buddies last night in the bar. He was telling them about fussing at me like *I* was the one who'd done something wrong."

Artie Bauer shook his head. "Didn't he see your folks sitting there? I guess not."

"No," Leah said. "He's never met my parents, and they weren't here for the past week or so for him to see them picking me up or dropping me off. So, he was running his big mouth last night at the bar—about how spoiled Arbor High kids are—and then Dad heard him say all that mean stuff about Reuben. Mom started crying and went to the ladies room, and then Foxx said *I* was a 'bulimic little brat' who had everybody snowed. That really made Dad see red, and—"

"And *then* he cold-cocked Foxx," said Ty.

"Just hold on," Nicie said, slapping Ty on the arm. "Let her talk."

Leah looked past her friends across the table and scanned the upper level to see where Jamie Foxx and Julia Safin were seated. She couldn't find the pair in the cafeteria.

"No," Leah went on, "Dad said he walked over to the bar and tapped Coach Foxx on the shoulder, and said, 'Hey, pal, aren't you the new basketball coach at Arbor High? Foxx—that's your name, right?' Coach Foxx said, 'Yeah, that's right. How do you know me?' And Dad said, 'My daughter's a student at Arbor. She brings the school paper home for us to read. We like to read that newspaper, especially the sports pages—always have. Wanna know why? Because our daughter is the sportswriter. And our son was one of the best athletes in Oleander County.' Then he stuck out his hand and said, 'Oh, I haven't introduced myself. I'm John Russo, and I'll thank you to keep your big trap shut about my children.'"

"Oooooh," said Nicie, "and *that's* when he hit him, right?"

Leah shook her head. "No, not yet," she said. "You know how Reuben was always good at staying calm in tight ballgames? Well, he got that trait honest, I guess, because Dad kept his cool and still didn't pop Coach Foxx in the mouth. It turned out he didn't have to."

"Wait," said Ty. "What? So, why isn't the coach here today? Did he fall off the barstool and break something?"

"That's not too far off," Leah said. "Coach Foxx and his buddies had been drinking for a good while, so he wasn't very steady. When Dad introduced himself, it took Foxx a few seconds to figure out who the school paper's sportswriter was and who Dad was. When it finally dawned on him that he'd screwed up, he slapped Dad's hand away and stood up. And then he made the mistake of turning and trying to give Dad a shove. Well, Dad stepped aside real quick, and ol' Foxx tripped over his own feet and face-planted right there on the floor of the bar—busted his nose and bled all over the place. I'm guessing he woke up with a couple black eyes, too."

"Did he go to the hospital?" asked Artie.

"I don't know if he did or not," said Leah. "His buddies picked him up off the floor and hustled him out of there before hotel security arrived. Dad said the bartender called the cops, but Coach Foxx was long gone by the time the squad car pulled up out front. One of his friends must have driven him home or to the emergency room, because Dad said Foxx was in no shape to drive himself. He was *that* drunk."

Artie nodded. "Your dad didn't get in trouble for what happened, did he? It wasn't his fault Coach Foxx ran his mouth and then tried to pick a fight."

Leah shook her head again. "That depends on how you define *trouble*," she said. "Foxx was blubbering all sorts of crazy stuff as his friends dragged him out of there. One thing he said was, 'I'll get even with your daughter,' and he shook his fist a couple times. And then he pointed at a big poster on the wall of the bar near the door, and he said, 'And I'll get her, too.' On their way out later, Mom and Dad looked at that poster." Leah turned to her friend Nicie and asked, "Do you know the poster I'm talking about?"

The big girl nodded solemnly. "I do," Nicie said. "It's from last summer when the hotel put on that beach volleyball tournament over the Fourth of July weekend. Those huge posters were everywhere—in every bar from Mimosa Beach to Iron Harbor. That tournament was a big deal. There were teams from up and down the coast. And me and my partner beat them all."

"Who was your partner?" asked Artie.

Nicie huffed. "You didn't come to our ballgame the other night, did you?" she asked him. "Well, Mimosa Beach's big girl is the best center in the conference. And she's the *second best* beach volleyball player in Oleander County." She smiled. "So, yeah, we won that volleyball tournament and split the prize money. But if Coach Foxx tries to report me for being a pro, he'll be turning in the Mimosa Beach girl, too. He's not gonna do that. He didn't turn us in last year when we were both on *his* team. He knew the hotel paid us to compete, and he didn't care."

Bennie Pressler, with his walker, Tommy White and Ricky Duran arrived from the lunch line and laid their food trays at their places. "What's this about?" asked Bennie. "Who got paid to compete? Are you guys talking about Brett? I didn't think he'd gotten a surfing sponsorship yet, but he told me he's trying. Has he told you he got one, Leah? That'd be great!"

Confused, Leah just shook her head at Bennie. "No, this isn't about Brett Woods," she said, "and, no, he hasn't written back to me yet. That FidoNet you hooked me up with is slower than regular mail. We aren't talking about surfing competitions—here or in Hawaii. We're talking about basketball and beach volleyball." She caught the boys up on the previous night's events.

"Oh, don't worry about that," Bennie told Nicie. "Brett and I looked it up in the rulebook, and you're okay because Arbor doesn't have a volleyball team. It's okay to take prize money or have a sponsor in a sport that your school doesn't compete in. That's how Brett and some other surfers can have equipment sponsorships and win prize money in surfing competitions, and not lose their amateur status in other sports—like football or basketball or baseball. We don't have a surfing team here at Arbor, even though a bunch of guys here surf. Speaking of that, Brett says he's finding out firsthand that surfing here is nothing like the surfing on the North Shore. That's the big leagues. I can't wait to get out there next week and see those monster waves."

Quiet until then, Ricky Duran set his milk carton down after taking a sip and turned to Tommy White. "Hey, my friend," said Ricky, "are you going to spend all your free time in Hawaii surfing, too?"

"Probably not," said Tommy. "As far as those huge waves go, I'm not the surfing type. I'm more of a laidback,stay-on-the-beach, luau kind of guy. But I'm gonna have to be careful and not eat too much while we're there."

Bennie laughed. "We'll do our best to find you a low-cal luau, bud," he said. "Anything to help out the Arbor High wrestling team, right? The poi and fish at a luau wouldn't be fattening, but we'll have to limit your roast pig and Spam consumption."

"Stop talking about eating," said Artie Bauer. "Remember, we're wrestling Port Oleander tonight. I probably gained ten pounds just thinking about a luau. Geez."

The friends were silent for a minute. The three wrestlers at the table pushed their food around their trays and tried not to think about the hunger pangs that would grow all afternoon until they could eat a protein bar or peanut butter sandwich after the weigh-in for that night's home match. Leah Russo went back to reading her book and sipping her water. She opened the pack of saltines and nibbled at one plain cracker. Bennie Pressler sliced into sections the round of mystery meat and studied one piece on the end of his white plastic spork. Ty Green and Nicie Evans chewed bites of the peanut butter and jelly sandwiches she always brought from home.

Leah was the first to notice Julia Safin gliding across the crowded lunchroom toward the Barf Table. Julia was alone for a change, not accompanied by her exchange sister, Jamie Foxx. Her hands were free, as she had not come to the cafeteria to eat. Without asking for the gang's permission, she pulled out Brett Woods's empty chair and sat, scooting the chair closer to the table so that she could lean forward and rest her elbows on the tabletop.

"Hello, everyone," Julia said, looking around the table. Her eyes came to rest on Nicie for a moment, then on Leah. "I will come to the point," said the Russian. "My American sister Jamie is embarrassed over what her father did last night at the hotel in Mimosa Beach. His actions are not to be excused, but she is afraid to speak out against him. That is why I am here now."

Julia paused to study the two girls' expressions. "We have noticed," she continued, "that we have been welcomed as teammates, even though the circumstances of our coming here to Arbor High School are, shall I say, unusual. You can be assured that *both* of us want to be here. Jamie realizes that we can be the best team in the conference, better than Mimosa Beach."

Leah and Nicie gave each other confused looks, as if they still didn't understand why Julia had come to them. She answered their unspoken question in what she said next. "Jamie wishes for me to apologize," said Julia, "and to ask that you not treat her badly because her father is an *eee*-diot—her word, not mine. That is all I wanted to say. I will see you both after school at practice."

As she scooted back her chair and rose, Julia Safin glanced at Artie Bauer and flashed him a sultry smile. "Good luck tonight, Arthur," she said, touching his shoulder as she turned to leave. "I will stay after practice and watch you wrestle tonight—that is, if someone can give me a ride home after your match." She smiled at him again and walked away.

As they watched her graceful exit, Ricky nudged Artie and said, "If you want to give her a ride home tonight, Artie, I will be happy to sit on her lap."

Artie laughed. "Yeah, well, we can fit three people on the bench seat of my old pickup," Artie said, "but I think she'd rather ride home with a girl. Besides, little guy, you'll be riding home with either your mom or your dad, remember? But nice try."

Nicie spoke up. "Come on now, Artie. I saw the way she looked at you—and that smile. You play your cards right, and you'll have a date for the Valentine's Day dance. Too bad Arbor doesn't have a dance before the holidays. Mimosa Beach does, but I don't dare go there now."

Then Nicie snapped her fingers. "Hey, why don't we have our own holiday party?" she said. "We could have it next Wednesday night at the clubhouse before Bennie and Tommy take off for Hawaii the next day. What do you think?"

The six others agreed that a party—a holiday luau, even—would be fun, though Bennie Pressler suggested that they invite their parents and guardians to see both their new clubhouse and Dr. Marecek's new office. He was sure his own parents would like that idea.

It was Bennie and Tommy's last Thirsty Thursday until mid-January when they planned to return to Arbor High from their vacation in Hawaii. In the 9th graders' honor, a group of senior boys pooled their money and bought twelve cans of Yoo-hoo from the vending machines in the cafeteria lobby. With five minutes to go before the release bell, they ordered Bennie and Tommy to chug six drinks apiece, one after another.

Bennie had no trouble killing all six of his drinks by the bell. Weight-conscious Tommy, however, took his time savoring one can of the chocolate-flavored liquid while the rest of the Barf Table gang downed the other five drinks for him. Even teammates Artie and little Ricky assisted Ty, Nicie and Leah in lending their friend some help.

The senior pranksters—some of them wrestlers themselves—saw that keeping Tommy's weight down would help their team effort, and so they applauded the five table mates' quick thinking and camaraderie. Their kindness also meant that Tommy was free to help walker-bound Bennie hurry to the restroom right after the release bell when the boy's tight, churning stomach threatened to show in living color how the Barf Table had gotten its name.

Chapter 22

TRUE TO HER WORD, Bruinette Julia Safin changed into her school clothes after basketball practice that Thursday night and waited to watch Artie Bauer wrestle. But she wasn't alone in the student section of the Bears Den bleachers, as Ty Green and Nicie Evans also were on hand to support their four friends on the wrestling team—Artie, as well as Ricky Duran, Tommy White and even heavyweight Wilma Marecek, who would wrestle first in an exhibition match.

Port Oleander High was the only other Suncoast Conference school to have a female wrestler. Like Wilma, the Pilots grappler was a heavyweight who wasn't quite good enough or strong enough to appear in the regular lineup. This girl wasn't better or stronger than Wilma either, but she was rounder and much heavier, as big as Artie and Port Oleander's first-string heavyweight, though shorter.

As usual, Bennie Pressler ran the scoreboard clock and announced each individual bout during the match, while Leah Russo sat next to him and kept the official scorebook. Since there were no junior varsity wrestling teams in the conference, exhibition bouts were held first at dual-team events, with three ninety-second—instead of the regular two-minute—periods. Otherwise, an exhibition got just as much attention as a regular match, maybe more being the first action of the night. Having two girls wrestle one another was an added spectacle, putting more pressure on poor Wilma, who was already having doubts about her place on the Bruins team.

"Dawg," said Coach Jug Johnson, standing within earshot of Bennie and Leah at the scorer's table. "That's a big girl." Leah heard him instruct Wilma to wrestle as if her opponent were Artie—and as if Artie had "bad-mouthed your mama."

Wilma looked unsure of herself from the start of the match, refusing to shoot and take the big girl down when she had the chance early on. Neither wrestler, in fact, was anxious to go to the mat, as they circled and circled around the inner ring until the referee told them both to quit stalling and to start wrestling. Otherwise, there was no point in holding the exhibition.

Dr. Minnie Marecek attended all of her niece's matches that she could, if for no other reason than to know exactly how to congratulate or console Wilma on her performance. Like Wilma's other friends, the doctor knew that saying she supported her niece would mean little if she weren't willing to give Wilma her time and undivided attention. Ricky Duran's parents took turns attending his matches, with the absent parent staying with Artie's grandfather on the farm. Abe Pressler would show up early or late to watch foster son Tommy White's matches, but the busy entrepreneur usually did not stay for the entire dual-team match, and either he or his wife would come back to the school to pick up Bennie and Tommy at the end of the night.

"*Boj*," Minnie Marecek shouted at Wilma—the Czech word sounding like "boy" in English. What it meant—"fight"—was unclear to everyone except Wilma and Leah. During her therapy session the previous Saturday, Leah had remembered to ask Minnie why she'd called Wilma a boy during her exhibition match against Solid Rock.

When Wilma heard her aunt's instruction, she dropped into a lower crouch with her right foot in front and then shot forward at the big girl's knees, wrapping her arms around one trunk-like leg and trying to lift the girl off her feet. Instead, the Pilots wrestler spread both feet and fell forward onto her over-extended opponent, pinning her face-down on the mat. Having lost hold of the one leg, Wilma tried to crawl out from under the huge body, but the girl's weight was too much for her to cast off. Wilma managed to rise onto her hands and knees to keep from being rolled over and pinned, but she couldn't break away before the ninety-second exhibition period ended. Their individual match score then was the Port Oleander girl 2, Wilma 0.

"*Boj*," Minnie yelled again, as the referee flipped his coin and then asked Wilma to choose how to begin the second period. Her four choices were to start with the two wrestlers standing again; with Wilma on her hands and knees in the "down" position; in the "up" position atop her kneeling opponent; or with her deferring her choice until the third period and letting the Port Oleander girl choose right then. Wilma looked over at Coach Johnson and clearly said, "I defer." The other girl immediately yelped, "Up," and pointed at the ceiling, meaning she planned to use her superior weight to ride Wilma into the mat again. It wouldn't be a takedown, but it would keep Wilma from scoring herself if she couldn't escape from under the big girl.

But Wilma's quickness and technical skill from having practiced with Artie for so many years helped her escape and end up on top herself. The two common wrestling moves—a sit out and turn in—also put Wilma back in the match by tying the score 2-2.

"*Jit*," shouted Minnie when she saw Wilma get the reversal. The Czech word meant "go," but sounded like "eat" to the untrained American ear.

Leah Russo had not shared her limited knowledge of the Czech language with Bennie Pressler, and so, like many others in the gym, he assumed that his therapist was yelling either code words at Wilma or insults at the big Port Oleander girl. "Why is Minnie telling either one of those girls to *eat*?" whispered Bennie to Leah, his hand covering the table microphone.

"That's *go* in Czech, silly," said Leah. "And B-O-J *boj* is *fight*, not B-O-Y *boy*." She shook her head and smiled. "But don't feel bad. I had to ask Minnie about that, too."

With the score still tied 2-2, Wilma chose to start the third and final period in the neutral, or standing, position. This time she didn't let her opponent lull her into circling and wasting time. Instead, when Minnie Marecek called out another Czech term that sounded like "steal it," Wilma shot low and drove the Port Oleander big girl onto her back. Wilma made another quick move to take control of the floundering Pilot. Two seconds later, the referee tapped hard on the mat and declared Wilma the winner by pin fall. The Arbor High crowd cheered as he raised Wilma's right arm in victory. She removed the green ankle bands and tossed them into the mat's center circle for the next home wrestler to wear. She did not look happy, but appeared to be aggravated.

Jug Johnson met Wilma and shook her hand as she walked to the chairs that had been set up off the mat for the Bruins grapplers. He even tried to pat the tall girl on her bare shoulder and say some words of encouragement, but she pulled away and went straight to her seat at the end of the line, pulling on her warm-up pants and jacket over her green and gold singlet. She removed the headgear that had protected her ears and the cap that had covered her hair, and tossed both pieces of equipment toward her duffel bag.

Bennie introduced the final exhibition match's competitors on the PA, then leaned over to Leah again. "What's Wilma upset about?" he asked. "She won."

"I don't know," said Leah. "And before you ask, I have no idea what 'steal it' means. We can ask Minnie later."

"Maybe that's 'you suck' in Czech," he said. "Remember, Coach Johnson wanted her to get mad. That would make *me* mad—if my aunt yelled something like that at me."

Leah shook her head. "He wanted her to get mad *at the other girl*, not at anybody else and certainly not at herself. Besides, Minnie wouldn't say something mean like that to anybody." Leah made a notation in the scorebook when the Pilots wrestler scored a quick takedown in the exhibition bout underway. "Stay in the match, Bennie," she said, "or I'll tell you to 'steal it,' too."

"*Two points for the takedown,*" Bennie intoned over the PA. He gave Leah the side-eye before turning his attention back to the mat.

Two matches later, Ricky Duran remained undefeated at 113 pounds, winning again off a takedown and quick pin from the standing start. When Tommy White's turn on the mat came about an hour later, the husky 9th grader pinned his more experienced opponent in the second period to continue what had shaped up to be an Arbor High rout.

That left only the heavyweight bout, with Artie Bauer facing a younger, lighter boy whom he had beaten in all four meetings the previous year. The Pilots wrestler had improved but still hadn't reached Artie's level of expertise. His one advantage was his quickness, which he used to put distance between Artie and himself at every opportunity throughout most of the match. It was also common knowledge that Artie had suffered an ankle injury during football season, and the younger boy tried his best to shoot at Artie's lower legs whenever he had to engage from the neutral position. The problem was, the boy didn't know which ankle Artie had injured, and so his offensive maneuvers were no more effective than they might have been otherwise. But he could shoot and withdraw before Artie could get him under control or push him down onto the mat.

For most spectators, it was a boring match—two big guys springing at one another and jumping away without either one scoring any points. But to Julia Safin, the match seemed to be something else entirely. Leah Russo couldn't help but to sneak looks at the exchange student who had expressed an odd interest that day in the leader of the Barf Table gang. The amused look on Julia's perfectly symmetrical face suggested that she saw the bout as if the wrestlers were two pandas playfully poking each other and rolling around their zoo enclosure. She was quiet throughout the match, even when the referee stopped the inaction with one minute left in the third period and ordered the boys to engage from a standing start.

"*Strilet*, Artie!" shouted Wilma Marecek, standing at her chair off the mat and shaking a fist in the air. "Shoot! Come on, Artie! Shoot!" Her initial utterance, in Czech, sounded much like "steal it," the same thing Wilma's aunt had yelled at her during the exhibition.

Artie Bauer may or may not have heard Wilma's instruction, but he did, in fact, shoot at the Port Oleander wrestler's tiring legs and did manage to take him down for two points. Artie even turned the boy over onto his back and would have pinned him if the buzzer hadn't sounded ending the match. Awarded two points for the near fall, Artie won 4-0. However, like Wilma, his cheerleader, he was anything but pleased.

Julia Safin was still smiling as the teams formed two lines and shook hands after the match. She stood and waited at her seat low in the bleachers to see if Artie would come and talk to her before going to the locker room. Likewise, Leah Russo took her time totaling up numbers in the scorebook so that she could see if this budding romance blossomed or died on the vine. Bennie watched, too, as he packed up and even muttered to himself, "Come on, big guy. You're *this close* to the Big Leagues. Go for it, buddy."

They watched Artie gather up his gear and push it into his duffel bag. He looked toward the home bleachers and smiled when he saw that Julia had stayed for the entire team match to watch him wrestle. He gave her a friendly wave, as if he hadn't noticed her presence earlier.

"He's blushing," Leah told Bennie. "Look at him. He's embarrassed."

"Oh," said Bennie, "Artie *always* looks like that after a match or game. But, yeah, I'll bet his heart's skipping a beat or two right now. Mine would be."

Artie did approach Julia, but he remained on the floor to lean toward her and exchange a few words. With his back to them, neither Leah nor Bennie could hear what Artie said to her, but it must not have disappointed Julia, because she held that same sultry smile and even touched his shoulder again, as she had done that day in the cafeteria. She nodded as Artie reached up and took her other hand, held it for only a moment, then turned and headed for the locker room. She watched him walk across the mat on his way out of the gym.

"He *shook her hand*," Bennie said incredulously.

"No, he didn't," said Leah. "That was sweet. She touched him, and he touched her hand. That was a big deal for Artie Bauer. He's super shy."

"Yeah, but he—"

"But nothing," Leah said. "Just shut up and watch. If she sits back down, she's waiting for Artie to shower and dress and take her home. If she leaves the gym, she'll get a ride home with somebody else. Simple as that."

Before Bennie could argue, Julia stepped down from the bleachers and walked up the sideline toward them. As she passed, she glanced over at Bennie and blinked slowly once like a bored cat. Then she stopped and turned—not to speak to Bennie, but to address Leah.

"I forgot to tell you something today at lunch," Julia said to Leah. "I think my father would have liked your father. Papa loved and fought for my mother and me, as your father stood up for you and your brother. Do not forget that he loves you."

Taken aback by the girl's unexpected kindness, Leah couldn't think of anything to say at first. Instead, her eyes welled up. She simply nodded, whispered her thanks and looked away.

Despite his tendency to use comedy in awkward situations, Bennie made no jokes about what Julia had said and how Leah had reacted. He patted his friend's shoulder and went back to unhooking the scoreboard and sound equipment.

Bennie Pressler did, however, shake his head sadly as he worked, reasonably sure, like Leah Russo, that their pal Artie Bauer had missed out on the hottest date of his young life.

Chapter 23

AS IT TURNED OUT, Artie Bauer and Julia Safin did spend more time together that Thursday night after the match, but not the way Bennie Pressler would have fantasized. After leaving the gym, Julia had waited outside in the White Whale with Nicie Evans and Ty Green in the parking lot. When they had seen Artie emerge from the building and trudge across the lot toward his old pickup truck, Ty had called out to him to come over and talk. Artie had been surprised to find Julia sitting alone in the Whale's big back seat, her beauty illuminated by the glow of the car's cracked plastic dome light. With that vision before him, the big farm boy had succumbed to her feminine wiles and agreed to a quick ride to the beach before heading home to the farm. Or at least that's what Ty told the rest of the Barf Table crew at lunch on Friday.

"So did you run out of gas?" asked Bennie, after hearing Ty's romanticized account of the night before. "Did you run out going *to* the beach, or coming back? Gee, who went for the gas, and who stayed in the car?"

"We *didn't* run out of gas, dork," said Ty. "We parked at Woody's and sat out on the deck and looked at the ocean for a while. It was kinda breezy and a little cold on the beach, but Nicie and I didn't mind bundling up. Did we, babe?" He winked at Nicie sitting next to him.

She stared at Ty for a moment and shook her head. "And you call *him* a dork?" she said, nodding across the table at Bennie. "It was so cold out there that we only stayed a minute. We got back in the car and drove straight back to the school. Artie got into his pickup without a word to Julia and drove home. I took her to Jamie's house in my car. And the *Love Doctor* here? We left him sitting all sad and alone in that land yacht of his."

"Like Jonah in the White Whale?" asked Leah Russo, having heard Nicie use that simile before. Leah looked at Ty and Artie, and saw that they weren't amused.

"Yeah, something like that," Nicie said, "except Ty had to open his big yap and ask Julia if she wanted to eat lunch with us here at the Barf Table every day."

"Well," said Ty in his own defense, "we have an empty seat, at least until Brett comes back. And we'll have two more empty spots for a few weeks while Bennie and Tommy are in Hawaii. It's gonna be downright lonely sitting here. Right, Artie?"

Artie shook his head. "Don't drag me into this," he said. "I feel bad enough now for not acting like some kind of lover boy last night. That just isn't me. Now tell 'em what Julia said, Ty—when you invited her to eat lunch with us. Good thing I didn't hear it."

Ty shrugged. "She said she needed to sit with Jamie at lunch," he replied. "She'd already asked Jamie if she could sit with us, because for *some* odd reason, she likes this big oaf here." He jerked his thumb toward Artie but didn't look at him. "Jamie told her that only losers sit at this table and that Coach Foxx would not be happy if Julia made friends with some of us." He glanced toward Nicie but didn't look her straight in the eye, either.

Leah spoke up. "Was this little bit of advice from Jamie *before* or *after* she got Julia to apologize for her yesterday? Or did Julia just make that stuff up so she could come over here and hit on Artie?"

Nicie replied, "Yeah, Julia probably made up most of that to get on our good sides—or on *Artie's* good side. And I'm guessing Jamie gave her heck yesterday after she talked to us."

"And you *still* took her home?" asked Leah.

"Yes, I did," Nicie said. "My problems are with Jamie and Coach Foxx, not with Julia. I kinda like her. Besides, anybody who likes ol' Yogi Bear here can't be all bad." She turned to Artie. "So, big fella, you can give Julia a call anytime you want, and I won't be upset with you. She is a pretty girl—don't you think?"

She waited for his reply.

But Ricky Duran answered before Artie could untangle his tongue. "We can all agree," said little Ricky, "that Julia Safin is the most beautiful Russian girl we have ever seen."

Nicie razzed. "She's the *only* Russian girl *you've* ever seen, little man—but I like your style. Maybe you can give ol' Yogi lessons on how to flirt with a girl—and on how to dance, too, while you're at it. I know ol' Boo-Boo here hasn't taught Artie very much all these years they've been friends. You'd think *something* would have rubbed off."

"Hey!" said Artie. "I'm sitting here, I'm sitting here."

Bennie laughed. "That's my line, buddy," he said, "but I'll let you use it until January 15th when we get back from Hawaii. Gosh, I can't wait to get out there. We'll be on the beach every day—won't we, Tommy?—and it'll be warm there, not like here in December and January. This is prime surfing season on the North Shore."

"I'm gonna miss you guys," Artie said to Bennie and Tommy. "Be careful playing in those big waves out there—both of you. And be sure to keep us posted on how you're both doing. You can do like Brett and send notes to Leah over the computer, right?"

Leah shook her head. "You need to do a better job of keeping in touch than Brett is," she said. "I'm still waiting to hear back from him. Maybe I'll get a note by tomorrow when we're at the farm. I guess we'll still have our sessions, even though Wilma and Tommy will be away with the wrestling team and won't be there to help. Artie and Ricky will be gone, too."

"Hey!" said Nicie Evans. "Maybe Ty and I can be the doctor's assistants tomorrow. I'm gonna help with Grandpa so Ricky's folks can go to the wrestling tournament, and Ty's gonna be there in the weight room, anyway. What do you think?"

Leah nodded and smiled. "Sure," she said. "That's a great idea."

Bennie eyed Nicie suspiciously. "Well," he began, "it's okay with me, as long as you guys don't try to play some silly joke and make my horse bolt or something. I'd hate to fall off ol' Belle and break a leg now that I'm getting them to work right. And Tommy wouldn't want to help push me up and down Sunset Beach in my wheelchair. Right, Tommy?"

Tommy didn't look thrilled at the prospect of pushing a wheelchair again on any surface, much less in the beige sand of that famous stretch of North Shore beach. "Yeah, you've got that right," Tommy said. "To tell you the truth, I'm not looking forward to being away at all."

"What?" said Bennie, confused. "Hold on. Do we need to talk about this later?" When Tommy nodded, Bennie continued, "But, yeah, I think having you guys help tomorrow will work just fine. And, Ty, I want you to give me some exercises I can do on my own in Hawaii. Okay?"

It was Fishy Friday in the Arbor High cafeteria, but the upperclassmen went easy on the four 9th graders at the Barf Table. Instead of doing something fishy with food items that were on the day's menu, three senior boys trooped down from the upper level with a huge, blowup shark float on their right shoulders, like Polynesian warriors carrying a dugout canoe. The inflatable toy was meant for the two boys who were headed for a month of sand and surf in Hawaii. But the other Barf Table mates knew that they could put the blowup shark to good use the next Wednesday night at their holiday luau in their new clubhouse on the farm. They wanted to do the affair up right, with party favors and the right décor, maybe even floral shirts for the boys and grass skirts for the girls. That way, the seven new friends—and maybe some old enemies, too—would have fun saying *bon voyage* to two of their own.

* * *

The basketball games that Friday night were on the road at Iron Harbor High School. As was the case in all team sports and in most individual ones, the Iron Harbor Gray Dukes boys' and girls' basketball teams were the class of the Suncoast Conference, mainly because this public school in the county seat was so much larger than the other four schools. Also, the City of Iron Harbor was the only real urban area in Oleander County, encompassing Iron Harbor A&M University, the Iron Harbor Naval Base, and the Port of Iron Harbor. Most of the male student-athletes who represented Iron Harbor High were every bit as tough as the name of the city and its institutions suggested. The Lady Gray Dukes—the girls' teams—were hardnosed but not as talented as their male counterparts every season. In other words, the girls were beatable.

Even the Iron Harbor cheerleaders looked like they were ready to rumble—a fact that Leah Russo knew she'd have to share with Bennie Pressler, who would be appearing with the Arbor cheering squad at away games once the new Bruno the Bruin suit arrived at Pressler's Department Store. Bennie didn't attend that Friday night's game because he had so much work to do in preparation for the family's trip to Hawaii, he claimed. That meant foster brother Tommy White also went home after a shortened wrestling practice. Artie Bauer and Ricky Duran went home themselves to catch up on farm chores before Saturday's four-team wrestling tournament outside the county. That left Ty Green and Leah Russo to witness Nicie Evans and the Bruinettes' first meeting of the season with the Lady Gray Dukes. Ty had plenty of work to do himself in the new weight room on the farm, but he wisely chose to "support his sweet, smart and really strong girlfriend over a bunch of old dumbbells," was how Bennie Pressler had phrased it at lunch. That might have been the first thing Bennie ever said that Nicie wholeheartedly agreed with.

From the scorer's table at courtside, Leah could tell from the opening tap that the Arbor girls were firing on all cylinders—with one exception. Bruinettes starters were freshman Sandy Cuthbert at point guard, replacing injured senior captain Mel Grayson; junior newcomer Jamie Foxx at shooting guard; senior Nicie Evans at small forward; exchange student Julia Safin at power forward; and freshman Ann Marie Childers at center. Little Sandy lived up to her nickname—"Cutthroat" Cuthbert—by repeatedly making steals, diving for loose balls and driving to the basket for contested layups that often sent her to the foul line for "and ones"—that is, for chances at three-point plays. Jamie Foxx played tough, too, having learned that even a five-star recruit needs the support of role players. Jamie seemed willing to let Nicie Evans keep being the team's star so long as the senior forward could keep coming through for the Bruinettes, as she had against

Mimosa Beach. As usual, Julia Safin was solid on both offense and defense. It was timid Ann Marie Childers, again, who couldn't hold her own against the Lady Gray Dukes.

To his credit, Coach Carson didn't leave Ann Marie in the game longer than it took him—and everyone else in the gym—to see that the 9th grader was outclassed in the pivot. As he'd done too late against Port Oleander, Carson started subbing in first Clara Harmon, then Sarah Harmon for Ann Marie midway through the first quarter. Getting those minutes on the bench to refocus gave the tentative freshman a chance to watch her more experienced teammates take on the Iron Harbor big girl, and to see what worked and what didn't.

By the end of the game, Ann Marie was playing better defense than she had at the start, though she was much more rested than the Lady Gray Dukes center.

Still, the Iron Harbor girls beat Arbor 65-60 on this Friday night. Nicie Evans was high scorer for the Bruinettes with 20 points, followed by Jamie Foxx with 13, Julia Safin and Sandy Cuthbert with 9 apiece, the Harmon twins with 4 points each, and Ann Marie with 1 point. The Lady Gray Dukes center tallied 32 points to lead all scorers.

As scorekeeper, Leah Russo saw all too plainly where the Bruinettes' weakness lay, and, as unofficial assistant coach, she knew that Coach Carson would be open to her assessment of Ann Marie Childers's play. Now was the time to make a change, Leah thought, because these first meetings with conference teams had been practice games, basically—non-conference contests to pad the schedules of the five schools in the small, county-aligned conference. Subsequent games with Solid Rock, Mimosa Beach, Port Oleander and Iron Harbor would count toward the conference championship and two state playoff berths, of which Iron Harbor almost always got one.

Later that night at home, Leah and her father watched the Iron Harbor TV station's late sportscast and learned that the Bruins boys and their new head coach had fallen to 0-4 on the young season, as they had lost 86-44 to the undefeated Gray Dukes. Leah was proud of her dad for not laughing—as she couldn't help but do—when an action clip from the game showed Coach Foxx wearing dark glasses on the Arbor bench, and the sportscaster quipped, "Even the Bruins' coach wanted to be incognito by the end of this blowout." At the very least, Foxx looked like he was in pain there on the bench. Leah wondered how long Principal Jerry Church would put up with his newest coach's bad decision-making and poor choices, both on and off the court.

Chapter 24

BRIGHT AND EARLY SATURDAY MORNING, the activity bus carrying Coach Jug Johnson and the Arbor Fighting Bruins pulled out of the gymnasium parking lot for its hour-long trip from Monk's Landing to Oakmont in neighboring Clay County. Four teams would participate in the all-day quad-match—Arbor High of the Suncoast Conference, host team Oakmont Prep School, Pinecrest Christian Academy from the next county over, and Saint Corbinian's Catholic School from Capital City. All four schools had solid wrestling programs within their leagues, as well as ranked grapplers on both regional and state levels.

Team statistician Leah Russo could have gone along with the Bruins, as usual; however, she didn't want to miss her last therapy session before Bennie Pressler and Tommy White left for Hawaii the next Thursday. She also wanted to get a head start on decorating the Barf Table gang's new clubhouse for the Wednesday evening party that would replace that day's horse therapy. Leah had one other responsibility—to scan and fax that week's assignments to Brett Woods from the clubhouse computer. Coach Johnson was understanding and said that keeping stats themselves would "keep the boys out of trouble." Leah wondered why he hadn't included Wilma Marecek in his pronouncement, though Wilma wasn't the troublemaking type.

Still, Leah got Nicie Evans to pick her up early Saturday morning and drive her over to the school so she could drop off the wrestling scorebook and wish the team well before they left for Oakmont. She was surprised when she didn't see Wilma on the bus, but she decided not to ask where the big girl was. She found out later that morning at the farm.

"I thought Wilma was looking forward to this tournament," Leah said to Nicie, as the blue sportster motored up Ebenezerville Road. "I wonder what happened. Maybe she got sick this morning."

"She was upset Wednesday night, remember?" said Nicie, her eyes on the road ahead. "And then that sumo wrestler girl from Port Oleander almost beat her Thursday night."

Leah nodded. "Yeah, she wasn't happy about that, and I don't blame her. Artie said he felt the same way—that he shouldn't have had such a hard time with the guy he wrestled." She was quiet for a second, then continued, "Wilma also said last week that she didn't feel like she was helping the team—that Artie didn't even need her as a practice partner now that Tommy is there. That's sad. Everybody wants to be needed."

"Well, like I've said before," Nicie stated, "we could use her on the basketball team right now. I'm tired of losing games because of Ann Marie Childers. She may be sweet as honey, but we can't wait for her to toughen up. Can I at least ask Wilma to consider giving basketball a try? I could call her at home tonight or tomorrow."

As it turned out, Nicie didn't have to wait to talk to Wilma. When the sportster pulled into a parking spot next to the Bauers' barn, the girls saw Wilma and Minnie Marecek sitting there in the doctor's pickup truck, waiting for their clients to arrive. Again, Leah was surprised, this time that Wilma didn't appear to be ill and that she even appeared to be in a good mood. Both she and her aunt turned and waved when Nicie's car pulled up next to them. The four got out of their vehicles and walked together toward the office trailer around back.

Wilma spoke first, looking straight at Leah. "I made a decision," the big girl said. "I talked to Coach Johnson yesterday, and I asked him if I could drop wrestling. He said he wanted me to do whatever was right for me—that he appreciated everything I've done for the team."

Leah nodded. "I wondered why I didn't see you on the bus this morning," she said, "but I knew you weren't happy from what you've said before." Leah thought Nicie might jump into the conversation, but she remained quiet. Leah went on to ask, "Have you told Artie? I hadn't heard anything from anybody."

"No," Wilma replied, "Coach said he'd tell the guys *after* today's matches so it wouldn't get anybody upset beforehand—Artie, I guess, and maybe Tommy, too. Coach said if anybody asked where I was, he'd just say something important had come up and I needed to stay home."

"Well, that's true," said Leah, turning to Dr. Marecek. "So, Minnie, will you come with me right now to go see Mr. Bauer? Artie says he's been out of sorts lately over some stuff we found in the attic—some old love letters he'd written to Mrs. Bauer when they were young. There's something else that Artie wants to show him—an old picture of Artie's mother and her friends—but he's afraid Mr. Bauer isn't ready to see it. It's kind of important, though."

The therapist agreed to go with Leah to visit Grandpa Bauer and had already started moving in that direction, but she asked, "What's so important about the picture?"

"Two things," Leah said. "One of the boys in the picture—he's Artie's mom's date—looks just like the guy who broke into my house and all those other houses, and killed all those dogs. He also assaulted Tommy outside Woody's Grill and tried to trick Artie into letting him into the farmhouse here after Mrs. Bauer died. So, that's a big deal, if Mr. Bauer remembers his name, and the cops can identify him."

By now the two were halfway down the farm lane to the house. "What's the other thing?" asked Minnie. "What you just said is enough, but what else makes that picture important?"

Leah chose her words carefully. "Well, nobody has said this out loud," she began, "and Artie certainly hasn't, but I'm sure he's thought about it." She paused again. "Artie's mom got pregnant with him around the time that picture was taken—maybe even that very night—so *I'm* wondering if that little weasel we've been calling 'the pizza guy' is Artie's father—even though Artie looks nothing like him."

"Did Artie recognize anyone else in the picture?" asked Minnie.

"Not Artie," said Leah, "but Tommy White did. *His* parents are one of the couples in the photo. So, apparently they all went to the prom together. But Arbor and Solid Rock didn't even exist back then, so that's something else we need to find out from Mr. Bauer—which high school his daughter attended, or whose prom she went to. Tommy would ask his parents, but they're both in prison—in Capital City."

"Yes," said Minnie, "that's why Tommy lives with the Presslers and has helped them so much with Bennie. I was aware of that."

As they turned down the sidewalk toward the back porch, Leah realized that she didn't have a way into the house that didn't require Grandpa Bauer to get out of bed. "Hey," she said, "I need to run back to the barn and see if Artie gave Nicie a key to the back door."

"No need to do that," said Minnie, "I know where they've hidden one out here. Mr. Bauer told me I could use it if I needed to get into the house to use the phone—or the bathroom—when they were gone. That was back before we got the trailer. Gee, telephones and indoor plumbing—such modern conveniences!"

The doctor smiled at Leah, then walked around the handicap ramp, leaned down behind the old rosebush at the kitchen window and picked up a palm-sized stone. Turning it over, she said, "See? It's one of those plastic rocks with a hidden compartment." She popped open the cover and took out the door key. "Don't let me forget to put this back," she added, as she laid the fake stone on the ramp's flat handrail.

On the back porch, Leah noticed that the small backpack that Artie carried at school sat in Grandpa's comfy old chair. The pack was partially unzipped, and sticking out on that side was one corner of the framed prom photo that Artie had wanted his grandfather to see. "Hey, here it is," said Leah. "I'm glad Artie left it here and not in Mr. Bauer's room."

Minnie wrinkled her brow. "Why is that?" she asked. "You don't think he'd destroy it, do you? Surely not."

"Maybe not destroy it," said Leah, "but from what Artie was saying, his grandpa is really depressed, especially after reading all those old love letters. Seeing this picture without having someone to talk to might push him over the edge. I mean, he's a tough old guy, but he has a heart like everybody else."

Minnie smiled again. "Yes," she said, "Harry Bauer surely did love Miss Pearl, and I'm sure he loved their daughter so very much, too. Her leaving like she did must have broken his heart. Seeing this photograph would stir up all those old feelings—for him and for Artie—but it needs to be done for both of their sakes."

"And we need to catch this guy," Leah said, removing the picture from the backpack and pointing at the pizza guy on the far left. "I mean, look—the jerk's even getting ready to kick the dog in the photo." She slid her finger to the right on the glass surface. "This is Artie's mom," she said, "and over here … these two are Tommy's parents."

"You're right," said Minnie. "Artie looks nothing like the little guy on the left—or little Miss Bauer either, for that matter." She studied the image for a moment. "Actually," she added, "Artie bears a closer resemblance to *Tommy's* father. Do you think…?"

"What?" said Leah. "That Artie and Tommy could be half-brothers? I don't know. What do you think?"

Minnie shook her head and gave a wry smile. "I think we need to quit gossiping and go see if Mr. Bauer is awake yet," she said, unlocking the door to the kitchen. "Oh," she added and then whispered, "Do *not* mention any of this to the others, not even to Artie. It isn't our place to find Artie's father—or to even speculate about it—not unless Mr. Bauer asks us to do that for him. It's his place to talk to Artie about that, whenever *he* feels the time is right."

"But we still need to find out who the pizza guy is," Leah countered. "We need to catch that little weasel before he hurts anyone else."

Harry Bauer was still asleep when Minnie Marecek and Leah Russo eased his bedroom door open and peeked at him—or so he appeared. Minnie checked to make sure that the tough old man's breathing and heartbeat were regular, but even her touch didn't awaken him. She told Leah to go back to the barn and begin working with Micki, her horse, and to send Nicie Evans to the house once Bennie Pressler arrived for his session.

"I'm going to stay here with Harry," said Minnie. "I'm worried about how unresponsive he has become. We might need to call an ambulance." At the word *ambulance*, Grandpa stirred a bit and coughed weakly once, as if he were waking up. "Oh, my," Minnie said. "I think he's going to be okay." She turned and winked at Leah.

Leah grinned and gave Minnie a little salute. "Great," said Leah. "I'll send Nicie back. If anybody can get Mr. Bauer up out of that bed, she can." Then she thought to add, "I'll leave this, uh, this *thing* we were looking at on the kitchen table, if you want to show it to Mr. Bauer. I can scan it later—to make extra copies. Okay?"

Minnie nodded, waved and turned her attention back to Grandpa, who had opened one crusty eye but seemed to be waiting for Leah to leave. "Tell Bennie I won't be long here," said Minnie. "I'm sure Harry will be in good hands with Nicie. She can tell him all about her basketball games and the wrestling matches this week. I'll see you and Bennie in a few minutes, Leah."

By the time Leah walked back to the barn, Bennie had arrived. He said his father had dropped him off on his way to their store in Ebenezerville. Standing in the stable with his horse Belle, Bennie pointed to a large shoebox sitting on a hay bale and identified it as the deflated, folded-up shark that he and Tommy had received on Fishy Friday. "After our sessions, we can do some decorating for the luau," Bennie said, "and fax Brett his school work."

Leah continued on through the stable and out the rear barn door to where Nicie Evans and Wilma Marecek stood talking. Nicie held a basketball in her hands and hefted it, as if she wanted to practice her free-throw shooting on the goal above the barn door. Standing next to Nicie, Wilma was both taller and broader, though her head was down-turned and she kicked at something with the toe of her sneaker as she listened to what Nicie was saying. Wilma wore her Arbor letter jacket against the chill of the December morning, and the added bulk made her look even bigger than she was.

"Hey, Nicie," called Leah. "Dr. Marecek is waiting for you at the house. She's staying with Mr. Bauer until you get there."

Nicie nodded and started toward Leah, then turned and tossed the basketball back to Wilma, who was surprised by the pass and bobbled the ball but made the catch. "Go ahead, Wilma," said Nicie. "Show her what you can do."

Standing fifteen feet from the goal, Wilma tentatively bounced the ball three times on the ground, turned the brown sphere in her large hands until it felt right, and then lofted the ball in a high arc toward the orange rim. The ball caromed loudly off the wooden backboard and through the basket, getting caught in the front of the net before dropping through it. The big girl seemed unfazed by her feat.

With a smile, Nicie turned back to Leah and held her arms out as if to ask for applause. "What do you know?" Nicie said. "She *can* hit the broad side of a barn—and she says she'll give basketball a shot. Isn't that great?"

Chapter 25

LATE SATURDAY AFTERNOON, Arbor High's Fighting Bruins returned to Monk's Landing victorious, having beaten two of the three other teams in the Oakmont quad-match. Individually, Artie Bauer won two of his three heavyweight bouts. Tommy White was 1-2, with his two losses to state-ranked grapplers. Little Ricky Duran remained undefeated, shooting his way to victories by quick pin-falls in all three matches. By Ricky's third time on the mat, the throng of wrestlers that gathered to watch him started calling the diminutive athlete "Shooter" because he never hesitated to make the move, and because his shots were so quick and deadly to opponents.

As far as nicknames went, Artie would always be "Yogi," if for no other reason than he'd been given that name years earlier on the baseball diamond by Coach Jug Johnson. Tommy's surname, his size and his tendency to circle the center ring with his opponent before lunging at the other boy's legs earned him the epithets "The Great White Shark" and, for short, "Jaws," though no one said them too loudly after his two close losses. His stubbled head and the scar from the pizza guy's assault and battery gave Tommy the tough look of someone called "The Shark," at least until his blond mullet grew back out. Besides that, he was becoming a good, young wrestler with help from Artie and even from Wilma Marecek, who had taught him all she could before that weekend when she decided to give up wrestling and take up basketball.

That very situation—Wilma's sudden absence from the team and Tommy's impending time off for holiday travel—weighed heavily on the rookie wrestler's mind late that Saturday evening when the Barf Table gang, now including Wilma, reassembled at their new clubhouse. Coach Johnson had told the boys on their bus ride home about Wilma's decision, and, according to Artie, had encouraged them to keep treating her as part of the team due to her past years of hard work and dedication. Artie added that Coach Johnson was big on loyalty, expecting it from his players and returning it both on and off the field or mat. When Artie learned from Nicie that Wilma would be trying out for the basketball team, he said that maybe he, Ricky and, later on, Tommy could attend the girls' home games to cheer Wilma and Nicie on. The "later on" part stung Tommy, who hung his head and began to squirm in his chair.

"What do we need to do tonight?" asked Ty Green, seated on one of his weight benches. "We've cleaned up the whole trailer and decorated all we can. What else can we do to get ready for the Christmas party?"

"The holiday *luau*," Nicie Evans corrected, "and there's a lot to do. We need food, something we all can drink—including our parents—and more decorations than just that blow-up shark hanging on the wall."

"And we all need something to wear," added Leah Russo, "something Hawaiian." She shot a look at Bennie Pressler. "And before you say anything, buddy, the girls *aren't* gonna wear coconuts. I'm thinking Hawaiian shirts for everybody. Maybe we can find some at a thrift store."

"*Oooo*," Nicie said, "and, Artie, don't forget to buy Grandpa a flower shirt, too, because I already told him today that he's coming—case closed. He's *my* date Wednesday night."

"Hey!" said Ty. "I'm sitting here, I'm sitting here." He smiled and lay back on the weight bench, pressing up against the heavy barbell but not lifting it. "Grandpa Bauer is the man. But, Nicie, I'm gonna have to keep my eye on you two after I get him pumping iron out here."

Artie laughed. "Don't worry, buddy," he said. "Grandpa's a one-woman man." But then the big farm boy's smile faded as he realized the sad truth of that statement.

They decided to pile into their vehicles and drive to Ebenezerville to shop for food and drinks, Hawaiian shirts and other decorations for the luau. Bennie said that he and Tommy would bring surfboards from home to set on sawhorses and use as tables. He also promised to ask his father about any fake palm trees, banana plants or tiki decorations that local Pressler's stores might not be using yet for their displays. Nicie said she could bring her family's assortment of beach towels and sand chairs. Ty said that he and his dad could use their gas grill to cook some pork, though it wouldn't be a whole pig or fixed in the traditional Hawaiian manner buried under hot coals and banana leaves. Ricky said he would help his mother prepare one of her dessert specialties, pineapple empanadas. Leah said she would bring her dad's VHS tapes of the Elvis Presley movies *Blue Hawaii* and *Paradise, Hawaiian Style*; and Wilma pledged to bring an old videocassette player and portable TV that she used in her guest bedroom at Minnie's house.

"That leaves me with nothing special to do for the luau," complained Artie. "I can't even order a pineapple pizza because Woody's is closed."

Nicie spoke up, "In the first place, *ewwww*. And in the second place, Artie, you're gonna have your hands full with Grandpa, so don't be feeling sorry for yourself just yet. We'll also be using your kitchen to fix and keep a lot of the food. Your job, buddy, will be *not* to eat all of it before the luau."

Artie laughed again and nodded. "Deal," he said. "Okay, so how are we gonna split up to go shopping? How many vehicles do we need?"

"Just one," said Wilma Marecek. "We can get everybody in mine."

"In your aunt's pickup?" asked Bennie Pressler. "What? Three in the cab and six in the bed? Not in the winter. I call shotgun."

Wilma shook her head. "No, not Aunt Minnie's truck," she said. "I drove the old Suburban my father bought for Mother and me before he left. It's old—he got it surplus—but it's big and it runs well. It'll seat nine people easy." She looked at little Ricky and winked at him. "And nobody will have to sit on anybody else's lap." Ricky snapped his fingers but grinned.

The white Chevrolet Suburban—sturdy as a tank and almost as large—was immediately named "Moby," to distinguish it from Ty Green's "White Whale" of a car. On their ride to the big shopping center in Ebenezerville, Wilma was at the wheel, with Leah and Nicie also up front. Bennie, Tommy and Ricky—the three freshmen boys—took the middle row because Bennie couldn't easily climb over seats; and seniors Artie and Ty stretched out in the rear seating area, an arrangement that suited them just fine.

The Ebenezerville Crossing Shopping Center—more commonly called E-ville Crossing, for short—had two anchor stores on opposite ends of its huge parking lot. One was a discount department store that was the main competition for the downtown Pressler's location. The other anchor was a large supermarket that had the best prices but the longest checkout lines in town. Between the two anchor stores sat a row of shops and small restaurants of all types, from fast-food joints to sit-down eateries of assorted menus. The group decided to shop for shirts first at the thrift store there, and then to order a pizza at a new place with a beach theme called Ricki's Tiki Tavern. The hostess and cashier—Ricki herself—eyed the teens suspiciously as they were seated but relaxed when she heard them order a large vegetarian pizza and sodas all around.

The gang shared a large rectangular table for a change, not a round one like a school. It sat in the middle of the dining area, which was situated past the hostess stand, cash register and Polynesian-themed bar. The dark room was lit by sconces that looked like tiki torches and flickering, tiki-shaped lights that were strung above the booths along both walls. At the back of the dining room was an all-you-can-eat salad bar that Artie and Ty agreed to revisit on a future trip to E-ville. The server brought their ice-cold sodas in tall, red, translucent glasses, while the friends chattered about their shopping spree just ahead.

"We need some lights like those," said Leah, pointing up at the string of tiki lights across from her. "Hey, guys, be sure to check the lawn and garden department. They might be on sale, too, since it's winter."

"What about a baby pool?" asked Ty. "We could fill it full of ice and put sodas in it. And then I could use it in my weight room as a spa or whirlpool."

Nicie slapped him. "I don't *even* want to know," she said, "how you're gonna make the water bubble and swirl. *Ewww.*" They all laughed.

"Well, I really like the shirts we found," said Artie, "and I think Grandpa will like his shirt, too. He'll look like Magnum, P.I., in that nice red shirt."

"Yeah," said Wilma, "and the rest of us will look just like Hawkeye and Trapper John on M*A*S*H. But I'd rather look like those guys than wear a grass skirt and coconuts like Klinger."

Bennie shook his head. "Coconuts get a bad rap," he said, waiting to see how the joke landed. When there was only silence, he just shrugged and took another sip of soda. The pizza arrived at the table right then and gave the hungry teens a new focus, as they quickly devoured the steaming wedges of cheesy pie.

After pooling their funds to pay the bill and tip the server, the gang split up to look for decorations at the discount store and for food at the supermarket. The boys—except for Bennie, who refused to "shop at the competition"—were assigned to buy balloons, paper streamers, silk flowers and cotton string for leis, and maybe the tiki lights, if they weren't too expensive. Bennie went to the supermarket with the girls to buy packages of frozen fish; cans of tropical fruit, sweet potatoes and vegetables; coffee, tea and soft drinks; and other items that were needed for their feast. Ty said his father already had a pork shoulder to roast. It was the same with Ricky's mom and the pineapple empanadas. Bennie said he'd bring his own Yoo-hoo and coconuts.

On the ride home in Wilma's Suburban, the teenagers were giddy about the prospects for their holiday luau—what would essentially be a bon voyage party for Bennie, Tommy and the Presslers. But then the topic turned to Wilma's upcoming role on the girls' basketball team and Tommy's impending absence from the wrestling team. Feeling guilty about her decision, Wilma offered to keep practicing with Artie until Tommy returned from Hawaii.

"You don't have to do that, Wilma," said Artie. He reached over the seat ahead of him and grabbed Tommy by the shoulders. "This guy has an announcement. Right, Tommy?"

The sudden attention appeared to embarrass the big freshman, and he turned to look at Bennie sitting next to him before he replied. "Yeah, I guess so," Tommy said. "I, uh, I think I'm gonna stay here so I can keep wrestling. I don't want to take such a long break."

Bennie looked surprised. "Hey, man, I knew you were having second thoughts," he said, "but where are you gonna stay while we're gone? You can't stay in our house by yourself—or I assume Mom and Dad wouldn't let you do that. Have you talked to them yet?"

Tommy nodded. "Yeah, I did," he said. "Well, I talked to your dad, anyway. I called him while we were in the store—from a pay phone—and I asked him if it would be okay for me to stay home—I mean, to stay here and keep wrestling if I could find a place to live. He said it would be fine. He said he'd call the airline tomorrow about my ticket."

Disappointed at Tommy's news, Bennie asked, "So, where are you gonna stay, then? You know, man, I was really looking forward to the three of us doing stuff together—you, me and Brett. It'll be a blast. Come on, now." The pleading in his voice kept the others quiet.

"Well," Tommy began, "Artie said I could stay on the farm. Another reason I don't want to leave right now is because of the pizza guy—and because of that picture we found with my folks in it. I kinda want to be here when the law catches him. They might need me here to identify that bum. Plus, I want to know how my parents are connected to him and…."

Artie finished his sentence. "And what Tommy's folks know about my mother and me," Artie said. "I haven't asked Grandpa yet if Tommy can stay with us, but I'm sure it'll be okay. Tommy spent the night with us about a week ago—the night all those break-ins happened—and Grandpa got a big kick out of talking to him."

"Besides, Bennie," said Tommy, "I can't spend so much time out in the sun until my hair grows back out." He rapped on his stubbled noggin. "This old coconut might crack wide open in all that nice Hawaiian sunshine."

Bennie's eyes narrowed. "I don't want to hear anything else about coconuts," he said, "not unless somebody wears them or claps them together like they're riding a horse. Got it?"

Once again, silence fell over the group, but it didn't matter because they were almost back to the farm. The friends recognized, though, that Benny was warming up to the idea of going to Hawaii without Tommy, because the funny man was trying again to make them laugh. No one saw any humor, though, in what Benny said after Wilma stopped the Suburban to turn left into the farm lane. A line of oncoming cars on Ebenezerville Road kept them from turning immediately. Seated on the left in the second row, Bennie had a clear view of all three cars in the procession. The second car, in particular, caught his attention. It was a coupe with darkly tinted windows. Not even the driver's silhouette was easy to make out.

"I think that was our guy," said Bennie. "Anybody else see him?"

"Our guy?" Wilma asked, as she made the left turn onto the unpaved lane. "What are you talking about?"

"The pizza guy," Bennie said. "The second car. It had tinted windows, and it didn't have a bumper. I looked."

"Did you get the tag number?" asked Artie Bauer.

"No tag," said Bennie, "and, yeah, I looked. Should I call the sheriff's department?" He took out his cell phone.

"Just wait," Artie said. "By the time they get out here, he'll be long gone. We can call and talk to the detective on Monday and see what's going on with the case. Maybe by then I can get Grandpa to talk, and I can tell them the guy's name—if Grandpa knows it."

Chapter 26

BEFORE LEAVING THE FARM on Saturday night, Leah Russo used the clubhouse computer to check her email. She had been sending Brett Woods regular notes via FidoNet but hadn't received a single response yet, not even that he had received his school assignments from her. On this night, however, a message from Brett waited in Leah's inbox when she logged into the Virtual Barf Table BBS. In a hurry to catch her ride home, Leah had glanced at the longer-than-usual note and had printed it out to take home.

Once Leah was alone in her bedroom, she took the printout from the back pocket of her jeans, unfolded the paper, smoothed it on the desktop next to her bed, and began to read:

"Hi Leah – Thanx for what you r doing. Up to my neck in homework but you and Vicki have me caught up. She calls every night M-F (night there – afternoon here) and talks my ears off. I hear Bennie will be Bruno at away games when he and Tommy get back. We'll give Bennie a hard time about that. I'm glad he's walking better now. I hope being in the water helps him get back what he lost.

"Vicki said a new girl named Julia might be the bear for boys home games. Who is Julia? Vicki only said she lives with the new coach and daughter. So how is the new coach doing with the boys? You said Ty quit the team. That must have hurt them. How are the girls doing? Is Nicie the star? You said she hated playing with the coach's daughter again. Nicie would LOVE Hawaii! She could make so much money playing beach volleyball here.

"I'm glad Ricky and Tommy are wrestling with Artie. Sorry Tommy's going to miss a few weeks. I feel bad for Artie losing his grandma after his grandpa had such a bad accident. Dad's worried about Mr. Bauer because he knew him when he was a boy and liked him a lot. My granddad and Mr. Bauer were friends. Dad would go bird hunting on the farm with them. That's why I'm writing – you said something about sending me a picture for Dad to look at. He said it would be better if you MAIL a good copy here instead of sending it on the computer. The pictures on the school work you send me aren't very good (not your fault!). He doesn't want to make a mistake.

The Christmas party sounds like fun! Wish I could be there. Maybe Bennie or Abe could call me and let me talk to everybody? (Dad is getting antsy about spending so much money here with his shop and grill closed there but we'll be OK.) Haven't been to a real luau yet. I think Dad wants to wait until the Presslers and Tommy are here. I spend most of my time on the beach. I've learned a few things but I'm not in these guys league. Or girls league either. I like to watch the lifeguards. I made friends with two and they teach me things (about surfing – HAHA!).

"If you need to reach me quick but can't call, tell Vicki. She can pass it along to me that night. I don't know how she's paying for all the phone calls but she keeps calling like we're dating or something. I like talking to her but I remember how she dumped me for that jerk at homecoming. Maybe she's trying to make up for that. What do you think? Has she changed? Is she hanging around any of guys at school? Not asking you to spy on her. Just wondering what's going on in her head. I'm sure Bennie will be able to tell me about DIGGER (haha!) when he and Tommy get here next week. Your friend – Brett."

Leah Russo didn't really know what to think about Brett Woods's long email message. Despite what Bennie Pressler had told Leah about Brett liking her, she was getting mixed signals from this note and its references to Vicki "Digger" Duke. Did popular Brett Woods like sad little Leah Russo as only a good friend, him seeing her as "one of the gang," or did he view her as a potential girlfriend whom he might take out on a Saturday night for a pizza and a movie or to a school dance? Was she pretty enough and athletic enough for him? Or was vivacious Vicki Duke, head cheerleader and homecoming queen, more the type of girl he wanted, even though Vicki had always behaved like a gold-digger, caring more about a boy's popularity and his family's wealth than anything else? Even Bennie Pressler couldn't help but flirt with Vicki Duke, even after she had dropped him as her boyfriend the previous summer following his surfing accident. He made fun of her and called her "Digger" but still flirted with her. And why had Brett asked about Julia Safin?

Afraid she might never understand boys and their desires, Leah folded up Brett's note and decided he could get answers to all his questions from Bennie, who would be with Brett in Hawaii by the end of the coming week. She went to bed and fell into a fitful sleep, knowing for a change that she was safe at home because her parents were downstairs in their bedroom. She knew that her father would protect her if the pizza guy tried to come back and finish whatever he had set out to do his first time at the Russo house. *Lady is safe, too, as long as Dad doesn't let her go outside to do her business all alone*, Leah thought. A black Lab puppy deserves every chance to be healthy and happy, but a teenage girl has to figure out how to take care of herself.

* * *

"This may be a good thing, or it may be bad," said Artie Bauer, after all his friends were seated with their lunches. The weather had turned cold overnight, and the student body seemed happy with the hot soup and grilled-cheese sandwiches being served on this Meatless Monday. Also, the mood at the Barf Table was subdued, because the three wrestlers—Artie, Ricky and Tommy— would be taking on their counterparts from Iron Harbor High in that night's dual-team match. But Artie wasn't talking about the cold weather or the warm food or even the tough Iron Harbor Gray Dukes.

"Are you worried about wrestling Mean Joe Greene tonight?" asked little Ricky Duran. He was referring to Iron Harbor's champion heavyweight, whom all three Bruins wrestlers had faced earlier that fall on the football field. Mean Joe—as everyone including his mother called him—was also the biggest and best defensive lineman in the Suncoast Conference. He got the nickname because he closely resembled the All-Pro Pittsburgh Steelers defensive tackle, even down to his beard and sweet tooth for soft drinks. No opponent called him by his real name—Louis—not after they saw him break through their offensive line and drive their quarterback or running back into the turf.

"You don't think he lost some weight and went down a class, do you?" Tommy White asked before Artie could answer Ricky's question. "If he did, I might go to Hawaii after all—and leave today." His smile showed he was kidding.

"No," said Artie, but instead of explaining what his initial statement had referred to, he stood and scanned the senior section of the lunchroom. "Hang on, guys. I want Wilma to hear this, too. She's one of us now."

Sitting at the end of a table next to the wall, Wilma Marecek was eating her soup and sandwich, but she also was keeping one eye on her seven new friends at the Barf Table. She smiled when Artie waved for her to join them. None of the seniors sitting near her appeared to notice when she stood without a word to them, lifted her tray and carried it down the stairs and across the cafeteria to the empty spot next to Artie.

"Hi, everybody," Wilma said. "It's chilly today, huh?" She sat and resumed eating, as if nothing were out of the ordinary.

"Yeah, it is," said Artie. "I had to get out my big coat this morning to do the milking." At school, he still wore his dressier green and gold letter jacket, as did Ty Green and Ricky Duran. Tommy White would have to wait at least one more season—maybe just wrestling season—for his first chenille block "A" to show off on a special jacket. Tommy had come close to lettering in football as a freshman, but Coach Jug Johnson had said he thought the boy should have a goal to work toward in upcoming seasons.

"I talked to Grandpa yesterday about the prom picture," Artie said. "We were right—he took that picture, even though he didn't want to. Grandma made him take it because she didn't know how to work the camera. He laughed when he saw the dog lunging at the pizza guy—said ol' Sergeant never did like that boy."

"So he knew his name—the pizza guy's?" asked Leah Russo.

Artie squinched up his face. "Well, kind of," he said. "He knew what my mother and the others called him, but it was just one name—*Rocket*. Grandpa said he didn't know if that was his last name or a nickname. All they called him was *Rocket* whenever he was around there.

"But get this," Artie continued. "Grandpa also said he's pretty sure this Rocket guy killed Sergeant—not on prom night, but after I was born the next year. A couple days after my mother ran off, Grandpa found the dog lying dead up near the barn. He'd been shot, but Grandpa hadn't heard any gunshots and couldn't tell from the wound what kind of gun had been used."

Leah frowned and said, "Anybody who'd shoot a poor dog should be horse-whipped. Artie, did your mother leave a note when she left?"

"No," said Artie, "she had gone off like that once before—without telling anybody—but had come back, so they didn't know she was gone for good. Grandpa said Sergeant barked a few times that last night, but he quit barking, and they figured it wasn't anything to worry about. Well, they were wrong—on both counts."

There were other obvious questions hanging like thought bubbles above the table at that moment, but Artie answered the most pressing one, though it hadn't been asked. "Yeah, I called the sheriff's department yesterday," he said. "I told them that Grandpa had identified the photo of a man who looks like the pizza guy, and I gave them the name. I also told them that we'd seen his car headed toward E-ville Saturday night. The detective wasn't in yesterday, but the deputy I talked to said they want to see the prom picture, and that I need to tell the detective Grandpa's story myself. They asked if I'd bring them the original photograph—not a copy—to the sheriff's office in Iron Harbor as soon as possible."

"Well," said Ty Green, "you're gonna be up there tonight for the wrestling match. Why don't you call the detective this afternoon and tell him to meet you over at the high school. You can give him the photo before you wrestle Mean Joe."

"Great idea," Bennie Pressler blurted. "*Before* might be better than *after*."

"Why's that?" asked Artie.

"You might not remember your *own* name *after* the match," said Bennie, with a sly grin. "I'm just teasing you, big guy. But you've got to admit—that guy *is* a real beast."

"I know, I know," said Artie, "but he wrestles clean, just like he played football clean. Me and him are pretty good friends, actually. I know he's a better wrestler than me, but it'll be a fair match, and I'm gonna do my best tonight against him.

"And Ty," added Artie, "I'm way ahead of you. That's what I suggested yesterday to the deputy. He said the detective will meet me outside the gym when the bus gets there." He turned to Tommy. "And you'll need to talk to him, too, buddy—to tell him your parents are also in that picture. That isn't a problem, is it?"

Tommy shrugged. "No, I don't guess so," he said. "That'll save me a trip to Capital City. I won't have to show my folks the prom picture to get them to ID the others. The detective can do that for me, if you give him the picture. Right?"

Artie nodded and said, "I don't see why not. That's what he's paid to do— investigate. It'll get you out of the middle of it. I mean, you're one of the victims. You shouldn't have to do all the legwork to catch this guy."

"No, *we* shouldn't," Leah Russo told Artie, "but I need to borrow that prom picture before you give it to the detective. I got a note from Brett over the weekend, and he said Woody wants me to mail him a good copy of the picture to see if he recognizes anybody we haven't already ID'd. That's *mail*, not *e-mail*."

Bennie laughed. "If you send that picture by snail-mail," he said, "I'll beat it to Hawaii. I could just take a copy with me on the plane and show it to Woody myself."

"That works," said Leah, "but we need to make copies." She rose from her seat. "Artie, do you have the picture here—in your backpack? I could take it to the guidance office. Miss Hopper has the best copier in the school building."

Bennie butted in, saying, "She has a scanner in her office, too. I could go with you and help you scan the photo. I have some blank floppies to save the file on. It's gonna be big. We'll have to zip it. Okay?"

Leah understood only half of what Bennie had said, but she agreed to let him go with her. Artie took the framed prom picture from his backpack and handed it to Leah as the release bell rang. Before any Meatless Monday pranks could occur and damage the photo, Leah and Bennie, still using his walker, made their way through the crowd of upperclassmen streaming toward the Barf Table and left the cafeteria. When they reached the guidance office, perky Miss Hopper greeted them like long-lost family and gave Bennie access to her copier, scanner and desktop computer, though she was careful to log out of all her school-related programs and email accounts. She even promised to write them late passes to their next classes if Bennie's computer work went past the bell for 4th Period.

Everything went smoothly, even after Vicki Duke reported early for her guidance office duties and refused to leave Bennie and Leah alone. At first, Leah wondered if Miss Hopper had told Vicki to supervise them so that Bennie didn't hack into the school network or change any of his grades. Miss Hopper herself hadn't appeared worried and, when Vicki arrived, had left the office to "confer with faculty members in the teachers' lounge," she said. *Yeah, right*, Leah had thought, but she didn't make any snarky remarks to Miss Hopper or about her to the equally effervescent head cheerleader.

"Oh, Bennie," said Vicki, "you're so smart. I wish I knew as much about computers as you do. You make me feel stupid."

I'll bet, thought Leah, but she said, "Don't be so hard on yourself, Vicki. Bennie just gets all these computer gadgets before everyone else does, because— you know—he's rich."

Concentrating on the task at hand, Bennie glanced up from the computer screen and gave Leah the side-eye. He waited for Vicki to scurry into the outer office to fuss over a teacher who had walked up to the counter, and he whispered to Leah, "I don't need that kind of help—especially with her talking to Brett every night."

Taken aback, Leah said, "So, you *know* about that. Have you been reading my emails?"

"No," said Bennie, "Brett told me himself—on the phone. He said it must be costing her a fortune, all those long-distance calls to Hawaii. He and I both know her family doesn't have that kind of money, but we can't figure out how she's doing it. Blue box, maybe?"

"What?" asked Leah. "What's a blue box?"

Bennie shook his head. "Never mind," he said. "If she can't figure out how to use this computer, she isn't going to be using a blue box. It's a device to make free long-distance calls. And it's illegal. She wouldn't do anything illegal, not after that mess at the homecoming dance."

"*Hmmm*," murmured Leah. "I wonder." She said nothing more to Bennie but decided to test Vicki's respect for the rule of law as soon as she returned from the outer office.

"Hey, Vicki," said Leah, pointing to the telephone on Miss Hopper's desk, "I need to call my dad to let him know when to pick me up tonight. Do you know what number to dial to get out on this phone? It'll be long distance, too, if that's all right."

Vicki Duke's bubbly manner burst like a needle pricking the cheerleader's conscience. "Students aren't allowed to make calls," said Vicki, "especially long-distance calls, not from a school phone. They cost a lot of money, you know."

"Then how am I supposed to call my dad?" asked Leah. "I don't have a cell phone." She was telling the truth, because she had given back her mother's borrowed cell phone.

Bennie stopped working and looked up. "You can use mi—"

"Shut up and finish, Bennie," said Leah. She looked back at Vicki and continued, "I don't have a cell phone, and I don't have any quarters for the pay phone in the gym lobby. Can't you punch in the code for me before Miss Hopper gets back? We won't tell her. And we won't look at the numbers you push—will we, Bennie?"

"Oh, no," Bennie said, not taking his eyes off the computer screen. "Better hurry, though. I'm almost done here." He swapped out the diskette in the small slot on the desktop's tower-like central processing unit and pressed Enter on the keyboard to finish transferring the large zip file from the computer.

"Well…," said Vicki, as if she were undecided. She looked toward the office door, to see if Miss Hopper might return and remove the temptation to reveal the office's dialing code. When the guidance counselor didn't appear, Vicki repeated, "Well, I *would* tell you, Leah, but I've been thinking about what you did to me at the homecoming dance—how you *tricked* me into drinking that cup of tobacco spit. Me, the homecoming queen."

"I didn't trick you into doing anything," Leah said pointedly. "That was all *you*, girl. And you got all of us in trouble because of *your* bad judgment—even Brett. He and I had to pick up trash in the parking lot for weeks after that."

Vicki's smile returned. "I'll bet you enjoyed every minute of that," the head cheerleader said, "getting to spend time with Brett Woods, I mean. He's so cute. And, you know, that's the *only* way a popular boy like him would—" She stopped mid-sentence. "Well, I'm not going to say what I'm thinking right now."

"That's a switch," Leah said.

"What do you mean?" asked Vicki. "That I talk too much?"

"No," said Leah, "that you're *thinking*." Leah figured she might as well have it out with Vicki, now that Leah had figured out how the girl was making all those long-distance calls to Brett Woods. The evidence would come in the school's next telephone bill with its log of calls to Hawaii and the times when all those calls were made after school hours. At the same time, Leah didn't want to get Brett into trouble along with Vicki.

Vicki's face was redder than if she'd just done cartwheels the length of the basketball court. Her back to the office door, she didn't see through the outer office's plate-glass windows that Miss Hopper was approaching from the hallway.

"Don't be ugly," Vicki told Leah. Then the cheerleader flashed her white teeth again and clarified, "I should have said, don't be *mean*, Leah. Brett says you aren't as mean as everyone thinks you are. He says I should try to get along with you because you're a really smart little girl and you can help people by writing good things about them in the newspaper."

"He said that, did he?" asked Leah, as she poked Bennie for making the sound of a cat's yowl under his breath.

Before Vicki could think up a smart answer, Miss Hopper announced her return and went straight to the copier as big as a chest freezer in the outer office. "Oh, Leah!" the perky guidance counselor sang. "Are you ready to copy that photograph? Did you take it out of the frame? Let me punch in my code so you can make a few copies while I'm standing here, okay?"

Then Miss Hopper glanced at Vicki, her office assistant. "Did everything go okay while I was in the teacher's lounge?" she asked, looking down to enter her code into the copy machine. "Nothing came up, I hope."

"Nothing came up, Miss Hopper," said smiling Vicki. Her eyes met Leah's for an instant, and she clarified, "Nothing important, anyway." When she said that, the upturned corners of her pretty mouth drooped just a bit, and Leah saw that Vicki knew she'd been busted.

Chapter 27

AT LUNCH ON KRAKATOA TUESDAY, little Ricky Duran tried not to look too happy. He had been the only Bruins wrestler to win his match the night before against the Iron Harbor Gray Dukes. Unlike his previous victories, it had been a close match, one that went all three periods and was decided in the final seconds. But again, Ricky won by shooting at his opponent, only this time by taking him down right before the final buzzer. He won the hard way—on points, not on a quick takedown and pin. Artie Bauer and Tommy White had wrestled hard, but they both lost to their vaunted adversaries. Neither was pinned, though Artie fared much better against Mean Joe Greene than Tommy did against his less fearsome opponent.

"Don't feel bad, guys," said Wilma Marecek. "Iron Harbor always has a great wrestling team. They were second in the state last year." She looked at Ricky. "And, little guy, you need to stick with wrestling. You're a natural." Ricky smiled and nodded, but remained quiet.

Ty Green took a bite of his sandwich and chewed thoughtfully. He swallowed and said, "I wonder if Iron Harbor would let me into their weight room to see how it's set up. I bet they even have a strength coach. Hey, Artie, has Mean Joe ever mentioned that?"

Artie shook his head. "No, buddy," said Artie, with a weary smile. "He's always too busy twisting my arms and legs behind my back to whisper any secrets in my ear. I feel like a human pretzel when I wrestle him."

Tommy gave a hollow laugh. "I felt like I was wrestling a spider," said Tommy. "Every time I tried to crawl out of bounds, he'd puu-u-u-l-l-l-l me back into the circle and keep trying to rearrange my arms and legs. It would have been a relief to get pinned, but I didn't want to let you guys down." He added for Wilma's benefit, "Or you, either."

"I wish I could've been there," said Wilma, "but my first basketball practice was pretty interesting. I'm glad I won't be playing tonight. Coach Carson said I need to learn the plays and defenses before he'll put me into a game. He said maybe he'll play me a little—but definitely not start—in the holiday tournament at A&M right after Christmas."

Leah put on her sportscaster hat and asked Nicie, "So, Ms. Evans, give us your honest assessment of Ms. Marecek's first practice with the Arbor High Bruinettes." Leah extended an imaginary microphone toward Nicie.

"Well," began Nicie, "Miss Wilma has a lot of work ahead of her on the offensive end of the floor. She needs to fine-tune her shooting and dribbling skills, and learn all of our extremely complicated offensive patterns and plays." She batted her eyes twice. "However, she herself is a natural when it comes to battling under the boards on both offense and defense, and in using her superior size and strength in the low-post position."

Ty seemed more proud of Nicie's commentary about Wilma than his girlfriend's own skills on the court. "When did you learn how to do that?" he asked Nicie. "I never know what to say when I get interviewed. I do more hemming and hawing than anything else."

Nicie shrugged. "The cable TV channel in Mimosa Beach always interviewed us on the beach after our volleyball matches," she said. "It gets easier the more interviews you do."

"Well, you're a real pro at it, babe, and I'm proud of you," said Ty. "So, Artie, how did your talk with the detective go last night?"

Artie exchanged a look with Tommy before answering. "He was waiting for us outside the gym like he said he would," Artie replied. "Coach let us go to an empty classroom and talk to him for a few minutes. I gave him the prom picture and ID'd my mother, and Tommy ID'd his parents. And, yeah, I told him what Grandpa had said about the pizza guy—that people called him Rocket—and I said again that we'd seen his car headed toward E-ville the other night."

Leah spoke up. "So," she said, "did the detective tell you anything about what's going on? Or are they still as much in the dark as we are?"

Tommy White waved Artie off to take Leah's questions himself. "He's driving up to Capital City today, he says, to interview my folks," said the big boy. "That's what he called it—interviewing them. He asked me if I had any idea who the other people are in the picture—other than Artie's mom, I mean. I couldn't help him, so he's gonna ask Mama and Daddy about them, too—the other people."

"Didn't your parents have any friends?" asked Leah Russo. "I'm talking about before they got into trouble with the law and got sent to prison. Didn't anybody ever hang around your house when you were all still together?"

Tommy frowned. "Well, first, they were *always* in trouble with the law," he said. "And as for friends? The people that came by our house weren't anybody Mama and Daddy wanted me to be around. They'd always send me outside when things were going on inside the house—all hours of the day, even at night."

"What did you do outside?" Bennie Pressler asked. "And for how long? You haven't told me about any of this stuff."

"You'd make fun of me," said Tommy. "Besides, it doesn't matter anymore, because our house burned to the ground after my folks got arrested. Some coincidence, huh?"

Artie stepped into the conversation. "Sure it matters," he said, "and we're not gonna make fun of you, Tommy. Are we, Bennie?"

"No," Bennie said. "Tommy, you're my brother now, and you've helped me more than anybody else since last summer. Believe me, I know how it feels to be the butt of jokes." He looked around the table. "Everybody here knows how that feels. So, I'm not gonna make fun of you for *anything*—even though I *am* the funniest guy at Arbor High."

"Oh, shut up, funny boy," said Leah Russo. "Tommy, what did you do? Did you have a basketball goal or something like that? Did you pitch horseshoes? Did you play catch, like with one of those pitch-back nets? My brother used to do that kind of stuff before I was big enough to play ball with him."

Ty Green jumped in. "Weights," he said, snapping his fingers and pointing. "You started lifting weights, right? First, it was fallen tree limbs. Then you moved up to railroad ties. *Then*, it was a small Japanese car—no, a Yugo—that a baby got trapped under out on E-ville Road one day. It was the start of a great professional wrestling career. Wooooo!" Everyone laughed.

"Stop it," said Tommy. "I'll tell you." He waited until the giggles subsided. "I grew flowers. And I raised bees, not just for the honey but for the pollination. Bees are important."

No one had a word to say for a few seconds as they took in Tommy's information. Then Leah asked, "But where did you go at night? I mean, you said they kicked you out of the house all hours of the day. Did you have a barn or something to sleep in, like on Artie's farm?"

Tommy shook his head. "Nope, no barn," he said. "It was a tree house—or a tree stand for deer hunters or a lookout post for pot growers, I don't know which. My little hiding place was out in the woods, as far away from the house as I could get. It was a clearing where I think my folks—or my dad, at least—used to grow marijuana back in the day. But they were into other stuff when they got caught—bad stuff with bad people."

Silence again. Finally, Wilma thought to ask, "What kind of flowers, Tommy?"

"All kinds," the big boy replied. "Everything from crocuses and daffodils in the spring, to irises and glads and lilies in the summer, to dahlias and daisies in the fall. My science teacher at school helped me with everything. Mom helped, too—with the flowers. She brought me some really nice irises—rare ones, even—that she'd transplanted at the house from somewhere else years ago. I liked wildflowers, too—and sunflowers. And I had a red rosebush just like the one at Artie's house. It looked like paradise when the flowers were blooming."

"How did you start keeping bees?" asked Ricky Duran. "My father has said he would like to have bees on the farm—that they would make the crops grow better."

"There were two old bee hives already there," said Tommy, "but they didn't have any bees left in them. I guess the pot growers needed bees but stopped taking care of them when they stopped growing pot. Anyway, my science teacher helped me with that, too. She caught a swarm of bees one spring and put them in one of my hives. Later on, she showed me how to move part of that first hive into the second one and start a new colony. I was just about to get some honey when my folks got arrested and I was put into foster care."

"What happened to your bees?" asked Artie Bauer. "We could move them over to the farm now—or whenever the best time would be. I don't think Grandpa would mind at all."

Tommy shook his head again. "No," he said. "It's too late. They're gone. I got up the nerve to call and ask my teacher if she'd go get my beehives and move them to her house, but she said they weren't there anymore. Bennie's dad told me later that the government *seized*—yeah, that's the word—they seized our property and auctioned it all off. I don't even know who owns the land now. That was after the house burned down."

Bennie reached over and patted the stubble on the crown of Tommy's head. "Old buddy, I think you just got yourself a new nickname," said Bennie. "*Shark* ain't gonna cut it now. I mean, flowers, bees, honey, this sexy crew cut? We're gonna have to start calling you *Buzz*." Everyone agreed, even Tommy White.

* * *

That night's basketball games were on the road again—against the Owls of Oakmont Prep. Like the season's first four games versus in-county rivals, this was a non-conference matchup that didn't affect the Arbor High squads' championship dreams or state playoff hopes. These were basically tune-ups for the conference slate, which would begin after the holiday break. Then the Oleander County schools would play each other twice—home and away—to determine the conference champion and two state playoff bids.

None of the head coaches liked playing "non-conference" games against conference foes; however, the first round of meetings was always good for school spirit and ticket sales, as well as for saving time and money on travel to non-conference schools outside Oleander County. Big-city Iron Harbor High's athletic program took on games against other metropolitan high schools across the region and fielded teams in sports that none of the other Suncoast Conference programs could support—like boys' soccer, girls' volleyball, and co-ed swimming and cross country. Those teams played complete schedules of non-conference matchups but could qualify for state playoff spots as only at-large additions.

Against the Oakmont Lady Owls on Tuesday night, the Arbor Bruinettes made a strong showing but came up short in the final point tally. They still missed injured Mel Grayson's court savvy at the point guard position, but backup Sandy Cuthbert was quickly becoming the team sparkplug on both offense and defense. Scorekeeper Leah Russo noticed that the scrappy freshman always seemed to be in the middle of scuffles and dustups on both ends of the court, and that she came out on top in almost all of them.

But as aggressive as Cutthroat Cuthbert was, freshman center Ann Marie Childers was just as passive, no matter what Coach Joe Carson said or did to motivate her. Not even Wilma's addition to the team seemed to goad Ann Marie into fighting harder to keep her starting spot. In fact, Ann Marie took to Wilma as if the former wrestler and top student were her new big sister. Leah wondered if the two big girls learning the center position at the same time might help them both and, in turn, help the team.

Jamie Foxx settled down and played a solid game against Oakmont. Her ball-handling was sound, and her shooting was on target. She took good shots and passed when Nicie Evans or Julia Safin were open for better shots. From the scorer's table, Leah couldn't find anything to complain about in Jamie's new style of play. Jamie's exchange sister Julia remained a role player at power forward. The Russian's individual play would have stood out more if she hadn't had to sag off her girl and help Ann Marie or a Harmon twin cover the Lady Owl post player.

Like Jamie Foxx, Nicie Evans played well but couldn't quite bring herself to take over the game and carry the Bruinettes to victory. Nicie showed flashes of brilliant play, always getting a step ahead of defenders, but then Ann Marie's lackluster performance would set the whole team two steps back. It was frustrating for everyone, knowing that Ann Marie and both Harmon twins were trying so hard to help the team but just didn't have the experience or expertise to compete with the Oakmont big girl—the same story as in previous losses. The Arbor High girls were now 2-3 on the young season.

Leah Russo and Nicie Evans were forced to stay for the boys' game because neither Ty Green nor Nicie's parents attended the game in Oakmont. Ty had stayed home to help his dad start cooking the pig for Wednesday night's holiday luau on the farm, and the Evanses couldn't take off work early enough to make the long drive and arrive before halftime. The two girls sat as far from the Bruins bench as they could, because Leah didn't want to deal with Coach Foxx's mean looks at her whenever his wife, still acting as team scorekeeper, asked a stupid question about something that had happened on the court. Mrs. Foxx must have needed eyeglasses and hearing aids, as she never seemed to see or hear the number of whichever player had just been assessed a personal foul. She reminded Leah of timid Ann Marie Childers, except twenty years older and twenty pounds heavier. Like Ann Marie, Mrs. Foxx was well-intentioned but out of her element. The difference was that Jimmy Foxx was much less patient with his spouse's slip-ups than Coach Carson and the girls were with their teammate's missteps.

The trade out for Leah and Nicie was that they now had to sit closer to the Arbor High cheerleaders, headed by homecoming queen and guidance office assistant Vicki "Digger" Duke. "Just look at her," said Nicie. "She thinks she's God's gift to men—all that prancing around and primping. I'm glad Ty isn't here. Even he gets all googly-eyed around her. I don't understand it."

"I know," Leah said. "She's about as phony as she can be. You should have heard her flirting with Bennie yesterday in the guidance office. 'Oh, Bennie. You're so smart.' And then she tried to make me jealous over her talking to Brett every night."

"He calls her on the phone?" asked Nicie. "From Hawaii?"

"No," said Leah, "she calls *him*, and I'm pretty sure she's been calling from the guidance office after school hours. There's just no proof yet—not until the school gets its next phone bill."

Nicie looked at her friend. "Are you gonna squeal on her?" she asked. "You know kids don't like snitches, right?"

Leah shrugged. "I don't know," she said. "But let me ask you something else. She told me yesterday that people think I'm mean—that *Brett said* people think I'm mean. Am I?"

Nicie chuckled. "You aren't exactly the warm and fuzzy type," she said, "at least not until somebody gets to know you pretty good. But me and you both know why that is."

"Yeah," said Leah, "but why would Brett Woods say that about me? He does know me pretty well—or he *should* by now. He's one of us."

Nicie shook her head. "No, he isn't," she said, "not yet. Now that he's some big hotshot surfer, he probably isn't sure where he'll fit in at Arbor High when he gets back. And—you just watch—his buddy Bennie Pressler will be looking for new friends, too, after a month away from us. He won't be using a wheelchair or walker, and he won't *have* to sit at our table anymore."

"Bennie doesn't have to sit with us now," said Leah, growing perplexed, "but I get what you're saying. I just hope neither one of them changes that much. And I hope Brett didn't really say that about me—or say it the way Vicki made it sound."

"You aren't mean," Nicie said firmly. "You just want to be left alone, and I know exactly how you feel. Everybody's always making a big deal over stupid things—stuff that doesn't mean anything, really. Well, *you* know what really matters, right? Artie's that way, too."

Leah's face relaxed, and she even managed a smile. "Yeah, you're right," Leah said to her friend. "How'd you get so smart about stuff like that? Have you lost somebody you loved?"

"No," said Nicie, "I've been lucky. But I do know what it's like to be put in a box and be expected to act a certain way. All my life people have taken one look at me and marked me off as being poor or stupid or, yeah, even mean, just because my mama and daddy have to work so hard at their jobs and because I play so hard at my sports. I don't like to be cheated out of things I work hard for, and neither do you."

The two girls turned their attention back to the action on the basketball court, where Coach Foxx's team was trying hard but failing to score its first win of the season. The young coach grew more and more frustrated as his charges struggled on the court and as Mrs. Foxx tested everyone's patience at the scorer's table. During timeouts, the Arbor High cheerleaders also tried but failed to resuscitate school spirit in the visitors' stands. By the end of the night, the smile on Vicki Duke's face was as weak as the downtrodden Arbor boys' grips in the post-game handshake line. The Bruins fell to 0-5.

Chapter 28

'WE'VE WUN OUT OF WAISINS,' was how Frankie the Death-Metal Cashier put it the next day when senior boys started asking why their trays had been shorted on cups of the dried fruit. "And don't throw the fruit cocktail instead," he would add, "unless you wanna help me mop the floor." That put the quietus on Arbor High's last Waisin Wednesday before the holidays.

Leah Russo and the four seniors at the Barf Table were laughing together when Benny Pressler, Tommy White and Ricky Duran joined them. "Oh, come on now, Artie," said Wilma Marecek. "It isn't like you and I haven't held each other close before. We've even rolled around on the floor in each other's arms."

"Ooooh," said Nicie Evans. "Artie Bauer—you dog, you."

Artie's face turned red. "Hey," he said to Nicie, "you know we were just wrestling."

Ty elbowed his buddy seated to his left. "Is that like 'running out of gas' on a date?" he asked. "One of those *euphoniums*?"

"What?" asked Artie, confused. "Euphonium? I think you've been hanging around Coach Johnson too long, Ty. You meant *euphemism*, right?"

Ty shrugged. "What do you think?" he said, grinning. He looked past Artie at Wilma and told her, "Don't listen to this guy. We'll get some Hawaiian Punch in him tonight, and he'll dance with you 'til the cows come home—which might not be all that late on the farm, come to think of it, but we'll get him out on the dance floor."

Artie shook his finger at Ty. "You'd better not spike the punch," warned Artie. "We don't need that kind of trouble tonight. Remember homecoming?"

"Don't worry, buddy," Ty said. "I was referring to all the sugar in those drinks we bought the other night. You diet-crazy wrestlers will be wound up all night just from one of them. Maybe Ricky better drink water, come to think of it."

Nicie Evans motioned toward Leah Russo and the three freshmen boys getting settled across the table. "Yeah, what about these little squirts?" said Nicie. "Who are they gonna dance with tonight? Leah can't do the hula with all three of these guys at the same time."

"You got *that* right," said Leah. "I can't do the hula—period."

Bennie jerked his thumb back at his walker. "Don't even start with that," he said to Leah. "If I can try to dance attached to this hunk of metal, *you* can get up and boogie, too. How about if you help *me* on the dance floor? Tommy never lets me lead. And he has two left feet."

"Hey!" said Tommy.

"It's a date," Leah said. "Now, what about ol' Buzz here? And little Shooter, too—not that Ricky needs any help getting a date. I'm just afraid he'll invite Icky Vicki."

"Or the whole cheerleading squad," said Nicie, winking at Ricky. "I'll never forget seeing you dance with *every single cheerleader* at homecoming—well, except Vicki Duke. That made Ty wish he was single. Didn't it, Ty?"

"I refuse to answer that question," Ty said, "on the grounds that you'll slap me upside the head again." He rubbed one ear, as if it still smarted from his girlfriend's imaginary punch at the homecoming dance.

Wilma briefly touched Artie's arm that rested on the tabletop. "Hey, I know," she said. "We can ask two of the 9th graders on the basketball team to be our guests tonight. I bet Ann Marie Childers and Sandy Cuthbert would come. Minnie and I can even pick them up and take them to the farm. I can take anybody else who needs a ride, too." Wilma looked straight at Leah, as if she expected the girl to say that her parents wouldn't be coming to the party.

"No," said Leah, shaking her head. "Mom and Dad are looking forward to being there. It surprised me when they said they'd go. So, I'll be riding out to the farm with them after practice. They might leave the luau early, though, and then I'd need a ride home."

"Well, we can take you home," said Wilma, "and there'd be room in the Suburban for a few more riders if any other parents need to leave early."

"Moby the Barf Table Party Bus!" said Bennie. "I can't wait until we go on a *real* road trip in that wagon—maybe next summer?"

Leah scowled. "First things first, Bennie," she said. "Okay, Wilma, you go over and invite Ann Marie, and I'll find Sandy and talk to her. We bought some extra Hawaiian shirts, so they don't have to worry about going home to change after basketball practice. You can even leave from here if you want."

Wilma nodded. She and Leah both rose to walk back toward the freshman tables. Nicie looked around the Barf Table at the five boys already busy feeding their faces. All five were at ease, not having to worry about the usual threat of *waisins waining* down on them and into their lunch trays when the release bell rang. They chewed their food in welcome peace.

Nicie called to the two girls walking away. "Tell them it'll be fun," she said, "even if they have to party with *these* guys."

Leah laughed as she spotted Sandy Cuthbert seated—for lack of a better term—at a far table near the cafeteria doors. The little point guard was bouncing up and down as she talked to a gaggle of girls around her. As animated as Sandy appeared to be right then, Leah wondered if little Ricky Duran would be able to keep up with her that night at the holiday luau, even after two or three cups of sugary punch.

* * *

The Barf Table gang's holiday luau that night was the perfect get-together for teenagers and adults alike. As the different families arrived in their floral shirts, the kids gave the grownups tours of the stable, corral and both sides of the doublewide office trailer. Each one received a lei of yellow silk flowers to wear, with the adornment presented by their child. Then the adults found seats in Dr. Minnie Marecek's comfortable waiting area to await the feast being set up next door in the weight room and clubhouse.

Wearing a bright red Hawaiian shirt with palm fronds and parrots, Harry Bauer was the last adult to get to the party. He was driven from the house to the trailer by grandson Artie and helped out of the red pickup truck by Nicie Evans and Leah Russo. Nicie gave Harry a lei from around her own neck to wear. Stopping his walker at the bottom of the handicap ramp out front, the old farmer motioned for Artie to draw closer and talked to him in a low voice for a few seconds.

Artie nodded and looked up at the adults who stood at Dr. Marecek's waiting room door to greet the elderly man. "Hi, everybody," Artie said. "Would you go get Bennie Pressler from the other room? Grandpa wants him to walk up this ramp with him."

When they heard Artie's request, Abe and Deborah Pressler smiled in a confused way but summoned their son, who appeared at the front door a minute later and hurried down the ramp as quickly as he could behind his walker. Bennie knew exactly why he had been asked to escort Grandpa Bauer up the ramp. He remembered his own recent first trip up a similar ramp into the Bauer farmhouse on Thanksgiving Day. That had been a big deal for Bennie then, and this was a big deal for Grandpa now.

"Mr. Bauer, did you think I would forget?" asked Bennie, with a big smile.

"No, son," said Grandpa, "but I wanted to make sure me and you had our chance to do this together before you leave on your big trip. I'm a man of my word. And seeing you walk up that ramp over at the house was what gave me the nerve to get back on my feet, too. Me and you both were in a fix, weren't we?"

"Yes, sir," said Bennie, as he turned to lead Grandpa up the ramp and into the trailer. Artie and the girls followed at a respectful distance.

Now that everyone was present, the adults were ushered back into the clubhouse area where surfboard tables loaded with food awaited them—sliced pork, fish filets, empanadas, corn on the cob and other vegetables, sweet potatoes, tropical fruits and Hawaiian sweet bread. The girls had made coffee and tea to offer the adults to drink, while the teens chose the soft drinks and punch that they had bought on their shopping excursion to E-ville. Minnie made up a plate of food for Grandpa and carried it to where he sat in the waiting room. She took the chair next to him and began telling him about her plans to move all of her operations there after the holidays.

The other grownups gravitated back to their previous seats and ate quietly while they watched a videocassette of *Blue Hawaii* with the sound turned low. Gradually, they ignored Elvis's gyrations and crooning, and they started talking to one another. By meal's end, the couples were much better acquainted with each other, especially with the one pair of parents that had been something of a mystery for the past year—the Russos. At one point, Elizabeth Russo looked at the yellow lei hanging around her own neck and broke down into tears as she thanked the others for looking after Leah during the couple's frequent attempts to put Monk's Landing and its sad memories behind them.

In the clubhouse, the ten teenagers—the eight Barf Table mates, along with Ann Marie Childers and Sandy Cuthbert—were oblivious to the grownups' conversation next door. In true luau fashion, the kids—even stiff-legged Bennie—sat on the floor to consume their feast and to conserve their energy for the dancing to follow. That, in fact, was the main topic of discussion in the clubhouse during the meal—to line dance or not to line dance. The girls wanted to teach the boys how to hula dance to "The Hukilau Song." Except for Ricky, who was eager to do anything on his feet, the boys were willing to line dance to "Electric Boogie (The Electric Slide)," because they'd already learned that routine at school.

"Oh, come on, guys," said Nicie Evans. "It'll be f—"

The office telephone rang loudly. Nicie jumped up and dashed into the office to answer the phone. Seconds later, she came back and stood in the doorway to the clubhouse area. "It's Brett," she announced to the group. "Everybody say 'hi.' He's on loudspeaker."

After exchanging hellos, Brett Woods told his Barf Table buddies that Bennie had given him their new office number and had encouraged him to call during the luau. He was especially pleased to hear that Grandpa Bauer, like Bennie, was up and walking, and he promised to pass that good news on to Woody, his father. Brett gave a shout-out to his football teammates—to Artie, Ty, Ricky and Tommy—and he said he was sorry that Tommy wouldn't be joining him and Bennie in Hawaii after all. Brett was surprised to learn that Wilma Marecek had quit wrestling to play basketball. He wished Wilma, Nicie and the other basketball players well on their upcoming conference schedule that winter. In the last few seconds of the call, Brett told Ty Green to stay out of trouble with all his new free time, at least until Brett could return home to get into trouble with him. He was off the phone before Leah Russo could speak up and ask if he'd rather have Vicki Duke send him his assignments instead of Leah herself.

"Don't worry about it," Nicie told Leah after rejoining her on the floor. "You know how guys are. They don't think. Maybe he meant to say something to you but just forg—"

The office phone rang again. "See," said Nicie. "I bet that's him calling back. Go grab it."

Leah rose and hurried into the office. Picking up the handset, she could feel her heart skip a beat. "Hello?" she said before the phone reached her ear. But there was no immediate response, as if the caller were surprised to hear Leah's voice.

"Hello?" Leah said again. "Who's calling?"

"Oh, I am sorry," said a sultry female voice with a foreign accent. "I might have dialed the wrong telephone number. I am trying to call the home of Arthur Bauer."

Leah immediately recognized the caller as Julia Safin. "Oh, hi, Julia," said Leah. "You have the right number—I guess. This is Leah Russo. I'll get Artie for you."

She called Artie to the phone. Before handing it to him, she covered the mouthpiece and whispered, "It's Julia Safin. She thought this was your home number."

"Yeah," Artie said, nodding, "she could have called that number—it's in the phonebook—but I fixed the phone in the farmhouse to forward our calls while Grandpa and I are here." Artie took the handset from Leah and waited for her to leave before he lifted it to his ear.

Back on the clubhouse floor next to Nicie, Leah continued to shake her head. "I just don't get it," she said. "I don't understand."

"Get what?" asked Nicie.

"Guys," said Leah, "and why they can't see what's right in front of them. I'm going to a lot of trouble for Brett, and he can't even say thanks. And Artie's with Wilma tonight—maybe just as friends—but right now he's in there talking to Julia Safin on the phone. What's up with that?"

Nicie nodded. "Ty used to be that way," she said, "until I got hold of him. Now I make him tell me what's going on in that goofy head of his, and I tell him what's bothering me when I get upset at him. Things work a lot better when two people don't keep secrets from each other."

Just then, Artie returned to the clubhouse from the office. He caught Leah's eye as he passed her but looked away, as if he didn't want to explain right then why the exchange student had called him. Nicie, however, had a different idea.

"Artie Bauer," said Nicie, "get your rusty dusty back over here and talk to me and Leah for one second." When he did, she continued in a lower tone, "You didn't invite that girl over here tonight, did you? You know that would be rude, right?" She cut her eyes toward Artie's empty cushion next to Wilma across the room.

"I know," Artie said, frowning. "I'd never do that. It wouldn't be fair to Wilma. Besides, I didn't tell Julia to call me, and I still haven't asked her out." Then he gave them an embarrassed smile. "She asked *me* out—for this Saturday night."

"Are you going?" Nicie asked.

"I don't know," said Artie. "I told her I'd talk to her tomorrow at school."

Now Nicie was the one shaking her head. She looked at Leah and said, "You're right, girl. Some guys don't see what's right in front of their faces. Poor Artie. Poor, poor Artie."

"What?" Artie said. But then he waved them off and turned away. "I need to go talk to Wilma," he said. "I still owe her a dance."

Before he'd taken two steps, though, the office phone rang a third time. So, Artie turned around again and trudged back to the office. He answered the phone but didn't do much talking during the brief call, at least not enough for Leah to overhear.

"You think that's Julia again?" asked Nicie under her breath. "Maybe the girl changed her mind when Artie didn't jump at the chance to date her. Some girls are like that, you know."

Leah leaned to one side for a better look at Artie standing at the office desk. "Well, something's up," Leah said. "He doesn't look happy. *Shhh.* Here he comes."

When Artie exited the office, his eyes met Leah's again, but this time he held the look longer than she found to be comfortable. Then he stopped, cleared his throat and asked for quiet in the clubhouse. "Look, guys," he said in all seriousness. "I need to go talk to our families in the other room. Something bad has happened." He looked at Leah and motioned to her, as well as to Nicie and Tommy. "You three need to hear this, too."

Artie and the others led the way into the waiting room next door, where all of the adults, surprisingly, were already quiet. Still seated along the wall, John Russo was holding one hand up for quiet as he held his cell phone to his ear with the other hand. Expressions of concern and disbelief on his face were unmistakable. "Oh, no," he said more than once. Then he said, "Yes, officer. We'll leave now. Thank you."

Leah's father rose and helped his wife to her feet. When he saw Leah standing with Artie at the door, he motioned to her to come with them. "That was the sheriff's department," John Russo said to the whole group. "There was another break-in at our house tonight." He paused. "Our neighbors called 9-1-1 when they saw a strange light, and the first deputy on the scene caught the intruder in the house. They want us to come home now."

"Why?" Leah asked. "Was it the same guy? Did he hurt Lady?"

John Russo shook his head. "No, she's okay," he said with a worried look, "but we need to go home right now. They need to talk to us—and to *you.*"

Artie stepped forward. "And us, too—me, Tommy and Nicie," he said. "I'm sorry we have to end the evening this way, but this is, uh, unavoidable. Thanks, everyone, for coming. And—Bennie and Mr. and Mrs. Pressler—have a safe trip to Hawaii. I'll get Tommy home after we talk to the detective. That's who I was talking to a minute ago."

Minnie Marecek agreed to stay on the farm with Grandpa Bauer while Wilma took Ann Marie and Sandy home in the Suburban. Ty Green offered to put Artie, Nicie and Tommy in the White Whale and drive them to the sheriff's department in Iron Harbor.

"We aren't going to the sheriff's department," corrected Artie. "They want us to go to the hospital to identify the guy—I mean, to see if he's our pizza guy, if he's *Rocket*." He took a quick breath and glanced at Grandpa. "Well, not to the hospital, exactly," he said. "To the morgue."

Chapter 29

JOHN RUSSO HAD TOLD LEAH THE TRUTH about Lady, the family's Labrador retriever. The dog was safe after the break-in, but only because Elizabeth Russo had put her in the backyard before they left for the farm. Rocket had parked up the street this time, not in the driveway, but had entered by jimmying open the front door again. After the earlier break-in, the neighbors had been on watch for anything out of the ordinary when the Russos were away. As John had said, the neighbors spotted Rocket's flashlight shining here and there in the dark living room, but their discovery hadn't been by chance. They had been alerted by Lady barking in the backyard.

When they got home from the party, the Russos learned that the responding deputy had arrived on the scene within minutes and had surprised the thief as he was headed out the back door to silence the dog. The shootout had happened there and then on the back porch.

Leah identified Rocket's car—the primer-colored coupe with tinted windows and no rear bumper—as being the one that she had seen parked in their driveway on that Friday night two weeks earlier. Still parked up the street in the Arbor Woods subdivision, the car—now encircled by yellow crime scene tape—was the one that Leah and her friends had spotted on the highway near the high school and near the farm, also at the beach after Tommy was assaulted.

"We opened the trunk," the deputy told the Russos, "and you wouldn't believe what all he had in there—wallets, handbags, wristwatches, jewelry; also, coin collections, stamp collections, baseball cards, autographed pictures of athletes and movie stars … anything collectible that was easy to carry out."

He added that the Russos' jewelry boxes were among the items still in the trunk, though he couldn't say if any jewelry was missing from them.

The Russos were spared seeing the body on the back porch, just the blood stains. The medical examiner and other investigators had finished photographing the scene, and they had sent the corpse on to the morgue at University Medical Center in Iron Harbor. The deputy said an autopsy had to be done—hopefully the next day—before the body could be released to a funeral home on behalf of the man's family, as soon as they could be found. He also noted that Rocket's name would not be released to the press until a positive identification was verified and his next of kin was notified.

Remembering her earlier conversation with Minnie Marecek about the prom photo and, specifically, about Rocket's relationship to Artie Bauer's mother, Leah Russo asked the deputy if he knew who the pizza guy really was—in other words, if the detective who had talked to Artie and Tommy White, and then had interviewed Tommy's parents in prison had learned Rocket's real name.

"Yes, ma'am," the deputy said, "we have a name for the young man in that photograph you're referring to. But now we need a positive identification of the man who died here tonight to see if they're the same individual. From what I understand, two family members are on their way to Iron Harbor as we speak, but that's all I can tell you right now. I'm sorry."

"I understand," said Leah. "I really do, but are you talking about my friends—about Artie Bauer and Tommy White? Are they the family members? Your detective called Artie tonight and asked him to take Tommy to the morgue to identify a body. Do you think the pizza guy is related to Artie somehow?"

The deputy wrinkled his brow. "Pizza guy?" he said, and then he nodded. "Oh, I get it—because he used a pizza box as a cover when someone turned out to be home, like out at the Bauer farm. Well, I can't answer that question. You'll need to talk to your friends when they get back from Iron Harbor, and they can tell you what they know. Again, I'm sorry."

John Russo, who hadn't objected to his daughter's questions, took her gently by the arm and started moving back down the sidewalk away from the suspect's car and toward their house. "Thank you, officer," John said. "If you have all you need from Leah, we'll head back inside. I think my wife might want us to pack up a few things and find somewhere else to stay tonight. I hope we can find a place that'll let us keep Lady in our room."

Elizabeth Russo was, in fact, waiting anxiously with the black Lab in the family's living room, sitting on the sofa with all the overhead lights downstairs turned on. She looked up from petting the dog when the deputy rapped twice on the front door and led John and Leah back into the house. "Artie Bauer just called," Elizabeth said, not so much to Leah as to all three. "He said to tell Leah it's definitely the pizza guy—whatever that means." With tearful eyes, she looked at John. "How much longer do we have to stay here?"

Leah was afraid that Elizabeth wasn't just referring to their home that night. Leah feared that her mother meant to leave the house in Arbor Woods and never return, or, even worse, to move away from Monk's Landing and Oleander County for good.

* * *

Thursday was moving day at Arbor High—for Bennie Pressler, who was on his way to Hawaii for a month; for Tommy White, who would spend that month on the Bauer farm; and for Leah Russo, whose parents were determined to find somewhere else to live. Late Wednesday night they had packed their suitcases—the same ones they had been using for their weekend getaways—and had hustled Leah, Lady the black Lab, and themselves, to the first pet-friendly hotel they found on the strand at Mimosa Beach. Still, Bennie's chair at the Barf Table was the only empty spot once Tommy White and Ricky Duran got through the long lunch line and took their seats with the others.

"Girl," Nicie said to Leah, "why did you even come to school today? Nobody would have cared one bit if you had stayed home—well, stayed out, I mean."

"I had an exam this morning," said Leah. "It wasn't any big deal—I could've made it up some other day—but Mom was falling apart, and I needed to get away from her." She laughed. "Isn't that funny? Until now, Mom has been the one wanting to get away from *me*."

Nicie shook her head. "Oh, don't talk like that," said Nicie. "You know she loves you. Mama said your mother was crying about you last night at the party—about how thankful she was that everybody cared about you and had helped out when they were off on all those trips."

"I'm afraid their next trip will be permanent," Leah said. "Mom is determined to move and start over somewhere else as soon as possible. That last night was the last straw for her. Dad's over there cleaning up the, well, cleaning the house right now. Then it'll be up for sale."

Wilma wiped her mouth with a napkin. "There are a couple of nice houses for sale in our subdivision on the river," she said. "Aunt Minnie even knows the homeowners. Wouldn't that be great—us being neighbors?"

"I wish," said Leah, "but Mom wants to leave Oleander County entirely. She's talking about moving up to the mountains—up near the lake where they rented a cabin almost every weekend this fall. Dad isn't sure how that's gonna work with his job, but he'll go wherever Mom tells him to go. I'm just along for the ride."

"Leah, you need to stay here—with all of *us*," Artie insisted. "I know what you're going through—like I've said—and I know it's really hard to deal with. I know that part better than ever now. But you've made a lot of progress. You aren't the same girl who sat in that chair on the first day of school."

Leah teared up at Artie's earnest declaration. As she tried to find the words to thank her friend and honorary big brother, she glanced past him and saw that Jamie Foxx and Julia Safin were headed across the cafeteria toward them. "Thanks, Artie," Leah croaked. "By the way, did you decide about Saturday night yet?"

"Huh?" he said. "What do you mean?"

Leah nodded toward the two girls approaching Artie from the rear. "Here comes Julia," Leah said, "with Jamie."

Nicie Evans added, "And they don't look happy."

"Uh-oh," Ty Green said to Artie. "Well, it's been nice knowing you, buddy."

The new girls from Mimosa Beach weren't there to discuss Artie Bauer and

Julia Safin's social lives. Along with the rest of the student body, Jamie Foxx had heard about the shooting at the Russo residence and that the dead man might have been the thief who had killed the Foxx's dog in the burglary spree earlier that month. Jamie wanted to know what the newspaper and TV stations weren't reporting just yet.

"Was it the same guy?" Jamie demanded. Julia was silent, and she studied Artie's face without even a hint of a smile.

"Yeah, same guy," said Artie. "All three of us saw him—me and Nicie and Tommy—and it was definitely him."

"Are you sure?" said Jamie, always pushing, never easing off.

Nicie spoke up. "Yes, Jamie," she said. "It was the same guy who attacked Tommy at the beach and then drove off in that same skeezy car we've seen him in all over the county."

"The same car he drove to my house two weeks ago," said Leah, "and again last night. It was the same guy. Right, Artie?"

"Yeah," Artie said. "I know it was, because I looked at his hand last night, and I saw the 'K' tattoo on the knuckle of his right index finger. That's what I noticed when he tried to open the door at my house that day." He looked straight at Jamie. "Is that enough proof for you?"

She nodded and glanced back at Julia. "Okay," Jamie began, "but we were wondering, too, if the cops told you how the guy killed our dog."

"Nathan, right?" asked Leah, remembering the dachshund from Jamie's previous visit to the Barf Table.

Julia Safin nodded sadly. "Yes, leetle Nathan," she said. "He was such a sweet dog. We miss him so." She looked at Artie and smiled.

"Yeah, I forgot about that," Artie said. "The detective explained why nobody heard any shots—why the dogs didn't have bullet wounds. It made sense, too, along with what Grandpa had told me about the guy—that everybody called him *Rocket*."

"Just tell me," insisted Jamie. "I don't care what his nickname was or any of that other crap. How did he kill my dog?"

Artie blinked twice, as if he were trying his best not to say what he was thinking. "They called him *Rocket*," said Artie, "because he used a slingshot to kill things—birds, squirrels, cats, even dogs. Tommy's dad told the detective that Rocket was always like that—a psychopath."

"So he killed my dog with a stupid slingshot?" said Jamie, incensed. "But I still don't know what that has to do with that gobbledygook about a nickname."

Ty motioned for Artie to stay quiet. "Jamie," said Ty, "if you were a country boy like me and Artie, you'd know that a *Wrist-Rocket* is a high-powered slingshot. Yeah, that makes perfect sense. But did Tommy's folks tell the cops Rocket's real name?"

Artie nodded. "Luther 'Rocket' Reep," he said. "I ran all that by Grandpa last night, and he didn't know the guy's real name—but he remembered the slingshot. He said that must have been how old Sergeant died, too—his German shepherd."

Jamie had heard enough. She turned away and tried to get Julia Safin to leave with her, but the Russian girl needed an answer of her own from Artie. "You go without me, Jamie," said Julia. "I will join you after the bell rings." She moved around the table and pulled out Bennie's empty chair next to Leah. She eased herself into the seat and looked up at Artie, as if the next move were his to make. She smiled.

Artie turned around and checked the clock on the far wall of the cafeteria. "The bell's gonna ring in a second," he said, turning back to face Julia. Then he looked at Wilma Marecek seated beside him. "I didn't get a chance to thank you and Minnie for staying with Grandpa last night," he said. "I really do appreciate everything you two do for us, and I'm glad Minnie will be out on the farm every day soon—and you, too."

The release bell rang. Wilma rose and picked up her tray to leave. "I'm looking forward to that, too, Artie," she said and waved goodbye to her teammates at the table. As they usually did, Nicie Evans and Ty Green got up and headed out themselves. Leah usually took off early, too, but decided to hang around until Julia Safin left. Still, she doubted that Artie and Julia would get into a heart-to-heart talk in front of the two freshman boys—Tommy White and Ricky Duran—because Artie had neither Tommy's naiveté nor little Ricky's confidence and charm.

"What are you grinning about?" Artie said, not to Julia but to Leah. "Don't you have a book to read?"

With both elbows on the tabletop, Leah rested her face in her hands, cheeks touching her open palms. "Oh, Artie," she said, "you're so smart."

Julia answered for him. "That is not very nice," Julia said. "Arthur is your friend, and you should not tease him so. That is why I like him—because he *is* intelligent. Also, he is the nicest boy that I have met here at Arbor High School." She said no more and again waited for Artie to speak. Her quiet smile made Leah wish that she herself had *that* kind of confidence.

"I don't know what to say," said Artie. "I … I … I'd like to g—"

"Artie, just say yes," Leah said. "Tommy and I will stay with your grandpa Saturday night, and you and Julia can go out and have a good time." Tommy nodded in agreement.

"And I will come over, too," said little Ricky Duran. "We can play cards or Monopoly or do whatever Mr. Harry Bauer would like to do. It will be fun."

Julia's smile grew wider. "Good," she said. "Then it is settled. You will pick me up at five o'clock, Arthur." There was a twinkle in her dark eyes. "And we, too, will have fun."

Chapter 30

ARBOR HIGH WAS WINDING DOWN for the long holiday break. There had been no wrestling match on Thursday night, and Friday night's basketball games were non-conference matchups against weak opponents. Both basketball teams from Pinecrest Christian Academy were usually easy to beat, whether at home or away. This night was no different, with Arbor hosting Pinecrest in the Bears Den and scoring almost at will. Coach Jimmy Foxx's Bruins won their first game of the season by a wide margin, while Coach Joe Carson's Bruinettes scored such a decisive win that every player on the bench—even senior rookie Wilma Marecek—saw some action. Wilma didn't score a single point, but she was thrilled to run the floor with her teammates and hear the cheers from the home stands. Likewise, Wilma's aunt, Dr. Minnie Marecek, liked watching the big girl work toward making a difference on the team that people would recognize, as opposed to Wilma's less obvious support of basically one wrestler, her friend and rival Artie Bauer.

The competition between Artie and Wilma for the Ebenezer Endowment had always been friendly, partly because Artie's chances of getting an athletic scholarship had grown with each year he played high school sports. Having a military father who was stationed abroad and a stay-at-home mother who preferred living with her accomplished sister-in-law, Wilma needed to win the four-year endowment to attend Iron Harbor A&M. Otherwise, she would either have to join the military herself or take out student loans that would put her deep in debt. The Ebenezer went to the best student-athletes in Oleander County; however, the award's focus was as much on academic excellence as on physical vigor. Strong leadership and good character also figured into the selection process. Usually only one endowment was awarded at each county school. So Wilma couldn't afford to quit the wrestling team without taking up another sport. And that was why Friday night's home game against Pinecrest Christian represented such a hopeful change.

Leah Russo was aware of the Ebenezer Endowment for two reasons—because she was the school newspaper's sportswriter and was expected to write an article about the award in the spring, and also because her brother Reuben Russo had been an Ebenezer nominee before his untimely death almost a year earlier. Being Artie's and Wilma's friend, Leah knew how much the scholarship meant to both seniors and how important it was for Wilma to succeed in basketball, at least to a greater extent than she had in wrestling. In other words, Wilma needed to get her name in the sports pages for some greater contribution to her team than as a practice partner.

On Saturday morning, Leah's father drove her out to the Bauer farm for her appointment with Minnie Marecek. From there, John Russo went back to the family's house in Arbor Woods to continue cleaning and packing for their eventual move. Elizabeth Russo had refused to return to the house and had chosen to stay with Lady at their hotel in Mimosa Beach, but John told Leah that they needed to give Elizabeth time to heal. John also suggested that Leah talk to Dr. Marecek about adding the young wife and mother to her client list after the holidays. That suggested to Leah that her dad might be open to staying in Oleander County after all, so she told him that she'd heard there were nice houses for sale in Minnie and Wilma's subdivision on the river. Leah watched his reaction and was encouraged when his eyes widened as if he were picturing a new life on the water, with a private pier and floating dock for the shiny, new fishing boat that he'd always talked about buying someday. Leah knew John Russo wasn't much of a fisherman, but that he had always wanted the laidback lifestyle of one.

"You're early," greeted Minnie Marecek, as Leah Russo walked into the stable to groom and saddle Micki. The therapist waved her hand holding the currycomb that she had been using to brush Bennie Pressler's mare. "I'm going to saddle Belle, anyway," Minnie said. "Maybe you and Wilma can go for a longer ride after your session—if you're up to it."

"I'd like that," Leah said. "Where *is* Wilma?"

"She's in the office," said Minnie. "The phone was ringing when we got here, and she can run a lot faster than I can." She laughed. "Turned out it was Bennie calling from Hawaii."

"Did he want to talk to me?" asked Leah.

"I don't think so," Minnie said, "but he *did* ask about you and your parents—if you all are okay. He was calling to give me instructions on how to hook up my computer and fax machine. With all the excitement the other night, he forgot to do that."

Minnie laughed and continued, "That's what Wilma is doing now—hooking them up for me. You know how I am with computers."

"Oh," Minnie added, "Bennie did say you shouldn't worry about sending assignments for Brett this week—Bennie called the high school Friday and got them. And he said he'll send you and Artie an email about that prom picture he took with him to show Woody."

"Did he tell you anything about that?" Leah said. "Any details?"

"No," said Minnie, "I got the impression that he hadn't shown that picture to Woody yet. I imagine, though, that if there's any big news about it, Woody will call Artie himself and tell him first. As I've said, it isn't our place to stick our noses in Artie and Harry's personal business. If they want us to know anything, they'll tell us. The dangerous part is solved now."

Leah trusted Minnie enough not to take her warning as a reprimand, but as a friendly reminder that they might not hear anything else about Artie's mother and his biological father, and that that would be quite okay.

Just then Wilma walked into the stable after crossing the barnyard from the office trailer. "Hi, Leah," said Wilma. "Aunt Minnie, we're all set now. Bennie's instructions were great. I got the computer and fax both hooked up. And they work! Bennie and I sent faxes back and forth."

Leah shook her head. "I can't believe he's up this early," she said. "It's the middle of the night in Hawaii right now."

"He told me he isn't on 'island time' yet," said Minnie. "Okay, ladies, let's get this session going. Leah, you finish up with Micki and meet me in the corral. Wilma, go ahead and saddle up Belle. She needs some exercise. Later, I'll work with the other horses while you two go for a ride around the farm. That'll be fun, won't it?"

Wilma was quick to agree. Leah wasn't too sure about "soloing" on Micki just yet, though Wilma would be riding beside her. During the therapy session, Micki seemed to sense her rider's anxiety. The horse was a bit agitated as soon as Leah mounted her, but both soon calmed down when Minnie reminded Leah to focus on breathing slowly and deeply. Leah had learned that her relationship with Micki reflected her dealings with everyone else in her life. She also knew that riding a horse wasn't as easy or as passive as, say, fishing could be, when it came to therapeutic activities. Leah needed Minnie, the therapist, to help her slow down and pay attention to the emotional "e-mail" between her subconscious mind and her fragile body. Leah knew riding a horse was all about balance and the trusting give-and-take between horse and rider. Maybe she needed to get her father to give up his dream of becoming a fisherman and join her on horseback. Maybe her mother would benefit from that kind of therapy, too.

Later, Leah and Wilma rode around the farm's perimeter through terraced fields of loamy soil and winter grasses. They did not push their horses to run or even to trot. Wilma knew from experience that each client's therapy moved at its own pace, just like the horse and its rider on whatever range. Right then, walking was fine.

Wilma broke the silence of the ride. "Leah, I hope your mother feels better today," Wilma said. "Does she still want to leave Oleander County? I hope not."

Leah kept her focus on the ground up ahead of them. "She still says we're leaving," said Leah, "but Dad perked up this morning when I told him about the houses for sale on the river. Thanks for telling me about that."

"Yeah, River Bend is a nice neighborhood," said Wilma. "I'm going to miss living there when Father gets back from overseas. Mother and I will have to move back onto the base then. Father refuses to buy a house until he retires. I'll be off on my own before that happens."

"What do you want to do—when you're on your own?" asked Leah.

Wilma thought for a second. "I'm kinda torn between two things," she said. "On the one hand, I'd like to be a psychologist and therapist like Aunt Minnie. But I also enjoy working with animals—of all kinds, not just horses. I'd love to live on a farm—well, like this one—and have my own veterinary practice." Wilma blushed a bit after mentioning how much she liked the farm. She knew Leah would make the leap to Wilma's relationship with Artie.

"I know you and Artie are friends," said Leah, "but do you want to be *more* than that with him?" She started to tell Wilma that Artie had been worried about hurting her feelings when Julia Safin had called him at the luau.

"What I want doesn't really matter now," Wilma said. "Artie's going out with Julia tonight, and I can't compete with her. She's so beautiful. She's a really good athlete, too. I can't wait to see her play tennis this spring."

Leah shook her head. "Oh, Wilma," she said, "just be patient. I know you two—you and Artie—and you're perfect for each other. But I feel the same way, like I can't compete with Icky Vicki Duke for the guy I like."

"Who's that?" asked Wilma. "The guy, I mean. Bennie?"

"No, but he and I had a long talk about that recently," said Leah. "He made it clear that we're just friends. He even told me he thinks the other guy—Brett Woods—likes me, whatever that means. But I keep getting mixed signals. And Vicki Duke has made it clear that she wants him back. I figure everything will work out one way or another by the Valentine's Dance."

Leah looked over at Wilma and saw the big girl smile. "So," Wilma said, "you and I have more in common than I thought." She studied her friend for a moment. "Tell you what, Leah. If you and I don't have dates for Valentine's, we'll find something *better* to do. I'm not sure what that would be, but we'll think of something."

"You got that right," said Leah, "and those boys won't know what they're missing out on."

* * *

Minnie came out of the office trailer onto the ramp out front as Leah and Wilma tied their horses to the fence railing at the corral. "Leah, your father called," Minnie said, some urgency in her voice. "You need to call him back immediately."

"What's wrong?" asked Leah, as she hurried up the ramp and into the trailer.

Minnie ushered the girl into her office and motioned for her to sit at the desk to use the phone. "All he'd say was that he needed to talk to you," said Minnie. "He sounded kind of broken up. He said to call him at home—the house, not the hotel." Minnie pressed and lit the button for Line 1, and gave the handset to Leah.

Leah could feel her heart beginning to race as dark thoughts crossed her mind. At the dial tone, she punched in the seven-digit number on the face of the desk phone and waited as the line made its connection and began to ring once, twice, three times.

"Yes?" said John Russo. Ordinarily, he would have answered, *Russo residence*, but both he and Leah knew that was no longer the case.

"Dad, what's wrong?" Leah said. "Are you okay? Is Mom okay?"

For a few moments there was silence, long enough to worry Leah even more. "Dad?" she said again.

"Elizabeth is fine—I guess," he said. "It's me. I just can't do this by myself."

"Do what?" asked Leah. "I thought you cleaned up the blood and all that yesterday."

"I did," said John Russo. "I tried, but I can't bring myself to pack up Reuben's things. And I can't ask Elizabeth—I can't ask your mom—to help me. She *won't* do it. She won't even walk in the front door now." He was quiet again for a second. "Can you come help me?"

Now it was Leah who fell silent. Tears had begun to roll down her cheeks. "I don't know if I can do that, either, Dad," said Leah, "but I'm on my way to help you pack. Artie or Wilma or somebody will give me a ride to the house. You stay right there. I'm coming. And whatever you do, don't call Mom." She hung up the phone and reached for a tissue to dry her eyes.

Having heard what was happening, Minnie Marecek took control. "Don't you worry about Micki and Belle," the therapist said. "Wilma and I will put them up, and then we'll both be on our way to help you and your dad. I'll call Ricardo Duran so he'll know what's going on. Right now, you need to go get Artie to drive you over there—to your father. Tommy can go, too. I'm sure Ricardo and Gabby will keep an eye on Mr. Bauer. Don't worry. I'll handle everything."

Things worked just as Minnie Marecek had said—with one big exception. Artie and Tommy dropped what they were doing and took Leah to the Arbor Woods house, where she comforted her father while the two boys began boxing up the memory-laden contents of Reuben Russo's bedroom—the trophies on the dresser; the photos, the framed newspaper clippings from sports pages on the wall; the letter jacket, the jerseys and worn sneakers that filled the closet of this son, brother and friend who had died too young. The exception to what Minnie had promised was that she and her niece didn't travel directly to Arbor Woods from the farm. Instead, they took the time to call around and get even more help. When Moby the Great White Suburban pulled up in front of the Russo house in Arbor Woods, the SUV contained nine more members of the Barf Table farmily: Minnie and Wilma; Ricardo, Gabby and Ricky; Nicie and Ty; and the old papa bear himself, Harry Bauer.

"We're here to help," announced Grandpa, as Ty Green helped him out of the vehicle and snapped open his walker. And help they all did, for the rest of the afternoon, all over the house and into the garage, using up most of the cardboard boxes that John had scrounged or bought the previous day. They barely took a break for lunch. No one asked why there were no holiday decorations or Christmas tree or wrapped presents anywhere to be seen.

The sun was low in the sky when Leah asked her father for the time. John checked his wristwatch and said, "Ten 'til five, honey. Do we need to stop and eat? It's getting late."

"Oh, no!" Leah said, then called across the living room. "Artie! It's almost five o'clock! Your date! You need to go!"

Artie Bauer shook his head and smiled. "No, I don't," he said. "I called her an hour ago, and she understands. We can go out some other time. This is more important."

Just then the doorbell rang. John Russo rose from the packed boxes upon which he had been sitting and walked across the living room to the foyer. Opening the front door, he spoke for a moment to the person outside. Then he turned and stepped aside to welcome the visitor in.

"Just to be clear, Arthur," said Julia Safin, "packing boxes is not fun—unless one is packing them to leave Siberia. You still owe me a *fun* date." In the girl's arms was yet another cardboard box, this one filled with cheeseburgers, French fries and soft drinks, enough food for the gathering.

Pushing his walker from the kitchen, Grandpa Bauer took one look at the box's contents and noted, "Well, pretty girl, I can tell you one thing about *that* box. Unpacking *it* is gonna be a lot o' fun. I'm half starved. You're *both* a sight for sore eyes—you *and* that box." He grinned.

Julia smiled back at Grandpa and said, "Hello, Meester Bauer. I am glad to meet you. I understand now why Arthur has such charm."

Standing off to the side, Ty Green nudged Artie and said under his breath, "You know what Jug Johnson would say right now, don't you?" When Artie shook his head, Ty said, "*Yogi Bauer, charming? From her luscious lips to God's ears.* Am I right?"

"Well, I don't know about the *luscious* part," Artie whispered back, his face turning red. He looked at Leah Russo sitting nearby to see if she had heard the exchange.

"Don't worry, buddy," said Ty, giving his best friend a big wink. "You play your cards right, and you will."

Chapter 31

ARBOR HIGH'S HOLIDAY BREAK—its first week, anyway—put all athletics on hold until the Monday after Christmas. There were no practices or games that week, giving players, coaches and fans the freedom to shop for gifts, the chance to celebrate with family and friends, and, for those who had nothing keeping them at home, the opportunity to travel near or far. The Woods and Pressler families, of course, were in Hawaii. The Evanses packed up their camping trailer and motored down the coast to warmer climes, taking Ty Green along against Donnell Evans's better judgment. The Mareceks—Minnie, Wilma and her mother—flew to Spain to spend part of the holiday with their favorite sailor, Capt. Stan Marecek, who granted himself three whole days of shore leave to host them in Seville. Ricardo, Gabby and Ricky Duran stayed busy working on the Bauer farm and volunteering in outreach ministries at their church in Ebenezerville, but they also welcomed Gabby's elderly parents and one of Ricardo's single brothers into their home for the holidays. Artie Bauer didn't want to go anywhere or do anything other than stay on the farm with Grandpa Harry and try to raise his spirits during this first Christmas without Grandma Pearl. That meant Tommy White, too, would be farm bound, until Artie and Grandpa decided to make a daytrip to Capital City and its two state prisons so that Tommy could visit both of his parents.

John, Elizabeth and Leah Russo were the last members of the Barf Table farmily to get down to the business of holiday cheer. Elizabeth never returned to the Arbor Woods house, not even to pack up the rest of her clothes and personal effects. As far as she was concerned, their house was cursed, haunted not only by ghosts of Christmases past but also by her present demons and her fear of the future. After the father and daughter finished cleaning out the house, John turned its sale over to Sandpiper Realty and bought three airline tickets to St. Louis, the nearest big city to where Elizabeth's mother and step-father lived. Leah loved her grandmother, with childhood memories of cross-country treks to Nana and Papa's house, and of the grandparents' visits to Monk's Landing for the occasional holiday and special birthday. But like the Bauers, this was the Russos' first Christmas without a particular loved one who had brought so much joy and pride to the family in times past.

Except for the Russos, everyone was back in Oleander County by the Monday after Christmas. Both of Arbor High's basketball teams were scheduled to participate in big holiday showcases that week—the boys in an actual tournament at Iron Harbor A&M's arena, the girls in two days of doubleheaders at the Mimosa Beach Convention Center. The Arbor High Fighting Bruins were slated for another quad-match all day Wednesday, this time at Saint Corbinian's in Capital City. Tommy White checked with both state prisons to see if either of his parents could attend one of his matches, but his requests for supervised releases were summarily denied.

All of the Arbor High teams resumed practices that Monday to knock off the dust from their off-week before going back into action. Leah, however, didn't set foot back in Oleander County until Tuesday afternoon—the day of the Bruinettes' first doubleheader game—when the commuter jet carrying her and John Russo landed at Iron Harbor International Airport. They had postponed two earlier flights—on Sunday and Monday—as they had tried to talk Elizabeth into returning home with them. She was determined, though, to ring in the New Year with her mother and to be somewhere that "feels like home." John made her promise to fly back home to Oleander County before Leah's school started back, so that the family could find an adequate place to live while their house was on the market.

"Welcome home, stranger," said Nicie Evans, as Leah Russo boarded the activity bus outside the Arbor gym. "Did you miss me out there in the Heartland?"

Leah pushed her bag into the overhead rack and sat down next to Nicie. "Heartland?" Leah said. "My heart is right here—in Monk's Landing, I mean, not on this bus." They laughed.

"Girl," said Nicie, "you should've seen my daddy and Ty Green on our camping trip. You would've thought he was Ty's daddy and not mine. They fished from sunup to sundown. They sat in their beach chairs and told each other stupid jokes and laughed their butts off, and then at night they made Mama and me play cards with them—every night!"

"What kind of cards?" asked Leah. "Go Fish?"

Nicie shook her head. "Real funny," she said, "but that's not the point. They didn't want to do *anything* with us. But on the bright side, Daddy *loves* Ty Green—probably more than I do."

"Well, that's something," said Leah. "I'm not sure my mom will be around long enough to meet anybody I date."

"She's not sick, is she?" Nicie asked. "I thought she was just depressed—unless you mean she might…"

"No, not that," Leah said, though the thought had occurred to her. "It's that she refused to come home with Dad and me. She says she will by the time school starts again, but I think she'll stay right where she is."

"At your grandmother's house?" asked Nicie.

"No," said Leah, "Nana and her husband live in a retirement village, and they can't have company for longer than a few days at a time. We stayed in a nice hotel—it had an indoor pool and everything—and that's where Mom is now."

Nicie laughed. "Shoot," she said, "you should have invited me along. I could've enjoyed that pool. And my daddy wouldn't have missed me one bit, as long as Ty still went camping with them. Mama might have missed me, though. We did a lot of shopping by ourselves."

"Did you have a nice Christmas?" Leah asked. "I mean, the actual day."

Nicie nodded. "Yeah, I guess so," she said. "Ty felt kinda funny about being away from his folks on Christmas Eve, but we came back Christmas Day, and he got to exchange presents with them and all that. How was it with you guys?"

Leah took a few seconds to answer. "We had Christmas at Nana's house," began Leah, "and Mom bought presents for them, even though she doesn't like Nana's new husband all that much." Leah frowned and added, "But she didn't give Dad and me anything, and he didn't want to argue with her about it. So, he and I are gonna celebrate Christmas for ourselves, even if it is a few days late."

"What did your grandma give you?" asked Nicie. "One of mine always gives me a card, with a dollar bill and a stick of gum. She does that for my birthday, too. But I don't mind. She has about fifty grandkids. And my other grandma gives me knee socks or pajamas that are always too small, like I'm still a little girl. But that's okay, too. What about yours?"

Again, Leah was quiet for a moment. "Nana gave me a card, too," said Leah, "but only because she didn't want Mom to see what was in it. She told me not to show it to Mom—that it would upset her."

"What was it?" Nicie asked. "A big check? A hundred dollar bill?"

"I wish," said Leah. "No, it was a reprint she'd had made of an old photo from when I was a baby, and she and Papa—that's my real grandfather—when they came to see me for the first time at the Arbor Woods house."

"But that sounds sweet," Nicie said, "unless just seeing a picture of your house would get your mama upset. Surely not."

Leah shook her head. "No, not seeing the house," she said. "The picture is of Nana and Papa, and of me as a baby just home from the hospital, and I'm being held by my big brother. He looks so proud, but at the same time he's holding me like I'm so fragile—like I might break."

"Oh, my," said Nicie, patting her own heart.

"But that isn't all," Leah continued. "Nana wrote a note on the back of the photo. It said, 'Stay strong, sweet little Leah, for now you have two proud angels watching over you,' and she underlined the word *two*."

Nicie covered her eyes and said, "Now *I'm* gonna cry. That's the sweetest thing I've ever heard." She wiped her cheeks with one palm and then smiled. "You have a good nana, girl."

"I know," said Leah. "I just wish some of the good in her had rubbed off on

Mom."

* * *

The Arbor High boys' basketball team lost in the first round of their single-elimination Christmas tournament on Tuesday afternoon. That freed them up to stay home at the Bears Den to practice every day for the rest of the holiday break, including practice on Friday, New Year's Day, a light workout and film session on Saturday, and an "optional" shoot-around on Sunday afternoon. The boys still weren't thrilled with their new coach, and Jimmy Foxx hadn't learned yet that girls were more team-oriented and easier to coach than boys were. The Bruins were 1-6 going into their conference schedule at the start of the new calendar year.

Coach Joe Carson's Bruinettes started the week with a 3-3 record. After winning both of their doubleheader games—one on Tuesday, the other on Wednesday—the Arbor High girls felt good about the changes that Coach Carson had made in the starting lineup, bringing in big and strong Wilma Marecek at center for timid Ann Marie Childers, and feisty Sandy Cuthbert at point guard for injured captain Mel Grayson. Wilma was a fast learner. Her ability to hold her own in the low post took much of the pressure off Nicie Evans and Jamie Foxx, the team's offensive leaders, as well as off Julia Safin. The new lineup also helped the Harmon twins, who could now rotate at the big forward spot and, along with Ann Marie, spell Wilma when she needed rest. It was a balanced team that would be even better when senior guard Mel Grayson returned to action late in the season. After the holiday doubleheaders, in which the Arbor and Mimosa Beach girls' teams swapped opponents, the Bruinettes ended this stage of their season at 5-3, the Lady Waverunners at 6-2. A noticeable difference, though, was that Arbor won its doubleheader games by wide margins, while Mimosa Beach struggled both nights to beat the same two teams.

At their quad-match in Capital City that Wednesday, the Fighting Bruins made Coach Jug Johnson proud. Ricky "Shooter" Duran remained undefeated at 113 pounds. Artie "Yogi" Bauer again went 2-1 in his three heavyweight bouts. Tommy "The Shark" White managed to score his second official win of the season in the 220-pound division, going 1-2 again for the quad-match. He joked to Ricky and Artie that he needed to switch his nickname to "Buzz," as Bennie Pressler had suggested, so that Tommy could "float like a butterfly and sting like a bee." Little Ricky had no idea what Tommy was talking about, and Artie was much too nice to burst Tommy's bubble. But when Jug Johnson heard Tommy use the line a second time on the bus, he turned around in his front seat and shouted, "Hey, White!" The bus fell silent. "You'd better not be stinging anybody with your fists like Muhammad Ali did," said Jug, "but you can float on the mat all you want, as long as it ain't belly up. Got that—Buzz?"

* * *

The waiter in a crisp, white shirt and black bow tie led John and Leah Russo to their round table brightened by candlelight. He pulled out Leah's chair and helped her slide it back into place, and he laid a sheet of paper on the red-and-white checkered tablecloth before her. Both she and her father carried gift bags that they sat on the tiled floor next to their chairs.

As soon as John sat down across the table from his daughter, the young man handed him a paper and asked, "May I get you both something to drink while you're looking over our specials for tonight?" He also placed two portfolio-like menus on the table. "Of course, you may order off our regular menu, if you wish."

"Yes, tap water, please—with lemon," said John Russo, looking at Leah for her approval. "We're here a day early. I hope one of your specials is a New Year's plate—you know, like brats and sauerkraut, or pork and Hoppin' John and greens."

The waiter nodded curtly. "Yes, sir," he said. "One of our specials tonight and tomorrow is *cotechino* and lentils—for good luck in the New Year, of course. Will that be to your liking? It is very tasty and our most popular New Year's Day dish here at Roberto's Italian Cucina." He smiled. "May I also bring *you*, sir, a wine list?"

"No, no," said John, "that's fine. And, yes, the lentils special sounds great." Again, he looked at his daughter before finalizing the order. "So, yes, we'll both have that," he continued, "but do you, by any chance, still have eggnog—even a small glass for each of us?"

Taking back the sheets of paper and menus, the waiter nodded. "I'll check, sir," he said. "My name is Tony, if you should need anything else—other than the eggnog. Now, please, enjoy your evening with us here at Roberto's." He gave a little bow, turned and left their table.

Leah eyed her father. "*Cotechino?*" she said. "What is that?"

John shrugged. "Some kind of pork," he replied. "Italian sausage, I think—like a German bratwurst or a Polish kielbasa, maybe? Why?"

"I don't eat meat," said Leah. "You know that. And *sausage* is the worst meat of all. It's the dipsy dumpster of meats."

"But it tastes *soooo* good," John said, with a chuckle. "Oh, by the way, that's *Dempster-Dumpster* of meats, not *dipsy dumpster*. You can look it up when we get back home. George Roby Dempster—my hero in business school. He turned trash to cash—just like sausage."

Leah was impressed with her dad's knowledge, but she still turned up her nose. "Well, I'm not gonna eat it," she said. "That Italian name sounds fancy, but it's still just parts of the pig you wouldn't eat any other way—snouts and ears and tails and feet. *Yuck!* But you enjoy your pig. I'll be just fine with the lentils and eggnog."

John surrendered. "Okay, okay," he said, still with a hint of a smile. "I'm sorry I forgot that you're a vegetarian now. You're not *vegan*, though—right? Then you'd be giving me a hard time about ordering eggnog, too. So you don't mind consuming eggs and cream?"

"No, not tonight, anyway," said Leah, though she *was* considering becoming a vegan as one of her New Year's resolutions.

"I'm just glad you're *eating*," John said, no longer smiling. "Your mother and I have been worried about you ever since…"

With her eyes closed, she nodded. "I know," said the girl, opening her eyes but looking away. "You and Mom have a funny way of showing it, though." Her words had no edge to them, because they stated a fact that could be neither denied nor changed.

"I'm sorry we haven't been here for you," said John, his face somber. "I don't like that expression—*being here or there for somebody*—because what the heck does it mean? But in our case, it means exactly that—*being here*, not off somewhere else when you were the one we needed to be taking care of. For as much as I loved Reuben—and *still* love that boy—I forgot that my little girl needed me, too—that you were hurting just as much as we were. Your mom is still struggling with that. I'm giving her time and space to heal, but that can't go on forever."

Through her tears, Leah studied her father across the table as the waiter brought their water glasses and two cups of eggnog. When young Tony had left, Leah reached for her cup and tipped it up to see the contents. "I don't guess he brought us the good stuff, huh?" she said, lifting the cup to her lips but waiting for John to follow suit.

"No, I guess not," he said, holding out his cup to toast the coming year with his daughter. "To the new year: No matter how hard the road ahead is, may we always remember that we're still a family even though we're apart, and never forget that it's okay for us to be happy again." They both took sips from their cups.

"Dad?" said Leah. "Is Mom ever coming back home?"

He shook his head but said, "I don't know, honey. She's really confused—about a lot of things. But I'm not giving up on her, and I'm not giving up on you—on this group of friends you have and on this new life you've started building for yourself. I won't take all that away from you. That wouldn't be fair. I want to be there—be *here*—for you, and when your mother comes to her senses, she will, too."

"So, what are we gonna do, Dad?" Leah asked. "Are we still selling the house? Where are we gonna live?"

John's eyes regained a bit of their old spark. "Your mom said she wouldn't set foot back in our house in Arbor Woods," he said, "but she didn't say anything about a cute little house at River Bend. It's right on the water, with a boat dock and screened-in porch overlooking the river. You and I will be happy as clams there while we wait for Mom to get herself together. It's just down the street from the Mareceks. You'll enjoy living close to Wilma. She's a nice girl."

Even though the thought of moving to River Bend thrilled her, Leah wasn't too sure that living there would pacify Elizabeth Russo. "But it's still in the same county," Leah told her father. "You know what Mom said about that—about wanting to leave Oleander County."

"Don't worry about it," John said. "If she comes back and pitches a fit, I'll take her for a ride in the big fishing boat I'm gonna buy and just dare her not to have fun. All I gotta do is pick out a nice boat and buy us a couple of fishing rods. Maybe we'll go to the spring boat show they have every year down in Mimosa Beach."

At his mention of fishing, Leah perked up. "No," she said, "all you'll need is *one* fishing pole—for Mom." Leah reached down for the gift bag next to her and handed it to her father.

Taking it, John looked confused. "Then what am *I* gonna use when we go fishing?" he asked. He opened the bag, reached inside and took out a black, plastic case that contained an ultra-light rod-and-reel combo. "Oh, my," he said. "Thank you, honey. This will be perfect to use on the dock. Won't that be nice, too—sitting on the dock with my line in the water, watching the sunset together? You *will* come sit with your old man sometimes, won't you?"

"You know I will, Dad," said Leah, eyeing the gift bag that her father had carried into the restaurant. It was much smaller than the one she had just given him. It wasn't large enough to hold an article of clothing or anything too bulky, but the bag could definitely hold a cell phone or Walkman or piece of jewelry. "Is that for me?" she asked, nodding down at the bag.

John smiled. "Yep," he said. "This *is* our Christmas Eve, right? And we're exchanging Christmas presents even though we're a week late." He picked up the bag and handed it to her. "I know you like to read," he said, "but you haven't read *this* book yet." His eyes twinkled when he saw her wince.

Opening the small bag, Leah looked inside and saw a thin, paperback with a plain, white cover. She took out the booklet and studied the three block letters on the cover, and she looked up at her father again with tears in her eyes. "Really, Dad?" she said. "You bought this for me? Isn't it too expensive?"

"Nope," John Russo said, with a grin. "That manual was free. The *laptop computer* that's waiting for you back at the hotel was the really expensive part. I bought you a fax modem for it, too." He reached across the table and took his daughter's thin hand. "You're gonna be a writer, Leah, and you need a writer's tools. I'm so proud of you, honey. But something else to keep in mind—this thing may be called a ThinkPad, but it can't think for you. That part's all up to you."

Chapter 32

FIRST DAYS BACK from long holiday breaks weren't tedious enough, so Principal Jerry Church approved Miss Thelma Hopper's request to hold a winter sports pep rally during the last half of 4th Period that Monday. The Arbor High Pep Band was out of practice from having taken all of the holiday break off, but they managed a recognizable rendition of the school fight song by the fourth time they blasted it from their dark corner of the Bears Den. Led by perky Vicki Duke, the cheerleaders pranced in front of the bleachers and pushed the different grade levels of students to clap and shout as the two basketball squads and the wrestling team entered the gym behind Bruno the Bruin in its brand-new bear costume. Before leaving for Hawaii, Abe Pressler had left word with his secretary for the bear suit to be delivered if it came in before he got back home.

Seated on the floor around the center jump circle, the groups of athletes punched and poked each other and whispered among themselves as Bruno and the cheerleaders did a new dance routine. For as excited as Vicki Duke had been to get that new suit for the school mascot, she was slightly perturbed by the attention Bruno now got from the assembly. Everyone laughed and cheered when Bruno lumbered over to the girls' basketball team and jerked Wilma Marecek up to dance something like the jitterbug. Then Bruno whirled Wilma back toward her spot on the floor and jogged across court to the wrestling team, motioning for Artie Bauer to stand up and dance. The boys in the stands hooted when Bruno grabbed Artie and started dancing something akin to the tango with him. Despite protesting that he had two left feet, Artie played along for a few seconds before trying to pull away.

The crowd booed Artie when he spurned Bruno, and jeered even louder when the bear mascot pretended to break down and cry, rubbing its oven mitt-like paws in its big, cartoon-bear eyes. They cheered when Artie shrugged and shouted, "I'm sorry, Bruno. Do you forgive me?"

Nodding its fuzzy, brown head, the mascot held out its arms and offered the big farm boy a conciliatory bear hug. The crowd chanted, "Bear hug! Bear hug! Bear hug!" until Artie started moving toward Bruno. Leah laughed when she realized that Bennie Pressler—at away games, at least—would now be expected to give bear hugs to Bruins fans and athletes alike. He would have enjoyed hugging and dancing with the cheerleaders, especially the captain, Leah figured, but now he would have to snuggle and boogie with everybody.

Covering the pep rally for the school newspaper, Leah adjusted the camera she held and aimed the lens at Bruno and Artie approaching one another with their arms extended. A trombone in the pep band began playing glissandos, sliding up and back down, like wolf whistles, and then the entire group broke into "Gimme Some Lovin'." The cheerleaders waved their pom-poms high above their heads and danced into a semi-circle behind the mascot and wrestler who were on the verge of embracing. Artie tried to peer into the bear's frozen-open mouth, a narrow gap through which the person wearing the suit could see out. As they hugged, Artie said, "Ty Green, I'm gonna get you for this."

With both arms around the wrestler's shoulders, Bruno grasped Artie so tightly that he was afraid he might lose his balance. The furry mascot then steadied the big boy and pulled him close to shout through the noise, "Arthur, thees is fun, but you still owe me a real date."

Artie's eyes widened, even more so when he spotted his buddy Ty Green standing next to the gym door. "Julia?" croaked Artie, returning her embrace. The crowd roared as Bruno finally released Artie and then led him in doing the Twist to the pep band's strains. Artie laughed and threw up one hand as he danced, holding Julia's paw in the other. This was the photo that made the front page of the school paper.

* * *

By the time Waisin Wednesday rolled around two days later, Arbor High students were ready to rock and roll again because Frankie the cashier hadn't reordered the students' favorite dried fruit. Rumor had it that Principal Church had noticed how peaceful the lunchroom had been on the Wednesday before break, so he had decided that a Hump Day tradition other than throwing sticky raisins was in order. The seniors took a poll and decided to wait and see if a pattern developed on the Wednesday menu each week, or if the administration gave in and let Frankie order more raisins. That day's luncheon plate featured square-sliced pizza, French fries, two shortbread cookies and a scoop of lime sherbet—everything the kids were more likely to eat and less likely to waste. The warm aroma of cheese pizza tempted even vegetarian Leah Russo to put off veganism for another meal, but she hadn't brought any lunch money that day.

That wasn't the only lunchtime change that first Wednesday of the new year. Because the Barf Table was now home to two new members—Wilma Marecek and Julia Safin—the gang decided to rearrange seats, at least until Bennie Pressler and Brett Woods came back to school. If the round table were a clock, the five seniors sat at the bottom of the dial from nine o'clock to three o'clock, with Artie Bauer at six o'clock. The three freshmen sat at the top from ten-thirty to one-thirty, with Tommy White at high noon.

Seated next to the Russian exchange student, Artie tried to think of something intelligent to say. "So, Julia," said Artie, "you really did a good job as Bruno at the pep rally and again last night during the boys' game. Weren't you tired after playing so hard against Solid Rock?"

Julia looked up from her lunch plate and smiled. "Yes, I was very tired," she said, "but I was happy that we had won, and dancing with people as Bruno is great fun. It makes them so very happy. Even *you* smiled when we were dancing, no?"

"No—I mean, *yes*," Artie said, "I did enjoy dancing with you at the pep rally, and I swear, Julia, we *will* go out on that date I owe you."

Wilma Marecek, seated on the other side of Julia, leaned forward. "Hey, Artie, you don't owe me a date, but you do owe me some dances. Remember the luau? I was looking forward to seeing you do the hula, big guy."

Ty Green, at Artie's right elbow, spoke up. "Yeah, Wilma," he said, "all of us were looking forward to seeing that, too. Artie here is good with the hand motions—I mean, he's been milking cows since he was a kid—but his footwork sure does need some polishing. He barely beat that chubby 10th grader from Solid Rock Monday night."

Across the table, Ricky offered his analysis. "That is because Artie had to chase that boy all around the mat," he said. "It was like a foot race."

"But Artie finally wore that boy down and pinned him," said Tommy White at the head of the table, where Leah used to sit. "That's how my guy was, too. He didn't want to tie me up, and I had to go after him."

"And you did a great job," Artie said to Tommy. "Every athlete here at the table ought to be proud of the way they performed the past couple nights. I hope the rest of the week goes just as well against Mimosa Beach." He turned back to question Julia. "That reminds me," he said. "Is everything okay at your house— with the Foxxes?"

"Jamie is not happy that I wish to sit with you all," said Julia. "She says this is the table for losers." She touched Wilma's hand on the tabletop, as her dark eyes moved from Artie to Ty to Nicie. "But that is not how any of you look to me."

Motioning toward the three freshmen, Julia added, "Even these young ones are so very good at what they do—Ricky and Tommy and even Leah, who helps all the athletic teams here at Arbor High School with her writing. She will be a great writer someday."

Nicie was concerned. "So, Jamie and her folks aren't giving you a hard time, are they?" she asked. "Jamie's behaving herself on the basketball court. What about at home?"

Julia shrugged. "I don't know," she said. "Jamie is aware that when basketball season is over, I will be participating in tennis tournaments every weekend throughout the region, and she will be playing on the—what is it called?—the *travel team* that her father will be coaching—that is, if he is not asked to coach the baseball team here."

"Well, that ain't gonna happen," Ty Green blurted.

Nicie nodded and asked, "So, does Coach Foxx yell at home like he does when he's in the gym? That would drive me crazy."

"Yes," Julia said, "he yells at us, but Jamie yells back at both of them—her father and her mother. I never spoke to my parents as she speaks to hers, even when I disagreed with my mother and step-father."

"Remember?" said Nicie. "Your first day at practice, Jamie called Coach Foxx an idiot in front of our whole team. Now, I may have *muttered* stuff like that about him when he coached me at Mimosa Beach, but I never said it right out loud in front of *everybody*. That's just stupid."

"And disrespectful," added Wilma. "Being an officer in the U.S. Navy, my father wouldn't tolerate that kind of behavior from me, much less from anyone on his ship. He's always saying that *respect* is the biggest part of good leadership."

Julia nodded at Wilma. "Your father is right," the Russian girl said, "but Jamie does not respect her father *or* her mother. Coach Foxx thinks that he can force people to respect him by shouting at them. But that is not respect—that is fear. And Meessus Foxx does not tell him to stop. I think she is afraid of him."

Leah had been listening to the conversation, knowing that her own home situation had been dysfunctional but in a different way. "Do you and Mrs. Foxx get along okay?" Leah asked Julia. "She doesn't yell, too, does she?"

"No, she does not," said Julia, "and, yes, she and I are friends. In fact, Meessus Foxx has agreed to accompany me to my tennis tournaments this spring and summer. She will be my *chaperone*, she says—although I do not think I need one." She looked at Artie with amusement. "Do not worry, Arthur," she said, lifting one eyebrow. "She will not chaperone us on our date."

Artie laughed. "Maybe I'm the one who needs the chaperone," he said. The big farm boy cast around the table at his friends. "Anybody want to volunteer? Ty? Wanna help me out?"

Ty Green shook his head. "Nope," he said, "you're on your own, ol' buddy. But we could double-date. This Saturday night, maybe? We could pick you up in the Whale and go to a movie in E-ville." He looked at Nicie, and she nodded.

"I accept—again," said Julia, not giving Artie a chance to back out. Then she turned to him and added, "I am looking forward to seeing your farm, Arthur. When I was a child in Siberia, my father worked on a farm, and he would take me with him some days in the summer when my mother was busy teaching her classes. He worked very, very hard, but he enjoyed growing the crops and bringing them home for us to eat." Then she looked at Ty Green and added, "Like Arthur, my father milked cows. His hands, too, were strong. And he danced with my mother."

That night during her therapy session on the farm, Leah asked Dr. Marecek about her own upbringing and how happy her immigrant parents had been, coming to the United States from Czechoslovakia after the war. Leah asked the therapist what her father and mother were like. Did they love each other and love their children equally—both Capt. Stan Marecek and Dr. Minnie Marecek—or did the parents show any favoritism? Minnie's answers didn't help Leah as much as they might have, because each was prefaced with something like, "They had lived in a much different place and at a much different time."

But Minnie did assure her young client that a strong woman who perseveres can surmount most obstacles placed in her path by any man. "And as for the ones that can't be overcome," Minnie Marecek stated, "I bide my time until I can find a way forward. I don't let *anyone* push me backward."

* * *

That Thursday night's dual-team wrestling match at Mimosa Beach wasn't even close. Ricky Duran remained unbeaten with another quick pin. In his match, Artie Bauer took only two periods to pin the Waverunner heavyweight. And Tommy White won again on points. At this stage of the season, Artie, Ricky and Tommy were three of a half dozen Fighting Bruins who had good chances to do well and qualify for the post-season regional and state championships.

The Arbor High activity bus hit the road for Mimosa Beach again on Friday night, as the girls' and boys' basketball teams faced off against their Waverunners counterparts. The Arbor boys lost again, partly because Coach Jimmy Foxx spent more time before and after his team's game—as well as at halftime—talking to the Mimosa Beach principal and athletic director. From their seats in the visitor stands, Leah Russo, Nicie Evans and Ty Green strained to hear Foxx's conversations, but they couldn't make out enough to figure out what he was up to.

Once late in the boys' game, Coach Foxx gave three shrill whistles in the direction of the Bruins point guard. When the boy didn't respond as Foxx wished, the irritated coach yelled at him to run a particular set play. The point guard promptly threw the ball in the wrong direction and chalked up another Bruins turnover. Foxx immediately called timeout and gave the boy a tongue-lashing in front of the MBHS stands. Even across the court, Leah could hear what Foxx was screaming, as could everyone else in the gym. The frustrated boy shouted back, "I don't understand your whistling, Coach! Or when you yell at me!" Neither did anyone else in the gym.

One reason Coach Foxx felt more pressure to win that night was because the Bruinettes had defeated the Lady Waverunners handily in the evening's first matchup. The Mimosa Beach center, who had dominated Bruinette Ann Marie Childers in their first meeting, learned that she couldn't push big Wilma Marecek around the same way on either end of the court. With some tips from Nicie Evans, Wilma knew how to guard the MBHS big girl and how to push her away from the basket without being whistled for fouls. In turn, the Lady Waverunner tried to hip-check Wilma whenever the two jostled for rebounding position under the boards, but the former Bruins heavyweight wrestler didn't budge like timid Ann Marie had.

Leah had fun keeping score for that game and listening to Coach Joe Carson's chatter on the bench. By the end of the game, he and the subs were laughing about how Wilma was "Mareceking" the Mimosa Beach big girl. Nicie Evans, Jamie Foxx and Julia Safin all scored in double figures. Sandy Cuthbert racked up four steals and a season high thirteen assists at point guard. And tired but happy Wilma Marecek scored five points, all on free throws, pulled down twelve rebounds and blocked three shots. Her presence had made a difference.

After Leah's therapy session on Saturday, the Barf Table gang got together for lunch in their clubhouse on the farm. Minnie Marecek carried sandwiches, chips and drinks to the house for Grandpa Bauer and her to eat while the teenagers spent an hour laughing and talking before going their separate ways for the remainder of the weekend.

"I can't believe how good we played last night," said Nicie, after everyone had sat down at the clubhouse table. "Just think how good—and how deep— we'll be when Mel's able to play." She handed Artie a sandwich. "You should have seen Wilma play," Nicie told Artie. "She was a beast under the basket. Three blocks and a dozen rebounds!"

Wilma laughed. "I know that was meant to be a compliment, Nicie," she said, "but *beast* isn't exactly what I'm shooting for. But, hey, playing next to Julia *is* kind of like we're *Beauty and the Beast*, I guess. It sure did work for us last night."

"I didn't mean it *that* way," said Nicie, giving Wilma's big arm a squeeze. "Julia *is* a pretty girl, though." She turned to Artie again. "Speaking of *Beauty and the Beast*, what are you gonna wear on our double date tonight, Artie?" she asked. "I've told Ty to put on a nice shirt under that old letter jacket he always wears."

Artie unwrapped his sandwich and studied it for a moment. "*Hmmm,*" he said. "I think my nice shirt's clean. I'll check after lunch." Artie took a bite of the sandwich to indicate that he had nothing more to say on the subject.

"Okay, Romeo," said Nicie. "Remember now. Ty will take me home to change, and then we'll go pick up Julia at the Foxxes' house and be back here to get you by five-thirty. That'll get us to E-ville by six to eat and to the movie theater by seven. Do we know what's playing tonight, Ty? Or does it matter?"

With a mouthful of sandwich, Ty shrugged and struggled to swallow without choking. "A lot of good movies," he said finally. "Can't go wrong with anything that's out now—well, except that one about the, uh, well, you know." He changed the subject. "So, why didn't Julia come out here to eat lunch? She's one of us now, isn't she? Or was she just sitting at our table because she likes this big lug."

He jerked his thumb backwards at Artie.

Wilma laughed again. "Well, that's a good enough reason, isn't it?" she said. "That's why I'm here." She looked at Artie and mugged. "Oh, Artie, you're so smart."

"Not feeling the love," Artie said, not entirely sure that Wilma was kidding. He also was surprised to learn that she had such a good memory and good hearing—that she had overheard Leah Russo teasing him about girls before the holiday break.

Wanting to lift weights after lunch, Ty, Ricky and Tommy kept quiet and concentrated on eating their food. Then Tommy looked up and noticed the copied prom photo that Bennie and Leah had framed and hung on the wall near the clubhouse table. "It was the same thing as with *them*," Tommy said, pointing to the group in the picture.

"What do you mean?" asked Artie. "Dating? That was just them going to the prom."

Tommy shook his head. "Remember when you and Grandpa took me to visit my folks in prison before Christmas?" Tommy said. "What I'm talking about has to do with being a part of a group—like us at the Barf Table, or *them* in that picture right there."

Artie frowned. "I still don't understand," he said. "You didn't say anything about this on our way home from Capital City—just that it was weird seeing your mom and dad like that."

"I know," said Tommy, "but the whole thing was kind of overwhelming, and I didn't know how Grandpa would take this part—if it would upset him on the ride home or not."

"What?" Artie asked again.

Tommy glanced around the table, then looked Artie in the eye. "My mom told me about *your* mom," Tommy began. "They were best friends in the 9th grade at Mimosa Beach High, and they started going out with older boys from Ebenezerville every weekend. But Grandpa and your grandma didn't know that, because our mothers would sneak around and say they were staying at each other's house when they were actually partying with my dad and *his* group of friends."

"So what are you saying?" said Artie, frowning even more.

"My mom became part of my dad's group, simply because they were dating," Tommy said. "And *your* mom became part of that group because she was best friends with *my* mom. They *both* got pulled into that mess."

Tommy explained further, "Mom said the three couples who went to the E-ville High prom together—the people in that picture—were part of my dad's gang, except that Mom and Dad were the only real couple standing together in the picture. They didn't want to make Grandpa mad. Mom said Luther—that's what she called Rocket—didn't really date your mother. He dated the girl who's standing with the guy on the far right in the picture. That was how they got your mom and that other guy into the prom—by having them go with Luther and his girl, who were both seniors at the old E-ville High and could take anybody they wanted to take, no matter how old they were."

Leah Russo interjected, "So the pizza guy *never* dated Artie's mom?"

"That's right," said Tommy, "and she hadn't been dating that other guy in the picture, either—the one on the far right. But then Mom told me tha—"

"Hold on," said Artie, lifting his hand to stop Tommy's explanation. "Why would Grandpa get mad about who Mom was standing with? As it was, Grandpa didn't like Luther or Rocket or the pizza guy or whatever his name was. He told me so. Sergeant didn't like him, either."

"Well," said Tommy, "they were together—your mom and Rocket—because he was still in high school. Like I said, he was a senior at E-ville, and your mom was just a 9th grader. But the other guy—who got into the prom with Rocket's girl—he had been out of school for four or five years. He was twenty-three. Your mom was fourteen or fifteen. They knew Grandpa would get mad about her being with somebody that old and that he wouldn't let her out of the house."

"He almost didn't, anyway," said Artie, growing uncomfortable over Tommy's revelation. "So who *is* the older guy—the one on the right?

Tommy looked around the table again, seeing that everyone was waiting for his answer. He had already revealed too much not to tell everything he had learned from his mother in his prison visit. "That's my dad's older brother—my uncle," said Tommy. "His name is P.J. White. He was the supplier for all the parties in Oleander County back then—and I'm not talking about balloons and streamers, if you know what I mean. I've never met him, and I didn't even know he existed until Mom told me who he was."

"Is he in prison now, too?" asked Artie.

"Mom didn't know," Tommy replied, "and when I saw Dad and asked him, he said—and I quote—'Keep your mouth shut about him. It'll get you killed.' He wouldn't say anything else."

Chapter 33

IT WAS A GOOD THING that Sundays were a day of rest in Oleander County. Leah Russo found out Monday at school that Artie Bauer and Ty Green had needed a day off to rest up from their double-date the night before, but not from romantic interactions with Julia Safin and Nicie Evans. Not only did the White Whale run out of gas, the old LTD's fuel line broke and emptied the tank all over the side of the road where Ty had pulled off when he started smelling gasoline and saw the needle on the fuel gauge begin to drop. This happened after the boys had taken home their dates and were driving back up Ebenezerville Road toward the Bauer farm. The pothole that sank the White Whale halfway between Monk's Landing and the farm had been growing deeper and deeper for the past month, but Ty had always been able to avoid it. On Saturday night, however, he had been distracted, Artie said. He shared this with Leah at lunch on Monday before anyone else joined them at the Barf Table.

"I can't believe it," Leah said, with a laugh. "He *really* ran out of gas?"

Artie nodded. "Yeah," he said, "it would have been funny if we hadn't had to walk so far in the dark to get to the farm. It was cold, too."

"So, you called Nicie's dad?" Leah asked. "Did he tow the Whale back to his garage?"

Artie nodded again and said, "Yeah, but me and Ty drove back in Grandpa's pickup and stood there with flashlights in case somebody tossed a cigarette out near the car. It would have gone up like a Roman candle, with all that gas on the ground." He shook his head. "It took Mr. Evans an hour to get there with his tow truck, and he took the Whale back to his garage to fix the fuel line. It must not be fixed yet, because Ty didn't drive to school this morning."

The other seniors—Ty, Nicie, Julia and Wilma Marecek—started to arrive at the table, so Leah and Artie ended their discussion and began greeting their friends.

As she took her seat next to Leah, Wilma smiled at Artie and Ty. "I heard you boys had an interesting date the other night—that you were out really late."

Julia Safin walked up just then and overheard Wilma's remark. "Yes," Julia said, "I have heard of this American tradition of running out of gas—but I thought we girls were supposed to also be in the car." She smiled and batted her dark eyelashes.

Artie laughed and responded, "Yeah, that's what my grandpa said, too. He told Ty and me that we needed some lessons on where and when to go parking— like he was an expert on it. He was just kidding, though, because Grandma wouldn't have stood for that. She was prim and proper, and was proud of being a church-going girl."

At the mention of Artie's grandmother, the others grew quiet, knowing it was good that the big farm boy was finally talking about her openly. "I bet Grandpa was quite a lady's man," said Nicie Evans, "before Miss Pearl settled him down." She looked at Ty and punched his arm. "Some guys," she added, "take longer than others to figure stuff out. But, Ty Green, you're still my man, even though you *don't* know where and when to run out of gas."

Tommy White and Ricky Duran arrived at the Barf Table with their lunch trays. The pair had already been discussing that night's wrestling match at Port Oleander High, and they didn't bother asking about their tablemates' love lives, possibly because Artie had already told them on Sunday how well Saturday's double-date—prior to the pothole incident—had gone.

Nicie told Leah later that Ty and Artie had taken her and Julia to the nice steakhouse in Ebenezerville, and so they had missed the seven o'clock movie at the twin cinemas. While they had waited for the nine o'clock showing to start, they had gotten dessert at the ice-cream parlor in the E-ville shopping center—hot fudge sundaes and hot chocolate to warm the four teens up against the January night's chill.

Leah had only one other question about the date. "Did Artie give Julia a good-night kiss when you guys took her home?" asked Leah in private.

Nicie winked. "He thought really hard about it," she said. "We watched him stand there under the porch light for what seemed like forever, and we thought Julia was gonna give up and grab him before he made his move." She snorted. "Right when he *finally* leaned toward her, the porch light blinked a couple times and then the door opened. Yeah, it was Jamie, and she was laughing at them, like she knew exactly what was going on and what she'd done."

"Artie was probably relieved," said Leah. "He's awfully shy, and Julia is such a pretty girl. I wish I looked like her."

Nicie studied her young friend's face for a moment. "You're a pretty girl, too, Leah," said Nicie. "You always have been, and you always will be. And Artie isn't the only shy person at our table. You're shy, too, just in a different way."

"I know, and I'm working on it," said Leah. "That's why Dr. Marecek gave me Micki to be my horse. She was shy, too—Micki was, I mean. But once we trusted each other, we were okay together. We're best friends now."

Nicie nodded. "And that's how it'll be when you finally meet the right guy," she said. "The movies want you to think it's all about *love*, but it isn't." She winked again. "It's all about trust."

* * *

Monday night's wrestling match at Port Oleander saw the three Barf Table grapplers—Artie Bauer, Ricky Duran and Tommy White—continue their winning ways. On Tuesday night, the Arbor basketball teams also went to Port Oleander. With Wilma Marecek quickly improving in the pivot, the Bruinettes got revenge for their earlier home loss when the Lady Pilots center had been able to push Ann Marie Childers around. The Arbor boys were more competitive this time but still fell short of a road win. From the visitor stands, Leah could tell that Coach Foxx's patience with his Bruins—what little restraint he had left—was wearing thin. She figured it was just a matter of time before he snapped both figuratively and literally, and she hoped no one she liked was standing close to him when his meltdown occurred.

On Thursday night at home, the Arbor wrestling trio got their comeuppance—all three of them. Artie lost again on points to Iron Harbor's answer to Mean Joe Greene. Tommy went up against a different wrestler this time but was still pinned. Little Ricky also wrestled a new man—this one moving down from the next weight division—and lost in the match's third and final overtime because he was unable to "ride out" his larger opponent for thirty seconds. It was Ricky's first loss of the season, and it was against the best team in the conference.

Before Friday's home basketball games against Iron Harbor High, Leah Russo took her spot behind the scorer's table and waited for the Gray Dukes scorekeeper to arrive so that they could copy each other's rosters and starting lineups. Leah missed her buddy, Bennie Pressler, whose family was scheduled to return home Sunday from their month in Hawaii. With her new laptop computer and modem, Leah had logged onto the Barf Table BBS from home for the past two weeks and had sent Bennie Pressler's and Brett Woods's school assignments to them via FidoNet. The two boys had faxed their completed homework to Miss Thelma Hopper's office in the guidance department. Whether her assistant, Vicki Duke, had maintained any contact with either boy or not no longer worried Leah. She decided that once Bennie got back home, Brett could get Vicki to start calling him again every weekday and get all his assignments from her. During his absence, Brett hadn't stayed in touch with Leah, except through Bennie's regular email messages that kept her abreast of the two boys' adventures in paradise. Bennie had said nothing, though, about the prom picture of Artie Bauer's mother and Tommy White's parents that he had copied and taken to show to Brett's father, Woody Woods. Even when Leah asked Bennie about it point blank in one of her messages, he ignored her inquiry in his next note.

To Leah's annoyance, Principal Jerry Church had filled in for Bennie as the Bears Den scoreboard operator and its public address announcer at home basketball games and wrestling matches. She would have preferred having her friend Bennie sitting beside her; however, being so close to the principal for so many hours gave each one a better understanding of the other's mannerisms, if nothing else. Also, Mr. Church let it slip that he didn't particularly enjoy sitting beside Mrs. Foxx as she kept score during the boys' game. As Leah was leaving between games once, she had off-handedly told the principal to "have fun tonight," and he had rolled his eyes and muttered, "Yeah, right." Leah was positive that Mrs. Foxx hadn't heard his response simply because she hadn't arrived yet, but Coach Foxx had been seated nearby on the Bruins bench while the boys warmed up on the court. Maybe Jerry Church didn't mind sitting with Mrs. Foxx as much as he minded watching her husband mishandle the boys' team.

But Bennie Pressler would be back in his seat at the Bears Den scorer's table for the non-conference home game the next Tuesday against Oakmont Prep. The following Friday he would debut on the road at Pinecrest Christian Academy as Bruno the Dancing Bear. It was a volunteer assignment that Julia Safin had been fulfilling at boys' home games since the new mascot costume had arrived at the start of the year. Everyone loved her as Bruno—or maybe it was just a nicer-smelling Bruno that they loved—but Leah was looking forward to seeing how well Bennie handled this challenge of performing with the cheerleaders and, specifically, interacting with head cheerleader Vicki Duke. Leah wondered if Bennie would flirt with Vicki behind his old friend Brett's back, or if Bennie would be the dutiful wingman and clear the way for his buddy's approach and landing at the Valentine's Dance the next month.

When Bruno finally emerged from the girls' locker room between the Iron Harbor twin-bill that Friday night, Leah could tell that the dancing bear was in the best of moods, and rightly so. The Arbor Bruinettes had beaten the Iron Harbor Lady Gray Dukes going away, thanks to center Wilma Marecek's tough play but also because forward Julia Safin had played her best game of the season on both offense and defense. As usual, Nicie Evans and Jamie Foxx had led the way in the point totals, but on this night Julia Safin had turned in a complete game with sixteen points, twelve rebounds and ten assists—a "triple double" that earned her a post-game interview with the Iron Harbor TV sports reporter. The interview had delayed her change into Bruno, but it was a welcome interruption.

When Julia eventually danced onto the court as Bruno, Leah called across the floor to her, "Hey, Ju—I mean, hey, Bruno!" Leah waved her Russian friend over to the scorer's table, where Leah was picking up her things and preparing to leave. "You were great tonight!" said Leah. "I wish Artie could've stayed, but he said to tell you he had to hurry on home to help his grandfather with something."

"Is Meester Bauer all right?" said Julia from inside the mascot head. Leah thought she sounded concerned, as there could be no discernible change in the bear's sewn-on expression.

"Yes, he's okay," Leah said. "Artie is running interference for his granddad. I don't know what you call that in Russia, but basically he's making sure Mr. Bauer doesn't have to be alone with this church lady who has the hots for him."

"For Arthur?" asked Julia. Rather than let fans see her standing still in the bear suit, she started dancing in place—an action that confused but amused Leah.

"No," Leah said, with a giggle. "His grandpa. When I was there Wednesday night for my equine therapy—you know what that is, right?—my *horse* therapy, this old floozy drove up in her brown car and headed straight for the back door. She had on so much perfume and powder, we could smell her all the way out at the barn. Artie ran as fast as he could back to the house, but she walked on in, anyway, and woke Mr. Bauer up. He was asleep in his room and didn't know what was happening for a few minutes. She was lucky he didn't go for his shotgun."

Julia switched to a slow soft-shoe dance, a difficult step with floppy bear feet. "So, did thees woman move in with the Bauers?" she asked. "Why did Arthur go home tonight?"

Leah laughed again. "He ran the old woman off Wednesday night," she said, "but you know how nice Artie is. He can't be mean to anybody. The old lady told them she'd be coming back tonight with supper for them. But Artie's granddad doesn't like pushy women—even if they *can* cook—and right now he isn't in the market for *any* old woman. That's what Artie told me."

"I see," said Julia, halting her dance for the moment. "Meester Bauer is still married in his heart." She held up a mitton-like paw and said, "I will call Arthur tonight when I get home. Thank you, Leah, for giving me his message. Goodbye."

She danced toward the line of cheerleaders in front of the home stands.

Leah left the gym shortly after her talk with Julia and not a minute too soon. She heard later that Coach Foxx had gotten into a row with his wife at the scorer's table. He was angry with her for being late to the game, even though she had a good excuse—getting stuck in traffic behind a wreck on Ebenezerville Road. Principal Church had stepped into the argument in Mrs. Foxx's defense—a decision that made the situation worse, because Jimmy Foxx had responded by telling his boss to "mind your own business, pal."

"What happens in this gymnasium *is* my business, Coach," the principal had said, "and I'll thank you to focus on coaching your team tonight, because I'm also responsible for ensuring that we field the best athletic program possible on behalf of our parents, athletes and students."

Final score: Iron Harbor 102, Arbor 48. Coach Foxx had no post-game comments for the Iron Harbor TV sports reporter—not that any were requested.

* * *

"Thanks for calling me last night," Leah said to Nicie Saturday afternoon on the farm. "I was gonna watch the late sports to see Julia's interview, but they wouldn't have shown *that part* of the excitement—you know, the Foxx family feuding in front of Lurch Church."

Leah and Nicie had been cleaning the gang's clubhouse and weight room since Leah's therapy session that morning followed by lunch. The other teenagers had either gone home or were watching pro football playoff games that afternoon with Grandpa Bauer in the farmhouse. Wilma and Minnie Marecek were still there—on their own side of the office trailer—but they were busy with housekeeping duties themselves. Leah would wait and leave the farm that afternoon when Wilma and Minnie did, as the Mareceks were giving her a ride back to River Bend, where Leah and her father were now leasing a new house. Leah's mother, Elizabeth Russo, had not returned to Oleander County by the time classes had started back earlier that month as she'd promised. Instead, she was still staying near her parents in the St. Louis area.

"How's your daddy taking all the excitement in *your* family?" asked Nicie.

"Did he talk to your mama this week?"

Leah shook her head. "No," she said. "Dad's trying to give her the space she wants—or that's what she *says* she wants, anyway. But he needs to call her tonight or tomorrow, because she's really running up our credit card bill, Dad says. That hotel she's staying in is expensive."

"Is he gonna tell her to come home?" asked Nicie.

Leah was quiet for a moment. "I don't know," she said. "I *think* he's gonna tell her that she *should* come home—that we're in a new place and that it's really nice, being on the river and all. But I don't think he can *make* her do anything—not right now, anyway."

"He can cancel her credit card," Nicie said. "That's one thing he can do. Then she'd have to make a decision—either come home where she doesn't have to work, or stay there and get a job to support herself. She can't move in with your grandmother, can she?"

"No," said Leah, "because they live in that retirement village, remember? Besides, Nana told Dad the other night that Mom is mad at *her* now. She tried to convince Mom to come back here, and Mom said she wasn't ready yet—or at least that's what Nana told Dad. He's had to talk to Nana a couple of times since we moved, because Mom hasn't been returning his calls."

"That's too bad," Nicie said. "I sure am glad my folks get along. Just look at all the family problems that our little group has to deal with—you and your folks, Julia and the Foxxes, Artie and his real parents, wherever they are, and Tommy's folks in prison. Wilma doesn't even have a normal kind of home life—not with her daddy stationed on a boat halfway around the world. I feel sorry for kids whose parents aren't around to be a part of their lives."

Leah frowned. "Yeah, well," she said, "my family's problem is that one *kid* isn't around anymore to be a part of his *parents'* lives—and *I'm* not special enough to make up for him being gone. I mean, Dad and I are finally getting close again—like he really does care about me—and that makes me feel better, but Mom's drifting farther and farther away from *both* of us." She was quiet for a second. "I hope Dad's able to talk to her tonight—I hope she takes his call—because tomorrow would be the absolute *worst* day to argue with her about coming back home—back to Monk's Landing, that is."

"Why?" asked Nicie. "Why's tomorrow so bad?"

The pained look on Leah's face was enough to break Nicie's heart, but Leah held back her own tears long enough to tell her friend the sad reason. "Tomorrow is a year since Reuben's wreck," Leah said, avoiding the word *death*. "I dread tomorrow. But I'm glad it's a Sunday, not a school day. Dad and I can stay home. I don't want to be anywhere near the high school and that intersection. I don't want to go out, not unless we go over there to sit with him—you know, Dad and me together. Mom should be here, too—of all people—but that's on her."

Nicie studied her friend's face. "Your mama will come around," she said. "She'll get her stuff together and be back here before long, because you *are* special, little girl. You're gonna make your mama and daddy awful proud before you're done, and it won't be how anyone else would do it. You're gonna make them proud like only *you* can."

"Thanks, Nicie," said Leah, "but I think you're giving Mom a little too much credit. She's messed up and won't let anyone help her."

"At least you still have a mother," Nicie said. "Look at Artie. He's never known his mama, just his grandma—and now he and Grandpa have lost her. And Tommy's mother is in prison for the next how many years? Your mama could be in worse shape."

"She's in prison, too," said Leah about her own mother. "She built it herself, and now she doesn't care if she ever gets out."

Chapter 34

MEATLESS MONDAY'S MAIN EVENT was the return of freshman funnyman Bennie Pressler, even though the Arbor wrestling team would be going up against cross-county rival Solid Rock that night—never a laughing matter. After their month away, Bennie and his parents had flown into Iron Harbor International Airport late Sunday and had driven home to Sandpiper Beach too late to get foster son Tommy White from the Bauer farm. Bennie had phoned Leah Russo from the airport to let her know they had landed safely, but he didn't say much else except that he would see everyone Monday at lunch—that he'd be coming to school late "with a big surprise."

As usual, Leah was the first member of the gang to take her seat at the Barf Table. All five seniors arrived soon thereafter, with Tommy White and Ricky Duran creeping forward at the back of the lunch line. On this chilly January day, the tomato soup was hot and good, and the grilled-cheese sandwiches warmed students' bellies with a favorite comfort food, giving them no incentive to do anything but eat their lunches.

"Where's Bennie?" Nicie Evans asked Leah Russo. "I figured him and his walker would be in front of Tommy and Ricky over there in line."

"He called me last night," replied Leah, "and said he'd be here for lunch, but that he'd be late. I don't know why—except that their flight didn't get in until about nine o'clock."

Nicie raised her eyebrows. "Sleeping in, huh?" she said. "Didn't I tell you that boy would change after spending a month in Hawaii? I bet he thinks he's too good to sit with us now."

Artie Bauer heard Nicie's remark and looked around the table. "Hey, guys," he said, "we need to round up another chair and make room for Bennie. We don't want him to think that *we* replaced *him*. And we'll have to do the same next month when Brett gets back."

"Well, we'll see," Nicie said to Artie. She turned back to Leah. "Hey, girl," she said, "are you feeling okay today? I thought about calling you yesterday to see if you wanted me to come get you. But I remembered that you and your daddy had something to do. Did that go okay?"

Leah nodded as she scooted her chair to one side, to make room for another seat at the table. "It went all right," said Leah, "considering…." She opened her ever-present paperback and reached into the pocket of her Arbor Bruins hoodie for a packet of saltines.

Bennie Pressler still hadn't arrived by the time all eight teenagers were seated and most had finished their lunches. As usual on a match day, the three Fighting Bruins—Artie, Ricky and Tommy—discussed their opponents for that night's dual-team match against Solid Rock. Ricky, in particular, was anxious to get back out on the mat, to make up for his close loss the previous week against Iron Harbor High. In fact, Artie said something to that effect—about Ricky "getting himself back into the win column"—and the little wrestler loudly declared, "Win column, nothing. I'm getting back into the *pin* column tonight."

"Just make sure *you're* not the one who gets pinned, little man," said Bennie Pressler, as he gingerly approached the Barf Table from the service area. He carried before him a lunch tray covered with eight small nut cans with plastic tops.

Artie greeted their friend. "Where'd *you* come from?" Artie said happily. "And you aren't using the walker now! Nothing at all! That's great!"

Bennie beamed as he leaned between Leah and Tommy to set the tray down. "I came in the back door," he said. "Frankie let me in and let me grab this tray. These are macadamia nuts. From Hawaii. One for everybody."

"Wow, thanks," said Ty Green. "You even have the right number for our new members. Let me go grab another chair."

Bennie waved him off. "No, that's okay," he said. "I can get it myself. But I need to hurry before the bell rings." Still walking as if he were a bit unsteady, Bennie eased himself over to the vacant faculty table near the cashier's stand, looked to Frankie for his approval, and slid a chair back to the spot that Leah had cleared for him.

Wilma, having helped with Bennie's therapy on the farm, was overjoyed. "I'm so proud of you, buddy," she said. "I never expected this."

"Oh, calm down, Wilma," said Bennie, with a straight face. "It's just a can of macadamia nuts." He winked at her and added, "No, I'm kidding. I know what you mean. I wanted this to be a little surprise, like at Thanksgiving—except now it's me walking without any help at all."

"How'd you do it?" asked Ty. "Weight training? Water therapy?"

Bennie nodded. "A little bit of both, I guess," he said. "I didn't do much surfing, though—couldn't stand up on the board. But Dad rented me a surfski to paddle around on—you know, like on *Magnum, P.I.* Brett helped me lift weights when he had time. He's lifting, too, because he wants to be ready for football next year."

Though she was glad to see her friend, Leah was confused about one thing. "So, how'd you know about Wilma and Julia?" said Leah. "I haven't told you about them joining us here at the table." Leah watched Bennie squirm in his seat. But then the release bell rang, giving him a few more minutes to come up with an explanation.

When the din of the upperclassmen returning their lunch trays and leaving the cafeteria finally faded, Bennie decided to tell his friends the truth. "Look, I talked to Vicki Duke on Friday morning," he said. "She didn't call *me*. I called *her*—well, I called Miss Hopper, actually, to make sure all my teachers know I'm back as of today."

"So, how did the Barf Table come up?" asked Leah. "Is Icky Vicki trying to convince you to sit somewhere else?" She shot Nicie Evans a "you-told-me-so" look.

"No," said Bennie. "As a matter of fact, Vicki was telling me about the great job that Julia is doing as Bruno at the boys' home games, and she mentioned that Julia and Wilma are sitting here now—also, that Wilma is doing great on the girls' basketball team. She figured I'd want to know that as, uh, as *The Voice of Arbor High*—that's what *she* called me. But I knew she was just buttering me up. That's the way she is, even though she's still stuck on Brett."

Julia spoke up. "Did Vicki remind you about the game this Friday?" she asked. "It is an away game, and so you are supposed to be Bruno. I will be sure to deesinfect the bear suit after I wear it tomorrow night. It will be very clean for you to wear."

"I just hope nobody's expecting me to dance like you do," said Bennie, "but maybe you can show me a few easy moves before Friday." He smiled. "Don't worry about cleaning the suit. I'm sure it smells *nothing* like the old one did. When can we get together—for you to help me?"

Tommy White laughed and said, "I know what, Julia. Since I'm moving back in with the Presslers, my shotgun seat in Artie's truck needs to be filled. You can ride out to the farm with Artie and Ricky on Wednesday night after practice, and then you can show Bennie some easy dance steps after his therapy session. You're part of our group now, aren't you?" He glanced over at Artie. "What do you think, big guy?"

Ricky Duran interrupted. "I think that is a great idea!" he said.

"Well, I think…," Artie began, pausing, "that you boys need to let me arrange my own dates." With an embarrassed smile, he turned to Julia and asked. "Would you want to do that? It'll be dark outside, but I can show you around inside the barn and stables, and Grandpa would enjoy seeing you again. We could do that before you teach Bennie … and Leah … and Tommy to dance." He nodded and grinned at his young friends.

"And *you* could learn, too," Julia replied, eliciting giggles from all four freshmen, including Ricky Duran, the dancing machine. Julia continued, "I seem to remember something about your footwork, Arthur—that it needs to be polished. Then you will be able to dance with both Wilma and me on Valentine's Day. You do owe her a dance, do you not?"

Wilma smiled and reached over to tap Julia's hand on the tabletop. Artie sighed, as if to say he knew when he was licked. "Yeah," Artie said. "I still owe Wilma one." Then he looked at Julia, his girlfriend, in a different light and added, "And maybe I owe you one, too."

Leah could tell from the brief look that Artie and Julia exchanged that his remark hadn't been mean or misunderstood—that the big farm boy was expressing to his persistent Russian friend how much he appreciated her spunk. Leah knew that Artie, for whatever reason, tended to put obstacles in the paths of girls who were interested in him. Like Artie, Leah was glad that Julia was a young woman who was determined to persevere.

* * *

The Arbor High Fighting Bruins lost a close dual-team meet that Monday night at Solid Rock Academy in E-ville, even though Artie Bauer, Ricky Duran and Tommy White tallied wins in their individual matches. At home against Oakmont Prep on Tuesday night, the girls' basketball team once again avenged an earlier loss by defeating the Lady Owls in a close game. The difference was new center Wilma Marecek, who managed to hold her own against Oakmont's big girl. The Arbor girls were now 10-3 on the season. The Arbor boys, however, couldn't take advantage of their home court to turn the season around against Oakmont, despite having PA announcer and scoreboard operator Bennie Pressler back at his usual station. By the start of the fourth quarter, Julia Safin—as Bruno the dancing mascot—got more attention on the hardwood than the Arbor cagers did. Most of the fans that stayed until the final horn did so mainly to watch Bruno's antics with Vicki Duke and the other cheerleaders during timeouts. Bennie's occasional quips over the PA—mostly about Bruno and Vicki's dance moves— also entertained the dwindling crowd.

The boys' season record fell to 1-12 with the loss, and Coach Jimmy Foxx wasn't in the mood for postgame frivolity of any sort, not even from the Arbor cheerleaders or the school's big Teddy bear of a mascot. Foxx knew that Julia, his exchange-student daughter, was the person inside the Bruno suit, but that fact didn't make him any less annoyed right then with this dancing bear for upstaging his luckless Bruins. When Bruno skipped over to console the angry coach as he stomped toward the locker room, Foxx waved the mascot off and shouted, "Not now, Julia. I am not in the mood." He even gave Bruno a small shove to make some space between them. The bear stopped dead in its tracks, hung its head and waved one big paw, as if it might never dance again. Leah Russo and some Arbor fans who were still in the stands saw the exchange and booed the ill-tempered coach.

After team practices on Wednesday, Julia Safin did as she had promised and rode from the high school to the farm with Artie Bauer and Ricky Duran. She had agreed to teach Bennie Pressler some easy dance moves after his and Leah Russo's horse therapy sessions. Julia also intended to let any other Barf Table mates join in the lessons if they wanted. As usual, Tommy White and Wilma Marecek were there to help Dr. Minnie Marecek. Ty Green and Nicie Evans came to watch Julia's dance class and give the hesitant dancers "moral support"—or at least that was what Ty had called it at lunch.

Wearing a white, tennis warm-up suit, Julia stood before her students and demonstrated each move in detail before asking them to attempt it themselves. Wilma, Nicie, Ty and Ricky sat off to one side on seats and weight benches that they had moved to make room for the dance class. They couldn't help but giggle at times. In an assortment of warmup attire—from plain gray sweat suits to designer exercise clothes—Artie, Tommy, Leah and Bennie spread out along the back wall of the weight room and clubhouse area. They tried to imitate their graceful teacher's footwork but, with the exception of Leah, didn't come close. The boys looked like actual dancing bears, even without having to wear furry suits.

"That was very good, Leah," said Julia, about a simple crossover step that the younger girl had completed with ease. "Now, boys, we will try it again. Arthur, do not stand quite so stiffly. Tommy, do not laugh at Arthur. You, too, must move with more grace."

Then Julia looked at shaky Bennie, who would more than likely be expected to perform this move at the Pinecrest games on Friday night. "You are doing quite well, Bennie," said Julia, "but all your movements must be bigger and more noticeable. Do not be afraid of falling. Wilma and Ty will stand with you, in case you lose your balance." Both friends rose to help.

"I forget," Bennie shot back. "Is that bear suit padded? In the seat, at least?"

Julia smiled. "Yes, there is padding," she said, "but you will not need it. Soon you will be able to dance like Baryshnikov or Godunov."

"Yeah, that's all I want to be—good enough," said Bennie. When he saw the Russian girl's brow furrow, he added, "Ha! Gotcha, Julia. I know who Alexander Godunov is—that good-looking, blond-headed guy in all the movies. Mikhail Baryshnikov, too. He's even more famous."

Like a patient teacher, Julia shook her head. "Bennie Pressler, you are a funny boy," she said. "Now, let us continue with the crossover step. Watch as I demonstrate again." For Bennie alone, she showed how to move with bear-like grace and ursine hand gestures.

By the end of Julia's lesson that evening, everyone including Bennie knew that Bruno the mascot wouldn't be tripping the light fantastic on Friday night at Pinecrest. However, this boy who had needed to use a wheelchair and then a walker not that long ago would now be able to stand on two feet like any self-respecting dancing bear, and that his footwork—on this first time out, anyway—would be good enough.

Chapter 35

THE THREE BARF TABLE WRESTLERS had no real trouble winning their matches against Mimosa Beach on Thursday night in the Bears Den. Ricky Duran's match took less than a minute to complete, as he pinned his opponent in short order. There was a long wait through the heavier weight classifications until Tommy White's bout, which the freshman won convincingly on points despite going up against a more experienced junior wrestler. Heavyweight Artie Bauer's match was next—the featured event that everyone wanted to see. Artie's opponent was the previous year's conference champion in the lower weight division in which Tommy was now wrestling. The new Waverunners heavyweight got off to a fast start by shooting for Artie's legs right after the opening whistle, taking him down and almost pinning him. But Artie escaped the lighter boy's hold and went on to wrestle a strong match once he had settled himself down. As Tommy had done, Artie had to wrestle all three periods but won on points.

It was Bennie Pressler's first wrestling match back at the scorer's table operating the scoreboard and public address system next to Leah Russo. As the home team's statistician, Leah kept the official scoresheet that she would fax to the Suncoast Conference office in Iron Harbor the next day—or later that night from home, using her new laptop. She was happy to have her best male friend by her side again after too many home matches with Principal Jerry Church filling in for Bennie. The principal still came to the match; however, he was free to move around the gym and rub elbows with whomever he pleased. Leah noticed that one such person was Coach Jimmy Foxx, who had discussions with Principal Church at least twice that evening.

Leah also saw Foxx bending the Mimosa Beach wrestling coach's ear about something that appeared to be serious right after the dual-team match ended. Neither Leah nor Bennie—when she alerted him—could hear what the two coaches were discussing. Leah knew from her father's account of the incident that the Waverunners wrestling coach had been one of the men with Coach Foxx in the Mimosa Beach hotel bar before Christmas, when they had been bad-mouthing her, Nicie Evans and even the memory of Reuben Russo. In fact, Leah saw Foxx point at Nicie when she and Ty Green hurried down from their seats in the home stands and went to congratulate the Barf Table wrestlers before leaving the gym. Wilma Marecek and Julia Safin were there, too, but stayed in the stands to let the crowd clear before approaching their three favorite grapplers. Also, Julia had to keep one eye on Foxx, who was her ride home.

* * *

On the long ride to Pinecrest that Friday night, Bennie Pressler did his best to entertain the girls' basketball team and cheerleading squad—and to divert attention from the fact that this was his first time on a high school activity bus. At Coach Foxx's insistence, the boys' basketball team took a separate van to Pinecrest Academy later so that the girls' team could leave around halftime of the boys' game in that same smaller vehicle. Principal Church had agreed that there was no point in making the Bruinettes stay until the very end of the boys' game, even though the Bruins were favored to beat Pinecrest again. Their earlier meeting in Monk's Landing had been the Arbor boys' lone victory of the season so far.

"Hey, Julia!" called Bennie, from a back seat. "Bruno and I have enough room back here, if you want to come give us another dancing lesson." The bear costume occupied its own back seat across from Bennie, the only male on the bus besides Coach Joe Carson, who was driving.

Seated midway back next to Jamie Foxx, the exchange student twisted around in her seat to respond. "You will do fine, Bennie," said Julia. "Just remember that Bruno's feet are much beeger than yours. When you do the crossover step, do not hurry. Take your time."

Head cheerleader Vicki Duke spoke up, even though she hadn't been consulted. "Once we get to the gym, you and I can find somewhere private to practice," Vicki said. "I *know* you can do this, Bennie. It'll be so much fun!" She squealed with delight at the prospect of dancing with the wealthiest bear in Oleander County.

Leah, who sat in front of Bennie, turned and rolled her eyes. "Oh, Bennie," said Leah, "you're so lucky to get to dance with Digger Duke. Oh, joy!"

"I'm just glad to be dancing, period," Bennie said. "I hope I don't trip over my own feet—like Julia warned me about—and make a fool of myself. I like making people laugh, but not that way." He reached across the aisle and patted Bruno's huge head. "You're a good boy," he said. "We're gonna have fun tonight, aren't we, boy?" He made the head nod and added, "I'll buy you a hotdog with everything on it as soon as we get to the gym. Good boy."

"You're a mess," Leah said, before turning back around in her seat.

Leah's offhand pronouncement was almost prophetic that night during the second half of the girls' contest. The game itself was never in doubt, with the Bruinettes dominating the action from the opening tipoff. As she'd offered to do, Vicki Duke had practiced with Bennie in a side hallway outside the gym, and she had taken care not to expect him to move as quickly and gracefully as Julia always had in the bear suit. What no one thought to remind Bennie about, though, was to be sure and take care of all his restroom needs *before* he climbed into the suit prior to the girls' game. Why? Because Bruno and the cheerleaders would be performing for fans at halftime and again between the two contests, and removing the bear suit was no easy feat to do alone—not when the wearer was in a hurry, at least.

At the scorer's table, Leah herself was the first to learn about Bruno's plight. Instead of dancing with the Arbor cheerleaders during a third-quarter timeout, Bruno headed straight for Leah. "You gotta help me," said Bennie from inside the mascot's huge head. "Get Mrs. Foxx to keep score for you. She just came in with the team."

Leah looked around and saw Coach Jimmy Foxx and the boys' squad finish entering the gym and head for their visiting locker room. Mrs. Foxx arrived with them, but she walked straight toward the scorer's table to take a seat behind Leah, where the coach's wife would wait for the girls' game to end.

"I'm not gonna ask her to do that," Leah told Bennie. "What's the matter?"

"I've got a problem," he said. "I've gotta *go*."

"Go where?" asked Leah. She noticed that Bruno had kept dancing—shifting his weight from one foot to the other, at least—throughout their exchange.

"To the *bathroom*," Bennie said, "and I can't get out of this suit by myself— not yet, anyway." At that point, he started hopping a bit on one foot, then the other.

"I can't go now," said Leah. "The horn's about to sound. Just go on to the locker room—the *girls'* locker room—and I'll get Mel to come help you. Okay?"

As Bennie hurried off the court as quickly as he could, Leah waved team captain Mel Grayson over and explained the situation. That week Mel's cast had been removed from her left arm, and she had started working toward rejoining the team but wasn't able to play just yet. The senior guard couldn't have known that the first game action she saw would involve wrestling the team mascot out of his bear suit in the girls' locker room. As far as that went, Bennie didn't care which locker room he used, as long as he got out of the suit in time.

Bruno and Mel didn't return to the gym until the final horn sounded and the Bruinettes celebrated another win. When the mascot reached the scorer's table to thank his friend for her help, Bennie wasn't exactly dancing in the bear suit, but he wasn't squirming, either. He waved at fans in the stands and, when he neared the sideline, stooped to pat children on the head before talking with Leah. She finished her work as the girls' statistician and prepared to give her seat to Coach Foxx's wife.

Without looking up, Leah asked, "What took you so long? I was getting worried."

Bruno waved to Mrs. Foxx and then placed his huge paws on each side of his head and shook it. "Bruno sick," said Bennie, in a funny, growling voice. "No more pregame chili dogs for Bruno, kosher or not."

Leah laughed. She reached out and patted Bruno on a furry arm and said, "So, Bruno's a bad boy, huh? Aren't you glad Mel was here, and we didn't have to get Icky Vicki to help. We both know what *she* would've done in the locker room. *Ewww*."

Right then, as the Bruinettes left the floor, the Arbor boys exited their locker room on the other end of the court and began their usual warm-up routine of a four-way passing drill followed by layups and jump shots. Jimmy Foxx stood with his arms crossed at the Arbor baseline as he watched his players, looking confident for a coach whose season record was 1-12. But he knew that his Arbor Bruins could beat these Pinecrest Patriots—or, at least, they had done so in their first meeting of the season. In the throes of their worst season ever, Pinecrest was the only area team that had not yet won a single game.

This year's Pinecrest Patriots were young, short and slow. But on this particular Friday night in their home gym, they could shoot and seemingly not miss, even from three-point range. Before halftime, they led Coach Foxx's snake-bitten Bruins by twenty points. The Arbor squad's showing was so embarrassing that Bruno and the cheerleaders had trouble keeping the visiting fans involved in the game on any level. Many of the Arbor High folks packed up and left before the first half ended.

Coach Joe Carson passed the word among the Bruinettes seated in the visiting stands that they would head for the school van as soon as the first-half horn sounded. Jamie Foxx and Julia Safin had already gone out to wait in the gym lobby, not wanting to witness any more of the boys' massacre. When they'd gotten up, both had flipped up their hoodies. Leah had asked why they were sneaking out, and Jamie had said, "*Sshhh*. We're in enough trouble for such a big win as it is." Julia had agreed and added, "Yes, Meester Foxx is already upset because his boys are playing so badly. But he will take it out on *us*, not on them."

To add insult to injury, a Pinecrest guard tossed in a last-second, half-court bank shot to put the Patriots up by twenty-three at the half. The home fans roared, and the Pinecrest boys shouted, shook their fists, chest-bumped and high-fived each other all the way across the court to the locker room door, as if they'd won the whole game. From the glare that Coach Foxx shot at his wife, the team statistician, he thought the game was over, too. As Leah and the rest of the Bruinettes made their way toward the exit, Leah could tell that Foxx was looking for someone to yell at before having to face his players in the locker room. It was Bennie Pressler's misfortune to be that person, though by mistake.

"Give me the scorebook!" Foxx shouted at his wife. "I'm gonna show those losers exactly how bad they're playing."

Mrs. Foxx jumped up from the bench behind the courtside scorer's table and leaned far forward to hand the spiral-bound notebook off to her fast-approaching husband. As he snatched it away from her and wheeled to catch up with his players, Foxx made the mistake of trying to jog through the crush of fans on their way to the concession stand outside and then through the Arbor cheerleaders and mascot moving into position on-court to perform their visitors' halftime routine. Coach Foxx and Bruno the dancing bear came face to face, though neither knew which way to zig or to zag to get past the other. To be honest, Bruno wasn't dancing, but he appeared to be, at least from where Leah stood, as the standoff— or dance-off—transpired.

Sensing what was about to happen, Leah dropped her things and pulled Wilma Maracek with her toward where Bruno and Foxx faced off near center court. The girls were a second too late. Aggravated by the holdup, Foxx blew his stack and shouted, "Get out of my way!" and gave the mascot a shove to one side. To his credit, Bruno did try to do a crossover step but got those big, bear feet tangled up, and tumbled awkwardly to the hardwood floor. Foxx made no attempt to help Bruno stand, instead snapping, "Get up, Julia. You're not hurt," as he moved away.

Like Leah and Wilma, Mrs. Foxx had seen what was unfolding on the court and had also come running. When she heard her husband yell at the mascot, who was now being assisted by Leah and Wilma, Mrs. Foxx shouted, "Jimmy, you idiot, that's not Julia! That's Bennie Pressler!"

Coach Foxx stopped, turned and looked down at Bruno in time to see Leah and Wilma remove his big mascot head. Bennie appeared to be uninjured, thanks to the bear costume's thick padding, but Leah could tell that the ungainly fall had scared him. She let Wilma take over with Bennie and rose to face Foxx herself.

"Who do you think you are?!" Leah screamed. "Where do you get off pushing *anybody* around—Bennie or Julia or me?! You're nothing but a bully—*and* an idiot!"

Having seen the dustup from the gym door, Coach Carson hurried over and put his hand on Leah's shoulder to calm her. "Get your things," he said in a controlled tone, "and go on out to the van. I'll take care of this." Carson glanced over at Foxx's fuming wife, and he added, "Make that, Ms. Foxx and I will *both* handle it. And Wilma and I will get Bennie here out to the van. He's done for the night."

Leah found out later that Coach Carson dressed down Foxx in front of the fans still on hand in the Pinecrest Christian Academy gym. Though it was only halftime, Carson sent Foxx home with his wife and promised the young coach that the whole mess would be sorted out with Principal Church before noon Monday. Also, Carson switched buses with Frankie Hughes, who had driven the boys' team to Pinecrest because Foxx had been too good to do the driving himself. Having Frankie take the girls and Bennie back to Monk's Landing allowed old Joe Carson to swallow his pride and coach the second half of the boys' game for Foxx—or for whoever would replace the sore-headed loser on Monday. Arbor didn't win the game, but with Carson's level-headed coaching, they rallied to within eight points at the final horn.

When Leah heard the final score, she knew that she had misjudged Joe Carson earlier in the year when she had thought him to be little more than a jaded old teacher and coach. But she realized that his long years of experience in public education and in high school athletics had helped him know when to stand back and when to step up. That night in Pinecrest, Coach Carson had made all the right decisions. He had sent the girls home without him and taken the wheel of the boys' bus. He had declared that Bennie was done for the night. And that weekend, the wily old coach would see to it that Jimmy Foxx was done for the season, if not for the rest of the school year.

* * *

Early that Saturday morning, Nicie Evans's mother rapped on the door to her daughter's bedroom. "Nicie, honey?" said Alicia Evans. "Are you girls awake? Breakfast is ready. I made biscuits. Get 'em while they're hot!"

Behind the locked door, Nicie and Leah Russo shared the double bed. On the carpeted floor in a pair of sleeping bags were Julia Safin and Jamie Foxx.

After the blowup at Pinecrest the previous night, Jamie had waited until her parents were back home and had called to ask her mother for permission to stay at a hotel in Mimosa Beach. Coach Carson was still at Pinecrest Academy with the boys' team, so no one—not even Leah—could get into his office to make phone calls. Jamie had to borrow Bennie Pressler's cell phone. She tried to keep her voice down, but Leah and Nicie, who were waiting with Bennie for his own ride home, couldn't help but overhear Jamie pleading with her mother.

"Oh, come on, Mom," Jamie had said. "You know how he is. He'll take it out on us. It'll just be one night."

At that point, Nicie had stepped in and had invited Jamie and Julia to spend the night at the Evanses' house, even the entire weekend if they wished, an offer that had shocked Jamie—and had stunned Leah as well. Jamie had hesitated to accept at first, but with Julia's prompting, she had relented and gotten her mother's permission.

"Great!" Nicie had said. "Leah can stay, too, and it'll be like a regular sleepover."

The next morning as the four girls took turns in front of the bathroom mirror, the aroma of warm biscuits filled the modest house. "I love the smell of fresh bread in the morning," said Julia Safin. "It is one of my *good* memories of my home in Siberia." She smiled at Nicie.

"Yeah," said Nicie, "Mama's a good cook. She works hard cleaning rooms at the hotel, but she loves to cook for me and Daddy. She takes good care of us."

Julia nodded and turned to Leah. "Maybe Meesus Evans can teach these things to *your* mother," said Julia. "Her cooking has made Nicie so big and strong."

Leah tried to ignore Julia's observation. "Is Mrs. Foxx a good cook?" asked Leah, looking at Julia first, then at Jamie. "Do you get much home cooking? Or do you guys eat out a lot?"

"We don't eat out," said Jamie Foxx, "but we don't get much home cooking, either—not unless *we* do the cooking. Mom and Dad are hardly ever at home when we are."

Nicie asked, "Well, what do you eat, then?"

Jamie looked like she didn't want to say, so Julia answered for her. "We eat food from the freezer," Julia said. "Meesus Foxx calls them *frozen deenners*. They, too, remind me of my childhood in Siberia. *Everything* there was frozen in the winter." She smiled again.

At the breakfast table, Alicia Evans put out a platter of her golden-brown biscuits, two different homemade jams—blackberry and plum—a long stick of softened butter and a bear-shaped squeeze-bottle of honey. There were eggs but no bacon or sausage, because Alicia had remembered that Leah Russo did not eat meat.

As the girls were eating and chatting, Nicie's father strode into the kitchen from the back porch and laid a set of keys on the table next to his daughter. "Sorry we missed your game last night," said Donnell Evans, "but I'm glad I went to the auction and traded for this Wrangler. It's all clean and ready to roll. Now you won't have to try to squeeze everyone into that sportster all weekend when you're running around."

"Thank you, Daddy," said Nicie. "You're the best." She stood and gave him a peck on his unshaven cheek. "I need to run Leah out to the farm to work with her horse," she added. "Jamie and Julia said they'd come along."

"One other thing," Donnell Evans said. "It's gonna be a nice day and warmer than usual tonight, so how about if I clean up the camper, and you guys move your pajama party out there? You can use an electric heater. That way everybody has a real bed. How does that sound?"

"That sounds great!" said Nicie. "We'll build a fire outside the camper and make s'mores. It'll be just like we're on the beach."

Leah thought for a second. "Or how about this?" she began. "We could actually *go* to the beach this afternoon or tomorrow and see if anything's happening there—maybe on the strand at Woody's?" Leah knew Nicie would see that her mention of the oceanfront surf shop and grill was a reference to Brett Woods and his impending return from Hawaii, but she didn't mind.

"Well, sure," said Nicie. "We can do that—now that we've got some wheels that'll carry all four of us." She turned to Julia and asked, "Does Siberia have beaches?"

"Yes, but they, too, are frozen much of the year," Julia said, "and even in summer they do not look like the soft, sandy beaches here in your Oleander County."

Nicie reached for another biscuit and eyed Julia across the table. "You're a tennis player, right?" asked Nicie. "I bet you'd be good at beach volleyball, too. Maybe once basketball season is over and Woody's opens in a few weeks, we can all go over there after school and play some beach volleyball—at least until softball starts. I'm gonna need a new partner this summer."

"No," said Julia, "I will be playing tennis every day, not just three times a week whenever I can, as I do now. And I will be going to tennis tournaments almost every weekend." She turned to Jamie and said for her benefit, "Maybe my sister can be your partner, Nicie. Now that you are friends, maybe you two can be as good together at volleyball as you are at basketball."

Like Leah, Jamie was surprised by Julia's optimism and didn't know how to respond right away. "Well, we aren't exactly *friends*—not yet," said Jamie, her eyes shifting from Julia to Leah, finally settling on Nicie, her former nemesis. "But I'm willing to give it a try. I'm tired of fighting."

Chapter 36

TWO NIGHTS IN A CAMPER TRAILER were exactly what Nicie Evans and Jamie Foxx needed to start building an actual friendship, not just an on-court relationship that had helped push the Arbor High Bruinettes to the top of the Oleander Conference standings. Along with Leah Russo and Julia Safin, the four girls stayed up all Saturday night and then into the wee hours Monday morning, sharing secrets, hopes and fears as close pals do. The breakthrough was when Jamie and Leah realized that their home situations were much the same—with both sets of parents on the verge of breaking up, whether for the short term or for good. Julia had already experienced the loss of both parents—her father dying in Siberia, her mother choosing to stay in Russia with her new husband—and so Julia could offer both younger girls the benefit of her experience. The weekend also helped Nicie see again just how lucky she was to have two loving, hard-working, supportive parents at home. The four girls' closeness carried over into Meatless Monday in the Arbor High cafeteria.

"I'm glad you came over to eat lunch with us, Jamie," said Nicie. "Just sit in one of those three seats right there. The boys can grab another chair from the teachers' table when they get through the lunch line."

Jamie pulled out the chair next to Leah—where Tommy would ordinarily sit—and looked around the table at Nicie, Ty, Artie, Julia and Wilma. "I'm sorry I said this was a table for losers," Jamie told the upperclassmen and Leah. "I hope you guys will forgive me for being such a brat. I guess I take after my dad."

Nicie, who had the most to forgive, smiled as she opened the paper grocery bag that her mother had packed that morning for the four girls and Ty. "Today's lunch is special," Nicie said, as she handed out wrapped sandwiches, "so don't start expecting this every day, Ty Green."

Without unwrapping his sandwich, Ty turned it over and sniffed the oil that had started to soak through the wax paper. "Tuna salad?" he asked. "*Mmm*. Yeah, I could get used to this."

Nicie popped his arm. "Well, tomorrow it's gonna be peanut butter and jelly again," she said, turning from Ty to Leah. "And, little girl, you can just learn to eat fish every now and then. It won't hurt you, and that big ol' tuna fish didn't feel a thing."

Wilma, who had gone through the lunch line, spoke up. "Yeah, Leah," said Wilma, "but if you don't want to be a *pescatarian*—that's basically a vegetarian who eats seafood—I'll be glad to trade you my grilled-cheese sandwich for your tuna salad. I can use the extra protein."

"Pescatarian?" Ty said, unwrapping his sandwich and sniffing it again. "That sounds like some kind of funny religion." He took a bite and chewed happily. After swallowing, he said, "But I'd go to a pescatarian church if all the food tasted like this. *Mm-mm*." He took another big bite.

The three freshmen boys finally got to the table with their food trays and took seats after rounding up another chair for Tommy. There were now ten members of the Barf Table, with only one old table mate missing—Brett Woods, whose first day back would be in exactly three weeks on the Monday after the Valentine's Dance. This particular year, the actual holiday—Valentine's Day—would fall on a Sunday, so the school dance would be held the night before, on Saturday.

As had happened over the weekend with the four girls in the camper, the discussion at the Barf Table on this first day of the week soon turned to who would be going to the Valentine's Dance with whom. Of course, Nicie and Ty were a couple. Julia and Artie had just become one. Wilma now had no date, since Artie—her escort at the December luau—was taken. So that left Bennie, Tommy and Ricky going stag, unless they found girls. Leah and Jamie might also have to attend without dates, if they chose to go at all.

In the privacy of the camper on Sunday night, Leah Russo had confessed to the girls that she wished Brett Woods would dump Vicki Duke and ask Leah to go with him to the dance instead. Jamie Foxx had admitted that she did like someone at Arbor High—an athlete, in fact—but she had refused to reveal a name. In light of the problems involving Jamie's father, the other three girls had decided not to push her. That she had trusted them with that much information was enough. On other topics, Jamie was more forthcoming at lunch on Monday.

"I called Mom this morning at break," said Jamie, "and she told me what's going on with Dad." She had talked to her mother a couple of times over the weekend, but hadn't been able to find out much about her parents' decisions concerning his job and their living arrangements.

Artie offered what he knew. "I was in the guidance office to pick up some college forms," he said, "and I heard Miss Hopper talking to Mr. Church. She asked if he minded coaching the boys' team the rest of the season. He said he'd enjoy doing it, even though it would put a cramp in his real estate work."

Jamie nodded. "Yeah," she said, "Dad was gonna be suspended, anyway, but Mom said he resigned this morning. He's going back to Mimosa Beach High— not as the basketball coach, though. They offered him the baseball coaching job this spring, and he took it."

Artie and Ty exchanged a knowing look, both of them having rightly said there would be no way that Jimmy Foxx would coach baseball at Arbor High as he had wanted to do, at least not while their old coach Jug Johnson was still there. But they hadn't considered facing Foxx on the diamond that spring as the coach of a rival team.

Nicie Evans was concerned about what she was hearing. "I don't like this at all," she said. "We've just started being friends, and now you're leaving—and Julia, too."

"Meesus Foxx said we do not have to leave Arbor High," said Julia Safin. "Isn't that right, Jamie? Isn't that what you told me this morning?"

"Yes," Jamie replied. "Mom said we can stay here until the end of the season, or until the end of the school year, or until I graduate next year—it's whatever *we* want, for a change." She looked around the table and added, "And we want to stay—the rest of the year. *Both* of us do."

Leah thought about her own situation and wondered if Jamie and Julia would have to find a new place to live, at least temporarily. "What about your folks?" Leah asked. "Are they doing okay—I mean, are they getting along after that mess at Pinecrest?" When Jamie didn't answer right away, Leah continued, "Like I told you the other night, I'm sorry I lost my temper, but Coach Foxx could have hurt Bennie really bad, pushing him down like that."

Because he had been at the center of Friday night's halftime altercation, Bennie Pressler had kept quiet until then. "I didn't mean to get in Coach Foxx's way," said Bennie, "but falling like that did scare the pants right off me—if Bruno had been wearing any pants." An odd smile crept across his lips, and he turned to Julia. "By the way," he said to her, "Bruno's suit will be clean as a whistle for you Friday night, inside and out—unless I mess it up tomorrow night in E-ville. My mom took Bruno to the cleaners this morning." He smiled sheepishly and looked away.

Julia's expression didn't change. "I am not worried about Bruno," she said. "I am worried about finding someone to be my tennis chaperone—that is, if Meesus Foxx can no longer do so, as she indicated this morning."

Since Julia had broached the subject, Jamie explained that her father had agreed, at her mother's insistence, to go into marriage counseling and anger-management therapy. "That's not all," Jamie said. "Dad's gonna go into rehab for a few weeks before he starts back to work at the high school—rehab for his drinking, not drugs. He'll be in Mimosa Beach, just not at our house."

"So, what's the problem?" asked Leah. "That sounds like your mom has things under control. Why does Julia need a new chaperone?"

"Because Mom's gonna have to go back to work," said Jamie, "and she'll be busy with all the counseling sessions and other things to get Dad back on his feet. She's gonna start selling real estate again, as soon as she talks to her old broker. It's the same real estate office that Mr. Church has been working for part-time— Sandpiper Realty on the beach."

"Yeah," said Leah, "that place next to Woody's." That reminded her of the one Barf Table mate who was missing. "By the way, I finally got an email from Brett today," she said. "Actually, it came yesterday, but I didn't have my laptop on our big camping trip." She winked at the other three girls who had stayed in the camper at the Evanses' house.

Leah continued, "Brett mentioned the prom picture we found on the farm—you know, the one with Artie's mother and Tommy's parents? But that's all he did—*mention* it. He said his dad clammed up after he saw who was in the picture. Woody told him to mind his own business."

"Well, that gets us nowhere," said Artie, "and my mother's diary was no real help, either. Remember, we found it in the cedar chest with that prom photo? Grandpa read it from cover to cover and didn't find anything about the pizza guy or prom night or anything after that, really. It just made him upset. He said the last thing she wrote in it was something about how much she *loved* drinking 'party juice.' That's what Grandpa called it—*party juice*. None of it made much sense. She was really messed up."

Leah nodded sadly. "I know how that feels," she said. "I might as well go ahead and tell you guys about this." By *guys,* she was referring just to the boys at the table, because she had already told Wilma during Saturday's therapy session and the other girls during their weekend sleepover. "My mom isn't coming back home," Leah said. "She told Dad she wants a divorce. He tried to get her to go into therapy—like your folks, Jamie—but Mom said there wasn't any point in it—that she just doesn't love us anymore." No one said a word.

Leah continued, "And, yeah, when she said she didn't love us, she meant *both* of us."

* * *

Wrestlers Artie Bauer, Tommy White and Ricky Duran were winners again that Monday night at home against Port Oleander. On Tuesday night, Bennie Pressler was back in the Bruno suit at Solid Rock, as the Bruinettes beat the Lady Harvesters for a third time. With Principal Jerry Church as interim coach, the Arbor boys' team didn't win but took the game to overtime and lost by only a point. Likewise, Bennie didn't exactly do the Lindy Hop with the cheerleaders, not even with Vicki Duke, but he did start giving bear hugs to Bruins fans and players alike. His biggest hugs went to Leah Russo, who agreed to replace Mrs. Foxx as the boys' statistician, and to his other Barf Table girlfriends at the game. Artie Bauer and Ty Green didn't object when Bruno grabbed Julia Safin and Nicie Evans during halftime of the boys' contest. Wilma Marecek, Tommy White and Ricky Duran did an impromptu line dance with Bruno—but carefully.

The best news from the girls' game—other than that the victory extended the Bruinettes' ten-game winning streak—was that senior captain Mel Grayson saw a few minutes of action again at point guard after sitting out eleven games with an injury. She had been hurt in the second game of the season at Mimosa Beach High. Against Solid Rock, Mel had subbed in for freshman Sandy Cuthbert, who had grown into a solid if inexperienced floor general. Sandy was fierce on offense and scrappy on defense, but Mel remained an unflappable competitor whose seasoned leadership and court awareness made the Bruinettes that much stronger at either guard position. Coach Joe Carson would have a tough decision to make that Friday night when his girls would face Mimosa Beach for a third time. Would he start Sandy or Mel at point guard?

On Thursday night, the Fighting Bruins went to Iron Harbor to wrestle the Gray Dukes again. This third time was not a charm for Artie as he lost again on points to the Iron Harbor heavyweight, Mean Joe Greene, who remained undefeated on the season. Ricky Duran won his match at 113 pounds, making up for his previous loss against Iron Harbor—his only loss that season. At 220 pounds, Tommy for some reason wrestled with less confidence than he'd been showing and was pinned midway through the second period after falling well behind on points.

At lunch on Friday, Tommy's lackluster performance on the mat was the first thing he wanted to talk about. "Hey, guys," he said, setting his tray on the table and taking his seat, "I'm sorry about last night. I really stunk the place up."

Artie looked up from the coleslaw he was shoveling around with his spork. "You don't have anything to apologize for," said Artie. "You've wrestled better this year against those guys than I have. I don't think I'm ever gonna beat that guy. I mean, he's beaten me sixteen straight times. Jeez."

Bennie laughed. "Sixteen straight times?" he said. "Really? Gee, when you wrestle him in the conference tournament coming up, you need to pin him. Then you stand up and point at him and say, 'Let *that* be a lesson to you. Nobody beats Artie Bauer seventeen straight times'—you know, like that tennis player said to the guy who was always beating him."

"Don't tease Arthur about his wrestling matches," said Julia Safin. "This Louis is the best heavyweight wrestler in the state, but Arthur is good as well. I know how that feels—to play and lose to a champion over and over. It is often that way in tennis—as you said, Bennie. Everyone cannot be the champion."

Nicie Evans piped up. "You're right about that, girl," she said, "and those Waverunner gals from Mimosa Beach are gonna find out tonight what it's like to get beat over and over by us. We may not be the champions yet—conference champions—but we're getting close. One more win, and we'll at least tie for first place, even if Iron Harbor beats us next week. Isn't that right, Jamie?"

"Yeah," said Jamie Foxx, the table newcomer, "but something fishy is going on there—at Mimosa Beach, I mean. Mom has been talking to Dad, and she asked me if Coach Carson has said anything to us about a complaint that's being filed with the conference office. She said she didn't know any details, just that Dad said it was pretty serious. He was laughing about it."

Bennie Pressler blurted, "Well, it *is* Fishy Friday, right?" When Jamie didn't make the connection, Bennie explained, "You said something *fishy* is going on at Mimosa Beach, and today's Fishy Friday. Get it?"

Jamie rolled her eyes. "Whatever," she said. "There's no telling what Mimosa Beach is up to. They can't stand losing, and they'll do whatever it takes to win. I honestly think Dad would be better off not going back there, even though he'll be coaching baseball, not basketball. That place is toxic. I didn't know that until I got away from it."

The others nodded and didn't comment on Jamie's confession. But she wasn't finished. "I just have one question," Jamie continued. "Nicie, do you think Coach Carson will start Mel at point guard tonight instead of Sandy? Or at shooting guard instead of me?"

"He's not gonna sit you down now," Nicie told Jamie. "You've been doing everything you're supposed to do and doing it well. Tonight's not the night to stir things up, and Coach Carson knows that—not against Mimosa Beach. Remember, they beat Iron Harbor Tuesday night, and we had our hands full the first time we played them."

Wilma Marecek and Julia Safin remained silent, neither wanting to speculate about their own chances of losing their starting spots. Nicie put the discussion to rest. "Coach Carson will do the right thing," she said. "He's a good coach, and I remember him saying it isn't who starts the game, it's who finishes it. He got that from some other old coach, and it's true."

Chapter 37

LOOKING MORE THAN CONFIDENT, the Mimosa Beach coach handed that night's starting lineup to his scorekeeper, who, in turn, gave it to Leah Russo for the official home scorebook. Coach Joe Carson had already named his starters, but he lingered near the scorer's table and watched the opposing Lady Waverunners finish their warm-ups in front of him. On the other end of the court, Carson's Bruinettes likewise had spread out and were lofting jump shots and free throws to loosen up, settle their nerves and get used to the far basket from their bench.

"Hey, Mr. Carson," called the young Mimosa Beach coach. "Could we have a word?" He walked to a spot on the painted sideline in front of the scorer's table and stopped, as if he didn't want to enter enemy territory.

"Why, sure, Phil," said Coach Carson, turning away from the court and glancing up at the scoreboard clock. "Better make it quick, though. The horn's gonna sound in a minute."

Behind the scoreboard control panel, Bennie Pressler leaned toward Leah Russo and intoned, "One minute and eight … seven … si—"

"Quiet, Bennie," whispered Leah, cutting him off. "I want to hear." The Mimosa Beach scorekeeper gave them both a superior look, as if she knew what was coming.

"We need to talk about your roster, Coach," said young Phil, seeming to buck himself up to prepare for battle with the older and more experienced coach. "Jimmy Foxx tells me that you have two ineligible players on your team—Donicia Evans and Yuliya Safin."

Carson's eyebrows rose. "The beach volleyball?" he said. "Is that what this is all about? And I guess you're gonna tell me that Julia Safin got paid to play tennis in Russia. Right? Well, we don't have volleyball and tennis teams at Arbor High. Neither does Mimosa Beach. So they can play *basketball* and not worry about amateur or professional status. You need to look it up for yourself before you file any complaints, Philip."

"But Coach Foxx told m—" Phil said, his face beginning to flush in anger.

"Jimmy Foxx is an idiot," said Carson. "Ask anybody. He's just trying to get even with Arbor High for suspending him last week. That mess at Pinecrest was all his fault, and it was *his* decision to quit over the weekend."

"But … but …," Phil sputtered, "but if you go ahead and play those two girls tonight, we'll be playing this game under protest." He didn't look so sure of himself. "If you win, I'll file a formal protest first thing Monday morning, and then we'll see who can play and who can't."

The horn sounded to end warm-ups. As the Mimosa Beach coach turned away to meet his players coming to their bench, Coach Carson called to him, "Well, Philip, you do what you gotta do. But just know that you'll be cutting your nose off to spite your face."

Phil turned and gave Carson an annoyed look. "What?" Phil said. "*My* face?"

Nodding, Coach Carson pointed at the Mimosa Beach center, the team's best player. "You've got one, too," said Carson. "She was Nicie's *partner* all summer long. Didn't Jimmy Foxx tell you that, too?"

The Mimosa Beach coach shook his head again and turned away, muttering to himself as he waved his girls in. They removed their warm-up suits and took their places on the bench. The coach took his big girl aside and exchanged some words. At first, he looked concerned, but then he patted her shoulder and nodded for her to join the other starters.

On the Bruinettes bench, Jamie Foxx mopped her face with a towel and looked up at Coach Carson. "What was that about, Coach?" she asked. "Did my dad have anything to do with what you and Phil were talking about?"

"This isn't the time or the place," said Carson. "We've got a big game to play, girls. And when we win tonight, we're the conference champions. Nobody can take that away from us."

At the scorer's table, Leah Russo leaned toward Bennie Pressler this time and muttered, "He *hopes*. He knows what a jerk Jimmy Foxx is."

Whether he had heard her or not, Carson glanced up at Leah and paused for a second before taking a knee in front of his starters. "Look here, girls," he said finally. "I'm gonna tell you what's up, even though it might upset a couple of you." He looked from one girl to the next. "You ladies might have heard that Mimosa Beach was up to something. Well, I just found out from the coach what it is. They're saying that two of us—Nicie and Julia—aren't eligible to play ball for us tonight because they're professional athletes in other sports—that's beach volleyball and tennis. I looked this stuff up before I ever wrote their names on our eligibility list and turned it in, and we aren't breaking any rules."

The girls' faces all relaxed, and Coach Carson continued, "But you know how some girls talk trash out on the court. Some of those Mimosa Beach girls may call you a cheater, but they don't know any better. They're just repeating what they've been told. And they're wrong." The old coach held out his hand for his players to touch before breaking the huddle. "We're glad to have Mel back," he said, "even though she'll be coming off the bench tonight. All you girls know what to do. Just don't let trash talk take you out of your game. Stay under control."

Upon hearing Carson's remarks, Leah Russo wasn't sure the coach should have told his players about Mimosa Beach's false accusation. But right after the opening tip-off, Leah saw the Mimosa Beach player guarding Nicie Evans—not the big center—mouth the word "cheater" as Nicie took a pass on the wing from Sandy Cuthbert at the point. Nicie gave the defender a head fake and tried to drive past her but tripped and fell when the girl stuck out her leg. Both players tumbled to the floor. Neither was hurt, but Leah knew right away it was going to be a long night.

The nearer official whistled a violation, placing one hand behind his head and pointing at Nicie. He let the whistle drop to his chest and called out, "Charging. Three-zero white." Facing the scorer's table, he repeated the offensive foul call and held up three fingers, then his fist to indicate the number on Nicie's home white jersey. "Charging. Three-zero white."

Nicie started to object, but she looked over at the bench and remembered the coach's admonition. In the home stands, Ty Green and the three Barf Table wrestlers howled at the bad call along with the rest of the Arbor High faithful. "Come on, ref!" shouted Ty. "Get in the game!"

On the ensuing possession, the Lady Waverunners quickly worked the ball down low to their big center. She spun—hooking Wilma Marecek with one arm—and cut under the basket along the baseline. Julia Safin moved over to pick up the center and contest her shot, but the big girl did a twisting, reverse layup and scored without being touched. Another whistle blew, this time for a foul on Julia. The home stands erupted again. Coach Carson got up from the bench and took two steps across the sideline to wave over the referee who had called both fouls. Leah couldn't hear over the din what Carson was saying to the ref, but the coach pointed at the spots on both ends of the court where the two calls had been made and threw his hands in the air to show his exasperation. Leah could, however, hear girls on the Lady Waverunners bench yelling, "Cheaters! Cheaters!" but not about the bogus foul calls. They were aiming their insults at the Arbor starting five, who had gathered for a quick huddle in the free throw lane.

Once players lined up on both sides of the paint for the free throw attempt, the offending official bounced the ball from where he stood on the baseline to the Mimosa Beach center at the top of the key. She caught the ball as she stepped up to the free throw line. She stopped and set her feet, dribbled the ball four times, and hefted it for a second before beginning her motion. Right then, she looked down the lane at Nicie and smirked, then puckered her lips and smacked them at her summertime partner. She lifted the ball over her head and lofted it toward the rim. It dropped through the cords without touching the iron. Mimosa Beach led 3-0.

With no defensive pressure, Sandy Cuthbert dribbled the ball down court and signaled for the Bruinettes to run their zone offense as she crossed the half-court line. As soon as she did so, the Lady Waverunners broke out of their two-one-two zone and matched up in a one-to-one defense, intending to trap if they could catch a Bruinette alone in a corner of the court. The move took Sandy by surprise. She tried to pass to Jamie Foxx on the wing but lost control and ended up throwing the ball away. A Lady Waverunner guard snagged the errant pass and flew up court for an untouched layup. Trailing 5-0, Coach Carson stood as if he were going to call a timeout, but he seemed to change his mind and simply shouted encouragement. "Come on, ladies," he called out. "Shake it off. Settle down."

This time down the court, the Bruinettes were ready for the Lady Waverunners' trapping defense. Sandy got the ball to Nicie, who held the ball high for a second and then snapped it to Julia Safin at the high post. Wilma moved away from the basket toward the opposite wing to set a screen for Jamie, just as Julia pivoted and started down the lane to the basket. Once again, the same referee's whistle stopped the action. "Traveling," the man called, rolling his forearms in front of himself to signal the violation. Tossing the ball to the other official near the sideline for Mimosa Beach's in-bounds pass, the partisan referee pointed at the other end of the floor and shouted, "Blue ball," to announce the change in possession. The home crowd roared in dismay.

"Whoa," said Bennie to Leah, "who ordered takeout?"

"What?" she said, not understanding his question.

"Takeout," he repeated. "Somebody *must* have ordered takeout, because this sure isn't home-cooking. Remember? They got home-cooking at their place at the start of the season. All the calls went their way."

Mimosa Beach brought the ball up-court and scored on a long three-pointer, upping their lead to eight. With the Bruinettes still not on the scoreboard, Coach Carson now called a timeout and waved the girls over to the bench.

"Well, ladies," Carson said, "it looks like we got our work cut out for us tonight. But we've been in worse spots—maybe not lately but back when we didn't know who we were." He looked at them. "We know who we are now. Yes, we do. We're winners, and we aren't gonna let a few bad calls keep us from getting back on track. We're just gonna worry about running our offense and playing tough defense, and we'll be okay." They broke the huddle and returned to the floor.

The Bruinettes got the ball down court, worked it around and managed a clear shot, but Jamie's jumper bounded high off the rim. Both Wilma and Nicie fought with their defenders for rebounding position, and both leapt for the ball at the same time. Nicie had the better angle and snagged the rebound, though she also jostled aside Wilma, her own teammate, as she brought down the ball and turned to make her outlet pass to Julia. The whistle blared again. Another foul on Nicie, the same official reported. He made the appropriate hand signals to the scorer's table.

Leah slapped Bennie's hand down as he started to make a signal of his own. "You can't foul one of your own players!" Bennie shouted, again not over the PA system but loudly enough that everyone nearby heard him—including the crooked official.

The referee looked straight at Bennie and blew another blast on his whistle, then formed a "T" with both hands. "Technical foul on the Arbor High sideline," announced the referee. "The scoreboard operator or PA announcer or whatever he is, is not allowed to disrupt the game by criticizing the officiating. One free throw, possession of the ball, and the Arbor coach must now remain seated for the duration of the game."

Standing with the other official on the opposite end of the court, the Lady Waverunners center stepped up to the free throw line and stripped the net on the technical foul shot, making the score 9-0. She took the ball out on the sideline and found a Mimosa Beach guard breaking to the basket off a high screen. Nicie left her player to help out with the Lady Waverunner who was driving the lane. The Arbor star went up to contest the shot, caught the player's arm and drew her third foul. On the layup, the ball bounced twice on the rim before falling through the basket. The horn sounded, and Mel Grayson was headed toward Nicie before the teams could line up for the free throw.

Leah heard Coach Carson apologize to Nicie for not taking her out of the game earlier when the technical foul was being shot. "I wasn't thinking," Carson told the girl, as she caught the rolled-up towel she was thrown and took a seat beside him. "Good lord, it's not like I turn cartwheels on the sideline—making me stay in my seat. Now they've got *me* flummoxed."

After the MBHS player's free throw made the score 12-0, the Bruinettes pushed the ball down court and managed to get into their offense before a whistle stopped play. This time it was a double-dribble violation on Sandy Cuthbert after she had passed to Mel Grayson on the wing and had taken the return pass. With a defender hanging all over her, Sandy had been forced to pick up her dribble before trying to swing the ball to Jamie Foxx on the opposite wing, and the turnover was an honest one. But the scrappy little freshman didn't hang her head, and Sandy made up for the turnover by intercepting the inbounds pass and streaking to the basket for her team's first points of the night. She was even fouled on the layup, but no whistle was blown. The score: Mimosa Beach 12, Arbor 2.

Bringing the ball back up the court, the Lady Waverunners point guard dribbled in place at the top of the key and looked to both wings before driving to the basket herself. Coming from down low, the Mimosa Beach center moved forward to act as a screen for the point guard. The big girl knocked Sandy Cuthbert to the floor with a moving pick. As she had done before, Julia Safin rotated away from her player to help defend the basket, but she and Wilma Marecek could do little when the point guard flipped the ball out to her unguarded teammate in the corner for a three-point attempt. Julia scrambled to recover. Too far away to reach the shooter in time, the Russian girl jumped straight up to contest the shot. Neither her hands nor her body came close to touching the shooter, whose effort was short and caromed off the rim. But again the bum ref's whistle sounded. No one on the home side—or visiting side—was the least bit surprised when he charged Julia with her second foul and awarded three foul shots to the untouched shooter.

The Arbor crowd went berserk. On their feet, students and adults alike screamed at the bad official. They waved their arms and shook their fists at him. Even fans from Mimosa Beach booed and yelled for that one referee to let the girls play ball—that they didn't want their Lady Waverunners to win the game that way. Ball under one arm, the bad referee conferred with his partner, and then the pair walked together to the scorer's table, where the young Mimosa Beach coach met them. Even though it would have been okay for Coach Carson to rise, he remained seated on the Arbor bench until the officials waved him over. Leah and Bennie could hear every word of the conference.

"What's your problem?" the bad ref asked Carson. "Didn't you see we need to talk?"

"You, sir, told me to stay in my seat for the rest of the game," said Coach Carson. "I was just following your orders, sir." Leah could tell that the coach was peeved, but his voice sounded calm to anyone who didn't know him better.

The uproar from the stands had subsided only a bit, and both officials looked nervous. "I want you to get on the PA," said the bad ref, "and tell your fans to settle down. This is a warning. If they don't get quiet and let us continue the game, I'm going to hit you with another technical. If *that* doesn't shut them up, we can always *call* the game. You'd forfeit to the visiting team."

Carson was taken aback. "Look, pal," he said, "*you're* the one causing this commotion—not my girls, not me and not our fans. I'll make an announcement, but we aren't the only ones yelling at you. Look across the court." He pointed at the Mimosa Beach stands. "They're upset, too. What kind of win would it be for them if you boys don't even let us play?"

The bad ref scoffed. "Let you play?" he said. "You've got two girls who shouldn't even be on the floor tonight." He pointed at Nicie, then at Julia.

"Where'd you get *that* information?" asked Carson. He looked from the one official to the partner, who only shrugged. "Oh, so that's why you're the only one who can't stop blowing your whistle. You know about what Phil, here, and I talked about before the game, and you're taking matters into your own hands."

Rather than back off, the bad ref doubled down. "Yeah, well, you're treading on thin ice, Coach," said the crooked referee. "I could hit you with another technical and send you home for questioning my officiating. So, are you gonna make that PA announcement or not?"

"Yeah, I am," said Carson, already reaching up for the desk mic in front of Bennie on the scorer's table. "But *you* need to know that Mimosa Beach also has a beach volleyball player who took money to play. Isn't that right, Phil?" The other coach shrugged a bit but didn't deny the assertion.

Carson continued, "And you also need to know that I've already looked into this—for both Miss Evans and Miss Safin—and both of these young ladies are amateurs, at least as far as high school basketball is concerned."

"That's neither here nor there," said the referee, growing flustered at the sustained noise level in the gym. "Right now, you need to get on the PA and get your people calmed down."

Carson nodded and took the microphone in one hand, pulling its cord for some slack and pressing down the talk button with his other hand. *"Let me have your attention, please,"* he said evenly. *"Please, folks, quiet down and listen to me now."* He waited for a lull and continued, *"I've been asked to announce that this game will be a forfeit—to Mimosa Beach—if we can't keep the noise to a respectable level."* He waited again and turned to see if the official was satisfied.

There was still an angry shout now and then from the home stands, but most of the fans complied by merely grumbling. *"Thanks, folks,"* Carson said, before sliding the mic back across the table to Bennie.

The old coach indicated he would return to his seat on the bench, but held up to share one last thought with the officials. "Thanks for the warning," he told them. "I think we can finish the game now. But I should warn you that I have two parents who religiously videotape our games for their girls—even though they don't play much." He pointed to the two dads who both sat high in the bleachers but with different angles. Both waved but didn't stop filming the meeting at the scorer's table.

"That happens everywhere now," said the bad ref. "So, what's the warning?"

Coach Carson smiled. "You're right," he said. "This isn't really a warning. I just want you to know that a tape of this whole game is going to the conference office in Iron Harbor first thing Monday morning. I know we can't redo what's already been done. But the rest of this game had better *look* like you're making good calls. We all know what's going on here, and we heard what you said. And we have witnesses." He pointed at Bennie, Leah and the MBHS scorekeeper.

Before turning away, a gleam appeared in the old coach's eyes. "Of course, I can make *another* announcement for you later, if you want," said Carson. "I can tell the folks to be sure *not* to mess with the vehicles parked in the 'Game Officials Only' spaces out back. You let me know if I need to do that, okay?" He didn't see the wide-eyed looks on both men's faces, but Leah and Bennie did.

"Thank you, Bruinettes and Lady Waverunners fans," announced Bennie over the PA. *"That official timeout was brought to you by the colors black and white—with apologies to our friends at* Sesame Street." Instead of raging again, most of the spectators laughed out loud at Bennie's joke. Leah slapped his arm and dared him to say anything else that might stir up the crowd or the forewarned referees.

With Nicie Evans still on the bench, Sara Harmon replaced Julia Safin in the Bruinettes lineup. The teams took their places for the Mimosa Beach player's three free throws on the bogus foul that had caused the lengthy delay. She sank only the first shot to increase the Lady Waverunners' lead to 11. Wilma Marecek pulled down the rebound on the third try and tossed a quick outlet pass to Mel Grayson, who turned and spotted Sandy Cuthbert near the center jump circle and Jamie Foxx streaking toward the basket. The ball sailed well over Sandy's head, but it dropped perfectly in front of Jamie. She caught the ball without breaking stride and took the two long steps to the hoop for an uncontested layup. Mimosa Beach 13, Arbor 4.

Minutes later at the end of the first quarter, Arbor had closed to within five points, trailing 15-10. By halftime, the Bruinettes had pulled to within a single point, with Mimosa Beach leading 25-24. Arbor fans had reason to be optimistic. Wilma was playing her best game of the season against the Lady Waverunners center. At the guard spots, Mel and Sandy complemented each other well, even though neither could score like Nicie. Coach Carson was able to get productive minutes out of both Harmon twins and a quick breather for Wilma out of Anne Marie Childers.

The main reason for Arbor's comeback was the play of Jamie Foxx. She didn't light up the scoreboard with three-pointers or other long-range jumpers, but she did everything a star player should do to lead her team. She took good shots and made more than she missed. She looked for open teammates and gave up the ball so that they could take the higher-percentage shot. She went to the boards when she could and boxed out opposing players. She guarded her girl closely and helped out on defense when a teammate ran into a screen or fell a step behind the player she was guarding. Jamie played as if she had something to prove—and, of course, she did, to her teammates and to her other Barf Table friends.

At halftime, the tired Bruinettes on the court returned to the bench for their warm-up jackets and then headed with their teammates toward the locker room. Leah noticed that Jamie, in particular, seemed to be scanning the visiting bleachers for someone—her parents, Leah assumed. But no adults waved down at the former Mimosa Beach player or shouted to get her attention. Even the MBHS students seemed to ignore her. That might have been because Jamie had become their enemy's best weapon that night. Or maybe it was because Jamie's mom and dad were much like Leah's parents after all—too preoccupied with their own problems to cheer their daughter to victory in her biggest public battle so far.

Chapter 38

TRAILING BY A POINT, the Bruinettes opened the second half with the original starting lineup. Jamie Foxx wasted no time giving Arbor its first lead, as she sank a three-pointer from the wing on her first touch. On their possession, Mimosa Beach tried to work the ball inside to their big center to level the score, but Wilma Marecek knocked the ball away from her so that Nicie Evans could grab it and start a fast break in the other direction. Nicie flipped the ball to Sandy Cuthbert, who drove up the middle of the floor toward the Arbor basket. Jamie and Nicie filled the fast-break lanes on the left and right, looking to see if Sandy would take the ball to the hole herself or dish it off to one teammate or the other.

A single Mimosa Beach player stood between Sandy and the basket. The scrappy Arbor guard waited until the defender committed by moving up and cutting her off. Sandy faked a pass to Nicie and bounced the ball to Jamie on the left. Coming in fast, Jamie took the ball on the run and stepped toward what promised to be an uncontested layup. The lone defender had taken Sandy's fake and moved to the right to block Nicie's path to the hoop. The Mimosa Beach girl planted her feet and braced herself for contact. Unable to hold up or veer away, Nicie slammed into her. They collided and went to the floor in a heap an instant before Jamie left her feet to lay the ball up off the glass and into the basket.

A whistle sounded. The official that had made such bad calls early in the game waved off the basket and called an offensive foul on Nicie—her fourth of the five a high school player was allowed before being disqualified. Jamie threw up her hands in aggravation at the call, and the Arbor crowd followed her lead with jeers aimed at the referee. On the Arbor bench, Coach Carson clapped three times deliberately and nodded. "That was the right call," Carson said, as if to himself, though Leah did hear him. Under the basket, Nicie rose and started to jog back down court, but held up, leaned over and extended her hand to the Lady Waverunner still on the floor. The girl hesitated a second, but with no Mimosa Beach players there, she took Nicie's hand and let her former teammate help her up. The crowd noticed this gesture of sportsmanship. They did not clap, but their boos and catcalls toward the official stopped.

Mel Grayson reported back into the game for Nicie Evans. The teams traded baskets on their next few possessions. Then Julia Safin committed a blocking foul—her third—by keeping her girl from cutting to the basket. Still seated, Coach Carson held his hands palms down in front of himself and patted the air, telling Julia to ease up and try not to pick up a fourth foul. He needed her to stay in the game and help Wilma Marecek with the Mimosa Beach center, since Nicie would be on the bench until midway through the fourth quarter. The third quarter was near its end now, and the Bruinettes couldn't afford to do without two starters for an extended period.

The Arbor girls were tiring—especially Mel, who hadn't played this much in weeks—but they pushed the ball up the floor on every possession when they couldn't run the break. Sandy Cuthbert played the point like a veteran. She penetrated the defense and worked the ball to girls for open shots. On defense, Wilma and Julia, in particular, took a pounding from both of the Mimosa Beach post players, as the Lady Waverunners tried to take advantage of Nicie's absence. Though she was basically a rookie, Wilma had learned to use her size and strength to her advantage. She couldn't shut down the Mimosa Beach center entirely, but she kept her from scoring at will, as the girl was used to doing against weaker opponents. Julia's help in the paint slowed down the MBHS standout further. But that help came at a cost.

Right before the third-quarter horn, Julia picked up her fourth foul. In the huddle on the bench between quarters, Coach Carson laid out his plan. "Okay, ladies," he said, "we're down by three—that's one possession—and we have the ball. Don't feel like you have to get all three points at once. Work the ball around, and look for a good shot, whether it's a two or a three. We have eight minutes to win this thing, and we can use every last second, if we need to."

Kneeling in front of the five who would return to the floor, Carson looked up at them and nodded his head. "We can do this," he said, his head turning to face Sara Harmon. "Young lady, the next four minutes are going to be the *best* four minutes of basketball you've ever played. We need you to give us four minutes of tough defense on Julia's girl. I mean it—play her clean and play her smart, but play her tough. This is your chance to shine, young lady."

He turned to Wilma. "You're playing a heckuva game, gal," he said. "Keep it up. I always hear folks say wrestlers are the best conditioned athletes, and, I swear, I do believe it now, after watching you run up and down the court and fight with that big girl for position under the boards. Leah told me just now that you have three fouls, but don't worry about that. You're doing great."

Carson glanced at the scoreboard clock to see how much time he had left. "One last thing," he said, extending his hand for everyone to touch. "Don't get down on yourself if things don't go our way right off. If we're within three possessions at the four-minute mark when Nicie and Julia get back into the game—that's nine points max—we can still win."

He nodded at Mel, Sandy and Jamie, and continued, "You three know how to handle the ball, and you three can shoot the eyes out of the basket when you need to. Look for good shots, and don't pass 'em up when you get 'em. Now, let's hear it—*team* on three. One, two, three…." The word *team* sounded above the expectant buzz of the Bears Den crowd, as the horn blared and Bennie reset the scoreboard clock for the final eight minutes of play.

* * *

When a whistle stopped the action with 4:03 left in the game, the Lady Waverunners were ahead by seven points—the three possessions that Coach Carson had warned his girls about. He reinserted Nicie and Julia into the lineup, telling the pair to play their games without worrying about the foul situation. "We need to make some stops," he told them. "We can't keep trading baskets with them." He also signaled for his team to begin pressing full-court. Sandy and Jamie positioned themselves up front to press the guards, Nicie and Julia in the middle of the court to pick up the forwards, and Wilma all the way back to guard the Mimosa Beach center. The Bruinettes weren't trying to trap the Lady Waverunners. They were merely picking up their girls one-to-one all over the court.

On that first possession, Sandy Cuthbert was all over the Mimosa Beach ball-handler who took the inbounds pass. The guard panicked and tried to pass the ball to her backcourt partner, but Sandy stuck out her hand and tipped the ball to Jamie, who took it in for a quick score. Mimosa Beach now led by five. The next time down the court, Nicie flashed in front of a Lady Waverunners forward and intercepted another harried pass from the same girl that Sandy was guarding. Nicie snapped the ball ahead to Jamie, who lured the Mimosa Beach defenders to her and then fed Sandy for another layup, cutting Arbor's deficit to three. The Mimosa Beach coach called a timeout so that his team could regroup, with 3:45 on the game clock.

"Here's what they'll probably do," Coach Carson told his girls during the timeout. "They'll let the big girl inbounds the ball, so she can step in and take a return pass, if necessary. Then they can clear everybody out and let her bring the ball up the floor against Wilma—that is, if we stay in man."

"You mean one-to-one, right?" interrupted Nicie, the hint of a smile on her lips.

Carson chuckled and nodded. "Yeah, sorry," he said. "I meant one-to-one. Anyway, we're gonna change things up and do a little trapping. I want Sandy, Jamie and Nicie up front, Julia near center court, and, Wilma, you stay back where you've been. Run this press the way we've practiced it—double-team the girl who takes the inbounds pass. Whichever one of you is free up front, try to cut off the pass to the big girl or to the other guard. Keep double-teaming up to half-court, if you can. Julia, you can poach from midcourt and try to pick off any passes to their forwards, but somebody needs to rotate and cover Julia's area of the court if she leaves to poach. Wilma, you're our last line of defense. Stay put and defend the basket. Everybody understand?"

All five players nodded. The Bruinettes broke the huddle with their "team" chant. Coach Carson looked up at Leah behind the scorer's table. "How many timeouts do we have left?" the coach asked Leah. "Both teams."

"One apiece, Coach," said Leah, after double-checking her scorebook.

Sure enough, the Mimosa Beach big girl stood behind the baseline and waited for the official to hand her the ball to be inbounded. But the Lady Waverunners guards were evenly spaced in the backcourt, and their forwards waited on opposite sides of the mid-court line. No one was back where Wilma stood. They, too, appeared to have guessed what changes their opponents would make after the timeout.

Instead of inbounding the ball to a guard, the Mimosa Beach center faked a pass to the guard on one side and then hit the forward coming toward her on the opposite side. When the Arbor guards and Nicie tried to trap, the forward passed to a guard coming off a screen. The girl with the ball raced down court toward Wilma. Two other Lady Waverunners filled the lanes, with the Bruinettes defenders unable to recover quickly enough. Wilma cut off the ballhandler, who dished to a teammate for the layup. Mimosa Beach 49, Arbor 44.

The clock continued to run, with 3:30 left in the contest. For the first time that night, the Lady Waverunners fell back into a one-three-one zone defense so that they could pressure the point guard and double-team the wings. They were willing to bet that Wilma wasn't enough of an offensive threat to outplay the Mimosa Beach forward whose position near the basket required her to run the baseline from side to side and cover both corners. She was fast, but not fast enough to keep Jamie Foxx from sinking a three-pointer from deep in the right corner. Arbor was now within two points. Less than three minutes remained. Coach Carson called off the full-court press and told the Bruinettes to pick up their girls at half-court.

Ironically, Julia Safin had managed to avoid her fifth personal foul when the Bruinettes had been pressing, but she committed it as soon as Carson ordered the Arbor girls back into a regular one-to-one defense. It was a non-shooting foul, meaning the Lady Waverunners would get no free throws but would retain possession of the ball. Leah was sure that Carson knew Julia had just fouled out; however, he kept his seat without seeming to react. He watched the referee record the foul with the scorekeepers and then be notified that it was Julia's fifth. Then Carson turned to Mel Grayson—a better ball-handler and shooter than Julia's usual sub, Sara Harmon—and conferred with the team captain before she reported into the game. The coach used every second he was allowed to make the substitution, so that his weary girls on the floor could get as much rest as possible without using his last timeout.

Play resumed. The teams traded baskets as the clock ticked down. At the two-minute mark, the Mimosa Beach coach ordered his players to slow down their play on offense and to take only wide-open shots. He wanted to force the Bruinettes guards to foul, and that's what happened—first, a foul by Mel Grayson that used up Arbor's allotment of non-shooting fouls. From then on, every Bruinettes foul would send the affected Lady Waverunner to the "charity stripe" for at least one guaranteed free throw, with a bonus shot for making that first one. Of course, players fouled in the act of shooting got two or even three shots, depending on whether the field goal attempt were from two- or three-point distance.

On the inbounds pass, Sandy Cuthbert shot out her hand to knock the ball away from her player but caught the girl on the arm and was whistled for the infraction. The Mimosa Beach guard went to the line, sank the first shot of the one-and-one, and missed the second shot. Wilma blocked out the big center, and Nicie grabbed the rebound. Nicie flipped an outlet pass to Mel, who passed ahead to Jamie beyond center court. As Jamie dribbled on an angle to the right, Sandy cut down the left side and along the baseline to the right corner, where Jamie hit her with a pass. Nicie ran to the low post on the right side of the paint and turned. She looked for a pass from Sandy but didn't get it because the big Mimosa Beach center had dropped down to cover Nicie, leaving the center of the lane open for the moment.

Trailing the play, Wilma Marecek saw the opening and headed into the paint straight for the basket. Sandy snapped the pass to her a step inside the free-throw line. In a split second, Wilma had to choose either to take the open twelve-foot jumper or to drive closer to the hoop, with the Lady Waverunners scrambling to recover. She decided against the shot and put the ball on the floor—a rookie mistake that allowed the big Mimosa Beach center to reach down and punch the ball away from her. Players dove for the rolling ball, including Mel Grayson, who had been hurt in a similar play in the first Mimosa Beach game. Mel managed to snag the ball and call timeout before an official could say she traveled. She was unhurt this time, and the Arbor girls retained possession of the ball. But they had used their last timeout with :59 on the clock.

On the sideline, Coach Carson called the inbounds play. "I want Nicie taking the ball out," he said. "You other four are in line going away from her, with Mel first, then Wilma, then Sandy, and then Jamie in back. You know how this goes. When Nicie slaps the ball to start the play, everybody except Wilma breaks— Mel toward the basket, Sandy toward the backcourt, and Jamie straight back. Nicie will hit whoever's open. Then she'll head for the basket herself. If we don't get a quick shot, we're in our offense. Remember, we've used all of our timeouts, so do *not* call a timeout for any reason—do *not*."

What the Bruinettes didn't count on was having the big Lady Waverunners center leave Wilma and contest the inbounds pass. Maybe the center's quick reactions—honed on the beach volleyball court—were what gave Nicie the most trouble, or maybe the girl's long wingspan was problem enough. From the scorer's table, it looked to Leah Russo as if the center's long arms were everywhere at the same time, and Leah wished Nicie could simply call a timeout to stop the ref's five-second count on the inbounds pass. However, Leah knew that calling a timeout that the team didn't have would result in a technical foul.

What Nicie chose to do surprised her beach volleyball partner more than anyone else. Rather than heave a pass onto the court out of desperation, Nicie went on the offensive and slung the ball as hard as she could at the big center's knees. It connected with the girl's legs and caromed out of bounds without touching Nicie first. The Mimosa Beach center huffed and shook her head, as if the schoolyard tactic were beneath a player of Nicie's caliber. The referee retrieved the ball and designated a new spot for Nicie to stand. Before he bounced her the ball, Nicie glanced at the Arbor bench and saw Coach Carson holding up two fingers. She turned to her teammates, who were lining up again to start the throw-in, and she called out, "Number two. Number two," and held up two fingers herself. She caught the ball from the ref, slapped it, and raised it over her head with both hands. The Lady Waverunners center didn't jump quite as high in front of Nicie this time.

When Leah saw the coach and then Nicie call the new inbounds play, she knew what to expect. Nicie bent this way and that to find space around the big center's arms. Wilma moved forward to set a screen for Mel, who broke straight toward the basket. Behind them, Sandy also stepped up to set another pick, this one for Jamie, who looped around behind both teammates and scooted down the sideline toward the left corner near the baseline. Wilma turned to face Nicie again, in case the throw-in came her way. Sandy faded toward the backcourt as a last option, if everyone else were covered. When Nicie spotted Jamie break away, she snapped the ball toward the corner and watched Jamie run it down like a soccer player chasing a ball headed out of bounds. Jamie grabbed the ball, squared up to the basket and lofted a high-arcing jumper that snapped the cords and brought the Bears Den crowd to their feet.

The fans roared, then collectively gasped as the referee standing near Nicie held up one arm, not two, and indicated that the goal was only a two-pointer. With :49 left on the clock, Arbor still trailed by a point.

"That was a three, Mr. Ref," said Nicie.

The man shot her an annoyed look. "Her foot was on the line," he said, as he turned to watch Mimosa Beach inbounds the ball under the basket.

With Coach Carson waving them forward, the Bruinettes picked up their girls at three-quarters court but did not try to double-team for fear of leaving someone open. The scoreboard clock ticked off the seconds as the Lady Waverunners dribbled in place and made short passes in the forecourt, forcing the Arbor girls to chase them and waste even more time. At :20 on the clock, Leah saw Coach Carson stand—though he wasn't supposed to—and lift his fingers to his mouth to whistle. His shrill signal alerted Mel and Nicie—his two senior leaders—to look over at him. When they did, they saw him standing with his forearms crossed to make an "X," calling for an intentional foul. They had practiced fouling by reaching for the ball, not by simply shoving the ball handler. That was the difference between sending the fouled player to the line in a one-and-one situation or giving her two guaranteed free throws.

Nicie and Mel both said, "Code red, code red," to their teammates—the verbal signal for an intentional foul. Ideally, a girl with fewer than four fouls—anyone but Nicie—would be the one to make the move on an opposing player to stop the clock. But with :12 left, the ball came to Nicie's girl, who dribbled away from everyone else. Nicie had no choice but to foul her as quickly as she could.

The official who had rung Nicie up with the two questionable fouls early in the game smiled as he pointed at her and turned to the scorer's table. "Personal foul, three-zero, white," he said. "Three-zero, white. One-and-one." Leah made the notation in her scorebook and held up five fingers to indicate that Nicie had fouled out.

When the referee nodded and turned to send Nicie to the bench, Leah looked to her left and was surprised to see Coach Carson standing not with Sara Harmon but with Anne Marie Childers. He talked to Anne Marie and gestured calmly, pointing toward the opponent's goal where the all-important free throws would be shot. A missed first shot and an Arbor rebound would give the Bruinettes eight seconds to get back up the court for a two- or three-point shot, either of which would win the game. The worst-case scenario had Mimosa Beach making both free throws and taking a three-point lead that would require Arbor to answer with a lower-percentage three-point shot to tie. Leah knew that a four-minute overtime period without Nicie and Julia in the lineup would be to the Lady Waverunners' advantage.

As Nicie approached the bench, Carson patted Anne Marie on the back and sent her onto the court. She handed Nicie a fresh towel as they passed one another. Nicie flipped the towel around her own neck in one motion and walked to the end of the bench to sit with Julia. Leah could tell they both were disappointed not to be on the court for the last seconds of the game, but Nicie, in particular, had done what she had to do to help her team. Both girls had played the best games they could have played on that winter night.

Bennie leaned over to Leah and quipped, "What did I tell you about ordering *takeout*? We sure could use some home-cookin' about now."

Leah shook her head. "That was the right call," she said. "I'm just glad he didn't call a technical on Coach Carson for standing up. Then we'd really be sunk. They'd get the foul shots *and* the ball."

The teams lined up for the Mimosa Beach forward's first free-throw attempt in the one-and-one. She dribbled more times than Leah thought necessary—as if the girl were still trying to kill time—before tossing the ball toward the goal. When the spinning ball struck the back of the rim, the players on both sides of the lane pushed and shoved for rebounding position. The two Arbor big girls—Wilma and Anne Marie—had lined up closest to the basket on opposite sides of the paint. Wilma used her strength to turn and push the Lady Waverunners center an extra step away from the backboard. Anne Marie, though, moved too far into the lane and got shoved into Wilma, effectively taking them both out of the play. Anne Marie's player jumped for the rebound as the ball bounced twice and rolled around the rim, but she came down without it when the ball dropped through the basket. Mimosa Beach now led by two, with a bonus free throw coming.

As the players lined up again, Leah saw Wilma wave to catch Anne Marie's attention. The former wrestler cupped her hands around her mouth and said something to her teammate that Leah couldn't make out above the crowd noise. The Arbor cheerleaders kicked their heels against the bleacher where they sat, and the home fans shouted, "Miss it! Miss it!" as the Lady Waverunner caught the bouncing ball from the referee and prepared to take her second shot. Leah saw Anne Marie nod and lean over to ready herself to move, extending her arms wide in front of herself but holding them steady so that the ref couldn't say she was trying to distract the shooter and award her another shot. The ball rose toward the rim. Leah held her breath.

Again, Wilma was able to hold off the Mimosa Beach center. The Lady

Waverunner next to Anne Marie tried to make the same move as before, but Anne Marie found the strength within herself to push back and move her opponent away from the basket. In fact, the Mimosa Beach forward stumbled over her own feet and fell to the floor in front of the shooter, who was moving down the lane to follow her missed shot. The ball clanged off the rim and bounced off the board to the left. Anne Marie, who had been the timid Bruinette, left the floor under control, reached up and grabbed the rebound. Without hesitation, she turned and hit Mel upcourt. The seconds were counting down. Arbor needed a two-pointer to tie, a three-pointer to win.

At :04, Mel Grayson lofted the ball into the air, not toward the basket but toward Jamie Foxx again in the left corner near the baseline. Jamie caught the ball, looked down at her feet, and—with the Mimosa Beach big girl closing in—uncorked another long jumper. Like the whole crowd, Leah rose from her seat when the shot went up. But hearts on the home side fell as the basketball caught iron and bounded high, going up and over the back board and out of bounds. With 1.5 seconds left on the game clock, the crooked referee signaled that the ball belonged to the Lady Waverunners—a call that would effectively end the game.

"Wait! Look!" shouted Bennie, pointing across the court. The other official was blowing his whistle and waving off the bad ref's call. He pointed toward the corner, where on the floor lay the big Mimosa Beach center, with the crumpled body of Jamie Foxx, the shooter, beneath her.

The referee faced the scorer's table and signaled the foul. "Personal foul, number two-three, blue," he said. "Two-three, blue. Three shots." He held up three fingers.

"Did you see that?!" said Bennie.

"No," Leah said, marking the foul in the scorebook. "I was watching the shot to see if it went in. I didn't see the girl foul Jamie."

Bennie shook his head and grinned. "No, not that," he said. "Did you see how our sweet Anne Marie *Mareceked* that girl on the rebound? That was awesome!"

The teams lined up again, this time on the Arbor end of the court. Helped up off the floor by her teammates, a noticeably shaky Jamie took several seconds to clear her head and walk to the free throw line. When she was ready, she nodded to the ref under the basket. He bounced her the ball, and she stood there for several more seconds, focusing her gaze on the front of the rim. Cradling the ball in her left hand, she feigned a practice shot in the air with her empty right hand, then dribbled the ball twice, cocked her right arm and shot. The ball stripped the net. The crowd cheered.

"Two shots," signaled the referee, retrieving the ball and bouncing it back to Jamie. She went through the same routine and swished the second free throw, tying the score. As the good official announced that Jamie had one shot left and as he prepared to return the ball to her, the bad ref's whistle blared.

"Timeout," the bad ref called. "Timeout, blue." He pointed at the Mimosa Beach bench.

Bennie leaned toward Leah again and said, "They're trying to ice her—give her time to think about that last shot."

"Hang on," said Leah. "I've gotta mark this down right." She tallied the timeout and held up her fist to the officials, pointing at one bench and then the other. The good referee came over to the scorer's table to verify that neither team had a timeout left. He notified both benches once they broke their huddles.

Back out on the court, the Arbor girls huddled again at the free-throw line. Leah hadn't listened in on Coach Carson's instructions, so she didn't know what he had told the girls to do in either case—whether Jamie made the shot or missed it. With 1.5 seconds left, Bennie kept quiet so he could watch for when the officials signaled for him to start the clock and then stop it again, if necessary. The home crowd buzzed in anticipation of this third and final shot coming up.

Jamie went through her free-throw routine. She cocked and fired. The ball arched toward the basket, hit the front iron and bounced to the back of the rim, hanging tantalizingly on the flat, orange section of the goal next to the backboard before rolling off to the left. The softness of the shot and the spin that Jamie had put on it held the ball on the rim longer than a less skilled free-throw shooter might have managed. It gave Anne Marie time to lean into her girl and move her too far under the basket for a rebound, and it gave Wilma the time and space to spin around the big center and come in behind Anne Marie.

Wilma jumped as high as she could and reached for the basketball as it fell from the rim. Her fingers tipped the ball up off the glass and into the goal. No whistles sounded to stop the clock after Bennie had started it. Only the wail of the scoreboard horn could be heard above the roar of the Bears Den crowd. The jubilant fans spilled onto the basketball court and surrounded their victorious Bruinettes, champions of the Suncoast Conference.

Chapter 39

THE JUBILATION AT ARBOR HIGH lasted until Monday afternoon when word came down that Mimosa Beach High had, in fact, filed a complaint against Coach Carson and the Bruinettes for having ineligible players on the team's official roster. Lost in the shuffle were the performances of Fighting Bruins Artie Bauer, Tommy White and Ricky Duran at the previous Saturday's conference wrestling tournament at Iron Harbor High. Ricky was the champion of his weight division, while Artie and Tommy were runners-up in theirs. All three boys qualified for the state's regional wrestling tournament, along with the wrestler whom Tommy had replaced in the 220-pound division early in the season. At lunch on Monday, Ricky and the Barf Table Bruinettes serenaded the cafeteria crowd with a passable rendition of "We Are the Champions." Bennie Pressler joked that Ricky and the girls should take their show on the road. He said Artie, Tommy and Ty could be the group's roadies—or groupies, as the case might have been.

Coach Carson explained to the girls at Monday's practice that the conference office had received the complaint first thing that morning from an "unspecified Mimosa Beach official," who Carson assumed was the Lady Waverunners coach. The conference director had conferred by telephone with all five board members—the principals of the five high schools—and had looked at the evidence that Mimosa Beach had presented before making his ruling. He told Carson that the Arbor High girls' basketball team would have to forfeit every game in which Nicie Evans and Julia Safin had played that season. The team's only remedy was for Principal Church to appeal the decision and present convincing evidence to refute Mimosa Beach's complaint. The coach said that he and Church discussed the matter, and that the principal had filed an appeal, as well as counter complaints against Mimosa Beach for the partisan game official's bad calls on Friday night and for the Lady Waverunners playing their big center, Nicie's beach volleyball partner. On the latter complaint, both schools would either be vindicated or punished, Carson said.

Nicie and Julia were forced to sit out Tuesday night's home game against Port Oleander while Arbor's appeal and counter complaints were being weighed by the Suncoast Conference's director and board. Likewise, the Mimosa Beach center was sidelined in the Lady Waverunners' road game at Solid Rock. Arbor beat Port Oleander without difficulty, even with Nicie and Julia in street clothes on the bench. Mimosa Beach, however, dropped their second close contest in a row, as a Solid Rock guard threw up a game-winning buzzer-beater from half court to sink the Lady Waverunners. Those results meant that if the decision against Arbor were reversed, the Bruinettes would win the conference championship outright, and Mimosa Beach would finish no higher than third in the league. But if the decision were upheld, both teams would undoubtedly finish at the bottom of the conference standings and miss out on the state playoffs entirely.

No word came from the conference office until late Friday afternoon, as the Bruinettes prepared to close out the regular season at Iron Harbor, and the Lady Waverunners got set to host Port Oleander in their final conference matchup. In fact, the Arbor girls were in their locker room at Iron Harbor High when the conference director—whose office was in a small building on the same campus—knocked on the door and asked where he could find Coach Carson. Minutes later, Carson himself appeared and relayed the conference's mixed decision.

Nicie Evans and the Mimosa Beach center had been found eligible to play basketball, Carson reported, because board members—that is, the school principals—had agreed that the two players wouldn't be in violation of the amateur-status rule unless they transferred to Iron Harbor High and tried to play volleyball there. The Mimosa Beach principal went along with that interpretation because he wanted his girl back in the lineup for that night's game, Carson added.

The situation with Julia Safin, though, was different. Coach Carson said he was told that something else had come up while investigating the exchange student's case—that her professional or amateur status playing tennis wasn't the only issue. As in Nicie's situation, Julia would not be allowed to play tennis at Iron Harbor High because she had received sponsorships and a modest amount of prize money in Russia. However, there was another concern that might keep her from playing basketball—or any other sport—for Arbor High. Carson said the director had made several official inquiries and was waiting to hear from those parties before making a final decision in Julia's case.

"He refused to tell me what the problem is," Carson told the girls in the locker room. "He says it's complicated and that they have to check on some things that involve other schools, but he wouldn't even say *which* other schools—so your guess is as good as mine." He shrugged.

"Nicie, gal, you can go ahead and suit up once I step back outside," Carson said, "and I'm so sorry, Julia, that you can't play tonight. Maybe this won't be our last game of the season. We'll all do our very best for you, okay?"

Julia nodded and managed a smile. "Maybe I will check with Bennie Pressler," she said, "and ask if he will allow me to be Bruno in his place tonight. Would there be anything wrong with that because I am a *Russian* dancing bear?"

Carson laughed. "Not in my book, young lady," he said. "Matter of fact, you're the best dancing bear I've ever seen—and that includes college and the pros."

The Bruinettes did beat Iron Harbor again that night. Nicie Evans, Wilma Marecek, and Jamie Foxx had wanted to leave after the girls' game with Ty Green, but they decided to stay and support Julia Safin, the best high school mascot in the Suncoast Conference, if not the whole state. With Jimmy and Louise Foxx gone now, Leah Russo kept the Arbor boys' scorebook again, as they lost another close one with Principal Church as interim coach.

* * *

Across town that Friday night in the arena at Iron Harbor A&M, the second round of the regional wrestling tournament was underway. Bennie Pressler had been happy to hand over the Bruno suit to Julia Safin and catch a ride with Ty Green to the university, because he could then attend the wrestling regionals and root for his foster brother, Tommy White. All three Barf Table grapplers were still wrestling—Tommy in the losers' bracket after a narrow loss to a Capital City High wrestler; Artie and Ricky in the winners' bracket after pinning wrestlers from Oakmont Prep and Saint Corbinian's Catholic School. The fourth wrestler representing Arbor High had also lost his first-round match and, like Tommy, could not afford a second loss until the tournament's final round. Only semi-finalists in each weight division would qualify for the state wrestling championships to be held the next weekend at State College in Capital City.

The tournament's Friday night second round was well attended from Monk's Landing. Ty Green and Bennie Pressler were there to cheer their friends on. Harry Bauer—now walking with a cane—rode to the event with Ricardo and Gabby Duran in their van. Harry wanted to see his grandson Artie wrestle, because they both knew these matches could be the last ones of Artie's high school wrestling career. But Grandpa also wanted to be on hand to root for neighbor Ricky and former houseguest Tommy. Abe and Deborah Pressler attended the tournament to watch Tommy, their foster son. And after taking in the girls' basketball game at Iron Harbor High, Dr. Minnie Marecek had convinced niece Wilma to attend the wrestling tourney after all, to support her friends and former teammates. The other girls—including Julia—sent word to Artie, Tommy and Ricky that all three had better win that night, so that the entire Barf Table farmily would be together on Saturday for the tournament's last three rounds.

All three boys did win their second round matches, though Ricky was the only one to win by pin fall. On Saturday morning, Ricky "shot" his way to another quick pin. Tommy continued to advance in the loser's bracket, with an easier than expected match against another precocious 9th-grade wrestler. Artie got a tough third-round draw, but won on points over the Capital City High heavyweight. Coach Jug Johnson came close once to throwing in the towel, so to speak, during Artie's match. Fortunately, old Jug held off, and Artie was able to free himself from the Red Cap wrestler's vise-like hold and untangle his right (throwing) arm from behind his own back. With team points being tallied in the regionals for school recognition, Jug hadn't wanted to lose his heavyweight and the Arbor High baseball team's star catcher in one fell swoop. That thought must have crossed Ty Green's mind, too, as he had been the Bruins' all-conference pitching ace for the past two seasons with best friend Artie as his battery mate.

During Saturday's long lunch break, the Barf Table farmily and friends found a quiet spot in the cavernous arena's stands to eat and talk. The wrestlers were careful about what they ate and drank. Their main concerns were rest and recuperation from the morning session as Artie, for one, looked toward a fourth-round match with the defending state champion, who also was Artie's friend and greatest conference foe, Iron Harbor High's Louis "Mean Joe Greene" Hines.

"What's for lunch?" asked Grandpa Bauer. "I'm half starved after watching Artie wrestle. For some reason, I'm craving one o' them soft pretzels—with lots o' mustard."

Artie chuckled as he took a sip of water. "Thanks, Grandpa," he said. "How about if you don't sit next to Bennie during my match against Louis this afternoon? I have a feeling Bennie's a bad influence on you." Tommy and Ricky agreed the joke sounded like one of Bennie's.

"Hey!" said Bennie. "I'm sitting here, I'm sitting here." He laughed and passed a couple of sandwiches to Leah, who passed them on to Ty and Nicie.

Leah screwed the cap back on her water bottle and set it down. "I wish my dad had come today," she said to the group. "He would have had fun with you guys, like at the luau—well, before we got *the call*."

Both sets of parents—the Presslers and the Durans—and Minnie Marecek were seated together so they could talk. Grandpa had chosen to sit close to the girls in the Barf Table gang, as he had always liked Nicie, Leah and Wilma, and had grown fond of Julia, too, since Artie had been dating her. Grandpa didn't know Jamie Foxx well yet, but he didn't seem to hold the girl's father or her former reputation against her.

Jamie was the one to address Leah's comment. "That man had it coming," Jamie said, "but I hate it happened at your house—him getting shot by the cops. I still miss little Nathan. He was such a sweet little dog." She glared at Bennie and as much as dared him to make a hotdog joke about her dachshund again.

"You're talking about Luther Reep?" asked Grandpa. "You're right. He was a good-for-nothing somebody, going back to the first time I met him. He killed my dog, too, with that dang slingshot of his. I don't know why my Ingrid had anything to do with that crowd. She should've found some friends like all you kids. Maybe me and Pearl should've pushed her to play sports like Artie does. She could hunt and fish, but she wasn't much for playing ball."

Artie sat up straight. "Grandpa!" he said, and nodded toward Tommy sitting nearby. The younger boy had heard the remark about his parents but had stayed quiet.

"I apologize, Tommy," said Harry Bauer. "Sometimes I talk before I think. A person can't help who their parents are or what kind of trouble those parents get themselves into. You don't have nothing to be ashamed of, Tommy. You're a good boy."

"And a *great* wrestler," added Wilma. She reached over and patted him on the back of his warm-up jacket. "I'm glad you came out for the team," she said, with a smile. "Otherwise, I wouldn't have quit wrestling, and I wouldn't have found out how much I like playing basketball. I just hope last night's game wasn't my last one."

At that, Jamie's face flushed. "I'm sorry, you guys," she told her teammates, then turned to her exchange sister. "I haven't even told you about this yet, Julia, but I overheard Mom talking on the phone to Dad last night." She paused. "*He* was the person from Mimosa Beach who filed the complaint about you and Nicie. It's all *his* fault, because he couldn't stand us being so good when his team was so bad. And he doesn't care how it affects me or you, his own daughters."

"I am not his daughter," said Julia Safin, "but you are my sister." She looked at the other girls and added, "You *all* are."

When the wrestling resumed that afternoon, Ricky "Shooter" Duran won his fourth-round match and advanced to that evening's championship bout, which he also won, to the thrill of the group that remained from Arbor High. As expected,

Artie Bauer lost to Louis Hines—Mean Joe Greene—in the fourth round. Artie then defeated the "winner" of the losers' bracket and had the dubious honor of facing Louis once again in the championship final. Completely worn out, Artie wrestled as well as he could but was pinned in the second period by the well-rested champion. Tommy White basically won his losers' bracket, but he was knocked out of the tournament for good when he fell to the semi-finalist who, like Artie, had lost on the winners' side.

On a positive note, Artie and Tommy did qualify along with Ricky for the state wrestling tournament, which would be held the next Thursday, Friday and Saturday. In the photograph that Leah Russo took late that Saturday night for the school newspaper, Coach Jug Johnson appeared to be as pleased as punch that three of the four wrestlers he'd brought to regionals were state qualifiers. The three boys themselves looked like tired puppies, but all three of them managed wide smiles for the camera of their Barf Table friend and favorite sports reporter.

Chapter 40

THE BRUINETTES MET ON MONDAY, not to practice for Wednesday's first round of the state playoffs but for a team meeting after school. Principal Jerry Church was in charge, even though Coach Joe Carson started the locker-room meeting by preparing the girls for bad news.

"First of all, ladies," said Coach Carson, "I'm as proud as I can be of every last one of you. We were undefeated in the conference, and we were 15-3 overall—probably the best girls' season Arbor High's ever had, all things considered. You did the school proud."

Carson studied his shoes, scuffing one toe on the polished gray floor. "Mr. Church has something to tell you," the coach continued, "and it's something that's hard to hear, 'specially at the end of a long season. But we all need to hold our heads high." He stepped aside so that the principal could stand before them.

Jerry Church held a sheaf of papers in one hand. "I received some faxes this afternoon from the conference office," he began, holding up the papers. "Before I tell you what these say, I want to be perfectly clear about one thing: No one in this locker room—and I mean *no one*—is to blame in any way for this situation." He glanced first at Jamie Foxx, then at Julia Safin.

"*The Suncoast Conference director and its board regret to inform you,*" Church read from the top sheet, "*that the official roster of the Arbor Charter High School women's basketball team includes one (1) ineligible player—Russian exchange student Yuliya Safin.*" He paused again to look around the room.

"*The attached documents show,*" Church continued, "*that Miss Safin's official sponsor in America resides solely at a Capital City address, not at a full- or part-time residence in Oleander County. As an official Capital City (Washington County) resident, Miss Safin is and has been ineligible to attend any Oleander County public or private high school; and, therefore, she is and has been ineligible to compete as a member of any athletic team at any Oleander County (i.e., Suncoast Conference) secondary school."*

Principal Church stopped reading again to let the girls digest what they had just heard. *"Consequently,"* he went on, *"the Arbor High Bruinettes do hereby forfeit all eighteen (18) varsity basketball games that the team played this season with Yuliya Safin's name on its official roster and eligibility list that were filed with the conference office. In that light, the Arbor Bruinettes are likewise ineligible to represent the Suncoast Conference in the upcoming state playoffs. These penalties do not extend beyond the current basketball season nor do they affect any other sport at Arbor Charter High School."*

Church shuffled through the sheets and concluded, "Well, girls, that's the most important information in this stack of paper. And, yes, this situation is regrettable, but, again, it isn't Julia's fault. Right, Julia?" He waited for her to nod but didn't ask her to speak. "Joe and I talked to her right after school today, and she said she went where the tennis coach at State College told her to go, and that was to come live with the Foxx family here in Oleander County. I do believe that."

Before giving up the floor, the principal said, "Miss Hopper in guidance is typing up an official letter for me to send home to your parents about this matter. But if any of you have a question right now, I'm happy to answer it—if I know the answer. Anybody?"

Leah Russo stood with her hand up. "Mr. Church," she said. "I'm asking this question as the team's official scorekeeper, but also as the school newspaper's sports reporter." He nodded, and she continued, "Was this information about Julia's official residence and her official sponsor something that either Coach Carson or I should have known? I mean, should we have seen the problem and headed it off? Should we have been better trouble shooters in this case?"

"No," Church said, "everybody here at Arbor High did what they were supposed to do. If you remember, Julia—and Jamie—transferred here when Jamie's father was hired to coach the boys' basketball team. We took his word that everything with the transfer was in order, and Miss Hopper accepted the documents that Coach Foxx brought with him concerning the move here."

Her head down, Jamie Foxx began to sob. One on each side, Julia and Wilma patted her shoulders. Then Julia stood and looked around at her teammates. "I am sorry about this," Julia said. "As Meester Church said, I did not know the rules about special forms or papers. I was told to come here—both to Mimosa Beach and to Arbor High—and I was told that Meester and Meesus Foxx were my sponsors."

She looked down at Jamie and added, "My sister Jamie has come to like this school as I do, and we do not wish to leave, but I may have to now. We shall see. Maybe it is not too late to fill out these special papers. There is so much more that I wish to do here at Arbor and so many people whom I have come to love." She sat back down.

Coach Carson brushed at one eye as if a speck of something had clouded his vision. "I wish we could roll back the clock and do things right," he said, "but it is what it is now, and we all need to move on—although I sure was looking forward to seeing just how far this team could go in the state playoffs."

Nicie had been quiet until then. "So, who gets our playoff spot, Coach?" she asked. "I guess Iron Harbor gets one of the spots. Does Mimosa Beach get the other one?" She frowned.

Carson smiled, now with a twinkle in his eye. "Nope," the coach said. "Jerry didn't tell you *that* part. It seems that Mimosa Beach had Julia on *their* eligibility list, too. Remember, she and Jamie were on their team until right before the first games of the season. That's when they came to us—and, like I said, I'm so happy they came here and let us get to know them."

Nicie shook her head. "I don't understand," she said. "Julia didn't play any games for them. She only played for us."

"That's right," said Carson. "But do you know what? Somebody down there at Mimosa Beach—the same somebody who filed the complaints against us—forgot to tell that new, young coach down there that he needed to redo his eligibility list and send in new paperwork to the conference. Julia and Jamie both were on Mimosa Beach's official roster all season long." He smiled again. "Now, maybe that was an oversight, or maybe it was on purpose, just in case these young ladies didn't like being here and decided to go back."

Leah piped up, "So, Mimosa Beach has to forfeit all their games, too?" When Carson nodded his head, Leah exclaimed, "Whoa! Ain't karma some kind of beast?"

Julia hugged Jamie again and then corrected Leah, the sports reporter. "No, my friend, karma is not a beast," Julia said evenly. "Karma is Bruno the dancing bear."

* * *

The big banner that the Arbor High cheerleaders had made especially for what was now being called *Tough Luck Tuesday* stretched across the back wall of the cafeteria. Hanging above the tray-return window, the banner read: "ARBOR BRUINETTES ARE THE CHAMPIONS OF OUR HEARTS!" in green and gold block letters. The white background was filled with red hearts and the autographs of almost every Arbor student. Miss Thelma Hopper and head cheerleader Vicki Duke had quietly spread the word for kids to come by the guidance office before school and between classes that morning to sign the banner.

In their uniforms, the Arbor cheerleaders stood at spots around the lunchroom and handed out heart-shaped boxes of chocolates and special Valentine's cards to team members as they took their seats. The cards carried encouraging notes and signatures from Principal Church, Miss Hopper and the school's coaches. Scorekeeper Leah Russo and PA announcer Bennie Pressler also received these gifts as tokens of the school's appreciation for the team's great season.

By the time everyone was seated with their lunches, the only team member absent was exchange student Julia Safin. Her empty seat at the Barf Table made all her friends—especially Artie Bauer—feel doubly bad, because they worried that she might have already withdrawn from Arbor in order to transfer to Capital City. In fact, Artie excused himself and left about five minutes before the senior release bell was to ring.

Leah asked Jamie Foxx if she knew where Julia was, and if she had heard any news from her mother about the exchange student's predicament. With red eyes, Jamie shook her head and said they knew nothing official yet. She added, though, that Julia had packed all her clothes and personal effects the night before, and was ready to move wherever she was told to go when the time came.

"She's taking it pretty well," said Jamie, "a lot better than we are—Mom and me, that is. I don't know what Dad thinks about it, and I don't really care. This mess is all his fault."

Leah nodded and—hearing a commotion—looked toward the cafeteria entrance. "Well, now I've seen it all," she said, her face beaming with surprise and delight. "Those two must have been practicing when we weren't around."

Just inside the cafeteria's double doors, Artie Bauer raised his right hand high and then swept it aside to let Bruno the dancing bear twirl beneath and skip away, twirl and skip as they bopped down the aisle toward the Barf Table. When they reached the table, Julia gave big bear hugs to each of her teammates there and waved the others in from their seats elsewhere in the lunchroom. Vicki Duke yelled for her own squad to assemble.

Leah scrambled to grab her camera and move away from the table, as Bruinettes and cheerleaders gathered on the floor beneath the banner. As Leah focused on the group, she felt a hand on her shoulder from behind. Turning, she saw Coach Carson's smile. Carson took the camera from her, waited a moment for Principal Church to catch up, and handed him the device so that Leah could be in the photo with him and the others.

"We need you and Bennie in the picture, too," Carson said, "because we're gonna put this photo in the trophy case. That's where it belongs. I'm as proud of this team as if we won the whole darn shooting match."

Principal Church adjusted the camera lens and tried to focus it. Frowning, he looked up and said, "Sorry, folks. Something isn't quite right." Then he smiled and pointed at Bruno, who was standing in the back at one end. "I need Bruno to move up front with the starters," he said, "and to take off that big old head of hers. It's okay, Julia, you're one of us."

The student body cheered. The cheerleaders waved their pom-poms. And when the principal held up his free hand and counted "one, two, three …," every last Bruinette knew to smile for the camera and say, "Team!"

* * *

Artie Bauer, Tommy White and Ricky Duran were set to leave for Capital City with Coach Jug Johnson after lunch that Wednesday. The coach had reserved a school van since there would be only the four of them on the trip. They had reservations for at least that night at the Collegiate Inn, with the option of extending their stay until Saturday, depending on how well the boys performed in the three-day tournament.

The first round started on Thursday morning at separate venues—State College Coliseum and Varsity Gymnasium. Championship matches in all weight divisions were slated for Saturday evening in the Coliseum. As it had been at regionals, the tournament format was double elimination. That meant a wrestler might be ready to go home at the end of the event's first day if he lost his first two matches—in the first round and again in the opening round of the losers' bracket. But Coach Johnson said that everyone would be staying as long as any one of them was still in contention for a state title.

Still waiting for the return of raisins to the mid-week menu at Arbor High, the student body decided to change that day's name to *Wiener Wednesday* in honor of the three Fighting Bruins on their way to the state championship wrestling tournament. It had been Bennie Pressler's idea—to get Frankie Hughes to ask the cafeteria supervisor to serve hotdogs at least that one day. She had reluctantly agreed, saying they might do so every Wednesday, in fact, if students did nothing gross with the boiled frankfurters. Everyone liked hotdogs, and so they behaved—until Bennie got another bright idea.

The main topic at the Barf Table that day was what to do if any or all of the boys made the wrestling finals on Saturday evening. Would the other students choose to attend the Valentine's Dance, or would they skip the dance so that they could attend the tournament finals and support whoever was vying for a championship?

Once again, Bennie Pressler spoke for the group—this time, more confident about his plan. "We're going to Capital City, right?" he said. "I mean, I'm supposed to be deejaying, but I already have my backup plan ready—a big boom box and two hours' worth of dance music on cassette tapes. A monkey could handle it—even the monkey that ruined our homecoming dance last fall with Icky Vicki." He didn't have to remind any of them about that debacle.

"Don't call her that," said Artie Bauer. "She's trying hard to make up for what happened at homecoming. What she did for you and the girls yesterday was really sweet of her. She didn't have to do that."

Bennie nodded. "Yeah, you're right," he said. "I just kinda come and go where that girl is concerned. She flirts with me, and then I hear she's been flirting with Brett—on the phone." He looked at Leah and shrugged. "She talks to him at home now," Bennie said. "He must be calling her, because I don't think she can afford to make those calls herself."

"Isn't he supposed to be back home this weekend?" asked Leah. "I remember her saying she was going to the Valentine's Dance with him, but that was a long time ago, and everything was up in the air back then."

Bennie shook his head. "All I know," he began, "is that Brett and his folks will be back at it on Monday—him here at school and Woody at the surf shop and grill on the beach. They have a lot of work to do before Woody can open for the season. Woody talks to Dad now and then." Without explanation, Bennie got up and walked back toward the serving line.

Ty Green took another sandwich from Nicie Evans and unwrapped it. "Well, I know what we'll be doing Saturday night," he said, inspecting the sandwich's wrapper for extra jelly. "Me and Nicie will be wherever our boy here is." He pointed at Artie.

"Where do you think that'll be?" asked Artie, preparing to take a last bite of hotdog.

"I think you'll be dancing," Ty said, quickly adding, "dancing around with a championship wrestling trophy in your arms at State College. I think you can beat Mean Joe Greene this time. Don't you?"

"I don't know," said Artie soberly. "I'm oh-and-nineteen against him right now in my high school wrestling career. But I guess stranger things have happened. Maybe he'll eat too many hotdogs or something on Saturday—if *I* get that far." He looked at the other two wrestlers and said, "We aren't taking anything for granted, right?"

Tommy, who was uneasy about his upcoming tournament appearance, nodded. Ricky, always confident, agreed with Artie, though on his own distinctive terms. "I do not take anything for granted," the boy announced. "I may not be as big and powerful as others are—like Artie and Louis and Tommy—but I am fast, and I am strong, and I can win if I'm given a fair shot at it."

All the girls at the table—all of them Bruinettes—knew exactly what little Ricky meant. In turn, they promised to get together and ride up to State College if any of the boys were in action on Saturday. Wilma Marecek said she'd drive Moby and take as many people as the Suburban could carry. Ty Green suggested that he might also drive the White Whale so that they could take even more supporters. Jamie Foxx and Julia Safin weren't in school that Wednesday, but no one thought Julia would want to miss Artie's big day, if he were fortunate enough to still be in the tournament on Saturday. They didn't know what Jamie might do, though.

Right then, Bennie Pressler returned from the cashier's stand, carrying a stack of three trays, three yellow mustard dispensers, and three hotdogs and buns on the top tray. "Are you guys ready?" Bennie asked his pals. "Are we ready to see who's the biggest wiener on this first *Wiener Wednesday*? We're gonna have a race—not a boring, old, hotdog-eating contest, but wild, wiener shootout!"

Artie sighed and motioned for the other two wrestlers to stand up with him. "Go easy on us, Bennie," said Artie. "We want everybody to have fun, but sometimes being a wiener isn't all it's cracked up to be."

Leah Russo, who ate only veggie dogs, wrinkled up her nose and said, "Ain't that the truth." She closed her paperback copy of *Moby-Dick* and prepared to watch the fun.

The hotdog contest was put on ten minutes before the release bell. Three largely empty trays, each bearing only a single hotdog on an open bun, were set up in the tray-return window. Armed with yellow mustard dispensers—plastic squeeze bottles with cone-shaped nozzles—the three wrestlers were supposed to stand behind a line drawn ten feet from the window and squirt mustard at their hotdogs. The yellow substance had to land on the wiener itself, not just on the bun or tray. As soon as referee Ty Green, standing to the side, verified that a hot dog had been hit, that boy would dash to the window, devour the hotdog and return to the starting line. The last "wiener" would have to mop the floor before leaving the lunchroom.

What Bennie didn't count on was that the game's demilitarized zone—the linoleum floor between the firing line and the window ledge—would be slimy with yellow mustard and become a treacherous minefield of spicy goo before any hotdogger scored a direct hit. As fate had it, all three boys splattered mustard on their hotdogs at the same time and took off toward the window as one, slipping and sliding in the mess they'd made. The raucous laughter at the student tables hushed when the cafeteria doors burst open and Principal Church strode into the lunchroom. He stopped at the Barf Table and glared at the boys on the floor.

Then Principal Church glanced over at Frankie the death-metal cashier and said, "Well, at least we didn't serve chili dogs today. Make sure it's cleaned up. Good luck tomorrow, boys." He turned to leave. Then he stopped again and looked down at Artie. "Young fellow," he said, pointing to his own face, "you've got a little *schmutz* on the end of your nose there. Let's keep our noses clean this weekend. Okay, boys?"

Always the gentleman, Artie said, "Thank you, sir. Yes, sir, we will," and wiped the yellow stain off his nose. With a smile, Church nodded, turned on his heel and left.

Chapter 41

THE THIRSTY THURSDAY BARF TABLE looked like a half-empty glass to the friends who still sat there that day. Artie Bauer, Tommy White and Ricky Duran were away for the first day of the state wrestling tournament in Capital City. Jamie Foxx and Julia Safin were absent from school for the second straight day without any of the remaining Barf Tablers knowing where they were.

The night before, Leah Russo and Bennie Pressler had even gone to visit Jamie and Julia—to take Jamie a special gift on Wiener Wednesday—but had encountered a dark house. No one had answered their knocks, and they had been forced to carry their present—a tiny dachshund puppy—back to the Presslers' van waiting for them on the street. Bennie and his parents were, in fact, cat people, but they agreed to board little Oscar another day or two. Leah was afraid she might become too attached to the puppy if she kept him until Jamie returned home from wherever they all were.

Jamie Foxx, by herself, was back at Arbor High on Fishy Friday. "We had to take Julia back to Capital City," Jamie told the group. "They say she has to stay with her official sponsor, at least until something else—something *legal*—can be arranged."

Being Artie Bauer's best friend, Ty Green knew the importance of the exchange student's case to the big farm boy. "Isn't she supposed to stay with the women's tennis coach at State College?" Ty asked. "Maybe she can go watch the guys wrestle this afternoon. All three of them were still in the tournament as of this morning."

Ty explained that Artie and Ricky were both 1-0 that morning before their second-round matches. At worst, they would appear in their weight divisions' consolation, or losers', brackets Friday afternoon. Tommy White was 1-1 going into Friday, after losing his first-round match on Thursday morning and then winning his first bout in the losers' bracket on Thursday afternoon. Tommy had also been slated to wrestle Friday morning, but Ty hadn't heard yet about any of the boys' outcomes on Friday morning.

"Did either of Tommy's parents get to see him wrestle yet?" asked Leah Russo. "I know how much he wants to show them how well he's doing. He really is a winner—even though he's in the losers' bracket."

Bennie raised his hand. "I'll take this one," he said of Leah's question. "You know, we've got stores all over the state. One of the biggest ones is at Capital Square Mall, not that far from the university." He paused to look around the table and continued, "Dad called the local-access, cable-TV station there, and he offered to have the Pressler's at Capital Square sponsor that TV station's live broadcast of the state wrestling tournament on Saturday."

"That's great," said Nicie Evans. "I didn't know Saturday's matches would be on TV."

"Neither did the TV station," said Bennie, with a laugh, "but Dad made them an offer they couldn't refuse. He had only two stipulations—that they show the losers' bracket matches, as well as the regular draw, and that they show all of our guys' matches. That way, Tommy's folks will get to watch him wrestle. Both prisons have cable TV in their dayrooms. Dad checked."

Jamie perked up. "Hey," she said, "that means Julia will get to see Artie and the boys wrestle after all—I mean, if the tennis coach won't give her a ride to the Coliseum. Their house is way out in the country. Julia said it reminded her of Siberia, without all the snow and ice."

The others laughed. "Well, then I hope our guys keep winning today," said Ty Green. "I talked to Artie last night, and he promised to call the school after their matches this afternoon, so we'll know what to expect tonight and tomorrow. I guess he'll call Miss Hopper's office."

Ty stood up and continued, "I'll go tell Vicki to let Artie know that Julia's there, too—well, *near* there, anyway—and that Saturday's matches will be on cable TV. Artie can tell Tommy. He *really* needs to know, 'cause he can only lose one more time. He has to win today *and* tonight."

"Hold up," Jamie called to Ty, who was already headed toward the lunchroom door. "I have Julia's new phone number. Let me give it to you, to give to Artie." She borrowed a pen and sheet of notebook paper from Leah and copied down the long-distance number.

Ty folded the paper and tucked it into his pocket. "Thanks, Jamie," he said. "I think both of them will appreciate this. Win or lose, he needs to talk to her, even if she can't go see him."

"That's right," said Wilma Marecek, from her seat across the table. "I have to admit, Julia has been good for Artie—good for us all, actually. Since I joined the basketball team, she's been like a member of the family."

Nicie laughed again. "You mean *farm*-ily, girl," Nicie said. "We're *all* sisters and brothers, and we need to remember that, no matter what."

As they watched Ty Green jog toward the cafeteria doors, Leah Russo remembered the gift that she and Bennie had taken to Jamie Foxx's house two days earlier. "Hey, Bennie," said Leah. "Does Jamie know about Oscar yet?" She watched his lips curl into a smile, and his eyes turn toward their new friend.

"No, she doesn't," said Bennie, touching Jamie's arm. "We drove down to see you the other night, Jamie, but nobody was home."

"Who did?" Jamie asked.

"Me and Leah—and Oscar," said Bennie, with a straight face.

"Oscar?" said Jamie. "Does he go to school here?"

Bennie shook his head. "No," Bennie said, "Oscar graduated last week— from obedience school. Oscar's your new puppy—a dachshund. Your mom said it would be okay. She just didn't know he'd be ready so soon. But it was Wiener Wednesday, and we just thought...."

Jamie threw an arm around each friend, one on each side of her, and pulled them into a big hug. "Thanks, you guys, so much," Jamie said, her voice cracking. "I'm sure Mom and I will love little Oscar as much as we did Nathan. When can

I get him?"

"How about Sunday?" asked Bennie. "Mom can take care of him tomorrow—you know, since we'll all be in Capital City, watching our guys wrestle. How does that sound?"

Jamie wiped her eyes. "That sounds just great," she said, sniffing. "The past few weeks have been really rough for Mom and me both. But we can wait two more days."

Knowing how it felt to lose a parent that way—one a father, the other a mother—Leah was thankful that she and Bennie were giving Jamie something happy to look forward to that Valentine's Day weekend. Neither girl had a date to the dance, and neither knew where she'd be on Saturday night—at the State College Coliseum or in the Arbor High gymnasium. Sunday would come soon enough for everyone.

* * *

Traffic on the interstate from Iron Harbor to Capital City was thin that Saturday morning, as the Barf Table gang's three-car caravan cruised up the road. With Ty Green at the wheel, the White Whale led the way, carrying Harry Bauer in the shotgun seat and Ty's mom Rachel Green and the Durans on the big bench seat in back. The picnic basket of tortas, or sandwiches, and empanadas that Gabby and Ricardo Duran had brought from home sat in the Whale's ample trunk, along with the rolling walker and seat that Minnie had found for Grandpa. Moby, the great white Suburban, occupied what truckers on their CB radios called the "rocking chair" in the convoy—between the White Whale and the Presslers' customized van, occupied by Bennie, Abe and Deborah Pressler, and Minnie Marecek. The Suburban was a "Girls Only" vehicle—despite Bennie's plea to be rescued from his dad's van—with Wilma Marecek as Moby's driver and Leah Russo, Nicie Evans, Mel Grayson, Jamie Foxx, Sandy Cuthbert, Anne Marie Childers, and Sara and Clara Harmon as passengers.

As the sun rose above the horizon and the morning mist started to burn off, Leah—in the front passenger seat of the Suburban—noticed the Whale slow and its right-turn signal begin to blink. Just then, the walkie-talkie that Abe Pressler had given Leah to use on the trip squawked. *"Breaker, breaker,"* said Bennie, in his best truck-driver voice. *"This is Rubber Duckie calling the White Whale. What are we stopping for, good buddy?"*

The radio crackled. *"This is the White Whale, coming back at you, Rubber Duck,"* said Ty, obviously trying not to laugh. *"Papa Bear, here, needs to make a pit stop. We thought you guys might want to pit, too. The rest area up ahead is the last one until Capital City. Ten-four?"*

"Ten-four, good buddy," replied Bennie. *"Hey, Moby-Dick? You got your ears on, sweet thing? Come back?"*

Leah raised the two-way radio to her mouth and pressed its transmit button. "Watch it, Rubber Duckie," she said, "or else you'll have to watch your back door the rest of the way up the highway. Over."

Bennie asked, *"Why's that, Moby? Over."*

"Because," said Leah, "we'll put Rubber Duckie in the rocking chair, and then you'll have a whole *load* of lady bears in your rear-view mirror all the way to State College. Over and out."

At the rest area, the teens milled around the vehicles and chatted about Friday's results and Saturday's upcoming matches. Artie and Ricky had continued to win Friday in the regular draw. Tommy had advanced in the losers' bracket, and his match later that morning would be televised on the local-access, cable-TV channel.

"I can't believe Louis got beat yesterday," Wilma said to Ty. "When you told us that back at the high school, I thought you were just kidding."

Ty shook his head. "No," he said, "Mom let me call Artie's hotel room last night, and that was about all we talked about. Everybody was shocked— including Mean Joe Greene."

"Don't call him that," said Wilma. "He can't help what he looks like."

Ty laughed. "He could shave his beard," he said, "but I probably wouldn't recognize him without it—he's had it for so long. You'd call him 'Mean Joe,' too, if he tackled you once or twice at full speed. Besides, Mean Joe Greene—the *real* Joe Greene—is a legend. He was the best."

Nicie offered Ty a swig from her water bottle. "Yeah, well," Nicie said, "Louis Hines is a legend, too. He's Iron Harbor's version of Artie—all-conference in three sports *and* he's a nice guy. But Louis is *all-state* in two of those sports—football and wrestling."

"That's right," said Ty. "He just signed his letter of intent to play football at State College. So losing yesterday didn't hurt anything but his pride. But to make it worse, Artie said Louis got cheated yesterday morning—by some jerk from Fairfield who thinks he's Ric Flair. The dude actually went, 'Woooooo!' when the referee raised his hand as the winner."

Leah spoke up. "How did he cheat?" she asked. "What did he do to Louis?"

"Artie told me the hold he used on Louis was technically *legal*," said Ty, "but it's one that really hurts—it can even injure your neck and spine—and this guy knew how to inflict more pain without looking like he was doing it on purpose. That's why he didn't get disqualified."

Wilma frowned. "That sucks," she said. "Is Louis hurt? Was he able to keep wrestling in the consolation bracket?"

Ty nodded. "Yeah," he said, "I mean, yeah, he wrestled again yesterday afternoon and won the match, but Artie said he didn't look like himself out on the mat. Louis isn't saying much about it, because he doesn't want to screw up his full ride to State—but he also doesn't want to quit. Artie said he wants to defend his state title since this is his senior year."

After visiting the restroom, Bennie walked up and had heard just enough to gather that Artie's main competition in the heavyweight class had lost on Friday. "Wow," said Bennie, "so how does Artie feel about his chances today? Is he glad Mean Joe's out?"

"He isn't *out*," corrected Ty. "Remember, it's double elimination—you have to lose *twice* to get knocked out of the tournament. And Louis can *still* make it to the finals and wrestle for the state title." Ty shook his head. "But, no, Artie's isn't celebrating just yet. He said he doesn't know *how* he feels, except that he's sorry Louis got cheated and is hurt now."

Back on the interstate highway, the caravan made good time, even though the traffic got heavier as they got closer to Capital City. Ty knew the way to State College Coliseum, having attended basketball games there on occasion all his life. His dream was either to play college football at Cardinal Stadium—thankfully now, on the same team as Louis Hines—or to pitch for the Cardinals at State College Field. He had shared his dreams with Artie, his best friend, and with Nicie, his girlfriend, but with no one else, not even his parents.

Meanwhile, back in the Suburban, Nicie, Leah and Wilma filled the other girls in on the situation involving Artie and Louis's rivalry—that Artie now had his best chance ever to defeat his long-time nemesis. Nicie also shared her views on being an elite athlete—in her case, in beach volleyball—and on dating a guy who had a good chance to be a college quarterback or pitcher, depending on how the spring of his senior year went. Both she and Leah—through her late brother Reuben—knew the risks and temptations that top college prospects faced in their senior seasons. Was competing all-out in a high school game or match worth the risk of losing a four-year athletic scholarship due to injury? Should a star athlete succumb to the temptation to push too hard for mere glory, or maybe not push hard enough in a less-important sport to them?

Everyone in the Suburban was silent as Wilma Marecek followed the White Whale into the Coliseum parking lot and pulled up beside the car. The Presslers' van pulled in beside them. Leah looked through Moby's windshield at the white dome of the huge Coliseum looming above the trees and walkways across the street. She watched as people in different high school colors and clothing hurried toward the building. She wondered if the dreams of their good friends—of Artie, Tommy and Ricky—would be dashed on that cold February Saturday, or if their dearest aspirations on this Valentine's Eve would finally come true.

* * *

With four wrestling mats laid out on the Coliseum floor, the farmily members and friends from Arbor High decided to find spots high enough to watch all the action. They sat in a block of seats halfway up the second level of the arena's cavernous, oblong interior. Wrestlers from high schools around the state gathered in pairs or groups with their coaches or teammates to stretch out along the sidelines and at each end of the competition surface. Arbor High hadn't been the only school to bring three state qualifiers to Capital City that year; in fact, three other teams—two of them being Iron Harbor High and Fairfield High—had brought four and five wrestlers, respectively. But Arbor was the only one that still had more than two wrestlers in the final day of competition. Artie Bauer and Ricky Duran were undefeated in the winners' bracket. Tommy White had one loss in the tournament but had advanced in the losers' rounds to Saturday's action. Of the three Fighting Bruins, Tommy was scheduled to wrestle first that morning, then Ricky in his own weight division, then Artie in the heavyweight class.

Leah Russo stood at her seat in the stands and scanned the sidelines for TV cameras. "There they are," she said, pointing out the four cameras being set up below them, one for each of the four mats. "Hey, Bennie, do you know how they're gonna show the matches? I mean, are they gonna skip around all four mats or stick with one match from start to finish?"

"Yes and no," said Bennie Pressler. "They're gonna split the screen in quarters and show all four mats at the same time. But when one of our guys is wrestling, they're gonna zoom in on just that one mat. Isn't that right, Dad?"

Abe Pressler nodded. "They'd better," Abe said. "We're paying that cable company a lot of money to sponsor this broadcast, and I assured Tommy's parents this morning that they'd be able to watch him wrestle. I just got off the phone with Connie a few minutes ago. The men's warden—or his assistant, rather—wouldn't let me speak to Bob, but they said they'd remind him about the wrestling matches this morning."

"Bob White?" said Grandpa Bauer, trying to remember the man by name. "I don't recall my girl Ingrid talking about anybody named Bob White back in the day, and I'm pretty sure that name isn't in that diary of hers. I *do* recall her writing about Connie all the time. But Bob White? Nah, that don't sound familiar."

With a laugh, Nicie Evans chirped, "Bob White? Like the bird?"

"Now *that* rings a bell," said Grandpa. "I stayed confused the whole time I was reading that diary the other week—or more confused than usual." He chuckled. "On about every other page, Ingrid went on and on about a bird. I didn't know she cared so much about birds, 'cept to go dove hunting with me and the boys. But she was always writing about either that one bird or about drinking alcohol—how much she *loved* drinking. Maybe that *bird* was Bob White."

"Maybe so," said Abe Pressler. "I think Bob's nickname in prison is Big Bird, because of his blond hair and his height. Tommy looks just like him, you know. I guess Bob could have had that nickname back in high school, too, but nobody called him that when he worked at our store in E-ville—not in front of me, anyway. And Connie was always such a sweet, hardworking girl."

Minnie Marecek leaned forward to look past Grandpa at Abe. "Do you have jobs for them when they get out of prison?" she asked the businessman. "You know how hard it is for felons to get jobs nowadays. Employment makes their transition easier."

"For Connie, definitely," said Abe, "and she only has about a year left to serve. I'm not so sure about Bob, though. After he left us, he fell in with an even rougher crowd than the one he'd grown up with. And from what I heard, his brother Pete was pretty bad."

"What happened to *him*—the brother?" asked Minnie.

Abe shrugged. "Good question," he replied. "Bob won't talk about him—as Tommy said he found out at Christmas. All *Connie* would tell Tommy about Pete was that he vanished years before Tommy was born—in fact, he disappeared not long after that picture was taken, the prom photo Tommy showed Connie and Bob."

Grandpa spoke up again. "So, that other boy in the picture I took was Tommy's daddy's brother?" asked Grandpa. "Not that little weasel they called Rocket or whatever, but the other big boy, the older-looking feller on the other end?"

"Yes," said Abe, "and he did such a good job of *vanishing*—as Connie said—that Social Services couldn't locate him at all when they were searching for Tommy's relatives, back when Tommy needed a place to live. That's how he came to stay with us."

Abe paused to watch with the others as Tommy White and Coach Jug Johnson walked together to the mat directly below where the group sat. The young wrestler and his old coach conferred as they waited for Tommy's opponent to appear.

"Social Services—and the DEA, too, for that matter—turned the White farm upside down looking for clues to Pete White's whereabouts," Abe continued, "but they didn't find anything—or so they said." He hesitated. "I don't want to say too much right now, but Deborah and I are trying to make sure Tommy's future is secure, no matter what happens with his folks. He really is a good kid."

Everyone within earshot of Abe agreed that Tommy needed to have good things happen in his life after such a tough start. With the exceptions of Julia Safin and Brett Woods, the entire Barf Table gang was together that morning in the Coliseum. Ricky Duran and Artie Bauer would be in action soon enough, but—like all the farmily members and friends in the stands—they fell silent and watched as Tommy White, in his yellow singlet, left Coach Johnson and walked to the center of the mat to meet the referee and shake his opponent's hand.

Bennie Pressler was the first to yell out. "Let's go, Tommy!" shouted Bennie. "Come on, Buzz! You can do this! Float like a butterfly, sting like a bee!"

Chapter 42

JULIA SAFIN ARRIVED at the Coliseum just as the referee lifted Tommy White's arm in victory. Standing inside one entrance, she clapped when she saw that Tommy was a wrestler on one of the four mats and that he had won his match. Then she scanned the seating areas, looking for the fans that were making so much noise in celebration of Tommy's win. She and Leah Russo spotted each other at the same time and waved. Leah motioned for Julia to hurry over and join the group so that they could watch Ricky Duran's match together. He was ready to wrestle on the adjacent mat in his weight division's semi-finals. A win there would put little Ricky Duran in the championship match that evening.

"We weren't sure you were coming," Leah said to Julia, as the former Bruinette took a seat with her friends from Arbor High.

Before responding to Leah's remark, Julia took the time to rise again and hug each of her former teammates—first her exchange sister Jamie Foxx, then Nicie Evans and the others. "I was not sure, either," said Julia. "My sponsor did not want to drive back into town today. And she likes to sleep late on Saturdays—or so she told me last night when I heard that Arthur had won his matches."

"I like to sleep in, too," said Nicie Evans, with a smile, "but this is more important than getting some beauty sleep." Nicie looked the Russian girl over and grinned. "Besides, Julia," Nicie added, "you don't need any more beauty sleep. Right, ladies?"

Wilma laughed. "Well, then," Wilma said, "I think I'd better go back to the Suburban and take a quick nap before Artie's match."

Julia leaned over to the big girl. "You will stay right where you are, my friend," said Julia, "because you are already so very beautiful."

"I was just kidding," said Wilma. "I wouldn't miss seeing little Ricky win his match for the world. But thank you, Julia. You're sweet." Then she added, "So, it looks like neither one of us is going to dance with Artie at the Valentine's Dance tonight—not if the boys keep winning."

Leah waggled her finger at Wilma. "Don't jinx them," said Leah. "Who really cares about that dumb old Valentine's Dance, anyway? We all know Vicki Duke will be the Valentine queen, and whoever her date is will be the king." Leah didn't want to say Brett Woods's name out loud, because she herself didn't want to jinx anything. She hadn't heard yet whether or not the Woods family had gotten back home from Hawaii.

Back on the mat, Ricky's match got underway, with the two grapplers facing each other in the standing, neutral position—one in Arbor Bruins yellow, the other in Fairfield Falcons red. Ricky took his shot and almost pinned the Fairfield boy before the bout was even thirty seconds old. But this opponent must have seen videotape of the Fighting Bruins phenom, and the Falcon knew how to fend off little Ricky's advances. At the end of the opening period, Ricky led 2-1 on points, on that initial takedown and the opponent's escape.

But Ricky Duran was persistent and wore the Fairfield boy down. The yellow-clad boy's quickness and strength—having been raised to work hard at home and on the farm—were too great for the Falcons wrestler to fight off time after time. Ricky's endurance and drive made the difference in the match. With less than a minute left in the final period, Ricky shot one last time and took the boy down, and then pinned him. A minute later, the referee raised Ricky's hand, as the Arbor fans chanted, "Ricky! Ricky! Ricky!" Bennie Pressler had started to shout, *Shooter! Shooter!* but had wisely thought better of yelling that incendiary word in the crowded arena.

The Arbor High students were thrilled that freshman Ricky would be wrestling for the state championship before the end of the day, as were all the adult fans from Oleander County. But proudest of all were Ricardo and Gabby Duran, who were so happy to see their boy succeed in another athletic endeavor, as he had in football the previous fall. Likewise, old Harry Bauer was bursting with pride. He had come to think of Ricky as an adopted grandson and true member of the Bauer family.

The group's interest in the action on the mats waned as they waited through all the other weight classes for Artie Bauer's heavyweight semi-final match. But then—on an outer mat in the losers' bracket—a tall, muscular heavyweight wearing a gray Iron Harbor singlet walked to the center circle and held out a huge hand to his much shorter opponent in a green uniform. Less than a minute later, on the mat at the opposite end of the arena, a sinewy heavyweight sporting Fairfield red hopped in place and punched the air as if he were preparing for a boxing match.

Bennie Pressler half stood and waved at Leah Russo to get her attention. "Mean Joe's over there on your end," Bennie called down the row of seats, though Leah had already spotted the Iron Harbor star. Bennie continued, "This is the Cox guy over here on my end who beat Joe yesterday morning—the cheater. Cox got beat last night."

Leah nodded and passed the word to Nicie and Ty, who were taking their seats again after visiting the concession area. "I know," said Ty Green, about Bennie's information. "The guy who beat Cox last night is the guy Artie is gonna wrestle in a few minutes. He's good, but not as good as Joe—I mean, *Louis*. Artie can beat him."

Louis Hines's match in the losers' bracket took longer to complete than anyone familiar with his wrestling career might have expected. Wilma Marecek—who had seen Louis in action more times through the years than anyone else in the Arbor High group—turned in her seat and got Leah's attention. "He's hurt," said Wilma. "I can just tell from the way he's moving. Why is he even out there?"

Seated next to her niece, Minnie Marecek agreed. "No, he definitely isn't one hundred percent," said Minnie, "not by a long shot. I've watched Louis Hines wrestle our boys—not just Artie—too many times, and that isn't Louis. I'm tempted to go have a talk with his coach."

Ty Green's mother Rachel, a nurse by profession, turned to join the conversation. "You'd think his football coach—the one here at State College— would stop him," said Mrs. Green. "He could be jeopardizing his football career."

But then Louis pinned his opponent and returned slowly to the locker room to recuperate before he would face the winner of the other consolation-bracket match—the one featuring Cox, the Fairfield cheater. That match went to the third period, with Cox starting on top and the other heavyweight down on his hands and knees. Using what must have been the same hold that had injured the Iron Harbor champion, Cox grappled with his opponent on the mat, managed to hook one arm around the other wrestler's neck, and then used his free hand to apply pressure. Within seconds, the boy in the chokehold slapped the mat twice to end the match. Cox sprang to his feet, bounced in place with both fists raised high and punched the air before moving to meet the referee and loser for the end-of-match routine. Cox's handshake was more a slap than a clasp, but the referee just shook his head and raised his own red-banded arm to indicate Cox's win.

"Why didn't the ref raise Cox's arm?" asked Leah Russo, bending forward to address Wilma and Minnie Marecek.

Still shaking her own head, Minnie turned and replied, "Probably because he knew that rotten kid was going to do it, anyway, as soon as he turned him loose. That move shouldn't be legal. It's called a *guillotine* for good reason."

"It *isn't* legal," interrupted Wilma, "if they take it too far. The ref's supposed to break them apart if the hold looks dangerous. But there are all sorts of ways to cheat. And I'm guessing that Louis didn't want to give in to that creep even though he was in a bad position. I can't figure out why the ref didn't stop the match yesterday and make them start again."

Within minutes, Artie Bauer and his opponent took the floor, wrestling on the same mat where Ricky Duran had won earlier in the morning. The semi-final match went the distance, with Artie falling behind in the first period, pulling even midway through the second frame, and using a quick takedown and near-pin in the third period to win on points. In the post-match ritual in the center circle, Artie shook the other big boy's hand and said a couple of words that elicited a nod and a weak smile from the opponent. Then Artie stood up straight and faced the scorer's table to let the referee raise his arm in victory. He waved to his friends in the stands, before turning to meet Coach Jug Johnson at the edge of the mat. They walked together toward the locker room door, where both Ricky and Tommy had been standing to watch their teammate win.

* * *

The morning session on all four mats ended by noon, and announcements over the PA reminded the crowd that tournament officials would be taking a break for lunch. Tommy White and Louis Hines would wrestle in their respective weight classes around one o'clock. The final round of the consolation bracket—slated to begin around three o'clock—would determine each division's challenger in the state championship finals. In other words, the winners of the losers' bracket would face wrestlers from the regular draw who were undefeated in the tournament to that point—competitors like Ricky Duran and Artie Bauer. If Ricky and Artie were to win their next matches—scheduled for around six o'clock—they would be state champions right then. But if a challenger from the losers' bracket were to beat one of the Arbor boys in that finals match, the challenger would have to turn around and defeat Ricky or Artie again to win the state title. That was how true double-elimination tournaments worked, with every participant staying in the running for the championship until they were defeated twice. Other states followed other rules.

After retrieving the picnic basket and other goodies that had been stowed in the White Whale's trunk, the Barf Table farmily and friends walked partway across campus to the College Dining Commons for a change of scenery. They found a long table in one corner, as far away from the tray-return window and garbage bins as was possible in the modern cafeteria, with its conveyor belt for dirty dishes and the separate waste chutes for different types of trash.

Senior Mel Grayson, who had already been accepted to attend State College as a pre-med student, wandered over to the serving areas to check out the food that she might be eating as a college freshman. Returning to the Arbor High table, she wrinkled up her nose and said, "I know now why this cafeteria's initials are CDC—like the Center for Disease Control. Gee whiz, our school lunchroom back home has better food. Pass me one of those empanadas, please."

"Hey, Mel!" said Bennie Pressler, seated across the table. "You just stole my joke! I'm supposed to be the comedian in this group."

Leah punched his shoulder. "Oh, be quiet and eat your sandwich," said Leah, looking around the large dining commons for other group members that had drifted away before being seated. Julia Safin was nowhere to be seen, as were Wilma and Minnie Marecek. Jamie Foxx, Sandy Cuthbert and Anne Marie Childers walked up to the table together and sat down. Sara and Clara Harmon had veered off toward the ladies' room in the CDC lobby and were still gone.

Other than Minnie being absent, the adults seemed to be getting along famously. Leah was happy to see Grandpa Bauer laughing and enjoying himself for a change, as he listened to the Durans, Presslers and Rachel Green share their own stories about Ricky, Tommy and Artie, in particular. Grandpa knew all three teens well enough right then, but he had not even met the two younger boys until after the tractor accident that had put him out of commission earlier that school year. Then, of course, Grandma Bauer had died before Thanksgiving, and both Grandpa and Artie had lost themselves for a good, long time. Leah hoped both were back now for good, though she knew from experience that mourning never truly ends after losing a loved one. Leah still missed her big brother Reuben, especially when something happened to remind her of good times with him. And now she—like Jamie Foxx—was dealing with another kind of loss, that of an absentee parent. Elizabeth Russo had even said she no longer loved her husband and daughter. Leah wondered if her mother had really meant that.

Bennie grabbed Leah by the arm and shook it. "Hey, in there!" he said. "Earth to Leah, Earth to Leah! Anybody home?"

Realizing how quickly her happy day had turned gloomy, Leah snapped back from all of her sad thoughts and answered her friend. "Yeah, yeah," Leah said. "We should've brought that bear suit for you to wear. You could make yourself useful and go grab me a sandwich out of that *pic-a-nic* basket over there."

"I'm speechless," said Bennie. "That's the first time I've ever heard you *ask* for something to eat. You're making progress, my friend."

Nicie Evans witnessed the exchange and chimed in, "You go, girl. But the question is, do you want your ham-and-cheese sandwich with the ham or without it, like Bennie's there?" Nicie winked and looked up as Wilma Marecek sat down with them. "So, Wilma, where did Julia and Minnie get off to? Do you know?"

Wilma shook her head. "Huh-uh," she said. "Aunt Minnie was all bent out of shape about Louis wrestling hurt, so I hope she's not trying to get him disqualified. That isn't her place. And I have no idea where Julia is. Maybe she had to go home—or maybe she went looking for Artie."

"Well," said Leah Russo, with a mischievous smile, "it's been quite a day so far. All three of our guys won their matches this morning, and Bennie Pressler was *speechless* for the first time in his life." She turned to her friend Nicie and added, "And I'll have my torta *without* the ham—like Bennie—if you don't mind. Everybody's got to stand for something, right?"

* * *

Tommy White's freshman season ended in his next match that afternoon. He wrestled a senior, a regional champion, who had lost in the state tournament all three of his previous years and was determined now to get one last shot at a state title. Tommy made the boy earn the win, though, giving him all he could handle right down to the final horn. The difference was the single point that the 12th grader scored by escaping from Tommy at the start of the third period. It was a fair match, and Tommy had no complaints—only that he hadn't been able to get a takedown in the final two minutes. He gave it his best shot, but his effort wasn't good enough this time.

After showering and dressing in street clothes, Tommy joined the rest of his Barf Table farmily in the stands. "You did great this year, Tommy," said Bennie Pressler, slapping his foster brother on the back. "Just imagine how well you'll do next year."

Wilma gave Tommy a hug and told him how much he had improved through the course of the season. "Thanks to *you*—and Artie," said Tommy. "I wouldn't have even come out for the team, if it hadn't been for you guys—I mean, for you *two*. Sorry, I didn't mean to call you a *guy*."

That Tommy might worry that he had hurt Wilma's feelings surprised Leah, as she was always using the same term to describe pairs or groups of her friends. "Well, Tommy, didn't you hear Wilma calling you a 'boy' during the match?" teased Leah, giving Wilma a wink.

"Don't even start with that, Leah," said Tommy, laughing. "I know what *boj* means. It's 'fight' in Czech. Artie *still* says that to me when I start slacking off in practice. And he also yells, '*Strilet! Strilet!*' from the sidelines, when I need to take a shot during a match."

Wilma beamed with pride, that her words had made a difference with both Tommy and Artie. "Maybe I'll dance with *you* instead of Artie tonight, Tommy," said Wilma, "that is, if I can steal you away from Anne Marie at the Valentine's Dance."

Now the big 9th-grade boy was truly embarrassed, not about losing the match, but about winning the girl—or a dance with her, at least. "Aw, that old dance will be over and done with by the time we get back to the high school," Tommy said. "I just hope we get to celebrate two state championships all the way down the road to Monk's Landing."

* * *

Louis "Mean Joe Greene" Hines's two big wins in the losers' bracket made what would have been a long afternoon more bearable for the Arbor High Fighting Bruins fans. The bout of particular interest to everyone in the Coliseum came right after Tommy's loss, when Louis found himself matched up again with Cox, the senior from Fairfield High. Despite his sore neck and shoulder, the Iron Harbor heavyweight came close to pinning the Fairfield boy before the end of the first period. But Cox—also an experienced 12th grader—was strong and fit, and he was able to squirm out of weakened Louis's grasp before the referee could tap him out.

Cox managed to hurt Louis with barely legal submission holds twice more, once in the second period and again in the third period when the wounded defending champion made the mistake, in this case, of choosing to start the round in the down position. The wrestling move wasn't a guillotine this time;

it was a Nelson hold that Cox made all the more effective by putting pressure on Louis's injured neck. Watching from the stands, even Leah and Bennie could tell that Louis was close to submitting, and both Wilma and Tommy confirmed their fears. Instead, Louis summoned a burst of strength that an ordinary grappler wouldn't have possessed, and freed himself from Cox's hold. As the Fairfield wrestler rose to his feet, Louis Hines suddenly shot at the opponent's legs and wrapped them up, took the surprised boy down, and ended the match—and Cox's high school wrestling career—by fall.

Two hours later, Louis returned to the mat and won his way into the state championship match against Artie—by beating the boy who had defeated Cox in the winner's bracket and then had lost to Artie in the semi-finals of the regular draw. This last match in the loser's bracket went all three periods, and Louis barely won on points. Everyone in the arena knew that Louis Hines was one of the best high school heavyweights ever, but—as farm boy Artie Bauer had learned at the regional tournament—wrestling up through the losers' bracket to win the championship was a Herculean feat. As they watched Louis Hines lift his arm in victory and then trudge back to the locker room for therapy on his injured neck, the Barf Table gang hoped that Artie Bauer was the very Bruin to take this Hercules on.

Minnie Marecek walked up not long after Louis Hines qualified for the finals. "That was some match, wasn't it?" Minnie said. "I watched it from floor level, and Louis was lucky to get the win. Even *I* can tell he's hurting, and I don't understand why the tournament officials let him keep wrestling. I didn't see it, but I heard someone on the floor say Cox had used a *full* Nelson against Louis this afternoon. That's illegal. But maybe that was just talk."

Minnie's niece shook her head. "No," said Wilma. "We all saw that match, and the hold *looked* legal—at least from up here. But Cox is sneaky. I'm glad Artie didn't have to wrestle that guy. Artie and Louis will have a good, fair match—even though Artie has never beaten him."

"Well," said Minnie, "maybe this will be Artie's night to shine." She smiled as if she really wasn't sure that Artie Bauer could beat even an injured Louis

Hines. "By the way," Minnie said, "Julia is outside waiting for someone to get here. She and I had a long talk this afternoon, and I made a few calls for her—to help with her living situation, hopefully."

"Is she coming back?" asked Leah. "I mean, is she coming back to watch Ricky and Artie wrestle tonight?"

"We'll see," Minnie said. "The tennis coach that Julia stays with was one of the people I talked to. She's not a bad person, really, but she's too young to *parent* a high school student, even a young lady as mature as Julia. That's what got Julia into this situation. The coach didn't want to be bothered with the responsibility—and the paperwork—of placing Julia the right way."

"Maybe if we go out and talk to the coach…?" said Leah. "Julia needs to be here with the rest of us for Ricky's and Artie's matches—especially *Artie's* match. Watching Artie win the state championship on TV just doesn't get it."

"No, it doesn't," said Minnie, an odd look in her eye. "I'm sure she'll be here if she can. We'll just have to hope that the tennis coach isn't too upset over my talk with her—and with several other folks, too. That's why it took me so long to get back here."

Wilma's eyes narrowed. "You didn't talk to the tournament officials about Louis, did you, Aunt Minnie?" asked Wilma.

Minnie shook her head. "No, I didn't," she said, "even though I sure did want to. I did see the State College football coach out in the lobby a while ago, so maybe *he'll* have something to say to the Iron Harbor coach. I'd hate to see Louis get seriously injured and ruin his future, but taking that risk is *his* decision to make, not mine."

Chapter 43

BENNIE PRESSLER HAD BEEN GONE for twenty minutes when the commotion occurred at the main entrance into the arena from the Coliseum lobby. Streaming through the doors were dozens of teenagers dressed in Arbor High green and gold. They laughed and looked up and pointed at the glittering black cube of a scoreboard suspended high above the arena floor from the white, domed roof lined with button-like rows of gymnasium lights. The teens shouted and clapped and waved at their schoolmates sitting in the stands and at their two heroes and their coach standing at the edge of the single mat now on the floor. Within another thirty minutes, the state championship matches would begin, with Ricky "Shooter" Duran and Artie "Yogi" Bauer vying for state wrestling titles in their respective weight classes. Ricky's match in the 113-pound division would be up second; Artie's heavyweight match against Louis Hines would come last.

Leah Russo had already grabbed her camera and waved for Tommy White to go with her when the uniformed Arbor cheerleaders, led by Vicki Duke, made their entrance—green and gold pom-poms popping up and rustling in the heavy air as the girls burst through the doors into the Coliseum. At the back of the pack ambled Bruno, the Arbor High mascot.

Leah laughed when she saw the bear and leaned toward Tommy as they descended the stairs to the arena floor. "I wondered where Bennie went," she said. "Did he tell you everybody was coming and that Vicki was bringing the suit for him?"

Tommy shook his head. "No," he said, "this is news to me. All he said when he went out a while ago was that he was going to see a man about a bear." He chuckled. "That makes a lot more sense now."

Bouncing toward Coach Johnson and the boys at the mat, Vicki Duke flashed her widest smile and held it, even when she reached the portable fencing that barred entry to the wrestling surface. "We're just so excited!" she squealed. "This is so much more fun than a silly old dance!" Then she spotted Leah and Tommy approaching her. "Why aren't you in your uniform, Tommy?" Vicki said. "I heard you won this morning."

Before Tommy could respond, Leah asked the girl, "Where'd you hear that? Did Bennie Pressler call you at lunch?"

Finding his voice, Tommy added, "I won this morning, but I didn't win this afternoon. I'm out now." He looked down at his Fighting Bruins warm-up jacket.

"Oh, Tommy," said Vicki, "you're *still* great! You're one of the best wrestlers in the whole state just by being here today!"

"Top six," Leah said, having already figured out Tommy's final standing. "But who called you, Vicki? It had to be one of us, right?"

Vicki reached over to hug Tommy. "Top six!" she repeated. "That's so impressive!" She let go of Tommy and turned to Leah. "Now, sweetie," said Vicki, "let me call Bruno and the girls over. I *know* you want them in your picture, too."

Not wanting to admit that Vicki was right, Leah nodded and asked Jug Johnson if she could take a group photo of them that close to Ricky's match. The coach smiled and told Ricky and Artie to follow him around the barrier. "No problem, little lady," said Jug. "This picture will go in the trophy case right next to the one you all took of the girls the other day."

Leah arranged the cheerleaders with their raised pom-poms behind the coach and his three wrestlers. Vicki stood on one end of the lineup next to Jug; Bruno stood on the other end next to Artie. Looking through the camera lens, Leah made her final adjustments for lighting and focus and held her hand up to get the group's attention. She stepped up onto a rolled-up mat to position herself higher than her subjects.

"I'm gonna take two shots," Leah said, "just in case somebody has their eyes closed. On three—and you can say *team* if you want, guys, instead of *cheese*." The boys jostled each other for a second until Jug told them to get serious and put on their game faces. Bruno punched Artie on the shoulder and waggled a disapproving mitten at him.

Leah counted, "One … two … three," and snapped the picture. "Okay," she said, "one more time—don't move," and started her count again. On three, Bruno quickly turned, grabbed Artie around the neck in a big bear hug—not unlike the chokehold that had overpowered Louis Hines—and planted the biggest smacker of a kiss square on the surprised boy's cheek.

"Bennie!" yelled Artie Bauer, his face turning red. "I'm gonna get you for that!"

Bruno took a step back, reached up and lifted off the costume's massive head, revealing that the person inside the suit wasn't Bennie Pressler at all. It was Julia Safin, the dancing bear.

"You do not have to *get* me, Arthur," said Julia. "I am already yours."

* * *

Leah Russo—and later Artie Bauer—learned that the surprise bear attack had been an inside job. Back in the stands, Vicki Duke relented and told Leah that she had talked to Julia at noon that day. "She told me all three of the boys were still in the running," said Vicki, "and that two of them—Artie and Ricky—were *definitely* in the championships tonight."

"So, what about the dance?" asked Leah. "What about Brett? Weren't you going to the dance with him?"

Now Vicki looked embarrassed. "Oh, Brett will be fine," Vicki said. "I called his house and left a message on their answering machine, but he didn't call me back. They were supposed to get back early this morning, so I don't know if they're home or not. We'll see Brett soon enough at school on Monday, right?"

Leah still wanted to know where Bennie Pressler fit into Julia and Vicki's plan, as he had said nothing to Leah, one of his closest friends, about the surprise. When Bennie returned to the stands from the lobby minutes before the first championship match was to start, Leah scolded him. "What's the idea?" she said. "I almost dropped the camera when Julia kissed Artie."

Bennie laughed. "Yeah, I saw it from the doors," he said. "They told me to hide until she took off the head. This was all Vicki's doings—and Julia's."

"I don't see how," said Leah. "When did they plan it?"

"Remember," Bennie said, "Ty took Julia's phone number down to the guidance office for Vicki to give to Artie? Well, Vicki called Julia and made arrangements for her to call if any of the guys made the championships. They thought it would be a good idea to bring a couple busloads of kids—and Bruno—to cheer the guys on. They told *me* so I wouldn't mess up the surprise."

The adults in the Arbor High group—Harry Bauer, Minnie Marecek, Rachel Green, the Durans and the Presslers—had moved down to a special section of folding chairs on the floor to be closer to the wrestling mat. In the stands remained the rest of the Barf Table gang along with their excited Arbor schoolmates. The students were joined by Coach Joe Carson and Frankie Hughes, the latter having traded out his usual black, death-metal T-shirt for a Fighting Bruins hoodie to mark the special day. Neither man seemed to mind giving up his Saturday to drive an activity bus to the state capital.

Leah Russo waited until the first match ended before she hurried down to the floor, camera in hand, and took a position alongside the other sports photographers covering the event. Sitting cross-legged on the floor just off the mat, Leah glanced over at the special seats to see how excited Ricardo and Gabby Duran were to watch their son wrestle in this big match. Grandpa Bauer was smiling and patting Gabby's shoulder, as if he were assuring her that Ricky would do well. But Grandpa suddenly stopped talking and turned to look at someone who had knelt down beside him. From her spot on the floor, Leah couldn't make out who the person was until he stood again to find an empty chair. The man was none other than a shaggy-headed and tanned Woody Woods, back from his family's three months on the winter beaches of Oahu.

Leah twisted around as best she could without getting up and looked back at the Arbor student section, where Vicki Duke and the cheerleaders were up front waving their pom-poms again to pump up the crowd. Bruno waved and danced in place. Through the fluttering haze of green and gold, Leah found Bennie Pressler in his place first, then spotted Nicie Evans and Ty Green and the other members of the Barf Table. Unlike most Arbor High students, none of the gang was looking down on the mat. Instead, they were all waving to their friend and Barf Table mate Brett Woods and beckoning for him to hurry and join them as he threaded his way from the aisle. When she finally saw this boy whom she had tried for so long not to miss, Leah's heart beat faster, but she knew she couldn't leave her post until after Ricky's match. Like the other photographers around her, she had a job to do.

* * *

Before Ricky Duran and his opponent—an 11th grader from Crestwood, near Fairfield—started their match, a tournament official walked to the scorer's table and took the microphone. "*I have an announcement,*" the man said. "*Quiet, please. This announcement involves tonight's heavyweight match between defending state champion Louis Hines of Iron Harbor High School and challenger Arthur Bauer of Arbor Charter High School.*"

A buzz circulated through the crowd as people who had seen Louis wrestle hurt earlier that day speculated that the champion might have decided to forfeit his title. From where she sat, Leah spotted Artie standing across the floor in the doorway of the hall to the locker area. He didn't look triumphant by any measure. He appeared stiff and less at ease than before any other match Leah had seen that season.

"*In light of the fact that* two *of our championship matches this evening feature wrestlers from Arbor High,*" the official continued, "*it was requested that we reschedule the heavyweight match to immediately follow the upcoming bout in the 113-pound division between Chuck Lyons of Crestwood Senior High and Ricardo Duran Jr., of Arbor Charter High. Both coaches and both competitors have agreed to this scheduling change, and it has been approved by this governing body. Thank you for your attention. And may the championship matches resume.*"

Leah overheard two photographers near her talking. "That's a big joke," one said, with a laugh. "They figure Hines will win." The other one replied, "Yeah, they don't want this thing to go all night with a rematch."

Leah shot a look back at the locker room door, but Artie had disappeared, at least for the moment. She turned her focus back to the center of the mat, where Ricky Duran shook Chuck Lyons's hand down low, the tops of their heads almost touching.

The whistle blew. The two wrestlers began to move slowly in a tight circle, facing one another, reaching out to nudge the other's head and grasping at but not gripping at each other's arms. Every couple of seconds, one would feint a shot and step back to keep the opponent out of reach. This went on until Ricky saw his opening and did not withdraw, but threw himself low at Lyons and wrapped his arms around the boy's torso. With quickness and power, Ricky drove Lyons to the mat for the takedown. The stunned Crestwood boy tried to roll over and scramble out of bounds, but like a cat, Ricky pulled his prey back across the outer circle, flipped him over, and lifted the boy's legs to pin his shoulders to the mat. Dropping onto his hands and knees, the referee peered across the padded surface for two long seconds and slapped the mat once to end the match.

Both boys rose to their feet, removed the red and green bands from around their ankles, and shook hands again. The referee raised the arm of Ricky Duran, state champion of the 113-pound weight classification, as the fans from Arbor High tried their best to raise the domed roof. Leah had fired off as many shots of Ricky's winning move as possible during the short bout, but her best photos of him that night showed him in the special seating, hugging both of his parents as Grandpa Bauer sat beaming next to them. The TV cameras that had been set up at the four corners of the mat all zoomed in on the jubilant scene.

* * *

The public-address announcer read off Artie's and Louis's full names and high schools, and noted again that Louis Hines—with a 31-1 record on the season—was the defending state heavyweight champion, as if anyone left in the Coliseum might doubt that fact. In comparison, Artie Bauer's season record was 23-7, with five of those losses having been to the very wrestler he was about to face for the sixth time.

But Leah Russo and everyone else who had seen Louis Hines wrestle that day knew in their hearts that Artie Bauer that night would face a diminished version of the indomitable man-ster whom the Barf Table boys had been calling Mean Joe Greene all year. Leah took a shot of Artie and Louis shaking hands at the start of the match, then of Artie's first shocking takedown of the defending champion a minute into the first period. The referee held up two fingers to the official scorer and moved to get a better view of the two heavyweights below him on the mat. As Artie struggled to find a good hold, Leah distinctly heard Louis utter the word *time* loudly enough for anyone near the mat to hear. Artie immediately released Louis from his grasp and pushed himself onto his hands and knees, then rose to his feet. Louis did likewise, though gingerly.

The Iron Harbor grappler spoke to the referee, who turned to the scorer's table again, raised one arm and twirled his index finger to start the clock on the injury timeout that Louis had just called. Leah knew from home matches she had worked that a wrestler could take only ninety seconds—a minute and a half—of accumulated injury time in an entire match before being disqualified. Also, the wrestler could stop the match only twice due to injury, no matter how little time he took to recover. On his third injury timeout, his opponent got the win.

With Artie leading in the match, Louis's second injury stoppage came midway through the second period. Louis's gray singlet was wet with sweat as he tried not to grimace from the pain he must have been feeling in his neck or shoulder. The referee summoned the tournament physician from the sidelines, and the man in a white shirt and tie looked Louis over and asked him if he wished to continue. Louis stubbornly nodded and turned back to face Artie once again. The referee signaled for the boys to take their original positions to start the period—with Artie up and Louis down—and blew his whistle for them to resume. Louis immediately went down again, but refused to submit or to call a third and disqualifying injury timeout.

Artie told Leah later that he had heard Louis whimper in pain on the restart, and that had been all the big farm boy could bear. Artie released his hold and stood, stepping back from this young man whom he had come to respect so much for his strength, for his determination to be the best at his sport, whether it was football or wrestling, and for his integrity as an elite athlete. Artie backed off, even though the crowd was screaming at him to finish the fight, to finish Louis off. He told Leah later that he'd even heard Arbor fans yell for him to fight, fight for the win, but he revealed no more than that.

Again, the mat-side physician examined Louis, and again he cleared him to continue wrestling. Artie, however, was done, and he told the referee so. What he said could be heard off the mat where Leah and the other photographers now knelt and also in the special section where the Arbor adults waited to see if the match would resume or not.

"You need to stop the match," Artie told the referee. "Either stop it right now and let Louis have time to recover, or I'll quit. I will. We can wrestle later tonight when we were supposed to—the last match of the evening. I'm not gonna hurt somebody just to win a trophy."

Still, the physician shook his head and refused to reverse his decision. Likewise, Louis claimed to be okay—good enough to wrestle, anyway. Leah knew, though, that Artie had also decided what he could and could not do. And so when the referee pointed to the center circle and motioned for the two wrestlers to take their same starting positions, Artie shook his head and walked away. The last photo that Leah shot of Artie was of him reaching for the locker room door, not even turning to look back.

The stunned crowd didn't know how to react. They stood in relative silence and watched the same tournament official who had rescheduled the heavyweight match now talk with the ref, the physician and both coaches. The fans—especially those from Oleander County—waited for the official to take up the mic again and tell them what was going on.

Instead, the referee stood in the center circle with Louis Hines and raised his hand, the winner by forfeit. It was then that the tournament official keyed the microphone and explained that since both Louis and Artie now had one loss apiece, their finals rematch at the end of the night would determine the state champion. *"To those of you who had requested the schedule change,"* the official added, *"I apologize for this bit of trouble we've encountered."*

Despite the announcement, Leah did not leave her position by the mat. She watched the Iron Harbor coach—who, like Jug Johnson, also coached football—motion to someone in the special seating. A large man in a red State College jacket rose and walked briskly around the edge of the mat to the scorer's table where Louis and his coach stood. The man in red was as tall as Louis and broader in the shoulders. Leah heard another photographer whisper, "That's Landis, State's football coach."

With a frown on his ruddy face, Landis laid one big hand on Louis's shoulder and neck area, and saw his future lineman, his most promising recruit, wince in pain. The college coach shook his head, directed a few words to both the high school coach and the athlete, and then he spoke to the tournament official. Nothing else was announced over the PA, but the official did take Jug Johnson aside to explain how the winner of the heavyweight division would have to be determined that night. Jug nodded and hurried to the locker room. Neither he nor Artie emerged until all the other championship matches had been fought. Everyone was forced to wait and see.

Chapter 44

IT WAS APPROPRIATE that the sun was shining on Valentine's Day after the long night before. Everyone from Arbor High had gotten home late. Some of them—mostly the adults like Grandpa Bauer and Minnie Marecek—had missed their usual bedtimes. Others had lay awake much of the night, whether from the previous evening's excitement or from weariness after their long rides home from Capital City. And then there were the few—like Artie Bauer, Ricky Duran and Tommy White—who couldn't believe how different their lives would be from then on, thanks to the opportunities that their success as wrestlers now afforded them.

Like Grandpa, the clock on the kitchen wall in the farmhouse was slow and had lost more than a few minutes in the three days that Artie had been away, but the big farm boy was glad to be home, even if he did have to rise early again to milk the cows and feed the chickens. "It's after one o'clock," Artie called to his grandfather in the bedroom off the kitchen. "You'd better get up, Grandpa. The rest of the gang will be here in a minute. Leah's already here."

Still in his pajamas, the old fellow appeared at the bedroom door, squinting and rubbing his bristly cheeks. "Gabby never made me get up early while you were in the big city," groused Harry Bauer, "not until Ricardo came in from the barn for lunch."

Then Grandpa noticed Leah sitting at the kitchen table and mumbled, "'Scuse me, little lady," and went back into his room, closing the door behind himself.

Artie laughed. "I never thought I'd live to see this day," Artie said to Leah, as he sat down next to her. "My grandpa, living the life of Riley."

Leah studied her friend for a few moments. "Did you get to talk much to Julia last night?" she asked. "Isn't that great about her coming to live with Minnie and Wilma?"

Artie took a second to answer, but Leah could tell from his shy smile and the pink in his cheeks that he was pleased. "It is," he said. "It really is. I just wish she could be here today—for Valentine's."

"You got to see her after midnight," Leah countered, "so, technically, you *were* with her on Valentine's Day." She saw from Artie's expression that a few minutes in a parking lot just wasn't the same as an evening of music and dancing, or even as a day of fun with friends.

"What about you and Brett Woods?" asked Artie. "Did you talk to him last night? He and Woody were gone when Coach Johnson and I—and Louis and his coach, too—came out for the rematch. It *was* awfully late."

Leah nodded. "Yeah," she said, "I heard Woody say they needed to get back, because they have a lot of work left to do at the grill. He wants to reopen soon." Leah realized that she hadn't answered Artie's questions, and continued, "But, no, I didn't talk to Brett. I stayed on the floor until the bitter end. I didn't want to miss *the* photo."

Artie laughed again. "Of what?" he said. "Of me forfeiting the state championship?"

"*You* didn't forfeit the match," said Leah. "You *both* did. You should've seen the look on that tournament official's face when you and Louis came out of the locker room for the rematch wearing white shirts and ties instead of your singlets. He almost had a cow."

"Yeah," Artie said, "and all the kids loved it—probably because they've never seen me wearing a nice shirt and tie before. I'm glad Coach Johnson made us all take some nice clothes for the kickoff dinner."

Leah nodded. "After they said you and Louis would *share* the state title this year, the whole place went crazy," she said. "That was the best way for the whole thing to end."

"I think so," said Artie. "The coaches—and that includes Coach Landis—

and Louis and I talked about it in the locker room. Louis wanted to go ahead and wrestle, even if it meant losing to me. But I could tell in that first championship match that I would hurt him—and probably hurt him bad—if I wrestled him straight up. I was holding back, and he was still in a lot of pain."

"Isn't that what wrestling's all about?" asked Leah.

"No, it isn't," Artie said, "not in high school or even in college. It's a sport. It's not life and death. And it isn't the fake stuff or the brutal stuff you see on TV—you know that." He changed the subject to keep from getting worked up. "But what about you and Brett? How do you feel about him now? Do you mind talking about it?"

Leah was quiet for a moment. "No, I don't mind," she said. "I could use a guy's point of view on this." She chose her words carefully. "I didn't tell you about the email he sent me," she continued. "It got hung up somewhere in the FidoSphere—or whatever it's called—and I didn't get it until Saturday morning, right before we left for Capital City."

"An email from Brett?" asked Artie. "What did he say?"

"Oh, just that he was looking forward to getting back home," she said, "and that he and I needed to have a *long talk*—that's what he said—have a *long talk*."

"About what?"

Leah shrugged and continued, "About *us,* believe it or not. And I didn't even know there *was* an *us* yet. I figured he'd want to d—"

Just then, the telephone on the kitchen wall rang. When Artie started to rise, Grandpa—still dressing in his room off the kitchen—picked up the extension on his nightstand and greeted the caller loudly enough that Artie sat back down. "That's probably one of the old ladies who's been chasing Grandpa," said Artie, with a chuckle. "So, is that all Brett had to say in his email?"

Leah shook her head. "No," she said. "He'll probably tell you this himself, but for the first time in his life, he's seeing that one of his dreams is out of his reach—his dream of being a professional surfer—and he doesn't really know who he is now. He said he feels like a real loser, because he couldn't keep up with all those big-time surfers on the North Shore. And he said he feels like he really does belong at the Barf Table now."

Artie laughed. "He knows better than that," the big farm boy said. "The Barf Table isn't for losers—and it never was."

Artie didn't need to point out that three of the state's best wrestlers and four members of the top girls' basketball team in the conference, along with three standouts in other endeavors—including Leah herself—would be sitting together at that lunch table come Monday.

"Yeah," said Leah, "we're gonna need a bigger table—if Brett does want to sit with us. So, is it ever a good thing when a guy wants to have a *long talk* with a girl?"

Before Artie could respond, Grandpa Bauer came out of his bedroom and hobbled over to the kitchen table. "You'll never guess who that was," Grandpa said, laying his hand on Artie's shoulder to steady himself. "I haven't talked to her in ages."

"Oh, Grandpa," said Artie, "you saw Miss Elsie a couple weeks ago when she brought us another casserole. What's she bringing us today?"

"That wasn't Elsie Bishop, young man," said Grandpa. "It was Connie Henderson—you know, Connie *White*, Tommy's mama. She saw me on the TV last night—after we moved to the seats next to the mat—and she heard the announcers talking about you and me and Pearl, that your grandma had passed recently. Connie got permission to call and express her condolences to you and me both. She always was a sweet girl when Ingrid would bring her around."

Artie looked surprised. "That was nice of her," he said. "Did you get a chance to ask her about the diary we found? Or if she knows where my mother ran off to? Or who my father is?"

Grandpa studied the crease in his grandson's brow. "No, sonny boy, I didn't," said the old man, "and I'm sorry. It wasn't that kind of a call." He patted Artie's shoulder and continued, "Connie *did* say one thing, though. She said something about that picture Tommy showed her at Christmas—you know, the picture I took of her and Ingrid and the others out in the yard, with ol' Sergeant getting after Rocket Reep, rest his worthless soul."

"What did she say?" said Artie. "How much ol' Sergeant hated that guy? Did she admit he shot him with that slingshot he always carried?"

"No, not hardly," Grandpa continued. "Like I said, it wasn't that kind of call. She said seeing all the flowers in that picture—Pearl's roses and her special irises—really took her back to those days and made her feel for one second like she wasn't locked up in prison. Connie said she'll never forget how Pearl gave her a cutting off that rosebush and some irises to transplant over at the White farm. And she was proud that she had passed that love on to Tommy, with his flower garden and his bees."

As Leah rose from the table to go look out the kitchen window toward the barn, Artie reached up and touched his grandfather's hand on his shoulder. "About that, Grandpa," said Artie. "Do you think we could find some space for Tommy to keep some bees here on the farm? You know he's not like his dad and his uncle. He's more like Connie—and us."

"That's a good idea," said Grandpa, "and I'm glad you mentioned Bob White and that brother of his. Yesterday, I talked to Abe Pressler about the White farm—if he could look into who owns it now—and he said not to worry, he's taking care of it. I also talked to Woody Woods last night when he got there. He cleared something up for me about that diary of Ingrid's, where she kept writing there toward the end about what she loved so much."

"Didn't you say it was *drinking* that she loved?" asked Artie. "Drinking alcohol?

Harry Bauer just stared for a second at this big boy he had raised. "Hold on, son," said Grandpa. "Let me go get it and show you. Woody said he wants to talk to you in person as soon as he gets the chance—that's why he wouldn't answer any questions about it while he was off on vacation—but I'll go ahead and show you." The man made his way back to the bedroom to retrieve his daughter's diary.

At the window, Leah turned and said softly, "Artie, the others are getting here. I can see Wilma's Suburban parked at the barn next to the Whale." She paused. "And Woody's old station wagon just turned off the highway. I guess he's coming to talk to you now."

Artie nodded and looked back at Grandpa returning with the old diary in the palm of one hand. The small, pink, cloth-bound book was open, and the old man's gnarled index finger was pressed to a line on one particular page. Grandpa leaned down and showed the phrase—"I love P.J."—to his grandson. The sentence was written at least ten times on the page, with hearts and flowers drawn in the margins.

Shaking his head, Grandpa explained, "I thought Ingrid was referring to that nasty party drink those kids was always mixing up. But Woody said, no, she was talking about P.J. White—Peter Jacob White. That's Bob White's brother, Tommy's uncle." There was nothing left to say.

Right then, there came a loud knock at the farmhouse's front door—three sharp raps that echoed down the hallway into the kitchen. Artie leaned back in his chair to look down the hall through the door's frosted window. Through it, he saw the hazy figure of a man standing on the front porch. The man appeared to be holding up something in one hand at chest level—a wide, flat object the size of a large pizza box, maybe two. That, in fact, was what the man held.

When Artie Bauer glanced back at his friend Leah Russo, she gave him a curious look. The knock came again. "I'll get it," said the girl, her expression now appearing oddly anxious. "You stay seated, Artie. I may as well get this over with."

Leah walked up the hallway and did not hesitate to unfasten the security chain and open the door wide. On the porch stood Brett Woods. The tall, muscular teenager's sun-bleached hair was shaggier than Leah remembered, and his chiseled face was tanned from days on the North Shore beaches. He wore jeans and a gray, short-sleeved T-shirt despite the nip in the air on this mid-February day.

When the door opened and he saw who stood there to greet him, Brett smiled and said, "Pizza delivery. Two, extra-large, heart-shaped pizzas—one pepperoni, one veggie." He lifted the lid of the box on top to show her the veggie pizza inside. "No charge," he said. "They're on the house."

He handed the boxes through the open door. She took them and started to turn away, but thought to ask, "Do you wanna come in? Artie and Mr. Bauer are in the kitchen. Or are you in a hurry to get back to the grill? I know you and your dad are busy."

"I'm not in that big of a hurry," said Brett, as he stepped through the door to follow Leah back down the hall to where Artie and Grandpa were. "These pizzas were a trial run for the oven after we cleaned it, and this delivery is *my* trial run as an official Woody's delivery man. I got my driver's license in Hawaii last week."

Without looking back at him, she added, "I noticed you have a tattoo—but not like the last guy who showed up here with a pizza from Woody's. I guess you know about that, right?"

"Yeah," said Brett, as they walked into the kitchen. "Hi, Artie. Hi, Mr. Bauer. It's good to see you again." He turned to Leah and held up his forearm. "It's henna," he said. "It'll wear off—but not right away, I hope. I got it the day before we left Hawaii—the day I sent you that email."

Grandpa Bauer checked out the simple tattoo on the smooth underside of the teen's arm—a single, unbroken line forming a heart around a curling wave. "What does that mean?" the old man asked. "That you love the ocean? Or do you have a young lady in mind? Is that a *V* right there or an *L*?" A part of the dark line could be read as either consonant, depending on the viewer's perspective.

Brett Woods looked up at Leah Russo again. "It's an *L*," Brett said, smiling when he saw the flash in the girl's dark eyes, "I mean, if she'll have me. And if not, then it's a *V*."

Grandpa cackled. "You're asking for trouble, boy," said the old man, with a wink, "but—shoot—that's what life is all about. Now, isn't it."

THE END